THIS CROOKED WAY

Also by James Enge

Blood of Ambrose

THIS CROOKED WAY

JAMES ENGE

an imprint of **Prometheus Books**
Amherst, NY

Published 2009 by Pyr®, an imprint of Prometheus Books

Portions of this book appeared as short stories in the following publications:

"Fire and Water" (as "Turn Up This Crooked Way"), *Black Gate* 8, Summer 2005; "Payment Deferred," *Black Gate* 9, Fall 2005; "The Lawless Hours," *Black Gate* 11, Summer 2007; "Payment in Full," *Black Gate* 12, Summer 2008; and "Destroyer," *Black Gate* 14 (Fall 2009). All are copyrighted © by James Enge.

Inquiries should be addressed to
Pyr
59 John Glenn Drive
Amherst, New York 14228–2119
VOICE: 716–691–0133, ext. 210
FAX: 716–691–0137
WWW.PYRSF.COM

13 12 11 10 09   5 4 3 2 1

Library of Congress Cataloging-in-Publication Data

Enge, James, 1960–
        This crooked way / by James Enge.
            p. cm.
        ISBN 978–1–59102–784–3 (pbk. : alk. paper)
        I. Title.

PS3605 .N43T47 2009
813'.6—dc22

2009022254

Printed in the United States on acid-free paper

To **Nicholas** and **Jessica**

May your ways take some interesting turns,
not wholly free from monsters and magic

Acknowledgments

he epigraph for chapter IV is from the version of *Gilgamesh* by N. K. Sanders (Penguin, 1960). The epigraph for chapter XVI is from the translation of Sophocles' *Antigone* by Dudley Fitts and Robert Fitzgerald (Harcourt Brace & Co., 1939).

Some of these chapters appeared, in somewhat different form, in the fantasy magazine *Black Gate*. Thanks are due the editors, John O'Neill and Howard A. Jones—how many, they know and I haven't words to say.

CONTENTS

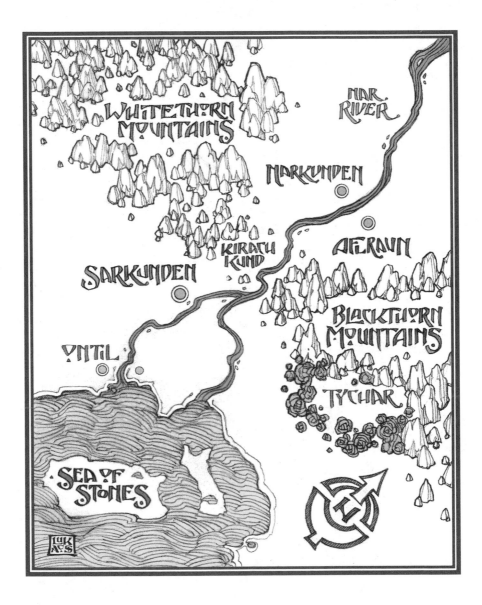

THIS CROOKED WAY

"NOW, SIRS," QUOD HE, "IF THAT YOU BE SO LIEF
TO FINDE DEATH, TURN UP THIS CROOKED WAY,
FOR IN THAT GROVE I LEFT HIM, BY MY FEY,
UNDER A TREE, AND THERE HE WILL ABIDE;
NOT FOR YOUR BOAST HE WILL HIM NOTHING HIDE."

—CHAUCER, "THE PARDONER'S TALE"

I

THE
WAR
IS
OVER

Nor, when the war is over, is it peace;
Nor will the vanquished bull his claim
    release:
But feeding in his breast his ancient fires
And cursing fate, from his proud foe
    retires.

—Vergil, *Georgics*

The crooked man rode out of the dead lands on a black horse with gray sarcastic eyes.

Winter was awaiting him, as he expected. In the dead lands it never rained or snowed, and the nearness to the sea kept the lifeless air mild. But it was the month of Brenting, late in winter, and as they crossed into the living lands the air took on a deadly chill and the snowdrifts soon became knee-high on his horse.

Morlock Ambrosius dismounted awkwardly and took the reins in his hand. "Sorry about this, Velox," he said to the horse.

Velox looked at him and made a rude noise with his lips.

"Eh," Morlock replied, "the same to you," and floundered forward through the snowdrifts, leading the beast. He was a pedestrian by temperament and had spent much of his long life walking from one place to another. He knew little about the care of horses, and what little he knew was not especially useful, as Velox was unusual in a number of ways. But, although he had considered it, he found he could not simply abandon Velox or trade him to some farmer for a basket of flatbread.

But Velox wanted food in alarming horse-sized amounts. Morlock had tried feeding him dried seaweed from the coastline, and Velox had eaten it, since there was little else. But Morlock suspected it wasn't enough for the grumpy beast, and he was going to have to go to a farm or even a town to buy some horse feed.

This was a problem, as Morlock was a criminal in the eyes of imperial law. He had reason to suppose the Emperor was not interested in seeing him dead, but no local Keeper of the Peace was likely to know this. It was dangerous for him to be seen, to be recognized.

On the other hand, his horse was hungry.

Nearly as grumpy as Velox, Morlock led the beast eastward through the bitter white fields until they reached the black muddy line of the Sar river, running south from the Kirach Kund. Alongside the river ran a hardly less muddy road; at intervals on the road were stations of the Imperial Post; clustering around some of these stations were towns where one could buy amenities like hay and oats.

Morlock mounted his horse and rode north toward Sarkunden. Presently he came, not to a town, but (even better for his purposes) to a barn. The doors of the barn were open and several dispirited farm workers were carrying pails of dung out of the barn and dumping it in a dark steaming heap that contrasted strangely with the recent snow.

Morlock reined in and said, "Good day. Can I buy some oats or something?"

The workers stopped their work and stared at him. Others came out of the barn, and also stopped and stared. After a while, one who seemed to be their leader (or thought he was), said, "Not from us, Crookback."

"Do you own this place?" Morlock asked.

"No, but we'll keep him from selling to *you*."

"Unlikely," Morlock replied, and dismounted. The men were gripping their dungforks and shovels and whatnot more like weapons now. If there was going to be a fight he wanted to be on his own feet, for a number of reasons.

"Know who I am, Crookback?" the leader of the workmen asked.

"No."

"This help?" He brushed some muck off his darkish outer garment. Morlock saw it was embroidered with a red lion.

"Not much," Morlock said.

"My name is Vost. I was Lord Urdhven's right-hand man. His closest friend. You killed him. Destroyed him. And now you come here. And ask me for oats."

"The man was dead before I met him," Morlock said. "We've no quarrel."

"You lie," Vost said, sort of, through clenched teeth.

"Then," Morlock replied. He drew the sword strapped to his crooked shoulders. The crystalline blade, black entwined with white, glittered in the thin winter sunlight.

"I hate you," Vost hissed, raising the dungfork in his hands like a stabbing spear. "I hate you. Nothing will stop me from trying to kill you until you're dead."

Morlock believed him. He was beginning to remember this Vost a little: a fanatical devotee of the late unlamented Lord Protector Urdhven; he had lived and died by his master's expressions of favor or disfavor. His life had lost its meaning when he had lost his master, and he had to blame someone for his freedom. Evidently he had settled on Morlock.

Morlock extended his sword arm and lunged, stabbing the man through his ribs. Vost's face stretched in surprise, then went slack with death. Morlock felt the horror of his dissolution through the medium of his sword, which was also a focus of power, very dangerous to use as a mundane weapon. A dying soul wants to carry others with it, and Morlock had to free himself of Vost's death shock and the dead soul's death grip before he was free to shake the corpse off the end of his sword and face Vost's companions.

They must have made some move toward attacking him, because Velox was in amongst them, rearing and kicking. One man already lay still in the dirty snow, a dark hoofmark on his forehead. As Morlock turned toward them, his sword dripping with Vost's blood and his face clenched in something not far removed from death agony, they took one look and fled, running up the road past the barn.

"Hey!" shouted a man coming out of the farmhouse with an axe in his hand. He was a prosperous gray-haired man with darkish skin, and he carried the axe like he knew how to use it. "Why are you killing my workmen?"

Morlock was cleaning his blade with some snow; he wiped it on his sleeve and sheathed it.

"The man annoyed me," he said at last.

"And the other one?"

"Annoyed my horse."

"You know what annoys me? People who come into my barnyard and leave dead bodies lying all over the place. I find that annoying."

"I was going to dump them into the river. Unless you have some strong objection."

The farmer blew out his cheeks and thought it over. "No, I guess not. They were no friends of mine, just some tramps working for the day."

"Then." Morlock hauled Vost's corpse out of the yard, across the road, and threw it face down into the muddy water of the Sar. The corpse sank almost out of sight; the sluggish waters tugged it away from the bank and it floated downstream. The last casualty in Protector Urdhven's civil war, or so Morlock hoped.

When he returned, he found the farmer had laid down his weapon and was crouching over the workman Velox had struck down. "This one's still breathing," the farmer said. "Your horse is hurt, though."

Morlock saw this was true: blood was dripping off Velox's neck and running down his left foreleg, staining the dirty snow. Morlock grabbed some snow from a clean patch and held it to the ragged wound on the horse's neck. It was already healing, but Morlock thought the cold might help counter the pain. If Velox felt pain: that was one of the things Morlock wasn't sure about.

Presently he turned away and grabbed a bagful of herbs from the pack strapped behind the saddle. He knelt down in the snow next to the fallen man and examined the wound on his head.

"The skull doesn't seem to be broken," Morlock said. "The man may wake up, or not. If he doesn't, he'll be dead in a few days; toss him in the river. If he does wake, give him tea made with this, once a day for a few days." He tossed the bag to the farmer. "It will help him heal."

"What is it?"

"Redleaf."

"Uh. All right. Wait a moment, I'm supposed to look after this tramp? I've got a farm to run."

Morlock reached into a pocket and tossed him a gold coin. "It's on me."

The farmer's eyes opened wide as he looked at the coin, weighed it in his hand. "All right," he said.

Morlock pointed at the red lion, faintly visible on the supine man's dirty surcoat. "You should get rid of this, in case an imperial patrol comes by. This man must be one of Lord Urdhven's soldiers, the dead-enders who wouldn't accept the new Emperor's amnesty."

"I didn't know."

"It's better if *they* don't know. Better for you. For him."

"I'll get rid of it. Let's carry this poor virp into the barn; it's a bit warmer there. And I don't want him in the house."

They bedded the fallen workman down in the loft, and then the farmer said, "It occurs to me that you came into my yard for some reason."

"I need some food for my horse, something I can carry with me. Oats or something."

"Not a horsey type, are you? That horse isn't going anywhere for a while. It's wounded pretty bad."

"He'll be fine by now."

The farmer shook his head and said, "You may be a murderous son-of-a-bitch, but you don't strike me as cruel. And I tell you it'd be cruel to expect him to carry you and your baggage for a while. Leave him with me; I'll take care of him. Or sell him to me, if you don't plan to be back this way. I'll give you a fair price."

"Just sell me some oats."

The farmer wanted to haggle over the price, but Morlock just handed him another gold coin and said, "As much as this will buy."

The farmer sputtered. "You *and* the horse couldn't carry that much."

"As much as he can carry, then."

"It shouldn't be carrying anything!"

Morlock went with the farmer down to look at Velox, who was quietly stealing some hay and hiding it inside himself. The wound had closed and a scar was forming.

"There's something weird about this," the farmer said.

"He's an unusual beast," Morlock conceded.

They bagged up some oats and strapped them across Velox's back. Morlock took the pack off, strapped it to his own back, and they threw more bags of oats onto Velox.

"That's thirsty work," the farmer remarked. "You want a mug of beer before you go?"

Morlock considered it and, when he realized he was considering it, said, "No."

"We've got a jar or two of wine from foreign parts—" the farmer continued, doubtful of his ground but willing to be sociable.

"If you offer me a drink again," Morlock said evenly, "I'll kill you."

The farmer did not offer him a drink again. He said nothing at all as Morlock led Velox out of the yard and away, northward up the road to Sarkunden.

II

Interlude: Telling the Tale

Imperious Prima flashes forth
  Her edict "to begin it":
In gentler tones Secunda hopes
  "There will be nonsense in it!"
  While Tertia interrupts the tale
  Not *more* than once a minute.

—Lewis Carroll

ore or less at the same time, young Dhyrvalona said,

"I don't understand?"
"Why didn't he take the drink?"
"Was he afraid it was poisoned?"

"A harmony," her nurse sang to her. "A harmony of meanings, Dhyrvalona dear. You may have three mouths, but I don't have three minds. Harmonize your questions the way you harmonize your voices; let your wisdom vibrate in the listener's mind, and she may return the favor."

Little Dhyrvalona's three adorable mouths harmonized three different but related obscenities she had heard her armed guards use.

Gathenavalona, Dhyrvalona's nurse, snapped her mandibles and extended all three of her arms in angular gestures of rebuke.

After a tense moment, young Dhyrvalona covered each of her three eyes with a palp-cluster, an expression of grief or sorrow—in this context, an apology. She peered through her palps to see how her nurse was taking it.

Gathenavalona relaxed the tension in her mandibles, giving her pyramidal face a less forbidding appearance. Her arms changed from harsh angles to soothing curves, and she stroked the top of Dhyrvalona's pointed head with one gentle palp-cluster.

Humbly, Dhyrvalona sang,

"But I still don't understand."
"Learning is a lasting joy."
"Ignorance is an endable grief."

Gathenavalona gestured strong approval and replied, more prosaically, "You know how the one-faced fill their one-mouths with rotten grape juice and old barley water?"

"Ick."
"So nasty."
"A single mouth! How ugly and stupid!"

The remarks didn't harmonize in sound or sense, but the nurse was not inclined to be strict with her charge these days. Young Dhyrvalona was growing up; soon she would take the place of old Valona in the Vale of the Mother. That would be a proud and sad day for the nurse, and she wanted the days and nights until then to be less proud and less sad.

"The juice makes some one-faceds happy; it makes some sad; it makes some sick. For Morlock—"

"Maker!"
"Traveller!"
"Destroyer!"

"—for Morlock Ambrosius, it does all these things. The farmer did not intend to harm him. His kindness would have harmed him, though. Do you understand?"

"No."
"Neither do you."
"The Destroyer is beyond understanding."

Gathenavalona sang.

"Empty your mind of lies."
"Fill your mind with truth."
"Nothing is beyond understanding."

Young Dhyrvalona opened her eyes and her ear-lids, indicating a willingness to be instructed.
The nurse sang.

"Kindness can kill."
"Enmity can heal."
"Surgeon and destroyer both wield sharp blades."

Young Dhyrvalona gestured acknowledgement, but incomplete understanding.
The nurse sang.

"We are nothing to Morlock."
"Morlock is nothing to us."
"Yet, on a day, we met and wounded each other."

The nurse paused and resumed.

"A mother was wounded."
"A mother was slain."
"A mother stood waiting in death's jaws."

The nurse paused and resumed.

"Morlock stole the hatred of the gods."
"The gods stole our hatred of Morlock."
"That end/beginning was our beginning/end."

The nurse paused and resumed.

"That is why, once a year, we wear the man-masks."
"That is why, once a year, we curse the gods-who-hate-us."
"That is why, once a year, we sing of who destroyed us."

Young Dhyrvalona cried out impatiently,

"All right, I'm trying to be good."
"Night is falling; the time for tales is ending."
"You haven't even told me about the horse!"

Gathenavalona blinked one eye in amusement and sang indulgently.

"A horse is almost like us."
"Horses have four legs, anyway, not two."
"For a man to lose a horse is a serious thing . . ."

Young Dhyrvalona snuggled down into her nest and prepared to be entertained. She knew this part of the story well, of course: the nurse told her a little more every year, but this was one of the earliest parts and she had heard it many times.

This year, her nurse had promised, she would tell her the whole tale, even if it took many nights, every night of the annual festival. The grown-ups of the Khroic clan of Valona's heard the whole story every year, and now she would too. That was because, the nurse had explained to her, she was almost a grown-up now. Young Valona could see that this made the nurse sad, but she herself was very happy; she couldn't wait to grow up. And she was so glad it was the season of Motherdeath, the happiest time of the year.

III

Blood from a Stone

He hath inclosed my ways with hewn stone,
he hath made my paths crooked.

—Lamentations

Morlock awoke because the earth was shuddering beneath him. He'd been raised under the mountains of Northhold and he knew in his bones that, if the ground moved, he had better move, too.

He rolled to one side to free himself from his sleeping cloak and leaped to his feet. By then the stone monster had plunged its fist or paw deep into the ground where Morlock had been lying.

The stone monster. It was clearly made of stone; at first he thought it was striped like a tiger, but then he saw that it was ringed or ridged down its long leonine body to the end of its four limbs. It swung its heavy maneless head toward him, clicking oddly as it moved; the stone teeth in its crooked ill-matched jaws streamed with some red fluid in the gray morning light. Its eyes gleamed like moonlit crystal or water as they focused on him and it prepared to leap.

"Tyrfing!" Morlock shouted, and held out his hand for his sword. It didn't come to him: even though he was not in rapture, he felt the talic impulse as it tried to reach him. Something was holding it back.

The stone beast jumped at him and he leaped to one side. The old wound in his leg was already aching; he hoped he wouldn't have to try to outrun this thing. He reached down and grabbed two fistfuls of dirty snow and threw them at the stone beast's eyes.

It responded strangely, like a startled animal, blinking fiercely and shaking its head to get the grit from its eyes.

In Morlock's opinion, those eyes were made of glass or crystal in some maker's workshop; the beast's whole body was a cunningly made puzzle, its joints clicking as pieces shifted so that it could move. He doubted that the thing could feel as an animal's body feels.

But it *acted* as if it could feel the dirt in its eyes; it expected to feel discomfort from the snow. At the very least, it was perplexed when something obscured its vision.

That told him something: he was not facing a golem. Golems do only what they have been designed to do, fulfilling the instructions on their life-scrolls. It was unlikely that a maker would waste scroll space telling a golem to react emotionally like an animal when something got in its eyes. Somehow a living entity was directing the motions of the stone monster.

And if it was alive, it could be killed.

Morlock's back was against the trunk of an oak tree, its crooked limbs leafless and whistling in the breeze of the winter morning. He reach up and tore one of the limbs loose from the trunk.

The stone beast, floundering through the snow, charged Morlock, who circled behind the tree. If he moved carefully, he could keep to the hardened crust of snow and move faster than the beast. It lunged toward him; he continued around the tree and, leaping into the trench of snow left in the stone beast's wake, he struck the beast as hard as he could across the back of its lumpy head.

The stone beast snarled, a grinding sound of rock on rock, and swung about to face him. Morlock fled back around the tree. The stone beast rose up on three legs and struck the trunk of the tree with its right forepaw. The oak tree shattered, the trunk split down the middle.

Giving vent to the turbulence of his emotions, Morlock said "Eh," and ran.

The beast was after him in a moment, but he took a twisting path though the nearby trees, keeping to the surface crust of snow when he could, and managed to stay barely ahead of the thing. Twice he managed to get in more blows to its head—once from the side, once from behind—and he thought that its movements were getting more sluggish, the beast groggier.

His twisting course took him toward the nearby Sar River. His thought was that, if worse came to worst, he could swim away from his stone enemy (although the cold water in this cold weather might kill him faster than the monster could).

As he zigged to avoid the stone beast's lumbering zag, he glanced over his shoulder and saw that one of the thing's glass eyes was cracked. The stone head kept twitching and shaking, as if to free the eye of some obstruction. (The shattered eye itself?)

He whirled about and swung the branch with both hands, striking the beast on the side of its head with the broken eye. The glass fell away and all that remained was a dark hole in the stone beast's face. It drew back, as if aghast. A thin trickle of blood, like tears, ran down the gray stone face from the empty eye socket.

Morlock turned on his heel and ran straight toward the river.

It was after him in a moment, but he had reached the icy marsh along the river's edge before it caught up with him. It came forward in a great leap and knocked him off his feet in the shallow ice-sheathed water as it landed behind him. The great stone body surged as Morlock scrabbled for his club on the icy surface of the water and struggled to regain his feet in the soft ground. The moments passed like hours; it seemed impossible that the beast would not recover and strike him dead before he could arm himself. But, in fact, it didn't. When he regained his feet he saw why.

The beast was stuck in the mud under the shallow water, unable to free its deadly limbs from the soft ground. Morlock realized this was his chance; he vaulted past the beast's snapping jaws and one-eyed face to land on its broad shoulders. Standing there he delivered savage blow after savage blow to the back of the beast's head. The stone body writhed and chittered beneath him, but in time it began to move slower and slower. At last it fell still; its snout slumped into the icy stream, and bloody water bubbled from the empty eye socket. The thing was dead.

Morlock staggered off the beast's back and tossed aside his now-splintered club. He took a few moments to breathe and gather his strength. But not too long: the cold was a pain gnawing at him, especially the limbs that had been soaked in the river.

He went to change into dry clothes, shivering by the smoking remains of last night's fire. He saw his sword, Tyrfing, bound in its sheath to a nearby boulder; he doubted that the stone beast's paws could have managed that, even if its brain could have planned it. That bothered him. He saw Velox nowhere, and that bothered him very much. He remembered the red fluid on the stone monster's stony teeth.

In dry clothes, after freeing Tyrfing, he went in search of Velox. And he found what he had feared he might: what was evidently the scene of a struggle, some distance away from Morlock's camp. There were the marks of savage bloody blows in the snow and the stiff unyielding earth below. There were some stray horsehairs, bloody hoofmarks in the snow and earth, but no body, not even stray bones or flesh.

He had seen something like this in his youth, where a monster had dismembered and eaten a horse on the long road facing the western edge of the world.

"Doubtful," Morlock reminded himself. There was more, or perhaps less, to this scene than met the eye.

He spent the rest of the morning dragging the dead body of the stone beast from the swampy margin of the river. He took his time because he wanted to avoid getting soaked again, using xakth-fiber ropes and a pulley system to haul the thing up from the water to an open area not far from his camp.

Not pausing for breakfast or lunch—eating didn't seem advisable, given his plans—he took Tyrfing and gutted the stone beast, laying bare its insides from its stumpy tail to its blunt snout.

There was indeed some kind of fleshy brain in the rocky skull. It was badly swollen from the beating Morlock had given it, but he didn't think it was a man's or a woman's brain. A dragon's? A dwarf's? Something else? Morlock couldn't tell. He was no connoisseur of brains.

The contents of the stone belly told an interesting tale indeed. There were multitudes of splintered bone fragments, a cracked hoof or two, an oddly familiar pair of black horse-ears, a brown equine eye, other more horrible things, all swimming in a strange pale fluid that stank like a torturer's conscience.

That was enough. Morlock wiped his sword carefully and sheathed it, then walked away. The stone belly told an interesting tale: that the beast had killed and eaten Velox before attacking Morlock. And the tale was a lie. Most black horses have brown eyes, but Velox did not, and there simply was not enough bulk in the stone beast's belly to account for an entire horse.

Morlock boiled water, washed his hands, made tea, and thought.

Every lie is shaped by the truth it is meant to conceal. What did the lie in the stone beast's belly tell him?

That Velox was probably alive, for one thing—seized by a maker skilled enough to make the stone beast and ruthless enough to use it. He knew of only one such, but there might be many; it would be best to keep an open mind.

Normally he would have sought out a crow who might have seen something, for he had an affinity for crows, but they were rarer in this region than they had been once. Using his Sight to search for the maker and his stolen horse might be a mistake, though. There were traps that could be set in the realms of vision that could capture or harm even the wary. Still, he needed more information before he set out in search of Velox. And there might be a way . . .

He went to his pack and sorted through it until he found a certain book.

He had written it himself in the profoundly subtle "palindromic" script of ancient Ontil. Each page was a mirror image of the one it faced; both pages had to be inscribed simultaneously. There was a page for each of the days of the year, and one for each day of the "counter-year" that runs backward as time moves forward. It was useful for reading the future or the past; merely to possess it sometimes gave one clairvoyant experiences. He had fashioned it over a long period, beginning last year, after he had some indication that he might have to confront a maker as gifted as himself whose talents in the Sight were even greater than his.

He turned to the day's date and read the palindromes for that day and its counter-day. Most of them meant nothing to him. But there was one that he came back to again and again.

Alfe runilmao vo inila. Alinio vo amlinu refla.

Which might be rendered: *From the skulls, {he} walked south. A maker goes into the north.*

"The skulls" might be "the River of Skulls": the Kirach Kund (to give it the Dwarvish name by which it was generally known). It was the high pass that divided the Whitethorn and Blackthorn ranges, the only way past those towering mountains . . . for those who had the courage to take it.

This didn't make his decision for him: like any omen it might mean anything or nothing. But his intuition confirmed it: he would go north.

Another man might have weighed the odds on recovering the horse against the fact that he preferred to walk. He would have thought twice about whether getting the horse back was worth it.

But there was a bond of loyalty between Morlock and Velox, and Morlock was not the sort to question that bond, or the obligations it might entail.

Also, he had nothing else to do. He struck camp and, before the sun had descended much from its zenith, he was walking along the river northward to Sarkunden.

IV

PAYMENT DEFERRED

THERE IS THE HOUSE WHOSE PEOPLE SIT IN DARKNESS;
DUST IS THEIR FOOD AND CLAY THEIR MEAT.

—*GILGAMESH*

he thug's first thrust sent his sword screeching past Morlock Ambrosius's left ear. He retreated rather than parry Morlock's riposte; then he thrust again in the same quadrant as before.

While the thug was still extended for his attack, Morlock deftly kicked him in the right knee. With a better swordsman this would have cost Morlock, but he had the measure of his opponent. The thug went sideways, squawking in dismay, into a pile of garbage.

The point of Morlock's blade, applied to the thug's wrist, persuaded him to release his sword. The toe of Morlock's left shoe, applied to the thug's chin, persuaded him to keep lying where he was.

"What's your story, Slash?" Morlock asked.

"Whatcha mean?"

Morlock's sword point shifted to the thug's throat. "I'm in Sarkunden for an hour. You pick me out of a street crowd, follow me into an alley, and try to kill me. Why?"

"Y're smart, eh? See a lot, eh?"

"Yes."

"Dontcha like it, eh? Dontcha like to fight, eh?"

"No."

"Call a Keep, hunchback!" the thug sneered. "Maybe, I dunno, maybe I oughta—" He raised his hand theatrically to his mouth and inhaled deeply, as if he were about to cry out.

Morlock's sword pressed harder against the thug's neck, just enough to break the skin. The shout never issued from the thug's mouth, but the thug sneered triumphantly. He'd made his point: Morlock, as an imperial outlaw, wanted to see the Keepers of the Peace—squads of imperial guards detailed to policing the streets—even less than this street punk with a dozen murders to his credit. (Morlock knew this from the cheek rings in the thug's face. The custom among the water gangs was one cheek ring per murder. Duels and fair fights did not count.)

"Ten days' law—that's what you got, eh?" the thug whispered. "Ten days to reach the border; then if they catch you inside it—zzccch! When'd your time run out, uh, was it twenny days ago? Thirty?"

"Two months."

"Sure. Call a Keep, scut-face. By sunrise they'll have your head drying on a stake upside the Kund-Way Gate."

"I won't be calling the Keepers of the Peace," Morlock agreed. The crooked half-smile on his face was as cold as his ice-gray eyes. "What will I do instead?"

"You can't kill me, crooky-boy—" the thug began, with suddenly shrill bravado.

"I *can* kill you. But I won't. I'll cut your tendons and pull your cheek rings. I can sell the metal for drinking money at any bar in this town, as long as the story goes with it. And I'll make sure everyone knows where I last saw you."

"There's a man; he wants to see you," said the thug, giving in disgustedly.

"Dead?"

"Alive. But I figure: the Empire pays more for you dead than this guy will alive."

"You're saying he's cheap."

"Cheap? He's riding his horse, right, and you cross the road after him and step in his horse-scut. He's gonna send a greck after you to charge you for the fertilizer. You see me?"

"I see you." Morlock briefly weighed his dangers against his needs. "Take me to this guy. I'll let you keep a cheek ring, and one tendon, maybe."

"Evil scut-sucking bastard," hissed the thug, unmistakably moved with gratitude.

"The guy's" house was a fortresslike palace of native blue-stone, not far inside the western wall of Sarkunden. Morlock and the limping thug were admitted through a heavy bronze door that swung down to make a narrow bridge across a dry moat. Bow slits lined the walls above the moat; through them Morlock saw the gleam of watching eyes.

"Nice place, eh?" the thug sneered.

"I like it."

The thug hissed his disgust at the emblems of security and anyone who needed them.

They waited in an unfinished stone anteroom with three hard-faced guards until an inner door opened and a tall fair-haired man stepped through it. He glanced briefly in cold recognition at the thug, but his eyes lit up as they fell on Morlock.

"Ah! Welcome, sir. Welcome to my home. Do come in."

"Money," said the thug in a businesslike tone.

"You'll be paid by your gang leader. That was the agreement."

"I better be," said the thug flatly. He walked back across the bronze door-bridge, strutting to conceal his limp.

"Come in, do come in," said the householder effusively. "People usually call me Charis."

Morlock noted the careful phrasing and replied as precisely, "I am Morlock Ambrosius."

"I know it, sir—I know it well. I wish I had the courage to do as you do. But few of those-who-know can afford to be known by their real names."

Those-who-know was a euphemism for practitioners of magic, especially solitary adepts. Morlock shrugged his crooked shoulders, dismissing the subject.

"I had a prevision you were coming to Sarkunden," said the sorcerer who called himself Charis, "and—yes, thank you, Veskin, you may raise the bridge again—I wanted to consult with you on a matter I have in hand. I hope that gangster didn't hurt you, bringing you in—I see you are limping."

"It's an old wound."

"Ah. Well, I'm sorry I had to put the word out to the water gangs, but they cover the town so much more thoroughly than the Keepers of the Peace. Then there was the matter of your—er—status. I hope, by the way, you aren't worried about that fellow shopping you to the imperial forces?"

"No."

Charis's narrow blond eyebrows arched slightly. "Your confidence is justified," he admitted, "but I don't quite see its source."

Morlock waved a hand. "This place—your house. No ordinary citizen would be allowed to have a fortress like this within the town's walls. You are not a member of the imperial family. So I guess you have a large chunk of the local guards in your pocket, and have had for at least ten years."

Charis nodded. "Doubly astute. You've assessed the age of my house to the year, and you're aware of its political implications. Of course, you were in the Emperor's service fairly recently, weren't you?"

"Yes, but let's not dwell on it."

Charis dwelled on it. Knotting his eyebrows theatrically, he said, "Let's see, what was it that persuaded him to exile you?"

"I had killed his worst enemy and secured his throne from an usurpation attempt."

"Oh, my God. Well, there you are. I don't claim your own level of political astuteness, you understand, but if I had been there to advise you I would have said, 'Don't do it!' I never do anything for anybody that they can't repay, and I never allow anybody to do anything for me that I can't repay. Gratitude is painless enough in short bursts, but few people can stand it on a day-to-day basis."

They ascended several flights of stairs, passing several groups of servants who greeted Charis with every appearance of cheerful respect. Finally they reached a tower room ringed with windows, with a fireplace in its center and two liveried pages in attendance. Charis seated Morlock in a comfortable chair and planted himself in its twin on the other side of the fireplace. He gestured negligently and the pages stood forward.

"May I offer you something?" Charis asked. "A glass of wine? The local grapes are particularly nasty, as you must know, but there's a vineyard in northern Kaen I've come to favor lately. I'd like your opinion on their work."

"I'm not a vintner. Some water for me, thanks."

This remark set Charis's eyebrows dancing again. "But surely . . ." he said, as the demure dark-eyed servant at his side handed him a glass-lined drinking cup.

"I don't drink when I'm working, and I gather you want me to do a job. What is it?"

Charis leaned back in his chair. "Let me begin to answer by asking a question: What do you think is the *most* remarkable thing about this remarkable house of mine?"

Morlock accepted a cup of water from a bold-eyed blond-haired page. He drank deeply as he mulled the question over, then replied, "I suppose the fact that all the servants are golems."

The comment caught his host in midswallow. Morlock watched with real interest as Charis choked down his wine, his astonishment, and an obvious burst of irritation more or less simultaneously.

"May I ask how you knew that?" Charis said carefully, when he was free for speech.

"From the fact that all the servants we've met, including your guards, have been golems, I deduced that your entire staff consisted of golems."

"Yes, but surely, sir, you understand the intent of my question: How did you *know* they were golems? For I think, sir, as a master in the arts of Making, you will admit they are excellent work—*extremely* lifelike." Charis's frank and inquisitive look had something of a glare in it. Clearly he had made the golems himself and was vexed because they had not deceived Morlock.

"Mostly the eyes," Morlock said. "The golems are well made, I grant you, and the life-scrolls must be remarkably complicated and various. But you can't quite get a natural effect with clay eyes."

Charis turned his gaze from Morlock to the dark-haired modest page at his left hand. Morlock watched the struggle in his host's face as he realized the truth of the observation.

"What would you use?" Charis asked finally. "If I may be so bold."

"Molten glass for the eyes proper—the eyeball and the cornea. I'd slice up some gems and use a fan-ring assembly for the irises. You're using black mirror-tube for the visual canals? I think that would work very well."

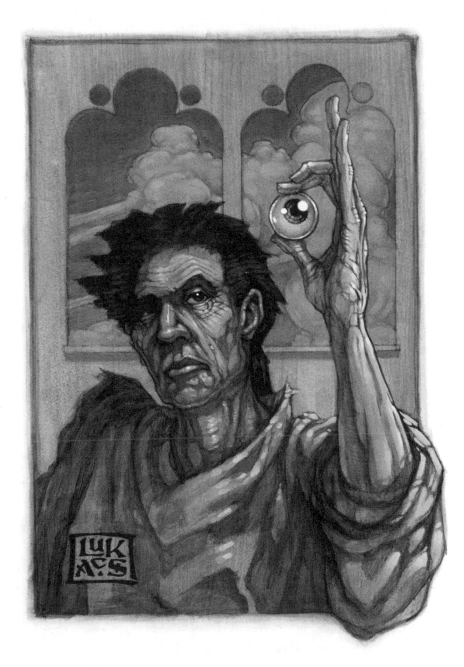

"You can't use glass," Charis said sharply, sitting on the edge of his chair. "I've tried it. The vivifying spell induces some flexibility in the material, but it's not sufficient."

"It would be necessary to keep it molten until the vivifying spell is activated," Morlock replied.

"It seems to me, frankly, that the problems are completely insuperable."

"I can show you," Morlock said indifferently.

"Frankly, you'll have to. That will have to be part of the deal. Frankly."

"What deal are you offering?"

Charis leapt to his feet, walked impatiently all around the room, and threw himself back down in his chair. "You have me at a disadvantage," he remarked. "As you no doubt intended."

"We both have something the other needs."

"Thank God! I thought for a moment—no matter what I thought. As you guessed: except for myself, all my household are golems. I do business every day in the city—a very large business in very small spells—and, frankly, when I come home I detest the human race. But I have the normal human desire for a sociable life."

Morlock, who had none of these problems, inclined his head to acknowledge them. "And the golems are your solution."

"A most effective one, by and large. Except that I will never be able to look one of the damned things in the eyes again!"

"That can be fixed," Morlock pointed out. "Also, there must have been something else, or you wouldn't have been looking for me."

"Yes. Yes. As you noticed, I've been at some pains to give each of my golems a distinctive character, physically and otherwise. A desert of a thousand identical faces and minds would hardly satisfy my social instincts."

"No golem has a mind," Morlock observed. "A limited set of responses can be incorporated into any life-scroll."

"A difference that is no difference, sir. What does it matter to me whether they really have minds or not? If they *seem* to have minds, my social instincts will be satisfied."

Morlock thought this unlikely, but did not say so. "Then?"

"The trouble is that, since *I* inscribed their life-scrolls, nothing they say or do can ever surprise me. You see? The illusion that they have identities collapses. My social instincts are not satisfied. Frankly, it's dull."

"Then. You would have me make a new set of lifelike golems, at least some of whose responses you will not expect."

"In an unthreatening and even charming way. Play fair, now."

"I can't undertake to provide charm," Morlock said. "We can rule out danger, insubordination, and incivility."

"Very well. I'm sure I can trust your esthetic instincts. Also, you must show me your method of constructing their eyes."

Morlock nodded.

"The question arises, 'What can I do for you?' I take it that mere gold will not . . . ? No."

Morlock shook his head. "I understand the Sarkunden garrison still runs scouting missions into the Kirach Kund," he said, naming the mountain pass to the north of Sarkunden.

"Ye-e-es," Charis said slowly.

"I can't remain in the empire, as you know. I can't go west—"

"No one goes into the Wardlands."

"In any case, I can't. I dislike Anhi and Tychar, and therefore would not go east."

"You intend to cross the Kirach Kund!"

"Yes. It is done from time to time, I believe."

"By armed companies. Nor do they always survive."

Morlock lifted his wry shoulders in a shrug. "I have done it. But I was once taken prisoner by the Khroi and am reluctant to risk it again."

"The Khroi take only prey, never prisoners. You will excuse my being so downright, but we live in the Khroi's shadow, here, and we know something about them."

"They made an exception for me, once. They may not make the same mistake again. It would be better for me if I knew what the imperial scouts know—what hordes are allied to each other, which are at war, where the latest fighting is, where dragon-cavalry has been seen."

"I see." Charis's face twisted. "I have never meddled with strictly military matters before. It will strain my relationship with the garrison commander."

Morlock lifted his crooked shoulders in a shrug. "You could hire a number of human servants. If—"

"No!" Charis shouted. "No people! I won't have it!" His nostrils flared with hatred; he neglected to move his eyebrows expressively.

"Very well," he said at last. "I'll get you your news. You make me my golems." And they settled down to haggle over details.

On the appointed day, Charis strode into Morlock's workroom, unable to disguise his feelings of triumph. "Oh, Morlock, you must come and see this. Say, you've been cleaning up in here!"

A shrug from the crooked shoulders. "My work's done. I hope you like your golems."

"They're *marvellous*. I'm so grateful. One of them speaks nothing but Kaenish! And I don't know a word!"

A smile was a rare crooked thing on Morlock's dark face. "You'll have to learn, I guess."

"Wonderful. But come along to my workshop. The guardsman will be along presently, and I badly want to show you this before you depart. Oh, do leave that," he said, as the other began to reach for the sword belt hanging on the wall. "You won't want it, and there's no place for it in my room."

They went together to Charis's workshop. Body parts fashioned in clay of various shades lay scattered all over the room. There was a positive clutter of arms on the worktable—Charis had mentioned to Morlock at supper last night that he was "on an arm jag," and now it could be seen what he meant.

Charis worked by inspiration, crafting dozens of arms or legs, for instance, as the mood took him, getting a feel for the body part and creating subtle differences between the members in the series. In the end he would construct golems like jigsaw puzzles out of pieces he had already made, and improvise a life-scroll that suited the body. His other skills as a sorcerer were quite minor, as he freely admitted, but his pride as a golem maker was fully justified.

So far, though, irises had defeated him. In everything else he had proved a ready pupil to Morlock, even in the manipulation of globes of molten glass, a difficult magic. But creating the fan-ring assemblies of paper-thin sheets of gem had proved the most challenging task of Making he had ever undertaken.

His latest efforts lay on the worktable, two small rings of purple amethyst flakes, glittering among the chaos of clay arms. He watched anxiously as the other bent down to examine them.

"Hm." A hand reached out. "An aculeus, please." Charis quickly handed over the needlelike probe. The skilled hands made the artificial irises expand, contract, expand again. Finally the maker's form straightened (insofar as it ever could, Charis thought, glancing scornfully at the crooked shoulders), saying, "Excellent. You should have no trouble now making lifelike eyes for your golems."

Charis sighed in relief. "I'm so glad to hear you say so. Really, I'm deeply in your debt."

A shrug. "You can pay me easily, with news from the pass."

"I'm afraid that would hardly cover it," Charis said regretfully, and pushed him over, onto the table. The clay arms instantly seized him and held him, a long one wrapping itself like a snake across his mouth, effectively gagging him.

Charis carefully swept the artificial irises off the table into his left hand and, moving back, commanded, "Table: stand."

The table-shaped golem tipped itself vertically and, unfolding two stumpy human legs from under one of its edges, stood. Its dozens of mismatched arms still firmly held Morlock's struggling form.

"I'm sorry about this—I really am," Charis said hastily, in genuine embarrassment. "When push came to shove, though, it occurred to me that my relationship with the garrison commander simply couldn't take the strain of fishing for secret military information. You've no idea how stuffy he is. Also, I'm not convinced the news would be as useful to you as you think, and you might hold a grudge against me. You've given me so much, and I'm afraid—that is, I don't like to think about you holding a grudge, that's all. So this is better—not for you, I quite see that. But for me. Guardsmen!"

From a side door three imperial guardsmen entered, the fist insignia of Keepers of the Peace inscribed on their breastplates. They eyed the inhuman golem and its struggling victim with distaste and fear.

"Have it let him go," the senior guard directed. "We'll take him in."

"Are you out of your mind?" Charis exploded. "This man is the most powerful maker in the worlds, and a dangerous swordsman besides. If you think that he is going to quietly walk between you to his place of execution, you—Look here: let's not quarrel. You'll get your reward whether you bring him in dead or alive. I simply can't risk his surviving to take revenge on me, don't you see? Cut his head off here. That's what we agreed. Don't worry about the golem; it was made for this purpose."

"They say Ambrosius's blood is poison," one of the other guardsmen offered quaveringly. "They say—"

"Gentlemen, it is your own blood you ought to be concerned about," Charis remarked. "This man is lethal. He has been condemned to death by the Emperor himself. You have him helpless. I've paid you well to come here, and you'll be paid even better when you bring his head to your captain. What more needs to be said?"

The senior guard nodded briskly and said, "Tervin: your sword."

"Hey!" shouted the junior addressed. "I'm not going to—"

"No. I am. But I'm not going to use my own sword. I paid a hundred eagles for that thing, and I don't want it wrecked if his blood eats metal, like they say. Your weapon's standard issue. Give it to me."

Tervin silently surrendered his sword; the senior guard stepped forward and remarking, in a conversational tone, "In the name of the Emperor," lopped off the head of the struggling victim. The sword bit deeply into the table-golem; several of the arms fell with the severed head to the floor.

The senior guard leapt back immediately to avoid the gush of poisonous Ambrosial blood, then took another step back when he saw that there *was* no gush of blood. The headless form in the table-golem's arms continued its useless struggle.

"No," croaked Charis, his throat dry. "This can't be happening."

He stepped forward, as if against his own will, and touched the gleaming edge of the severed neck. It was clay. He reached down into the open throat and drew out a life-scroll inscribed in Morlock Ambrosius's peculiar hooked style. The body ceased to move.

"They told me you were cheap," Morlock's voice sounded behind and below him.

He turned and, looking down, met the calm gray gaze of the severed head that looked like Morlock's.

"They told me you were cheap," the severed head remarked again, "so I expected this. I am somewhere you can't reach me. Have the information ready when I send for it and I'll hold no grudges. But do not betray me again."

"I won't," whispered Charis, knowing he would have nightmares about this moment as long as he lived. "I promise. I promise I won't." Then he turned away from the suddenly lifeless head to soothe the frightened guards with gold.

That night the unbeheaded and authentic Morlock lay dreaming in the high cold hills north of Sarkunden, but he wasn't aware of it. To him it seemed he was lying, wrapped in his sleeping cloak, watching the embers of his fire, wondering why he was still awake.

An old woman walked into the cool red circle of light around Morlock's dying campfire. He could not see her face. She bent down and took the book of palindromes from Morlock's backpack and flipped through it until she reached the page for that day. She carried it over and showed it to him. Her index finger pointed to a palindrome: *Molh lomolov alinio cret. Terco inila vo lom olhlom.*

Which might be rendered: *Blood red as sunset marks the road north. Son walks east into the eastering sun.*

He looked up from the book to her face. He still could not see it. He wasn't able to see it, he realized suddenly, because he never had seen it. Then he awoke.

He opened his eyes to find the book of palindromes open in his hand. It was his index finger resting on the palindrome he had read in his dream.

Morlock got up and restowed the book in his pack. Then he settled down and built up the fire to make tea: he doubted he would sleep any more that night.

He was caught up in some conflict he didn't understand with a seer whose skill surpassed his own. Any omen or vision he received was doubly important because of this, but it was doubly suspect as well.

He much preferred Making to Seeing: the subtleties of vision were often lost on him. In a way, he had made the book of palindromes so that he would have some of the advantages of Seeing through an instrument of Making. He thought the omen pointing him northward was a real omen, and it was possible that this one was, too. But it was possible that one or both had been sent by his enemy to mislead him.

Morlock drank his tea and thought the matter over all night. By sunrise he had struck camp and was walking along the crooked margin of the mountains eastward, keeping his eyes open for he knew not what.

V

FIRE
AND
WATER

THE ANCIENTS HELD NO OMEN WAS SO DIRE,
AS TO SPILL WATER, WHEN THEY TALKED OF
    FIRE.

—**BUTLER,** *POETICAL THESAURUS*

ne morning, after many days of travel eastward, Morlock awoke to find his pack had been slit and the book of palindromes stolen. He spent some time thinking about why the thief had stolen that one thing, and what the theft might mean. In the end, he shouldered his violated pack, belted on his sword, and took after the thief.

Morlock was a master of makers, not trackers, but the ground was soft in early spring and the track fairly easy to follow, perhaps too easy. The trail led north and east, toward a place Morlock had particularly wanted to avoid.

When the thief's trail took him as far as the winterwood, as he had known it must, Morlock Ambrosius sat down to think. To enter there was to gamble with his life, and Morlock hated gambling: it was wasteful and he was thrifty—some said cheap. Still, there was the book. . . . And the note. It had been staked to the ground, just next to his slit pack . . . staked with a glass thorn from the same pack. (The chamber of the thorn was broken and the face inside was dark and lifeless. Another score to settle!) The message was simply a stylized figure of a hand with the fingers pointing northward . . . toward the forest of Tychar, the winterwood. The meaning was as clear as the slap in the face the symbol represented: *Forget your book. It's gone where you can't follow.* The note was addressed "Ambrosius."

So it was someone who knew him, someone bold enough to rob him, someone who had preferred, when he was vulnerable, to insult him rather than kill him. He had a desire to meet this person.

As he sat, pondering the dark blue trunks of the winterwood, he found the desire had not faded.

He kindled a fire with the *Pursuer* instrumentality. As he was waiting for it to grow to optimal strength, he took off his pack and set about repairing the slit. There was a patch of gripgrass not far away; he spotted it by the long deerlike bones of an animal it had killed. He drew a few plants from the ground, taking care not to break the stems or tear the central roots. He sewed up the slit in his pack, carefully weaving the gripgrass plants into the seam.

The fire was high enough, then, so he took the thief's note and burned it in the *Pursuer* fire with a pinch of chevetra leaf. The smoke traveled north and east, against the wind, toward the forest: that was the way the thief had gone.

They called it "the winterwood." The trees stood on high rocky ground; it was cold there, even in summer. The trees there, of a kind that grew nowhere else, flowered in fall and faded in spring. They resembled dark oaks, except their leaves were a dim blue and their bark had a bluish cast.

Just now it was early spring; patches of snow lay, like chewed crusts, beneath the hungry-looking trees. The leaves, crooked blue veins showing along the withered gray surfaces, were like the hands of dying men. They rustled irritably in the chill persistent breeze, as if impatient to meet and merge with the earth.

Morlock did not share their impatience. When he saw the smoke from his magical fire enter the tree-shadowed arch of a pathway (a clear path leading deep into those untravelled woods) he shook his head suspiciously.

So he sat down again and took off his shoes. After writing his name and a few other words on the heel of his left shoe, he trimmed a strip of leather from the sole and tied it around his bare left foot at the arch. He did the same with the other shoe (and foot). He muttered a few more words (familiar to those-who-know). Then he picked up the shoes, one in each hand, and tossed them onto the path. They landed, side by side, toes forward, about two paces distant.

He stood up and moved his feet experimentally. The empty shoes mimicked the motion of his feet. He stepped forward onto the path; the shoes politely maintained the two-pace distance, hopping ahead of him step by step. Morlock nodded, content. Then he strapped his backpack to his slightly crooked shoulders and walked, barefoot, into the deadly woods.

Morlock first became aware of the trap through a sensation of walking on air.

He stopped in his tracks and looked at his shoes. They stood on an ordinary stretch of path, dry earth speckled with small sharp stones. But just in front of his bare feet he saw a dark shoe-shaped patch of nothingness.

Morlock nodded and scraped his right foot on the path; the right shoe mimicked it, brushing away a paper-thin surface of earth suspended in the air, revealing the nothingness beneath.

"Well made," Morlock the Maker conceded. No doubt the pit beneath the path concealed some deadly thing—that was rather crude. But Morlock liked the sheet of earth hanging in the air, and would have liked to know how it was done.

Carefully approaching the verge of the pit, he peered through the empty footprint. The pit was about twice as deep as Morlock was tall. At its bottom was a fire-breathing serpent with vestigial wings, perhaps as long as the pit was deep. The serpent wore a metal collar, apparently bolted to its spine; the collar was fastened to a chain anchored to the sheer stone wall of the pit. The serpent, seeing Morlock, roared its rage and disappointment.

"Who set you here, serpent?" Morlock asked.

"I set myself," the worm sneered. "This chain is a clever ruse to deceive the unwary."

"I have gold," Morlock observed.

The serpent fell quiet. Its red-slotted eyes took on a greenish tint.

Morlock reached into his pocket and brought forth a single coin. He swept away the dirt hanging in the air and held the coin out for the serpent to see.

It saw. Its tongue flickered desperately in and out. Finally it said, "Very well. Throw me the coin."

Morlock dropped the gold disc into the pit. "Tell me now."

The serpent roared in triumph, "*I tell you nothing!* Only a fool gives gold for nothing. Go away, fool."

Morlock (he knew the breed) patiently reached back into his pack and brought forth a handful of gold coins.

Silence fell like a thunderbolt. Morlock held the gold coins out and let the serpent stare at them through his fingers.

"Tell me *now*," Morlock said at last.

"It was a magician from beyond the Sea of Worlds," the serpent replied, too readily. "He said I could eat your flesh, but must leave the bones. I said I would break the bones and eat the marrow, and no power in the world could stop me. He called me a bold worm, strong and logical. He agreed about the bones. Then he rode away on a horse as tall as a tree."

Morlock allowed a single coin to fall into the pit.

"More!" The word rose on a tongue of flame through the mist of venom blanketing the serpent.

"I will give you two more. For the truth."

"All!" shouted the worm. "All! All! All!"

"The truth."

"It was a Master Dragon of the Blackthorn Range. He—"

Morlock snapped the fingers of his left hand twice. The two coins that had fallen into the pit rose glittering out of the cloud of venom and landed on his outstretched palm.

"Thief!" the serpent screamed.

"Liar," Morlock replied. In the language they were speaking it was the same word.

There was a long silence, broken by the serpent's roar of defeat. "I don't *know* who he was! He came on me while I was asleep. I didn't wake up until he drove this bolt into my neck. Take your gold and go!"

"What did he look like?" Morlock demanded. "Describe him."

"Describe him! Describe him!" the serpent hissed despairingly. "He was no different from you."

Morlock shrugged. He'd met serpents better able to distinguish between human beings. But he had never supposed his interlocutor a genius among worms. He opened both his hands and scattered gold into the pit.

As he rose to go the serpent called, "Wait!"

Morlock waited.

"I'm hungry," the serpent said insinuatingly.

"Then?"

"Must I be more explicit? I was promised a meal, yourself, if I permitted myself to be staked in this pit. I am staked in this pit, and have been denied the meal by the most offensive sort of trickery. You are the responsible party, and your double obligation is clear. I ask only that you remove any buckles or metal objects you may have about your person, for I have a bad tooth—"

"No."

"But this tooth—"

"You may not eat me."

"Be reasonable. I won't eat you all at once," the serpent offered hopefully.

Morlock shook his head, declining this reasonable offer. "Nevertheless," he added slowly (for it occurred to him this creature would certainly die if it remained staked in the pit), "I will set you free for some slight charge. Perhaps a single gold coin."

There was a pause as the worm struggled between the prospect of certain death or the loss of any part of its new wealth. "Never!" it snarled at last.

Morlock walked away. The worm's voice followed him, carrying threats and abuse but never an offer to change. Morlock ignored it and presently it ceased.

The path came to an end just beyond the pit. This left him at something of a loss as to where to go next, but there was one good thing about it: he could put his shoes back on.

He sat down and tugged the leather strips from his dusty feet, breaking the spell. He heard footsteps and looked up to see his shoes running away into the dense bluish woods.

Morlock was aghast. Some spirit or invisible creature had clearly stepped into his shoes as they preceded him down the path. When the spell was broken they had stolen the shoes.

He had to recover those shoes. He had made them with his own hands; he had worn them for months; he had written his own name and other magical words on them. He would never be safe if he did not recover them.

Leaping to his feet, he heard footsteps crackling eastward through the blue-green underbrush. Heedlessly he followed them.

It was not long before the poisonous blue leaves began to sting his bare feet. These had already been scratched and bruised by his barefoot walk down the stony path. The slight pain from the poison naggingly reminded him that if he walked for long in these woods without protection for his feet the poison would accumulate in his lower limbs and they would die. Then he would face the unpleasant alternatives of self-amputation or death.

The shoes seemed to be aware of his danger. At every turn they plunged into the thickest underbrush, treading down hard to leave a path sharp with broken sticks and poison leaves.

But their strategy was not an unqualified success. Whatever their guiding intelligence was, it did not provide Morlock's sheer physical mass: an undoubted advantage in storming through wild shrubbery. The shoes became entangled for long moments in places where Morlock simply brushed through or leapt over, and he closed steadily.

In a gap without trees he drew to a halt and listened, knee-deep in leafy poison. Silence fell in the winterwood. The crashing through blue bracken and greenish underbrush had ceased. His shoes had taken cover somewhere.

His heart fell. He was bound to lose a waiting game. He seized the first heavy branch that came to hand, tore it loose from its tree, and began to beat savagely about the dense covert of bushes.

It was sheer luck he glanced up to see his fugitive shoes weaving and dodging among the close-set trees on the opposite side of the narrow clearing. Morlock gave a crowlike caw of dismay and dashed off in pursuit. But almost as soon as he spotted them they disappeared in the woods beyond.

Morlock forced himself to halt at the place he had last seen the shoes. He listened. Again a sly chill quiet had descended on the winterwood. There was no light footfall, no crunch of leaf or snap of twig—not so much as the rustle of leather soles edging forward in the grass. The shoes had taken cover again. And they were nearby; he was sure of it.

He turned slowly, a full circle, examining every rock, stone, bush, or tree in sight. He saw no trace of his shoes. He moved forward, as quietly as possible, striving to make no sound that might cover the shoes' retreat. He saw nothing. He heard nothing.

After taking ten paces forward, he halted. He had missed them somehow; they could not have come much farther than this. He turned and looked back the way he had come. Then, on a bitterly sharp impulse, he glanced up at the forest roof. Far out of reach, the shoes stood nonchalantly upon a blue-black tree limb.

He crouched down and groped about on the forest floor. Latching on to a fist-sized rock, he rose again and pegged it with deadly accuracy at the rakishly tilted right shoe. Then he held the branch, like a crooked javelin, ready in his other hand in case he needed something to throw at the other shoe.

But he didn't. The right shoe tumbled almost to the ground before the other followed it, hurtling from the bough like a stone shot from a sling. Morlock wasted a moment wondering about the nature of the thing that had stepped into his shoes. Before he shook off his speculations the shoes began hopping like a pair of leather toads across the forest floor.

Then, in an instant, the chase was over.

The left shoe had hurled itself forward to land in a dimly blue patch of gripgrass (less greenish in color and finer than the weed carpeting the poisonous wood). In doing so it had bent the stems and torn the central roots of dozens of blades of the bluish grass.

Each offended blade divided into several long wire-tough lashes that instantly wrapped around the first solid object they touched. The left shoe was swiftly bound to the forest floor. Moreover, some of the released lashes inevitably snapped across their quiescent brethren; in less than a human vein-pulse the whole patch of gripgrass had come to greedy life. It snatched the right shoe, flying overhead, and bound it to the earth next to its mate. Even then a faint blue cloud of yearning tendrils floated on the air until the unoccupied blades re-formed themselves and slowly sank back into quiescence.

Their more fortunate kin clung tightly to their new prey, so that its death and corruption might provide food for the whole patch, not to mention serve as bait for an unwary carrion eater. This time they had caught nothing more nourishing than a pair of old shoes, but even if they had known they would not have cared; it is not in the nature of gripgrass to be choosy, and what they possess they do not surrender.

"*Hurs krakna!*" muttered Morlock, giving vent to one of the many untranslatable idioms of his native language. Then he sat down and began to bind up his feet, using strips torn from his cloak.

It is not every master maker who carries a choir of flames in his backpack. For one thing, few master makers have backpacks, being typically as sessile as clams. Also, flames are not readily portable; they require care of a peculiar sort; they are fickle and given to odd ideas. Nevertheless Morlock, a gifted maker of gems, knew that there was nothing so helpful in tending a seed-stone as a choir of wise old flames.

The sphere of smoke clinging to the choir nexus was dense and hot, so Morlock kept his face well out of the way as he removed the dragon-hide wrapping of the nexus; there were the signs of a heated conversation in progress.

"In a former—"

"How do you expect—"

"—life, I was a salamander. Mere words can't imagine how much I meant—"

"—expect me to *breathe?*"

"—to myself, bright as a brick in the Burning Wall . . ."

"Remember lumbering through fossil-bright burning fields?"

"I prefer wood to coal. Would you feed us more? Would you? Eh? *Would* you?"

A shower of bright sharp laughs, like sparks, flew up into the dim air of the winterwood.

"I'm hungry!" cried a lone flame, when the laughter had passed. "Feed me! I'M GOING OUT! *FEED* ME!"

Morlock glanced into the nexus. "Friends," he said patiently, "fully half the coal I gave you last night is unconsumed. You needn't go out."

"Coal is boring!" the desperate flame cried. "Death before boredom!"

"*Death before boredom!*" the choir cried as one.

"Most of us like coal, you understand," a flame confided agreeably. "But we all support the principle."

"Principle first, always," another flame agreed. "And more coal, please."

"It makes my light so dark and heavy. And all those strange memories!"

"Strange memories, yes. Remember all those fish!"

"I remember remembering. Strange to be a fish."

"No coal!" hollered the desperate flame. "No coal!"

"Snuff yourself."

"Friends," said Morlock, "I come to offer you variety."

"Variety," one observed snidely. "How dull!"

"I have a task for a single flame—outside the nexus."

This shocked them into silence. It was the nexus that sustained them beyond the ordinary term of flamehood, giving them time to develop their intelligence. In twenty years of life, many of them had never blown a spark outside the nexus.

"Well, what is it?" one flame demanded matter-of-factly.

With equal matter-of-factness, Morlock held up one of his clothbound feet. "My shoes have run away into a plot of gripgrass. I want one of you to eat them free."

He waited patiently while the choir exhausted itself in laughter and jeers.

"Gripgrass is something none of you has tasted," Morlock continued. "Furthermore, if one of you volunteers I will give the whole choir two double handfuls of leaves, the smoke of which is poisonous to man."

"Nonsense!" cried a panicky voice, in which Morlock thought he recognized the coal-hater. "Coal's good enough for us! Nothing better! More coal or nothing!"

"I like coal well enough," the matter-of-fact voice said, "but it will never taste so good to me unless I try gripgrass."

"Then," Morlock said, and snapped his fingers. The flame hurtled up and landed in Morlock's palm. Morlock immediately fed it with a strip of bark from the branch he still carried.

"This bark tastes a bit odd," remarked the flame smokily.

"It is kin to gripgrass," Morlock replied. "Do not talk, but listen. Time is your enemy as long as you are outside the nexus. Yonder is the gripgrass hiding my shoes. Do you see them?"

"Smell 'em."

"Then. I'll place you on the forest floor; work your way into the gripgrass and burn the shoes free, then proceed to the far side of the patch. The nexus will be there and you can climb back inside. Do not speak unless you are in trouble; then I will do what I can for you. *Do not propagate* or you will lose yourself in your progeny. Plain enough?"

The red wavering flame nodded and danced anxiously. Morlock put it down and watched it burn a black smoking beeline for the dim blue patch of gripgrass.

Morlock absently brushed the pile of ashes from his palm, but did not check for blisters. It took a flame hot enough to melt gold to do harm to his flesh; like his crooked shoulders and his skill at magic, that was the heritage of Ambrosius.

Having placed the nexus beyond the gripgrass patch, just out of lash-reach, Morlock sat down beside it and began to whittle idly at the branch he still held in his hand. The pale bluish scraps of wood he fed to the flames were still resident in the nexus.

"This wood has a cold marshy taste," a flame remarked, not disapprovingly.

"I don't think I like it," another said. "But I'd need more to be sure."

"Don't blow the smoke over here," said Morlock, annoyed. He'd taken enough poison today as it was; his feet were numb with it. He tossed another pile of wood scraps in the nexus; that was when the gripgrass plot lashed out again.

Morlock had been expecting this. If a plant's central stem was burned through it would not (because it could not) unleash. The central stem would respond to the burning of a peripheral stem, and some central stems would fall and set off the inevitable chain reaction.

Still it was alarming. The air currents totally dispersed the smoke trail by which Morlock had been gauging the flame's progress. Even after some moments the smoke did not return.

"Are you all right?" Morlock called out.

"Yes," replied the flame, its voice muffled by the tightly woven roof of gripgrass.

"Can you breathe?"

"*Yes*," replied the flame, with overtones of annoyance.

Morlock took the hint and returned to his whittling.

Presently the flame's bright wavering crown appeared, like the point of a knife, through the blue mat of gripgrass. It swiftly ran around and cut a smoking shoe-sized hole in the still tightly lashed grass.

"One shoe free," the flame announced curtly and disappeared.

Finally the wavering crown reappeared and repeated the procedure.

"Second shoe—" it began.

Then the flame was nearly extinguished by the passage of both shoes leaping backward up and out of the gripgrass patch. Landing with a double thump on the forest floor, they immediately began to run away again.

Morlock hurled the improvised javelin he had carved out of the tree branch, spearing the leather sole of one shoe. The other, farther off, kept on hopping away. Morlock bided his time. Finally throwing his knife, he transfixed the shoe, in midleap, to a nearby tree. Both shoes struggled briefly and fell still.

"You'd better get yourself some sensible shoes," suggested a matter-of-fact voice behind him. Before he could respond, the flame had reentered the nexus and was lost among the choir.

He fed the choir their double handfuls of leaves and sat aside while they smokily consumed and discussed them. As he waited he carefully removed every trace of the spell he had written on the shoes; he sewed up the holes with the leftover strips of leather from the spell.

The reek of poisonous smoke was still heavy in the air when he finished, and he glanced impatiently over toward the nexus. If he'd known they were going to take this long he would have picked drier leaves. (They preferred leaves moist or, as they said, "chewy.")

"We've been done for centuries!" cried a flame defensively as he approached. He saw this was essentially correct; the leaves had all been consumed, and they were working again on their lump of coal.

"We think the forest may be on fire," the matter-of-fact voice observed.

"It may be," Morlock agreed. "Friends, I am going to wrap you up again."

He took their complaints and bitter insults in good part. But he wrapped the nexus in its dragon-hide covering and stowed it in his backpack.

Shoes firmly fastened to his feet, pack comfortably strapped to his crooked shoulders, Morlock wandered casually toward the source of the poisonous smoke. On his way he was attacked by several white wolfish or canine beasts that had black beaks and narrow birdlike faces. He killed one of them with the accursed sword Tyrfing. He had no chance to examine the dead predator's body; although its companions fled howling, the corpse was immediately set upon by a cloud of small catlike creatures with long leathery wings ending in reticulated claws. These were apparently scavengers that followed the bird-wolf pack. They descended with pitiless delight on the dead predator; their brown triangular cat-faces were soon black with blood.

Several of the scavenger catbirds orbited around Morlock, as if searching for a place to land and feast. He knocked them away. One scored a long bloody gash along his left forearm, but as the wound was shallow he decided against treating it at that emergent moment.

He was further delayed by the passage of a fire-breathing serpent taller than himself and as long as a caravan. The approach of this monster was evident from five hundred paces away in the afternoon gloom of the woods. Deciding to take cover until the thing passed, he climbed a tree with comparatively dense foliage, most of which was still blue-black from winter, and wrapped himself in his black traveling cloak to complete the camouflage.

He could feel the blood from his wound soaking into the cloak, which began to cling to his skin. And his torn, bruised, and poisoned feet had had enough trouble today without perching for an appreciable chunk of the evening on a tree branch. Plus, there was the inevitable sharp object intruding on his wounded arm—he didn't want to move away from it in the serpent's presence. (Fire breathers do not hear or smell very well, but they have bitterly keen eyesight.) He grinned wryly and waited it out. Most annoyingly, and most trivially, leaves from the tree (he assumed that was what they were) kept brushing against him and tickling his skin unbearably.

The giant worm rumbled away into the woods. Morlock sighed with relief. Now for some free movement . . . and a good scratch!

He threw back his cloak. The catbirds that had settled down on and around him (whose feather-fur he had mistaken for leaves) leapt screaming into the air and began to circle the tree.

Morlock shouted several croaking insults a crow had once taught him, then plucked one of the catbirds out of the air and snapped its neck. He killed a second with a well-thrown knife and dropped the first body where the second one fell.

The scavengers having gathered on the ground to feed on their fallen comrades, and Morlock dropped down beside them, branch in hand. He killed several more scavengers by methodically flailing about before the survivors flew off to a safe distance. It was an ugly business, and as Morlock stood over the crushed catbirds and heard their fellows screaming at him from a nearby tree, he was not pleased with himself.

But it had been necessary. This demonstrated to the deadly catbirds that he was not merely a wounded prey staving off death but a predator in his own right. They would be more cautious in following him thereafter; perhaps they would leave his trail entirely. And if nothing else, these corpses would entertain the survivors while he got away.

Having retrieved, cleaned, and sheathed his knife (the grip was covered by razor-thin teethmarks), Morlock made his way into the woods. He looked back once and saw that the forest floor where the dead catbirds had been was alive with dark winged forms.

Heading straight into the smoke-bearing wind, he walked until he found the fire. By that time night had entirely risen, and he could see from a distance that it was a kind of campfire. A tree had been cut and sectioned, certain sections quartered and several of the quarters set afire, all with considerable labor, no doubt. The hapless campers, one man and one woman, lay unconscious before the fire. You might have thought them overcome by weariness until you noticed their faces, greenish even in the red firelight. Apparently they'd been poisoned by the fire they'd set and were in danger of dying.

Morlock felt the tug of sympathy; he also felt there was something wrong with this scene. But out of the corner of his eye he saw the cloud of scavenger catbirds settle silently down on a nearby tree. He found he couldn't walk away and leave these as catbird fodder.

He beat down the flames with his hands and heaved earth over the fuming coals. He sat down some distance away from the pair and bound up his wounded arm as he waited for them to awaken.

Morlock kept thinking he should get about his own business. But the scavengers were still out there in the darkness watching what he would do. He waited, thinking long, slow thoughts to pass the time. Twice he roused himself to kill several large carnivorous beetles the size and temperament of snapping turtles who were approaching him hungrily. He tossed the dead beetles out into the wood, where the catbirds devoured them.

Finally the woman stirred. A long yawn broke off in a gasp as she sat suddenly up.

"Vren," she said, in the *lingua franca* of the Ontilian Empire, "the fire has gone out!"

"Not exactly 'gone out,'" Morlock observed, in the same language. "I extinguished it."

Now both man and woman were standing. "Who are you?" the woman demanded. "*Where* are you?"

"I am a traveller," Morlock said cautiously. He rarely gave his name, south of the Whitethorn Range. "I am somewhat behind you and off to one side, as you can tell from my voice. Passing by, I noticed your fire and found you overcome with its fumes."

"Oh," said the woman. "Are the trees poisonous, too?"

"Yes. You will find all life in Tychar inimical to you."

"Including yourself?" she shot back.

"Possibly," Morlock admitted. "There are some strange things about you two. How did you happen to fell, section, and burn one of these trees without noticing its nature?"

"We tell you nothing," Vren said sullenly.

"Be quiet, Vren," the woman said without heat. "We had the *kembril* do it, traveller. We had a spell, and we spoke it, and the *kembril* came. It brought us fire and food, as we commanded. The food was good, at least. The fire was . . . local."

Morlock did not recognize the word *kembril*, but he thought he understood the gist of the story. "You are sorcerers, then?"

"We are thieves, mostly," the woman said frankly. "(Be quiet, Vren! He saved our lives.) But we steal magic by choice. We are going to rob a sorcerer who lives in the winterwood. Maybe then we'll be sorcerers, with a little practice."

"There is a sorcerer in the wood?"

"Yes," said the woman reverently, "the greatest and evillest in the world: Morlock Ambrosius himself. He has settled in Tychar."

"Hmph," said Morlock, glad of the darkness. "This is news to me."

"Well," said the woman complacently, "few know of it. We were lucky enough to rob one of his sorcerous correspondents in Sarkunden, our hometown. We thought . . . well, for such as us it is the opportunity of a lifetime. We have a map."

Morlock had expected nothing else, except an offer to join their quest. That was forthcoming in another moment; he accepted with a thoughtful glumness that seemed to surprise his new companions.

The two thieves, Urla and Vren, went back to sleep, trusting as children, after Morlock offered to stand guard for the rest of the night. Or perhaps they were not so childlike, Morlock reflected: he had already had his chance to rob or kill them; they had more reason to trust him than he did to trust them, which was why he had taken the watch.

They walked all the next day and into the next night, avoiding death narrowly on a number of occasions. Each time, however, the catbird scavengers fed well on the corpses of their attackers. Morlock believed they had come to look on him as their patron predator. He found this annoying; there was nothing he could do about it, though.

That night they slept in shifts. Morlock took the last watch—something of a risk, perhaps. He had come to trust his companions, although he had occasion to think them somewhat timorous.

And he needed sleep. It had been long since he had woken up, south of the forest, to find himself robbed. His arm wound was infected and the poison in his system was slow to dissipate. He expected that tomorrow would be a very bad day indeed.

It was all too soon when Urla's voice woke him from a hellish dream and he crawled out of his sleeping cloak to stand watch over his companions. He sharpened a stick and absentmindedly speared any of the carnivorous beetles who crawled too near him or the sleepers. There was no fire, so he watched by the starlight and moonlight that managed to filter through the blue-black branches and leaves. He found that his left arm was swollen and sluggish, and so used his right hand almost exclusively.

At last dawn came. Morlock, having viewed the thieves' crude map several times the previous day, spent the last few moments of his watch calculating how long it might take them to reach the house of "Morlock."

He glanced idly back along the way they had come, noting that their trail was vividly marked by silver dew on the blue-green coarse grass of the winterwood. His eyes moved on; it was time to wake Urla and Vren—then he looked sharply back. *His* trail was visible: grasses bent by his passage dark among their silvery kin, footprints clearly outlined in the mold of the forest floor. But there was no sign of any others beside his.

Troubled, he looked down on his companions, now waking on their own in the dim blue dawn. He was sure they were real—that is, they were not mere illusions; they did not have the talic aura an illusion must project. Yet if they had left no trail in the woods, they could hardly be real.

Real, yet not real. He stared at them as they greeted one another, chatted, shook the dew off their blankets. . . . The grass moved beneath their feet, he noticed. But did it move enough for a real man and woman?

Vren was groaning. "Back to the packs! I thought mine would split my shoulders yesterday."

Urla sympathized and Morlock stepped over. "Let's trade," he suggested. "I'll carry yours, and you mine."

Vren looked surprised, then glanced at Morlock's formidable pack. "It's probably worse than mine," he grumbled.

"It's not so bad as it looks," Morlock insisted. "Give it a heft."

Vren hesitated. Both he and Urla wore tense troubled expressions. Morlock bent down and picked up Vren's pack. It was as light as a spiderweb.

Morlock dropped it and straightened; reaching out with both hands, he seized his companions under their chins. Pulling up strongly, he tore off both their faces.

In the holes that had been faces there were forests of silvery spines. They vibrated tensely for a few moments, then grew still. The skins of Urla and Vren separated and fell away, exposing the creatures that had worn them as a hand wears a glove . . . or a puppet. These "hands" had small insectlike bodies and hundreds of long silvery legs that took a roughly spherical shape around the central body.

Morlock had heard of such things. Given the outer shell of a person, and having fed on that person's brain, they could sustain his or her living likeness. But they had no muscle or significant mass of their own, so that the seeming person would be light as gauze. They were marginally intelligent; at least they could feign an intelligence suited to the guise they wore. But shorn of their disguise they would unthinkingly return to their creator for protection and guidance.

So these did, rolling away in the dim blue woods. Morlock shouldered his pack and followed them. Out of the corner of his eye he saw a few of the catbirds drop down and devour the discarded skins. The rest of the cloud followed silently on his trail.

The silver-spine creatures were not moving quickly, but Morlock was dazed with poison and fever; he almost lost them twice. Using his left arm had torn the wound open again, and it throbbed with each leaden heartbeat. Still he kept moving. The hunt was almost over.

They came at last to a dark stone house in the dim blue woods. The spheres of silver tines paused, then began to wander aimlessly along the walls, seeking ingress.

Morlock found two dead bodies lying against the door of the house. One had been a man, the other a woman. They had been flayed, their skulls broken like eggshells and drained. Carrion eaters had torn their flesh. These, Morlock guessed, were the originals of Urla and Vren. Morlock covered the bodies with earth and deadwood, sealing their quasi-comradeship.

Then he turned to the wooden door of the stone house. It was locked; he crouched down to examine the lock with his fingers. Only then did he understand how ill he was; his right hand was trembling too much to perform any subtle work and his left hand was swollen into useless immobility.

Morlock stood back and unslung his pack. He drew out the choir nexus and unwrapped it. He explained the matter in a single terse sentence; a moment later, fifteen volunteer flames were eating their way into the door around the lock. When they had passed through Morlock cried "Stay clear!" and kicked in the door.

He paused for a moment on the threshold, shuddering with fever chill and pain. (The blood-beats of exertion were agony to his wounded arm.) Then he passed into the entry hall and swore. The flames had stayed clear all right. From burn marks in the many rugs and tapestries it appeared they had scattered in search of adventure and interesting combustibles.

Well, he had no time to look for them. He stowed the nexus in his backpack and took that on his shoulders again. The hallway led him to a winding stairway; Morlock ascended it, feeling that the sorcerer's workroom would be on the upper floor.

It was. In fact, the workroom occupied the entire upper floor of the house. As he entered it, his enemy, at the far end of the long room, rose to greet him.

The room was full of water. It was lit (quite apart from the tall unglazed windows) by glass cylinders filled with a bubbling white fluid that emitted a harsh bluish light; these were set like torches along the walls. The stained worktables that lined the room were crowded with retorts, alembics, beakers, tubes, and tubing, all of them emitting or gathering liquid. In the middle of the room was a circular sheet of gray bubbling water, suspended in midair. At the far end of the room was a crystal globe fill with very bright, very clear water. Morlock guessed this was the sorcerer's focus. At any rate, he was seated before it with a fixed inward stare when Morlock entered the room, and he turned around and smiled broadly, as if in welcome.

"There are flames like rats loose in my house," he explained, rising. "Fortunately they have proven rather easy to detect and extinguish. I hate flames, I suppose as much as you love them. Mine is a watery sort of magic, as you will have guessed."

The stranger advanced through the room as he spoke, his manner suggesting that Morlock was an expected guest and he himself was a slightly remiss host. He wore garments of white and blue; otherwise he was a mirror image of Morlock: the same dark unruly hair, the same weather-beaten features, the same alarmingly pale gray eyes. The stranger even had crooked shoulders and walked with a slight limp, as Morlock did.

"Unimpressive," Morlock remarked. "Certainly not original."

The stranger looked surprised, then amused. "Oh, my appearance. But I assure you, my dear fellow, it is no mere ploy. Years of labor have gone into this work, and perhaps the rest of my life will go into perfecting it. You see, I have decided to usurp your personality."

Morlock shrugged.

"I'm not joking, either," the stranger continued. "Not that I'm surprised by your indifference. That's what gave me the idea, in a way.

"You see, I was sitting in a tavern (forgive my loquacity, but I have so looked forward to telling you all this) and a drunk was singing some nasty ghost story you were supposed to have had a part in. And I was thinking how . . . well, how unlike your legend you are. (Most of those-who-know know that.) And I thought, too, how little use you have put your legend to. It really is a remarkable resource, coupled with your true abilities. You are truly feared, south of the Kirach Kund. Yet you wander from place to place like . . . like some kind of magical tinker, when you might command fear and respect the way a general commands an army."

Morlock shrugged irritably. "Why?"

"Why?" repeated the stranger incredibly. "For everything a man could want!"

"There is not much that I want."

"That is your problem. It is not mine. Mine is (or was) that I had no legend. Like most makers, I have pursued my studies in solitude; we are too unworldly, most of us. I would have labored in obscurity, only to totter into some local fame when I was too infirm to put it to effective use. You have the advantage of us there; we aren't all descended from demi-mortals like you are.

"Then I realized (sitting in the tavern, you understand) that if *you* weren't going to use your legend, it was only fair that *I* do so. And to that I have bent my life ever since. I built my house here in the winterwood; I changed my appearance; I began to conduct correspondence with other sorcerers in my new person. Things were developing nicely, even before I ran into you along the trail the other night."

"So it was an accident."

"Some such meeting was inevitable," the stranger said superciliously. "Anyway, I managed to slit your pack and extract the book of palindromes (which has proven most instructive, by the way). But the protective spell over your person was so subtle I could not even guess its attributes. So I decided to lure you into my own territory. . . ."

Morlock was smiling wryly.

"I suppose that sneer means there was no spell," the stranger said bitterly. "Well, that doesn't matter. You are here, now, and your pack is here, and there are no risks involved. Or maybe you're thinking I'm an inferior sorcerer because I had to appropriate your legend. But I'm not. Your legend is a historical accident. I can't be held responsible for not being the beneficiary of a historical accident."

"It was political slander, originally," Morlock observed, a little weary of the subject.

"Really? That's most interesting. Take some political slander, let simmer a few hundred years, add seasoning, and dish up. Fearful legend, serves one. Very nice.

"Now arises the question of whether I will spare your life or not. I feel you might possibly be a useful adviser, under restraint—sort of the world's expert on having been Morlock, if you see what I mean. Also, I'm sure some of the most interesting artifacts in your pack would be damaged in a mortal combat. So . . ."

Morlock said nothing.

"Oh, come now," the stranger said irritably. "*Don't* try to be forbidding. I know exactly what shape you're in. I watched every step of your journey; don't think I didn't. I knew the forest would do my fighting for me! I saw you scrabbling at the lock on my door (what a pitiful performance that was!) and I see now that you can barely stand.

"And where do you stand? In my place of power. Never doubt it, Morlock: I have a thousand deaths at my beck and call as I stand here. Do you doubt it? You still are silent?" The stranger shrugged. "Very well. Why should you take my word for it?" He waved his hand and spoke an unintelligible word.

The weight on Morlock's crooked shoulders was suddenly heavier by several pounds. In sudden alarm, he unslung his pack and lifted out the choir nexus. Water poured out through the dragon-hide wrapping. The choir was dead.

"You killed my flames," Morlock said hoarsely. His eyes were stung by abrupt surprising tears.

The stranger laughed incredulously. "'Killed'? The notion is jejune. I extinguished them. That water might as easily have gone in your lungs instead, or—heated to steam—in your heart or brain. Then it is you who would have been *extinguished*. I killed my hundreds perfecting the techniques, Morlock, and they work. Never doubt it—again."

"I doubt you will find your own death jejune," Morlock replied. Tears were still running down his face; he supposed it was a symptom of the fever.

"Don't threaten me, you battered tramp!" the stranger snarled. "You were about to hand me your pack, that I might spare you what remains of your life. Do so now."

A long moment passed, in which Morlock seemed to consider. Then he slowly lifted the pack, holding it out to the stranger.

The stranger laughed and took the proffered edge. This, the only convenient hold, happened to be the place where he had slit the pack two days ago. When his grip was firm, Morlock pulled back, as firmly. The stranger's grip, resisting the tug, tore the gripgrass woven into the sewn seam.

The gripgrass, starved for nutriment, exploded into dozens of thin wire-tough lashes, binding the stranger's hand inescapably to the repaired slit. The stranger emptied his lungs in an instinctive cry of pain and surprise.

Morlock pulled him off his feet, by way of the pack, hauled him over to the nearest window, and, still holding on to the pack, threw the stranger out. His body slammed against the stone wall of the house and he stared up at Morlock for a long moment, as if gathering breath to speak.

Then his body was dark with winged forms. The catbird scavengers had been waiting for their predator, and he had not disappointed them. In a matter of minutes the stranger was dead, dismembered, and devoured. Morlock drew in a pack stained with blood, shining blue threads of satiated gripgrass woven into the sewn-up slit.

Morlock carefully unwove the grass. It had caused him considerable trouble, preserving its integrity, and it served no purpose now. When he finally disentangled the gripgrass, a matter-of-fact voice near his feet inquired, "Do you want that?"

He looked down to see a single red flame burning a hole in the wooden floor. "Because if you don't want it," the matter-of-fact flame remarked, "I'll take it."

Morlock dropped the grass on the floor and the flame casually devoured it.

"A little *too* chewy," the flame remarked smokily.

"The whole business was somewhat chewy," Morlock replied. "But it's over now, I guess." Taking some water from a nearby table, he set about sponging the blood off his backpack.

Morlock set the flame-nexus out to dry and searched the dead sorcerer's house for his stolen book of palindromes. He found it finally, or what was left of it, in a glass jar submerged in watery acid that was eating away the book's pages. It had passed the point of uselessness, so Morlock left it where it was.

Had Morlock been led to the dead sorcerer, or he to Morlock? Was the whole purpose of the encounter to deprive Morlock of the book of palindromes? He suspected as much.

If so, he should trust the book's last omen and continue his journey eastward.

He didn't know what awaited him there, but he gave it some thought as he left the watery sorcerer's house burning behind him in the winterwood.

VI

AN OLD LADY AND A LAKE

As Love, if Love be perfect, casts out fear,
So Hate, if Hate be perfect, casts out fear.
—Tennyson, *Merlin and Vivien*

very night for many days, Morlock had been dreaming about a house and a horse. The horse might have been Velox: Morlock couldn't see him or hear him, but he knew he was there, behind the house. The house was just a house, a little weatherworn cottage on an island in a deep blue-water lake between the unclaimed woods and the fuming foothills of the Burning Range. Morlock dreamed he was walking around the house trying to see the horse, but the horse kept moving to keep out of sight. That was all there was to the dream.

The first time, the dream was frustrating. The second time was maddening. The third left him thoughtful. He was deliberately not reaching out with his Sight to make contact with the future, as he suspected his enemy was laying traps for him in the tal-realm. But it seemed as if an especially insistent future was reaching out to make contact with him. He began to have the dream every night, sometimes more than once, as he continued his journey eastward, going deep into the crooked margin of the mountains to avoid a region to the south that some friendly crows had warned him about. His insight also said the place was dense with talic danger.

The fifteenth morning after the dreams began, he walked into a clearing between the unclaimed woods and the fuming foothills of the Burning Range, and there he saw a deep blue-water lake with a small island in it.

There was a wooden footbridge from the mainland to the island, and in the middle of the island was the cottage of his dream.

Morlock stepped onto the bridge. At that instant, with a roar and a clanking of chains, a fair-sized troll leapt out from under the bridge and landed atop the wooden walkway.

"Now I eat you!" the troll proclaimed. "I was set here with the precise and specific mandate to eat anyone on my bridge who crosses it without my permission, as you have done, so now I will eat you!" Its ear-braids quivered with anticipation. "Do you follow me, or shall I explain again?"

"I have not yet crossed the bridge," Morlock pointed out.

"Oh!" The troll tugged fretfully in turn at the tufts of unbraided hair proceeding from several of its noses. "Oh. Damn it. And I'm hungry, too. All I've had to eat for the longest time has been fish, and a bite or two from the Pernicious Grishk that lives in the lake."

"What's a grishk?"

"It's pernicious and lives in the lake. And it gets a bite out of me at least as often as I get one from it, so I'm not sure that even counts. Are you going to cross the bridge or what?"

"If you'll stand aside and permit me."

The troll put several hands in its pockets, and the leftover hands behind its back, and stood toward the edge of the bridge. Morlock crossed over to the island and went up toward the cottage. The troll groaned when it realized how Morlock had tricked it and slunk down into the water under the bridge.

Morlock looked the cottage over carefully. He walked around it once, very slow, widdershins. He saw no hoofprints in the soft ground, of a horse or anything else.

That wasn't surprising. Morlock suspected the dream's meaning, if it meant anything, was that he would get news of Velox here.

He shrugged and knocked on the cottage door. It was opened by an extremely aged old woman with a bloodless wrinkled face and sunken gray eyes.

"Excuse me, madam," Morlock said, "but I'm looking for my horse—"

"Is that supposed to be funny?" the old woman screamed, hiding behind her half-opened door.

"No," Morlock said slowly. "Why would it be?"

"And that 'disguise,' I suppose you call it."

"I don't."

"You don't even not look like you!" she screamed.

"I'm not supposed to not look like me. If I understand what you're saying."

"Look at those shoulders!" she hooted. "Bent like an ill-made bow! You can wear a black wig and fake a limp until Hell freezes over but you'll never fool me! You never did! You've fooled me too many times before!"

"I don't suppose you've seen a horse around here," he said rather desperately. "A middle-aged black warhorse with silver eyes?"

"Is that supposed to be *funny*?"

"Good day, madam," he said, giving up. "I'm sorry to have bothered you." He started to turn away.

"Stop!" she said, peering at him with sea gray eyes out of an ashen face. "What was that you said?"

"I'm sorry to have bothered you."

"Can't be him," she muttered to herself. "*Can't* be him. On his best day he wouldn't apologize for disembowelling your pet weasel."

"I don't have a pet weasel, madam. Just a horse. I'll look elsewhere for him."

"You'd better come in, then," she said resignedly. "Your horse might be somewhere about the place. You must pardon me, young man; I'm almost completely crazy."

"I hadn't noticed, madam," he lied. It had been a long time since anyone had referred to Morlock as a *young man* but he took it in his somewhat irregular stride.

"Well, I wouldn't notice your horse if he were creeping around in my underwear. An intriguing thought, that."

Intriguing wasn't the word Morlock would have chosen, but he didn't know how to say so without seeming rude. At no time in his several centuries of life had a conversation ever gotten so completely away from him. The old lady waved her hands at him imperiously. He shrugged and stepped in through the door.

She led the way into the little room that made up the entirety of her little house and collapsed onto a stool by a table as if her legs wouldn't carry her any further. "What was it you wanted?" she demanded.

"I'm looking for my—"

"Oh, I remember all that. But you really mean it? It wasn't just a chance to get inside and rummage through my, er, things?"

Morlock thought it was possible she was moving her hips suggestively as she squatted on the stool. He decided that he had not noticed this, and that he wasn't going to, either. He shook his head decisively.

"Damn," she said thickly, and coughed. "I was hoping there was something here you wanted. Because—well, because there's something I want you to do to—for me."

"What's that?" Morlock asked.

"If experience is any guide, I'm about to die." She coughed again and rubbed at her nose. Something white fell out of it and wiggled on the table. "I was hoping you'd bury me. I hate the thought of lying around the house and rotting away." She coughed again. "And there's no one else to do it, you see."

The white wriggling thing on the table was unquestionably a maggot. Morlock looked at it a moment and said, "I'll bury you, madam. Assuming you die fairly soon, that is. I'm still looking for my horse."

"This hippophilia really becomes quite tiresome, after a while," the old lady said crossly. "Is it a nice horse?" she asked wistfully.

"Not very," Morlock admitted, "but we've been through a lot together. He was stolen from me by someone I think might harm him, so I'm trying to get him back. A dream led me here, but I suppose it was a false one."

"So," she said, nodding wisely, "you're a seer of visions. And, I suppose, a maker of things."

"Yes."

"The Two Arts! Seeing and Making, the Sight and the Strength! I knew something about them in my day."

"I'm sure you did."

"Meaning: you're sure you know more than I ever did. Well. Maybe you're right. But not everyone had my teacher, anyway. Although he taught Ambrosia twice as much as he did me—" She broke off in a coughing fit.

"Ambrosia, madam?" asked Morlock, when her coughing subsided. "Ambrosia Viviana? Do you know her?"

The old lady cackled. "Slightly. She's my daughter. That impresses you, eh? I wish she were here." She started coughing again.

Ambrosia Viviana was Morlock's sister. That meant this deranged rotting old woman was his mother.

"Hard to die without anyone near me—only a stranger—" she gasped between coughs.

What was he to say? *I'm not a stranger; I'm your son.* Then she might say, *My son is a stranger.*

She was still coughing, anyway, bent nearly double. He reached out in a mute meaningless gesture to comfort her, but she shied away and fell from the stool to the floor. "Oh, shit—" she gasped and then vomited a spray of maggots as her limbs spasmed briefly.

She wasn't coughing, or even moving now. Morlock bent down over her and wiped away the maggots from her face. She didn't seem to be breathing. There was no flutter of life beneath the withered breasts. His mother was dead.

There was a small well-kept garden outside the little house. He took the lifeless, strangely light body out there and buried it in the shade of a plum tree. He cut some slate from an outcropping he had seen up the weed-choked road and on it he carved an epitaph.

Here lies, far from her home,
Nimue Viviana
faithful traitor
loveless love
lost and found
Domina Laci
wife to Merlin Ambrosius
mother to Ambrosia Viviana
to Hope Nimuelle
and to Morlock Ambrosius,
who carved these words.
Requiescas in pace, mater perdita.

He set the stone above the fresh grave and then stepped back.

"Nice work," his father's voice said, in grudging tones, behind him. "She'd have liked the Latin, especially. Was it just a slip, or did you know that *mater perdita* means both 'lost mother' and 'damned mother'?"

"I didn't know her well enough for the second one," Morlock said, without turning.

"Oh, I think she would have enjoyed it," Merlin's voice replied. "She always liked a play on words."

"I wouldn't know."

"Don't get weepy on me, boy."

"I'm not a boy, so I get weepy when it suits me."

"Aren't you at least surprised I got here so fast?"

Morlock grunted skeptically. "Who says you're here?" he said, and turned.

Merlin's fetch was about a pace behind him.

The fetch is a mind's talic halo. Most people's fetches look like animals or gnomes or specters of some sort, and few ever see them except in dreams or the visionary state. Merlin's was more solid and useful; he had taught it to wear a cloak of visible light that resembled himself, and his conscious mind could dispatch it on errands.

"Did you take my horse?" Morlock asked Merlin's fetch.

Merlin's face twisted with annoyance. "Yes, and a lot of good it did me, too. I was hoping I could adapt its immortality to poor Nimue's case. But it died after only a few experiments, and now she's dead anyway. Oh well. Better luck next wife, I say."

"Eh."

"God Avenger, what a bore you are, Morlock! How am I supposed to make conversation with someone who just grunts at my witty remarks and wise sayings?"

Morlock shrugged indifferently. He was fairly sure Merlin was lying to him about something. Encouraging further witty remarks and wise sayings, if that's what they were, didn't seem like a good way of getting at the truth. In fact . . .

There were a limited number of ways by which a seer could project an

effective fetch very far from his body. The best way involved an anchor that
had been put in talic stranj with the seer's focus of power. Breaking the stone
would shatter the talic link and disperse the fetch.

Morlock drew Tyrfing and summoned the lowest level of vision.

It was what Merlin had been waiting for. The fetch bristled suddenly
with talic force, striking at Morlock's awareness through his vision. Morlock
deflected the lightning-like attack with Tyrfing and watched for lines of talic
emanation from Merlin's suddenly blazing fetch.

Aha. There.

Morlock dismissed his vision and walked toward an unremarkable blue-
gray stone at the edge of the woods.

"Oh, come now," Merlin's voice sounded irritably behind him. "That's no
way to win a quarrel! If you were any kind of—"

Morlock swung Tyrfing once, shattering the stone. Merlin's voice fell
silent, and when Morlock turned around the fetch had disappeared.

In all likelihood, Merlin had other anchors hidden nearby. But probably
he would wait to use them. Morlock was free from Merlin's peevish ranting,
if not from his observation, for a time.

Morlock went into the house and began to sort through his dead
mother's things. There was surprisingly little there: the place was almost like
the house-sized mausoleums he had seen in Anhi. The Anhikhs often surrounded a dead body with a replica of the place where it had lived, giving its
ghost the illusion of being home, so that it would not wander. Morlock found
some books and marked-up sheets of paper, a few clothes, some household
implements, cold-lamps for reading after dark, some firewood and firemakers
beside the narrow hearth. But he found few clothes and no food or drink at
all. It was incomplete, unreal.

One of the sheets of paper was a letter Nimue had written to herself.

Hello—

I am you. (Check your handwriting against mine and see if this isn't so.)
    *You are feeling confused right now and you don't remember much. Don't worry
about that. Your memories will return, or at least some of them will.*

Your name is Nimue Viviana. You live in this house. If you try to go far from it, someone will try to stop you. Sometimes he will call himself Merlin, sometimes other things. Whatever he says, don't believe him. He thinks he knows what is best for you, which means you cannot trust him about anything. But he can keep you from leaving this place and he will. There is a troll under the bridge and monsters in the water of the lake, and probably other guards besides.

The confusion you are feeling are the effects of the antideath spell that Merlin has put on you. You must find a way to break it somehow. The more you remember about Merlin the more impossible this will seem but, trust me, you know a lot of magic yourself. You just have to remember it. Don't be discouraged.

Good luck. I'll be rooting for you!

With sincere self-regard,

    NIMUE VIVIANA

Morlock was sitting by the window, rereading this odd letter for the second time, when a shadow fell on the page. He looked up to see his mother standing over him, as filthy as if she had just clawed her way out of the grave, which she evidently had. Her face was twisted with anger, and in her unsteady hands she held the shovel he had buried her with. She lifted the shovel and struck him with it.

The blow fell without much weight; he was more stunned by the event itself. When she began to wrestle the shovel aloft to hit him again, he stood up and took it from her.

"Who are you!" she shouted—an accusation of strangerhood more than a question. "Why are you here, going through my things!" She paused and put a filthy hand to her filthy forehead. "Who am I?" she asked, and it was a real question.

He handed her the letter and stood aside to let her sit by the window.

She read the letter through. "Get me something to write with, won't you, dear?" she said presently.

He already had a wax tablet and stylus in his hand, and he handed them to her. She scratched away for a while on the tablet, then looked at the letter, shrewdly comparing the scripts. "Looks the same," she said to Morlock, finally. "But maybe he wrote the letter. He's a pretty good forger, unless I'm thinking about someone else."

Guessing she meant Merlin, Morlock said, "He'd have told you to trust him."

"Unless he wanted to manipulate me by telling me something, as himself, that he really wanted me to disbelieve. I seem to remember now that he likes these little tricks and disguises and things."

"Yes, but—" Morlock began, and spread his hands.

"—but," she concluded for him, "he can never stand for these little theatrical games to go on for very long. Like any unprofessional actor, his favorite part of any performance is taking his bows. 'Oh, Merlin, how clever you are; you've fooled me again.' Asshole."

"Yes."

"I can see you know him well. Even if you don't say much, and you slouch. Stand straight, young man."

"I'm as straight as I'll ever be," Morlock replied sharply.

She glanced at him with a watery gray eye. "Oh? Are you one of *them*? The Ambrosii?"

"Yes."

"Which one?"

Reluctantly, he said, "Morlock."

She took it without flinching. "Well. We meet at last, eh? Not one for sentimental reunions, are you?"

"No."

"Good. I let Merlin think I was crazy about you because it seemed to irritate him, but it would be awkward to assume a doting-mother-with-dutiful-son act this late in our respective lives, wouldn't it? It was different with my daughters. I actually knew them. Are they still . . . ?"

"They were fine when I last saw them, early in winter."

"Who's in charge? Has Hope taken over?"

"Ambrosia is usually in charge."

"Still? Must be getting a little elderly, though. Thought Hope would show a little more backbone by now. Anyone would get tired of being pushed around by Ambrosia for—"

"I am very fond of Ambrosia," he interrupted her.

"Oh, who isn't? She sees to that. Never mind. I love them both better than you ever will, young man."

"Mother," he said (the word coming rather awkwardly to his lips), "I am over four hundred years old."

"What!" she shouted, then sat there bemused for a while, her lips twitching as if she were talking to herself, but no words could be heard.

"I suppose you must be," she said aloud at last. "Yes, it is starting to come back to me, I guess. I really thought I had beaten him, this time— thought I'd broken his antideath spell and I really was going to go west. Then this young fellow came to the door and I asked him to bury me—oh, that was you, wasn't it?"

"Yes."

"You were looking for your horse. Did you ever find it?"

"Merlin took him."

"Oh, I'm so sorry. You should see what he does with animals in his workshops; says it's all part of his craft of lifemaking. Cruelty, I call it. Was it a nice horse?" she asked wistfully.

"Not very, but we've been through a lot together."

"That's what you said last time—have we had this conversation before?"

"Part of it."

"You must pardon me, young man; I'm almost completely crazy. What was your name again?"

"Is that part of the antideath spell?"

"Is what? The craziness? Yes, exactly. I'm not all here, in any sense of the words. Merlin cut my selfhood in three parts and hid them from each other."

"Oh?"

"Don't believe me?" She shrugged and reached up both hands to the back of her head. She undid something there, and then abruptly turned her head inside out. There was no skull or apparently any sort of bone or organ inside the empty skin, at least as far as he could see down the fleshy tunnel of her throat. The inner surface of her skin did display a large number of maggots, however.

He was deeply horrified, but he tried not to show it. "No bones, eh?" he remarked.

"No nothing: just my shell," her voice replied, somewhat muffled.

"I suppose some spell transmitting magnified talic impulses provides the equivalent of skeletal support and organic functions?"

"I guess so," she said, refolding her head so that her face reappeared. "He wouldn't tell me about it—I suppose he thought I'd try to counter-inscribe the spell somehow. Which I have, a few times, but nothing seems to work."

"Hm. Er—"

"Oh, for Christ's sake, don't grunt at me. What is it?"

"You seem to have—there's an infestation of . . ."

"The maggots, you mean? Well, well, quite the observant one, aren't we? Yes, young fellow, one of the hazards of perpetually dying is the occasional infestation, as you so sweetly put it, of *maggots*."

"If you rinse yourself out with salt water, that may clear them away."

"If it were that easy—Salt water, you say?"

"Yes."

"Sting, won't it?"

"It won't kill you."

"Is that supposed to be *funny*? Oh, never mind; I guess it is, sort of."

"Where's the rest of you?"

"Which one of us is crazy, anyway? Haven't you been listening? I don't know. I'm just the shell of myself. There are three of me now: my shell, my impulse-cloud, and my core self. If there is a way for me to know where they are, I don't know it. I don't know half of what I used to know, and what I do know I often can't remember."

"But he couldn't have done this unless . . ." Morlock broke off.

But she had heard. "Unless I consented?" she asked. "Ah, but I did consent. Of course I did. Young man—what's your name?"

"Morlock."

"Morlock. That was my son's name. I haven't seen him since the day he was born, and yet sometimes I feel that I loved him the most of all my children. When—"

"Enough of that. Merlin's not here."

"Yes, perhaps you're right. Anyway, have you ever been in imminent danger of death?"

"Yes."

"Oh. Good. Excellent. Well: wouldn't you have done anything, absolutely anything in that moment to go on living?"

"No."

"What? You're lying."

"No."

"I can take your word on that, can I, Epimenides? Well, anyway, *I* was on the point of death, and he talked *me* into it. I was afraid, and he . . . he said he could cure death and even the common cold if he had enough time—this was just a temporary measure. A temporary measure. Do you know how long it's been since then?"

"If he built the house for this purpose: between one hundred fifty and two hundred years."

Nimue looked at him with somber gray eyes and said in a subdued voice, "That's about right. Say, you sounded a bit like him, just then. You're not him in disguise, are you? What's your name?"

"Morlock."

"Ha. That's a laugh. My son's name is Morlock."

"You mentioned that."

"I tend to repeat myself at times. You'll have to forgive me, young man, but I'm almost completely crazy."

"Because of the antideath spell."

"Yes! He was so clever. And I didn't notice: he never said it was a life-spell or a youth-spell. It prevents death, but doesn't really permit life."

"And you want to break the spell."

The old woman was silent for a time. "Sometimes I do. When I remember. Then I'm desperate to. But. The other parts of me. They drag me back to life. Anyway. I don't want to die. I just want to be. I just want to be *me* again, alive, and whole, and in one place, even if I die the next second."

"You probably will."

"Doesn't matter. I don't expect you to understand."

Morlock stared glumly out the window for a moment or two, considering the path that had led him here. At last he said, "I can probably arrange that."

"What?"

"I can bring the separate segments of your self to the same location. They will reunite and I suspect you will die shortly thereafter."

"Heh. He won't love you for it. Merlin, I mean."

"He hates me already."

"Oh? Then we shall be friends. What's your name?"

"Morlock Ambrosius. I'm your son."

"That explains why you'd bother, then. Excuse me, young man, I have to go down to the lake and wash. I've gotten all dirty somehow."

"Don't forget the salt."

"The salt. Oh, that's right. My son was just here telling me about maggot infestations, the insolent son-of-a-bitch, and I should know. Or was that a dream?"

Morlock didn't answer, and Nimue, taking a basin and a block of salt, went down to the lake behind the cottage. Morlock went down to the bridge. As soon as he stepped onto it, the troll appeared again and landed on the bridge ahead of him.

"Now I've got you!" the troll shouted.

"I still haven't crossed the bridge without permission," Morlock pointed out.

"No, but you *will*."

"I was going to, yes. I wanted to go into the woods and feed deeply and richly on walnuts and acorns until I had swollen up to twice my natural size. Otherwise I'd hardly be worth eating, as you see; I've been living on flatbread and dried meat—and not much of that—for months."

"You might be more worth eating then, but I'd never get the chance. If you get off the island you'll keep on going into the woods and someone else will get to eat you."

"No, I plan to come back and talk with the woman in the cottage."

"You won't be back. She's crazy, you know. I always hide when she comes down by the bridge here. She scares me."

"She's my mother."

"Oh. Sorry." Several of the troll's faces peered at him. "I guess I see the resemblance at that," it admitted. There was a long pause. "Walnuts, eh?" The troll licked several of its lips. "All right. Go on: don't be too long." It jumped off the side of the bridge and disappeared.

Morlock crossed back over the bridge and went off into the woods. He built a potter's wheel, found some clay, and threw a vase. It was long and narrow in external form, about two feet long; he folded the outside through a higher dimension so that the inside was about the size of a small room. He had no kiln, but he took out his choir of flames and explained to them what he needed. They were not very bright, as flames go: the few survivors from the debacle in the winterwood had propagated to fill the nexus, and most of the flames were rather youthful. But Morlock explained to them what he needed and stayed there to keep them on task, and by the following morning the vase was baked and glazed to Morlock's exacting specifications. He stowed the nexus and the jar in his backpack and returned to the wooden bridge leading to the island in the lake.

When he stepped onto the bridge the troll climbed out of the water and drew itself up onto the walkway. The majority of its eyes looked doubtfully at Morlock and it said, "You don't seem to be twice your previous size. What was that? Hyperbole? I dislike rhetorical tropes that verge on dishonesty."

"Unfortunately, there are no walnuts or acorns in the woods. It's spring and they won't be ripe until autumn."

"Now wait a moment. Just *wait* a moment."

"I expect my mother will give me a good breakfast. Mothers are famous for that."

"I wouldn't know," the troll replied. "We reproduce by fission."

"I'd heard. You must be pretty close to splitting, to judge by the number of extrusions from your central body."

"Yes, pretty close now, pretty close. *If I can ever get anything to eat.*"

"I'll be headed back this way after I speak with my mother, whether she gives me anything to eat or not."

The troll's mouths were tight with skeptical sneers. Morlock guessed that if he were trying to leave the island instead of entering it there would have been more discussion. As it was the troll nodded him on with one of its smaller heads and it climbed with quiet dignity back under the bridge.

The door was closed. He knocked on it. Nimue half opened the door and peered through the gap, her watery gray eyes unlit by any recognition. "Yes?" she asked suspiciously.

"I'm your son, Morlock Ambrosius. Yesterday I offered to reassemble the segments of your self."

"Is that supposed to be *funny?*"

He went through the whole matter with her again. Sometimes she remembered him; more often she did not; sometimes it seemed as if she did, but it turned out she was thinking of someone else. Not infrequently she railed at him, thinking he was Merlin.

He found it went easier if he didn't think of her as one person but as a group of people. He had to discuss the matter with all of them and bring them all to agreement before they could go on. Every now and then someone new would come in and he would have to start over. It was not the kind of work he had ever been good at, but there it was: the task he had to do, the task he had set himself.

Around noon they had reached a point in the conversation where Nimue said, "But how is this going to work? There is a troll down by the bridge who says the most offensive things about me whenever I go down there—I've had to speak quite sharply to him about it. I'm sure he wouldn't hesitate to eat either one of us. And Merlin must have set other protections around the place besides."

He showed her the jar and explained his plan.

She drew herself up and looked at him suspiciously. "Are you sure you're not Merlin? He was always putting me in jars."

He shrugged. "I think this will work. If you have another idea—"

"You shouldn't shrug like that. It draws attention to your shoulders."

He looked her in the eye and shrugged.

She snickered. "All right. I get the message. And no I don't have any ideas. If I had any ideas I would have told them to that young fellow who came here looking for his horse; he was much politer than you are."

Morlock took a stoppered green bottle out of his backpack and released the morpheus-bird, its wings feathered with every shade of dim green. It flew once around Nimue's head and then returned to its bottle. He restoppered the bottle as his mother's shell lumped to the ground.

He laid her out flat on the floor and rolled her up as tightly as he could, like a scroll of thick paper with irregular edges. Then he slid her into the narrow mouth of the jar he had made in the woods. There was a cap for the jar but he left it off, in case she needed to speak to him about anything when she awoke. He stowed the jar and the bottle in his pack and went back down to the bridge for the last time.

The troll was waiting for him in the center of the bridge. All of its eyes were on him as he approached. As soon as his shoes hit the planks of the walkway it said to him, "I'll eat you now, if you don't mind."

"I do, and you won't," Morlock replied. "By the terms you were set here, you may not."

"What?" roared the troll with all its mouths.

Morlock explained, "The spell binding you here permits you to eat anyone who has crossed the bridge without your permission. This creates two classes of bridge-crosser: those who have crossed without your permission, and those who have crossed with it. I am clearly in the latter class: you have permitted me to cross the bridge three times. Three is a magic number, you know."

"It *is*?"

"Everyone says so."

"Oh, pus and broken fangs. I suppose I should have paid more attention to my magic lessons. But I thought that I'd never use it, you see. I always wanted to be a bridge-troll."

Morlock shrugged and walked by. The troll clenched all its jaws as he passed, and he kept his hand free to summon Tyrfing, if need be. But he reached the far side without a struggle and walked away into the unclaimed woods.

Merlin was waiting for him there.

"You killed the troll, I suppose?" the old necromancer said, stepping out from behind a tree.

"Talked my way past it," Morlock said. He reached over his shoulder and drew Tyrfing. "If it had been smarter, I might have had to kill it."

"Morlock and God: protectors of fools. But who'll protect you, Morlock? Do you ever wonder that?"

Morlock shrugged and waited for his father to say something worth answering.

"At least," Merlin said at last, "the troll kept you busy until I had a chance to get here. Now you face me in my own person, Morlock—not a fetch or an illusion."

For answer Morlock reached out and passed his left hand through Merlin's chest. It was almost wholly insubstantial, a mere cloak of light and sound for his fetch.

Merlin's face took on the irritated expression it usually wore when he confronted his son. "How did you know?"

There were three or four ways Morlock had known: the absence of any movement among the grasses on which Merlin was supposedly standing was only the most obvious.

But he found that he could say nothing in response. The light particles had taken flight in a complicated four-dimensional pattern around his hand. The pattern drew his attention and held it. He could neither move nor speak.

"Morlock, Morlock," Merlin's voice chided him. "Of course, you are the master of all makers. I know you never say so, but *I* say so, and I would really rather say it about myself, as we both know. But I am the master seer and life-maker—necromancer, as some ignorantly call it. I knew you would come here: I saw it in my map of the future. I could not risk facing you here myself. So I set this trap for you.

"And the best part of it is, you set it off yourself. If you could have brought yourself to speak to me like a human being, your will would still be free. But I knew that you couldn't resist the temptation to brush my little simulacrum out of your way.

"Morlock, you are a maker and you think of light as physical. But it, like aether, casts a shadow on the talic and even the spiritual realms. I find it an easy thing to infect a cloud of light with my will, and now that cloud has infected you. You must remain where you are until I see fit to free you. Not even death will be a release: I think my binding spell will hold your self there even if your body rots away. Anyway, we'll see, won't we?"

What Merlin said was both true and false, Morlock felt. His body was bound by the light, but his mind was free. That meant he had at least one choice to make.

"Yes," Merlin drawled. "You could try that. If you think you can best me in my own art of Seeing."

Morlock didn't think that he could. It was simply that or surrender, and Morlock, when sober, wasn't the surrendering type.

Recklessly, he summoned the rapture of vision. The world of matter and energy fell away to dim shadows; he stepped into the bright world of understanding and intent, the borderland between the material and spiritual. His own fetch appeared: a black-and-white pillar of flames. Tyrfing, too, took on his monochrome talic presence as an extension of himself.

Merlin's fetch stood before him; shed of its illusory light-cloak, he was a pillar of red flames, his fiery hands grasping the staff and faceted crystal that were his own foci of power.

Pity there are no witnesses to this! Merlin's awareness remarked directly into Morlock's. *It will become a legendary battle among those-who-know.*

Morlock signalled his indifference: the talic equivalent of a shrug.

Merlin struck, a lightning-branch of terror leaping out to infect Morlock's talic limbs.

Morlock banished it with Tyrfing and riposted with a triple-fanged stab of guilt-shame-weariness.

Merlin absorbed it with his diamond-shaped focus and remarked pleasantly, *So much for old favorites. See how you like this!*

But that was the end of it.

They had forgotten they were not alone.

They had forgotten because Nimue was spread thin through the world, like a three-cornered spiderweb.

But the tal-world is nearer the spirit-world, where distances matter not at all, and Nimue's physical division did not diminish her talic power.

The three-cornered spiderweb that was Nimue's fetch radiated sudden refusal.

Stop this, she said, and Merlin's attack died aborning.

It might have been the time for Morlock to strike a final, perhaps a fatal blow, but he didn't want to draw her anger on himself. He dismissed his vision and fell back into the chaos of matter and energy that those-who-do-not-know call the real world.

He was lying on the ground in the forest, Tyrfing still gripped in his hand. Merlin's fetch had vanished and Morlock's body was free to move as he willed.

"Thanks, Mother," he rasped out when he could speak.

She didn't answer that he could tell.

He struggled to his feet and, sheathing his sword, headed through the woods westward.

Due west was the talic zone of danger he had avoided while travelling eastward. Now he hoped that whatever was projecting it would provide some cover from the malefic necromancer he knew at last for his enemy.

VII

INTERLUDE: BOOK OF WITNESS

Oh, to behold thy features in thy book!
Thy proper head and shoulders in a
    plate,
How it would look!

—THOMAS HOOD

very clutch of fosterlings, every phalanx of Virgin Sisters, every warrior-pod, every coven of seers and stand of elders had a copy of the book of Witness, and read this part of the tale from it in the season of Motherdeath. But this was *the* book itself, its leather cover cracked and often repaired, many of its pages inscribed by a pen held in a man's awkward stiff fingers. There were no harmony marks; it was traditional to read the words as written: flat, monovocal, with a single mouth. Some wore a dark-skinned man-mask for the purpose, but Gathenavalona, young Dhyrvalona's nurse, thought that was stupid.

She did think it was important for her charge to see the book itself, not a copy—and to hear it. The book had come into the horde's possession on the night of Motherdeath, and Roble's part of the story was already written within it in his own handwriting. After Motherdeath, when the seers were seeking to understand the catastrophe that had befallen them, they sought out other witnesses to the terrible events, speaking to them in dreams and recording their dream-voices in magic letters that could speak again, when called upon in the proper manner.

Marh Valone was the keeper of the book, and Gathenavalona stood now in his pavilion holding the book in her palp-clusters.

"I thank you again, Marh of Marhs!" she said gratefully. "This is a trust; I feel it deeply. I will return the book unscathed or die."

The horde-leader's pyramidal head inclined politely to acknowledge her courtesy. "Take it; keep it. Why should she-who-will-be-Valona not know of these things? Some of the elders disapprove, but I see no wrongness in it. Still, Gathenavalona—"

"Yes?" She paused fearfully in the act of backing out of his presence. She was not afraid of him physically: she was perhaps twice his size. She did fear what he might say to her, what sooner or later he must say to her.

He said it. "Old Valona is sterile. Her eggs have no life in them. Since the last implanting, some of the victims have died, some are sick, but there has been no new life. The tribe has no mother. There must be an anointing."

"Please, may it wait?" she begged, jangling the words disharmoniously from all her mouths. "I promised to tell her the tale of Motherdeath, the whole tale. Only a few more days—"

"Gathenavalona, Gathenavalona. Do you know what the last Marh Valone told me, on the night before I slew him and took his name?"

"Many things, I guess."

"So many, so many. But one thing he said was, 'Gathenavalona will always want more time.'"

"After her second birth, I fed her with my own blood," Gathenavalona said to the implacable Marh Valone. "I taught her to hunt; I kept her safe through all the days and night."

"Of course you did," said Marh Valone. "That is what Gathenavalona is for. Now the time is come for an anointing. That is what Dhyrvalona is for."

Gathenavalona closed all of her eyes, and opened them. She gestured submission, defeat.

Wordlessly the Marh stepped forward. He bent her arms until they gestured weary triumph. "That is the way," he said. "It is not a time for grieving. Your task is fulfilled and you may rest for a time."

"I will still grieve."

"As you like." His harmonies indicated sympathy, implacability.

"When?" she asked.

"Soon. Prepare yourself. I suggest you say nothing to her."

"Of course." What could she say?

She backed out of the Marh's presence.

Dhyrvalona was waiting for her back in the nest.

"Did you get it?" she asked excitedly, while another mouth said, "Is that it?" and her third mouth said, "Marh Valone is the best of marhs!"

"He is not a bad one, I think," Gathenavalona said wearily. "He cares for the horde, above all."

"Need we wait for evening?" whispered Dhyrvalona impishly. "Can you read me a tale now?"

She was astonished when her nurse replied with a single mouth, "No need to wait. This is Roble's tale: hear his voice: 'I will not live three hundred years. . . .'"

ROBLE'S STORY

VIII

THE LAWLESS HOURS

The laws of Nature break the laws of Reason.

—QUARLES, *FONS LACHRYMARUM*

I will not live three hundred years. I'll be dead before I'm eighty and, if I'm not, I'll wish I were. The Strange Gods of the Coranians never knew my name, and I don't know theirs.

I'm not a Coranian knight—I'm not a Coranian anything, but especially not a knight. I'm sick of that mistake. People see me in my armor, on my horse, and they scuttle away or call me "sir." Some of the Riders like that; it's the reason they ride. But I don't need it; if anybody calls me "sir" I tell them straight out. Nobody calls me "sir," not even my sister's boys.

That night I was riding with Liskin. I wasn't happy about it. Liskin was a whiner, a rule-keeper: I'd heard about him. A rule-keeper, but his regular partner, Ost, was a bloody-truncheon, a dead-or-aliver who had killed ten people on the Road, just for fun, in the past year. There was no mystery about it: this was the sort of thing Ost liked to brag about on his nights off. It's not a crime to kill on the roads or in the woods at night, as long as you bring the body back to a castleyard. It's not a crime, but it's not what the Riders are about, either. A couple of us got together (I wasn't there but I heard about it) and asked Liskin what he was going to do about Ost. "What Ost does is not against the rules," he said. So the rest of us did what we had to do about Ost. Liskin didn't join us; it was against the rules.

I was the lucky winner who drew Liskin as a new partner, at least temporarily. My regular partner, Alev, had gotten his legs broken in a Bargainer's man-trap the night before. That would never have happened if Alev weren't a rule-breaker and a bad example; we were strictly forbidden to enter the woods around the Bargainer village. But we brought his stray out, and brought him out alive. *That*'s what the Riders are about, and not keeping any particular set of rules.

Try and tell that to Liskin. He was on me from the moment I entered the courtyard of Rendel's Castle. My sword and shield were both shorter than regulations allowed, he said; my cloak was dark blue, not black, he said; worst of all I had a long scratch in the black enamel on my armor, he said.

I could have explained to him that long swords and long shields aren't handy for fighting in woodlands; a stabbing sword and a round shield are better. I could have told him that after sunset in the woods, dark blue *is* black, or so close as to make no difference. I could have said, in a reasonable tone, "Look, Liskin: it's twenty days until we get paid and I've got to help feed my sister's children. I can't afford to send my breastplate to the armorer's right now, not for a stupid scratch." I might have said all this, but I didn't have a chance. Liskin was still talking.

"Roble, you've got a slovenly appearance," Liskin said, proudly standing next to his own shield, which was leaning against the courtyard wall. "How do you expect anyone you meet on the road to believe you when you say you're not a robber?"

"Well—" I began, but he swept on.

"I tell you, Roble," he told me, "I never appear for duty without the proper gear in proper order. It isn't safe, and it just isn't right." He went on to tell me what he'd tolerate from the person he rode with, but I didn't have to listen to any of that. Because I *knew* what he'd tolerate.

I glanced over at his shield, standing tall and stainlessly black beside him. I drew my truncheon and struck it hard, back against the wall, scoring the enamel halfway down the shield. It bounced off the wall and fell face-down on the dirty cobblestones of the courtyard. Hitching my truncheon back on my belt, I looked at Liskin. He stood there, his mouth slightly open.

Neither of us spoke, or had to. Liskin had a spare shield back at the Riders Lodge (he had a spare at every lodge in Four Castles). He could run and get it. But then he wouldn't be back in time for evening muster, which was just about to happen. So he had to ride with a scratched shield or miss muster; either way he broke a rule.

I picked up his shield and handed it to him. After a moment's hesitation he took it. Slinging it over his shoulder, he walked off without another word toward the mustering square. I waited a couple moments before I did the same; by then the mustering officer had actually appeared.

That night we were mustered by old Marmon. He had been a Rider for twenty years, but the time came when he could no longer stand the rough-and-tumble of the roads. By law of the Four Castles, he could eat and sleep at any of the Riders Lodges for the rest of his life, but you no longer got paid after you stopped riding the roads. So Marmon mustered us now and then (which paid a little something), and introduced lonely colleagues to his two "nieces" (which paid considerably better). He was grayer than your grandfather and only forty-five years old.

Marmon walked down the steps of the stabler's house, hefting a hillconch shell to his lips. He blew a curt and negligent blast (strictly for form, as he saw we were all present). But the echoes were still ringing in the courtyard as we lined up on the mustering square.

"Who rides to the east?" he demanded.

"Arens," said one of the other pair, and, "Teck," said his partner. Marmon looked them over without enthusiasm.

"Who rides to the west?" Marmon asked eventually.

"Liskin!"

"Roble."

Marmon stepped over and eyed both of us. "Liskin, you seem to have a scratch on your shield," he said, and I'd swear the old pimp was smiling.

"Yes, sir. Roble—"

"I'm not your mother, Liskin," said Marmon sharply, and Liskin shut up.

Marmon stood back and spoke to us all. "Arens and Teck, you're fresh from a month off, so I'll just caution you not to play hero. It's one thing when you're boasting in the tavern; it's another thing when you're out there in the woods. Remember: if you're lost, that's one more for the enemy to feed on. When in doubt, save yourself at least; bring back the bodies if you can.

"More specifically, watch where you step. You'll be riding past the Bargainer village, and they've been setting man-traps all along the road and baiting them with real people. Take a long look at everything, especially the ground, confer with each other, and, when in doubt, *save yourselves*. Go ahead and saddle up."

They left and Marmon turned to us. Again, he was almost smiling as he looked at Liskin's shield. "You two are new partners," he said, "and something tells me you're not going to get along. That's fine with me; it's fine with the Four Barons. You don't have to like each other. But do your job. That's all." He waved us away.

"Marmon," I asked, "what's the road like between here and Caroc?"

"Nothing unusual. Some older children staying out late—'just walking in the woods, Mother,' you know. That's about it. Get on the road."

I turned away with Liskin and ran toward the stables. The sun had almost set.

"He didn't tell us not to be heroes," Liskin complained.

"I guess he forgot," I guessed.

It was twilight when Liskin and I rode out of the courtyard of Rendel's Castle and down the main road through Rendel's Town. Liskin and I were both blowing on hillconches as we rode, and off to the east we could hear Arens and Teck doing the same. We made quite a racket between us; there can't have been a person in castle or town who didn't hear us. That, of course, was the idea.

We rode on to the stretch of gravel road at the edge of town, then reined in and turned. Liskin blew another blast on his hillconch, and then I broke the law.

"By the authority of the Four Barons," I shouted, "Masters of Caroc, Rendel, Etain, and Bleisian (castles and towns and lands between), I declare the limit of the law. From town to town, through all the woods, from northern hill to southern plain, I say the law has vanished with the light and will return only with the sun. Until that time, those who enter the woods or walk the Road are guilty of their own suffering and loss, even to their deaths. Let their souls be cursed and their names be forgotten. I declare all this in the name of the Master of Rendel's Castle (here unspoken) and my own, Roble of the Riders."

Liskin blew a final blast on his hillconch and I shouted, "Naeli!" Liskin looked at me in surprise (for this was not part of the rite as he knew it), but he didn't say anything. We rode over a small wooden bridge that arched over a narrow stream and galloped down the road into the lawless woods.

The Riders began as a guild of gravediggers, and in a way that's what we still are. Our primary duty is to collect the dead bodies that accumulate along the road during the lawless hours. Equally important is to collect "strays"— people travelling, ignorant, on the road or lost in the woods. These we conduct to a place where law prevails. Finally, there are those who go beyond the law by choice: to kill or rob along the road during the lawless hours. These, too, we bring out of the woods. If they don't resist, then all's well. They have, after all, committed no crime, no matter what they have done. If they resist, we bring them anyway; if necessary, we kill them and bring the bodies out.

That's the one law the Riders carry with them through the lawless hours: *bring the bodies out*. For every body left in the woods after dark became the subject and sustenance of our enemy, the Boneless One, the Whisperer in the Woods.

That was why the Four Barons had long ago declared the woods and the road through them to be beyond the law after dark: to prevent people from straying there. Those who didn't fear the Enemy, whom they had never seen, would be held back by fear of their fellow man, whom they knew all too well.

It had been a good idea, I'd always thought—perhaps the only thing that could have kept Four Castles alive across the centuries. But it was an idea, some were beginning to suspect, that was doomed to failure. Because there are always outsiders who stumble into the woods without suspecting what dwells there. Because many who should know better simply do not do what is best for them. Because there will always be a few who say to themselves, *I won't be killed; I will kill*. (And if they're right they leave a body in the woods, and if they're wrong they leave a body in the woods. Either way the Enemy, the Boneless One, gets what it needs.) And, finally, because of the Bargainers, who grow more numerous every year.

The first trap was on the road itself. It looked like a woman in a white dress being dragged off the road by three men with the narrow filed teeth of Bargainers. Glancing over at Liskin, I saw he had drawn his sword and was preparing for a heroic charge. I whacked him across the visor and said, "It's a trap!" He gaped at me in surprise.

At the sound of my voice the "woman" turned toward us. Her hair and skin were as dark as mine; her nose was as high arched and delicate as my mother's had been. Her voice was ragged with desperation as she cried out, "Help me! Help me! Why won't you help me?"

I should know better by now, but it got to me. It always got to me. Alev, in contrast, was pretty callous and could even make conversation with the traps until they vanished in (I guess) frustration.

"Go to hell," I muttered desperately; it was the best I could do, usually.

"Help me!" she screamed. "Help me! Why won't you help me?"

"Shut up," I muttered. "You're not real."

It went on for a while longer until the Enemy gave up and the illusion-bait disappeared. Left behind (because it was real, not illusion) was an immense man-trap—or horse-trap, really, since it was made to catch our horses as we galloped to the rescue. I dismounted and went forward to move the thing out of the way and break it with my truncheon. Liskin remained on his horse as lookout, which was in accordance with the Rules and (for once) good sense besides.

"Be careful!" he called to me as I hustled the shattered trap over to the side of the road. "There's sure to be a Bargainer or two nearby in the wood!"

"You think?" I grunted as I hurled the broken metal into the woods. At that moment I was glaring eye-to-eye with a Bargainer crouching in the brush alongside the road. He made no move toward me, nor I to him, but he smiled at me, showing his teeth filed sharp as needles.

My irony had been lost on Liskin. "Of course!" he said. "There had to be someone on hand to attack us and haul the bodies into the wood!"

"I've learned a lot from riding with you, Liskin," I remarked, backing carefully toward my mount. I could not see any companions to my Bargainer out there. Possibly he was alone. If so, he could be killed and his body hauled out of the woods, which was a good thing, in theory. In practice, it was a little early in the night to start collecting corpses; no god knew how many we would be hauling by the end of the night. It would be extremely bad if we had to stop before dawn and burn some bodies on the road. Also, there was the possibility that the Bargainer I saw was not alone—that he was just another form of bait. I weighed the alternatives, reflected that it was Liskin, not Alev, who was watching my back, and decided to let the Bargainer go.

He apparently made a similar decision about me. At least, he made no move against us as I remounted and we rode away.

"We'll have to tell the pair riding east from Caroc tonight about this," Liskin said, after a while.

"Right."

Still later he asked, "How did you know it was a trap?"

"The woman was my sister."

He thought about this for a while, and then just had to say, "But she could have been travelling east from Caroc—"

"Naeli's been dead for six years or more," I told him. "She was lost in the woods."

Liskin was silent for a long time. Finally he said, "I'm sorry." (That's what you're supposed to say, isn't it? It's one of the Rules.)

"Her own damn fault," I replied, to get him to shut up. It worked. But it didn't work with Naeli. Nothing ever worked with her.

Naeli's last child, a girl, had been born two months after the death of the father. (He'd been a miner and was killed in a cave-in.) At that time she was living with her husband's stepparents, but about a month after the birth they began wondering aloud how she was going to help pay the expenses of the household. She took the hint, as only Naeli could, and stormed out of there. She stormed all the way from Rendel's to Caroc—not so easy, seeing that she had three boys and an infant girl to tend to—and moved in with me.

At the time I was a journeyman jeweller, working for a crafty old half-Coranian named Besk. I was doing well enough to support my sister's family.

And, although there was only one kind of work for women that paid a decent wage, Naeli helped out where she could. She worked a plot of ground behind the house, selling some of her produce, feeding the rest to us. (She referred to us collectively as the Enemy and pretended to mourn each individual vegetable. She would cry out absurd names she had invented for each tomato-root, then shout, "But no! Their suffering is on their heads! They were born like vegetables, let them die like vegetables! Let their piths be accursed and their names be forgotten!" And the children would laugh, scandalized, and even I would grin. Except for the people she cared about, Naeli took nothing in the world seriously, including the Enemy.)

Naeli was half crazy, anything but a rule-keeper. She was a good mother, though. She taught her children how to read, both Coranian and Castellan, and the two oldest sons were apprenticed out—one to a blacksmith, the other to a carpenter. It wasn't easy to achieve this: sons were supposed to follow the trade of their fathers; that was the first law of the Guilds. But Naeli was tireless in her petitioning, bribing when she could afford to; she insisted that none of her sons would go to the mines to die like their father (in a cave-in) or his father (withered away by some illness breathed in deep under the earth). And she had her way: her youngest son, Thend, we agreed would be Besk's apprentice, or mine, when the time came.

So she took care of her sons and loved them. But it was her daughter, Fasra, who truly held her heart. She doted on the girl, spoiled her, labored long hours at the petty labor permitted to women so that Fasra could have a dowry. And her affection was not misplaced: Fasra was a lovely child, with silver-pale hair, clear brown skin, and two black lightning bolts dwelling permanently in her storm-dark eyes. She was clever and engaging, too; everybody was fond of her.

But it was clear, from the moment she took to her own feet, that Fasra had a will of iron, which she was not inclined to have anyone temper. And Naeli could rarely bring herself to discipline the girl (at once the last remnant of her husband and the radiant mirror of her own youth) as she should have, so matters grew worse. Fasra, at first merely strong-willed, grew contrary; "no" meant *yes* to her, and "yes" meant *I won't*.

One day, when Fasra was around seven years old, she was invited on a picnic with some of her friends; they were going to pick wildberries in the woods. The mothers of the children were to accompany them, but Naeli could not go. It was market day and she had a load of vegetables ready to sell. So she told Fasra *she* couldn't go. Fasra disagreed, and finally Fasra had her way. Naeli committed her to the care of one of the other mothers in attendance, a friend of hers, one of the thousand and one people she knew in Four Castles.

The children went on their picnic. The forest is a strange and beautiful place during the day, but still forbidding in comparison to the ordered life of town and castle. During the morning the children stayed close to their protectors, terrified by the approach of the smallest chipmunk. But, as the day approached noon, the terror receded; the children wandered farther through the green woods and golden clearings, seeking out skeneberries and clusterfruit and the three types of mushroom they had been taught were good to eat.

As noon gave way to afternoon Fasra found herself with less in her basket than most. It wasn't because she wasn't clever or hadn't been taught. But she was moody and contrary. She looked for berries in the shade and mushrooms in the sunlight. It took her much of the day to learn that things grew where they grew, and not where she thought they should.

She explained her theory to her custodian, Naeli's friend, as they sat down for lunch. The berries, she said, were like bright little suns; they could warm up the woods when it was too cool. The mushrooms were chilly and gray, like clouds; they would be pleasant in the hot sun-drenched clearings.

Naeli's friend applauded the ingenuity of this idea, then asked how many berries and mushrooms Fasra had actually collected. Fasra reluctantly showed her basket. Then Naeli's friend showed Fasra her own daughter's basket: it was more than twice as full as Fasra's. Many children had brought in full baskets from the morning's berrying, Naeli's friend explained, perhaps a bit tactlessly, so a change of method seemed in order.

Fasra's face fell and she turned away. But she wasn't stupid; she could learn a hard lesson when she had to. And she had brought three baskets along, which she was determined to bring home full to Naeli, whom she loved as fiercely as Naeli loved her.

So she went to work in the afternoon in grim earnest. The nearby clearing had been plucked clean in the morning, so she searched the ones that were farther away. And she filled two baskets with clusterfruit and skeneber-ries, bringing them proudly back to her custodian.

It was the third basket that brought disaster. She had resolved to bring back a basket full of cleft-caps, the rarest edible mushroom in our woods. But she started on this too late in the day. That third basket—and her iron will—sealed her fate.

In midafternoon, the other children began to wander back, with berry-smeared faces and full baskets. They were happy, but tired, and a little fright-ened by the lengthening shadows. Darkness was rising from the earth; they wanted to go home; their custodians wanted to take them . . . but Fasra was missing.

Naeli's friend left her own daughter in someone else's care and ran to the place where Fasra had been last seen. She kept calling out Fasra's name until the girl finally appeared at the edge of a clearing, like a wood-sprite reluctant to leave the forest shadows.

"Come back," Naeli's friend said to the proud child. "We're going home."

"Not till I'm done. My basket's only half full."

Now, if I'd been there, I might have indulged the little girl with a few more moments to pick mushrooms. I might have helped her. I might have bribed her with the contents of my own baskets. And if the child had balked again at coming home I might have said, *You are more important to your mother than a basket of mushrooms.*

Or, weary from the long day, tired of the child's imperious manner, frightened by the onset of darkness, I might have done exactly what Naeli's friend did. Which was to shout, *"No! Come now!"*

"Just a moment," Fasra said icily. "I'm not finished."

"You're finished when I say you're finished!" Naeli's friend cried. "Dark-ness is rising! Come home."

"Not till I'm done."

"We're leaving," Naeli's friend said, walking toward the girl, who ran back a few steps into the wood.

"No!" shouted Fasra. "No! No! No!"

Naeli's friend turned and began to walk away. "Good-bye," she said, over her shoulder. "I hope you can make your way out of the forest by yourself."

There was no answer. After a few steps more she turned and looked back. Fasra had vanished.

They searched for her, of course. But the day was growing old, and they had other children to take care of, their own children. Finally they returned to Caroc without Fasra, and Naeli's friend brought the terrible news to my house around sunset.

Naeli came to Besk's shop immediately. She was weeping, but she managed to tell the story as she knew it.

"Naeli, I'm sorry," was all I could find to say, as she sobbed. "I loved her, too."

"Her name will be mentioned at the next Mysteries," Besk promised her, his pale brown face etched with grief. He was very fond of Naeli, and Fasra too.

"What do you mean?" cried Naeli, in fresh alarm. "Aren't you going to help me find her?'

Besk and I stared at each other in astonishment. Then Besk said firmly, "No. You must mourn her, Naeli. No one can help her now."

"White-faced Bargainer," she cursed him. "Stay here and lick your pennies! My brother will still help me!"

"Help you do what?" I shouted. "I won't help you commit suicide. It's already getting dark!"

"She's alone!" Naeli said. "She's never been alone this long. She'll be getting cold. She'll be afraid. And soon it *will* be dark and they *will* come for her. The Bargainers. The Enemy. The Whisperer in the Dark. They'll come for her!"

She stared at us in silence for a few moments as Besk and I refused to meet her eye. The thought of the beloved child dying alone in the dark woods was terrible. But there was nothing we could do. We knew that. We resented Naeli for not knowing it, too.

"Help me!" she screamed in my face. "Help me! Why won't you help me?" Then she ran from the shop, leaving the door swinging open behind her.

I turned resolutely back to the work we'd been doing, a commission from the Baron of Caroc which was to be ready the next day. But Besk reached over and grabbed me by the shoulder.

"Go after her," he said. "Go now. Hurry, Roble."

"No," I said stubbornly. "She'll come to her senses in a little while."

"She's in her senses now," Besk replied. "But that doesn't mean for her what it does for dull fellows like you and me. She is a great one, an empress or a merchant lady by rights. If she lived in the wide world, she would be one or the other by now, or something better than both. She knows everything you know, how the law is about to be broken in the woods. To you, that means she must not enter there. To her, it means she must. Go, Roble. Run. It may be too late as I stand here talking. . . ."

Besk was a good man, but he'd never sent me home early in the ten years I'd been working for him. This, more than anything else, struck me with urgency. I dropped my tools and ran out the open door.

The sun had set, and the narrow lanes of Caroc Town were heavy with shadow. The dark blue radiance left in the evening sky was already dim and fading. As I left the side-lanes for the Road I heard the hillconches ring out like thunder, breaking the law.

"Naeli!" I shouted as I ran. "Wait! Naeli!"

She didn't wait. At the edge of town there were only the black-armored Riders on their black steeds. I could hear the one's voice as I ran up to them, but made no sense of the words. (I realize now what he was saying, of course, having said it so many times myself.)

The one finished speaking and I asked them, "Have you seen a woman pass this way? I—"

The Rider who had not spoken drew his truncheon and pointed it at my throat. Neither of them said a word, and I found myself unable to speak either.

Now I know that the Rider was only threatening to kill me if I tried to enter the woods. But then his gesture seemed full of mystic import. I had never confronted one of these Riders in their dark regalia before, never thought about what they implied. The forest where Fasra had vanished had now taken Naeli, too. But it was their forest, I realized: only they could cross and recross it in the lawless hours. I didn't understand how they dared to do it. But I realized that I couldn't imitate them, that I must not. They had forbidden it. And in that strange moment they seemed to have more power than the Four Barons themselves. After all, the Barons could only say what the law was. The Riders said what it was not, and rode beyond its limits.

"Will you at least look for her?" I pleaded, when I found my voice again. "Her daughter is there, too, a girl of seven years . . . lost in the woods."

They still did not speak. I suppose they were simply hesitating, wondering whether to explain to me that they could not afford to wander from the Road, that they were powerless and couldn't really help. I suppose they resented me as I had resented Naeli, demanding more than I could give. But I felt none of this. I felt as if I had bowed down in prayer to two statues of the Strange Gods, or asked a favor of a stone wall.

Defeated, I turned and walked away in silence. They watched me go and then, no doubt, rode off down the lawless road. It was long after dark when I finally reached my house. My sister's sons were sitting huddled around the cold fireplace in the front room.

"Where is Naeli?" I asked stupidly, as if I didn't know. I guess part of me expected her to be there, to always be there.

"She went to find you," Stador, the eldest boy said. "She said you would help her. . . ."

I don't remember the rest of that night, or much of the following days. There were the funerals, strangely bitter with no bodies to bury. And I apprenticed my sister's youngest boy to Besk. A month and a half later I enlisted in the Riders.

I thought it would be difficult to join. But it wasn't. There were always places falling vacant.

The trouble with Liskin, I discovered, was that you could shut him up, but he wouldn't stay shut. He kept wanting to talk: about whether we were riding fast enough, about whether we were riding too fast, about whether we should have hunted down the Bargainers tending the trap. The subject didn't matter; he just wanted to run his mouth. But, when you're riding through the woods during the lawless hours, you have to pay attention to what's happening around you. You can't do that with someone nattering in your ear all the time.

Finally, I had to rein in and tell him. I added, as an afterthought, that it was crazy to try to carry on a conversation in full armor on trotting horses.

Up till then he had been nodding (like, chastened). But this he wanted to argue about. "Oh, I don't know, Roble—"

"Bargain it, Liskin," I swore, then stopped. Over his shoulder I could see a flicker of red light filtering through the night-black branches of the forest.

"Stray!" I said, and pointed.

He turned to look and said, "Or another trap."

"Either way, there are bodies to bring out." I dismounted.

Liskin didn't. "Roble," he said, "it's against the Rules to go that far from the Road."

"Then don't," I replied. "But if there were any rules in these woods we wouldn't be here." I drew my sword and left the Road, plunging into the forest that had swallowed my sister and her child.

The light was a longish way from the Road. It took me endless moments to wend through the close-set tree trunks until I approached close enough to see that the light was from a campfire. Someone was sitting beside it.

You get an eye for spotting illusions after you've been in the Riders for awhile. The illusion-bait is always something you want to see, the thing that's too good to be true. It's the image in your mind most likely to kick you forward before you have a chance to think.

There are a lot of variations the Enemy could play on this method: traps baited with simulacra of your enemies; traps baited with images of people you don't recognize; traps baited with sleeping or otherwise defenseless Bargainers, and so on. But the Enemy never does this; maybe it can't. Maybe the Enemy, for all its immortality and power, is a little stupid.

So I knew that what I saw before me was real. Because I was not in the least impressed.

The stray was about average height. He had white skin, like a Coranian, but it had been burned on his face and hands. He looked like he spent a lot of time outdoors: all his clothing (as dark as a Rider's) was travel-worn and weather-stained, and his shoes had been mended more than once. He had crooked shoulders and dark unruly hair. All in all: the sort of person you might expect to find at your back door, begging for a meal or a mug of beer. He was too unpleasant not to be real.

I looked the situation over carefully. Just because he wasn't an illusion, it didn't mean this wasn't a trap. Alev and I had found that out yesterday. And even if it wasn't a trap, Bargainers might have spotted the stray and staked him out, just as I had. Then, the stray himself might be dangerous (though he didn't look it).

I slowly made my way all around the campsite, assuring myself at every step that there were no Bargainers to compete with me for this stray. The stray himself didn't seem to notice me; he was intent on some carving he was doing with a long pointed knife.

Finally I stepped into the firelight. The stray looked up at me without surprise. I was wondering what language I should speak to him when he solved the problem by addressing me in a kind of Coranian.

"Do you speak for the singing wood?" he asked sleepily.

"No," I said, as clearly as I could. Obviously the vagrant was half-enchanted: his disturbingly pale gray eyes seemed to be glowing slightly. "I've come to take you out of the woods."

He shook his head. "I will stay here tonight and listen," he said sleepily. "And perhaps, tomorrow night, I will answer. If—"

"If you stay here tonight, you will die here tonight. I'm paid to prevent that. Come along with me and I'll take you to the nearest castle."

He shook his head again casually and said, "There is a great hunger in these woods, though. Felt it immediately. Something like it only once before. I fell asleep in the middle of a forest fire. I heard a deep golden voice calling to me. I passed from sleep to the rapture of vision, and tried to speak with it. But it knew nothing except hunger, an inhuman and utterly destructive hunger. Then I awoke and realized: I had been in talic stranj with the heart of the flames." He laughed fondly at the memory.

"Talic stranj, eh?" I said. "I know exactly what you mean. Happens to me all the damn time." This stray was probably crazy or a sorcerer or both. (They go together like shell brisket and earth-apples.) That meant that I would probably have to kill him to get him out. And I'd have to do it fast, before the Bargainers arrived. I covertly loosened my sword in its sheath.

He noticed, damn him. He was no longer as sleepy or as stupid as he had first seemed. We stayed that way for a moment, looking at each other, saying nothing.

When the Bargainers hit me from behind, the first thing that I thought was, *Bargain it! It is a trap!* That flashed through my mind as I fell like a stone, as if I were unconscious (though I wasn't). Three of them stayed to guard me, and the rest moved into the circle of firelight

I rolled to my feet (try it in full armor sometime; but I spent my off months exercising, not soaking up beer in the taverns) and drew my sword. I cut two of their throats before they were ready for me; the third turned to meet me, though, his club held high.

As we fought, I realized this wasn't a trap. The stray had a long sword with an odd flashing blade and was fighting the Bargainers as fiercely as I was. That was something. But there were so many of them!

I killed my third Bargainer easily enough. They're not usually armored and they don't carry weapons to kill, only a long club, like our truncheons, to knock people unconscious. (The Boneless One is said to prefer live victims.) They're best at stealth, and the Enemy helps them there. But right now stealth wasn't on the table; Bargainers were pouring out of the woods on several sides.

I ran into the clearing and was going to charge the Bargainers around the stray when someone called my name. I turned my head and saw what I most wanted to see: Alev limping toward me through the wood. "Roble!" he shouted. "Bargain it! It *is* a trap! Come this way!"

I took three steps without thinking. It was impossible not to. Then I did think. I turned back to the Bargainers and found several of them bearing down on me. I met the club of one with my truncheon and slashed wildly at another with my sword. Then they leapt back and encircled me, beginning a long, slow, carefully coordinated attack certain of victory. They had most of the night, and my attention was divided several ways. They had only to stay out of reach of my sword and wait for my inevitable mistake. I didn't need to glance back into the wood to know that Alev was not there, had never been there. His image had been a sending of the Enemy.

Over the shoulder of a Bargainer, I saw the stray do something pretty smart: he leaped up and caught hold of a branch with his left hand. Then he lifted himself into the tree as the Bargainers surrounding him swarmed in to grab him.

To start with, it's pretty impressive to see a grown man lift himself into a perch using one hand. But, more importantly, it meant he was probably safe now. The Bargainers didn't carry swords or axes or arrows; if they tried to climb up he could probably knock them off as they came. And the forest was so dense, he could go from tree to tree if he wanted to escape his pursuers on the ground.

Of course, it was also tough luck for me. Even if I had been able to hold off the Bargainers surrounding me, I wouldn't be able to fight the whole crowd. But I had known I was taking a risk coming into the wood. The stray was safe—that was the reason I had taken my risk—but he might not know it.

"You're all right!" I shouted at the stray. "Stay up there until dawn and they'll go away!"

The stray looked at me, right at me with those gray eyes that pierced like spear points. Then he scanned the clearing, looking at the Bargainers drifting away from the tree and toward me.

"Stay up there!" I shouted desperately. I was afraid he'd throw his safety away in a futile attempt to assist me. "I'm done! You're not! You can't help me!"

He sheathed his sword and braced his back against the tree trunk.

I had to duck from a club launched at me by a Bargainer, so I didn't see what happened next.

But I heard it. I heard part of it, anyway. It was a sound impossible to hear, but audible just the same. A word, spoken in a human voice, but a word that resonated with power, a bright black hammer of a word. I passed out before the word was finished.

When I came to myself I was lying in the clearing. Someone was moving about nearby. I struggled groggily to my feet and reached for a weapon.

But there was no need: the only person moving about was the stray. He was binding the hands of the Bargainers, who were strewn unconscious about the clearing.

"Good evening," he said, nodding toward me as his hands worked ceaselessly. "You might stand by to clop a few of these fellows on the head, if they start waking up before I can bind them. They should be coming out of it soon."

"It?" I said, picking up my truncheon.

"I spoke one of the Silent Words. Your helmet shielded you from some of it, so you woke up sooner, but these others aren't dead. They're just stunned, as you were. I am Morlock Ambrosius, by the way." He glanced directly at me, as if to see whether I recognized the name.

I didn't, so I just told him mine in return. Then I added hesitantly, "Um. Strictly speaking, I should kill these Bargainers."

"Oh?" Morlock didn't seem surprised—it was hard to read his expression, for a fact—but he didn't seem inclined to cooperate, either.

"Or I could herd them to Caroc Castle when they awake. It would be tricky work, but just possible."

"What would happen to them there?"

"They'd be killed."

Morlock shook his head. "I don't know what lies between your people and theirs, but I can't stand here while you kill"—he glanced around the clearing—"forty-seven people."

"It doesn't appeal to me, either," I grumbled. "Then I'd have to haul them out, or burn the bodies. . . . Let's just bind them and leave them. It's not the first Rule I've ever broken."

Somehow Morlock's face indicated approval without changing expression in the slightest. We bound the rest of the Bargainers (clubbing them into unconsciousness as necessary), Morlock recovered his pack and bedroll from the campsite, and we buried the fire in moist earth.

I led the way back to the Road. At first I thought that I had reached the wrong part—it's easy to lose your way in the woods after dark, and Liskin and my horse weren't anywhere to be found.

But there was some fresh horse dung on the Road, as if more than one horse had been there for a while recently. And I did recognize the place.

"Liskin, you worm," I muttered to myself.

"Liskin?"

"My partner. I left him holding my horse when I saw your campfire from the Road." I gestured at the horse crap on the Road. "Some of that's probably his."

"So we walk."

"Right." I thought about going back for the three bodies of the Bargainers I had killed and decided against it. There was no way we could bring those corpses out without a horse, and if we tried to burn them needle-toothed Bargainers would come like moths out of the wood. Much as I hated to, I'd just have to leave the Enemy a little snack tonight.

"You should dump some of that iron," Morlock suggested, gesturing at my armor. "You'll move faster."

"I'm used to it. Besides, I can't leave a Rider's armor on the Road—some Bargainer might find it and use it to trick someone."

Morlock nodded, and we started down the Road. Morlock kept his eyes on the right side of the Road, I watched the left, and every now and then one of us looked over his shoulder to check the Road behind us.

"These Bargainers," Morlock said presently, "they live in the wood?"

"Yes."

"Why are you at war with them?"

"They serve the Enemy who lives in the wood, the Boneless One. They take us, when they can, to feed it. We kill them, when we can, to prevent that." I gnawed my lip. "I should have done something about those damn Bargainers. I don't know why it made a difference that there were so many. They'd've taken forty-seven of us and bragged about it afterward."

"Probably," Morlock agreed flatly. I glanced at him, but his eyes were scanning the roadside. He seemed neither skeptical nor surprised to find people preying on each other the way the Bargainers did on us.

He seemed to be a pretty reasonable person. I wanted to ask him why he'd been talking so crazily when I first spoke to him, but I didn't want to insult him. "What's talic stranj?" I asked, eventually.

His grim face twisted in a one-sided grin. "You're wondering whether I'm crazy."

There didn't seem to be any point in denying it. "Yes."

"Some people who are crazy can't stay in their own heads. They keep drifting into other people's, or abroad in the world. Have you ever known anyone like that?"

"No. I haven't known that many crazy people."

"There can't be too many people like that in these woods. Your Whisperer—"

"He's not mine."

"—he would eat them, I think. But I was trained by such a person to ascend to the rapture of vision and see all three phases of the world."

"Uh-huh. Three phases?" I was getting nervous again. Walking through woods thick with Bargainers, with the Enemy lurking unseen, was bad enough; I didn't like adding a crazy Coranian to the mix.

He shrugged his wry shoulders and said, "Hear me out and decide if I'm crazy. There are matter and spirit, yes? The things we see and feel and touch, and the minds that lie behind them."

"All right. Say there are."

"But how does dead matter impinge on a living mind? How does a living mind make dead matter respond?"

"You tell me."

"Through the middle phase: tal. Tal is the medium through which the spirit realm takes action in the world of matter and the medium through which matter affects the spirit."

"So ghosts—"

"Not just ghosts. People. Squirrels. Dogs. Bugs. Any entity that can take volitional action in the material world is a fusion of three bodies: material, talic, and spiritual. Physical death occurs when tal is no longer able to unite matter and spirit. In rapture I can ascend from material perception to talic perception, with at least a glimpse of the spiritual realm beyond."

"Hm. Not my line of work."

He laughed, surprising me. "Yes it is." He waved his hand at the road. "You collect dead bodies—"

"When someone doesn't run off with my horse."

"—and people in the woods. Why?"

"So that the Enemy won't eat them. What's good for him is bad for us."

"What do you suppose the Enemy eats?"

"You're telling me you know?"

"I do know. I sensed its specific hunger when I was in rapture. It feeds on tal. The tal of living beings, men and women, when it can. A living consciousness is haloed in tal. But the dead still possess tal, which will fade over time, like the heat of a dead body."

"And it can live on this?"

"Yes. It would have some harmful effects, over time, but a person with certain skills could prolong his life indefinitely by absorbing the tal of others. It's the sort of magic Coranians have always been good at."

Coranians. He said it like it didn't include him. That set me back. He was pale skinned, like a Coranian himself; he spoke Coranian like it was his native language. "Aren't you a Coranian?" I asked. "You speak the language."

"I share the language," he said, not as if he were angry or embarrassed, just stating a fact. "But my people didn't call it Coranian. You must know some Coranians yourself: you speak the language well."

"They pretty much run Four Castles. The Four Barons and the gentry are all white-sk—Coranians."

"Hm."

"They live a long time," I added. "Three hundred years, or so some of them claim."

"Hm."

"You don't think—?" I began.

The Silent Word hit me again, like before but worse. It was like being buried in a bright avalanche of silence. I found myself sprawled on the ground and got up shaking my head.

"Look, I was just asking," I said stiffly. "You didn't have to pound my head with your magic word."

But Morlock was climbing to his feet as well. "I didn't," he said, a little unsteadily. "I think—"

It struck again, a dark inhuman voice shouting the silent word through the trees.

We rose from the ground a while later and looked at each other. Morlock dropped his backpack on the ground and began to paw through it frantically. We both lost consciousness several times as the voice in the woods shouted the Silent Word at us. But finally, as I watched him with a certain disinterest—I was getting a little groggy; it was like taking repeated punches to the head—he pulled something shiny out of the pack and put it to his lips.

It was a pennywhistle or a pipe or some other kind of cut-rate flute. He began to play a little tune on it just as the Silent Word rang again out of the woods.

I staggered a little but didn't fall. There was some sort of magic in the pipe's music that masked the stunning force of the Silent Word.

Using his right hand to finger the pipe as he continued to play, he reached down and slid one strap of his pack over his left shoulder. Then he switched hands and put the strap over his right shoulder.

"Your pack's open," I said. "I'll—"

He paused playing for a moment and said, "Have to get moving. Rats."

This last bit meant less than a Bargainer's promise to me, but I could see how it was a good idea to get moving. We walked westward, toward Caroc town.

Presently, I got to thinking, though. The pipe made magical music—what was the magic for? Just to cover up the magic of the Silent Word? I didn't think so. *Rats*, Morlock had said. It couldn't really be to—

I turned around and walked backward, keeping up with Morlock step for step. He was right: it would have been a bad idea to stop and tie up his pack while the music was playing. Because it was drawing rats out of the wood.

There were hundreds already, creeping along behind us—the road was dark with them. I looked at Morlock; he met my eye and shrugged without pausing the music.

I swung around and walked forward. Obviously, there was no point in speaking—and, frankly, I was glad of that.

Sure, I was grateful that his magic pipe was keeping me from going unconscious every other moment. I was grateful his magic word had saved me from the Bargainers. He had obviously thought it safe to use, as the Bargainers would no more be able to hear the word or remember it than I had. It would affect any man or woman that way, no doubt.

But the Whisperer in the Woods, the Boneless One, was not a man or a woman. *It* had heard the Silent Word and was learning how to use it. If it learned how to use it against townfolk without striking the Bargainers as well, even the walls of town and castle wouldn't protect us: walls mean nothing if there is no one standing on guard behind them. The long war between the Castles and the Enemy might be over at last, thanks to Morlock. And me.

I should have left him to the Bargainers, I thought over and over again as we trudged toward Caroc. That was the bitterest pill of all, because it meant, in spite of everything, that Liskin had been right.

Dawn came about an hour before we reached the edge of Caroc Town. I told Morlock he could stop playing—the Enemy was never active during the day. He blew a final shrieking blast on the pipe, very unlike the tripping persuasive music that had drawn the rats, and they fled in all directions.

I didn't have my hillconch with me—it was hooked to my horse's saddle—but I shouted the ritual restoring law to the road and the woods. Morlock listened with interest as he stored his pipe in an odd pocket in one of his sleeves and tied up his pack. Then we walked on to the town.

I was not surprised to learn, when we reached Caroc, that I had been horribly killed by Bargainers in the woods and Liskin, though striving valiantly to save me, had been forced to flee with my horse, for the safety of the Four Castles and, indeed, all humankind.

The sad news reached me through Besk, who was waiting for me at the east edge of town with a mug of beer and a piece of cheese. While I ate the cheese and drank the beer (I offered Morlock the first shot at both; he waved them away, but it looked to me like he really wanted the beer), Besk told us about how Liskin rode into the town before dawn reporting the terrible things he had seen.

A small crowd had gathered around by this time, enjoying the prospect of a man hearing about his own death. I could have said a lot of things, but what I did say was, "That Bargaining little weasel. Besk, Morlock. Morlock, Besk."

Besk's pale brown face went blank and then, for the first time, he looked straight at the stray I had recovered from the lawless woods.

"Morlock Ambrosius?" Besk asked.

Morlock shrugged his crooked shoulders.

Besk seemed to accept this as an answer; he nodded solemnly and said, "As a maker of sorts, I honor you, of course. As a Coranian of sorts, I've been taught to hate you. But I could never take that stuff as seriously as I should, I'm afraid. You'd better leave him at my place, Roble, before you go to report. The Barons won't treat him well."

"Can't," I said flatly. I was a little surprised that Besk had heard of Morlock, but not very: Coranians are supposed to get more news from the wide world than the rest of us, and what they get they share at their Mysteries.

(Besk had the wrong ancestors to ever be a full Initiate of one of the Inner Circles. But he, unlike me, had some of the right ancestors, so he could be a member of one of the Outer Circles.) I didn't know what Morlock had done to get on the wrong side of the Coranians or when he had done it; frankly, I didn't care. Something more important than him or me had come up, and now was not the time to hand in a false or, should I say, *Liskinized*, report. I'd never cared for the Baron of Caroc (who struck me as a stiff), but he needed to hear the truth from me now, including whatever Morlock could tell him about the Silent Words.

To my surprise, Morlock agreed. I thanked Besk for the breakfast (or is it supper when you've been awake all night?), left him among the crowd, and trudged toward the castle.

"Besk is a good man," I said, after we'd walked awhile in silence.

"He seems so," Morlock replied. "But . . ."

"But what?"

"There was something a little strange about him."

I should have been offended, but I knew what he meant. I shrugged and we went on without speaking.

The audience hall of the Baron of Caroc was full of rubberneckers and armed guards when I ushered Morlock in. The atmosphere was festive but unpleasant. It was like some creepy Coranian religious holiday (although there were almost as many brown faces as white ones in the audience hall).

I conducted Morlock up the hall to the throne where the Baron sat, ramrod straight.

"Sir," I said, a little embarrassed (I don't usually have to run my mouth with so many people listening), "I bring you news from the woods. And—"

"I know about your prisoner, Liskin," the Baron said. "Don't worry: you'll have your reward."

"The name's *Roble*," I snapped, my embarrassment vanishing in annoyance. (It was just like Liskin to cop the credit for my "prisoner," after abandoning us both in the woods.) "Someone's been feeding you false reports. Sir. And I don't know what you guys have against Morlock, here, but there's something more important going on in the woods."

"Nothing is more important than the capture of one of our enemies from the old time," the Baron said gloatingly. "But I suppose you will deny your identity, enemy?" he said, speaking directly to Morlock.

Morlock shrugged indifferently, much as he had when Besk asked his name. *From the old time*: how old was Morlock? Did they really hate him personally, or was it someone he was descended from?

"Why is he still armed?" the Baron demanded. "You—Riskin—Loble— whatever your name is. Take his sword. Take his backpack. Take anything he has on his person."

"Including his tin whistle?" I said sarcastically, but my heart was falling. I didn't like where this was going. The Baron had goons to lock people up and search them; that's not what the Riders are for, and I was annoyed the Baron was talking to me like one of his jailors. But I couldn't just stand here while they made plans to carve Morlock up, either. He'd saved my life when he could have let me die.

I didn't figure I owed any loyalty to the Baron. The people who lived in Four Castles came first, I figured, especially the people I cared about, then people I owed something to (like Morlock). The Baron of Caroc wasn't on either list.

No, what bothered me was what would happen when I refused. He'd just call in his goons and I might end up in a cell right next to Morlock. That wouldn't do anyone any good. But I didn't like the idea of knuckling under, either.

Just when the situation was bad, Morlock made it worse by drawing his sword. A gasp went around the crowded audience chamber.

It's a crime to draw a weapon in the presence of any of the Barons, of course, except in their defense. But that wasn't what shocked the crowd; at least I don't think so. It was the blade itself. They were all staring at it with their mouths open.

I admit it was weird. I hadn't had a chance to look at the blade before, when Morlock was fighting the Bargainers. The blade was like a long pointed slab of black basalt with veins of white crystal running through it. It seemed as if the white parts began to move, like white flames flickering against a black background. Morlock almost seemed to flicker a little bit, too, and his gray eyes actually seemed to glow. He closed his eyes and I could see the light of his irises shining eerily through the thin skin of his eyelids. His movements were sluggish, almost sleepy.

It reminded me of how he had been when I first saw him. He was going into the rapture state, I suddenly realized. Why?

. . . the sort of magic Coranians have always been good at . . . he'd said, right before the Silent Word struck us both down. He'd meant the kind of magic that preserved physical life by devouring someone else's . . . no, their tal. It was just what the Enemy did. I'd wondered then if the Enemy might once have been a Coranian, though I didn't have a chance to ask the question.

Did Morlock think the Enemy might be *here*—not in the woods but in Four Castles? Could he use his altered vision in the rapture state to find out?

The Baron was shouting for someone to take his sword. I didn't move to obey; if Morlock was doing what I thought he was, I wanted to know the answer at least as much as he did.

Eventually, though, three soldiers wearing the Baron's surcoat approached. The light in Morlock's eyes died; the light in the sword faded. I was wondering whether to intervene when he opened his eyes and peaceably surrendered the sword, hilt-first, to one of the guards (who seemed reluctant to touch it). He shrugged off his backpack and handed it to the second guard (who grabbed it with two hands and grunted a little; it seemed to be pretty heavy). He nodded politely to the third guard. Then he kicked him in the crotch, knocked him down, and ran past him.

I was as startled as anyone. (I'd figured Morlock was going to surrender and plead for the Baron's mercy. Not a shrewd move, necessarily, but one where I could lend my assistance without ending up in the slammer.) Before I knew it the crooked man was up on the dais, struggling with the Baron, with both of his hands on the Baron's left arm. Morlock wrenched the arm suddenly; there was an indescribable sound, like a moist crackle, and he had torn the arm from the Baron's body.

But there was no blood. And something dark dangled and writhed at the Baron's side, where his arm had been, like muscles with no bone or skin.

The guards had dumped Morlock's sword and backpack and (except for the one still rolling around on the floor with pain) were going to the Baron's rescue. But this stopped them. Like everyone else they stood gaping at the scene playing out on the dais.

Morlock stripped the severed arm of its sleeve and rapped it against the back of the throne. It was hard, chitinous, like a shell. He presented the torn end to those standing agape in the hall; we could see that it was hollow. The Baron of Caroc wasn't human—just a sort of land-crab that looked human. . . .

"Is your enemy the Boneless One who lives in the woods?" Morlock asked. "What of a boneless one who walks among you—misdirects your efforts—eats your lives?"

He took the Baron (who was striking at him with one remaining claw-like hand) by the armless shoulder. He tore the shoulder in two different directions, and the Baron's torso came apart. Morlock tipped him forward and something oozed out of the gaping tear in the chest, like the soft boneless body of an overcooked snail. It fell on the dais steps and slid down a few, leaving a gleaming trail of slime behind it.

It had human eyes, though. And its shapeless mouth screamed in the Baron's voice as Morlock stepped forward to crush it.

The crowd's horror burst into panic. I wasn't the first person to rush for the door, but I wasn't the last one, either. Pretty soon we were all charging toward the wide doors of the audience hall, forcing our way out, yelling our heads off. The crowd spun me around as I went through the door, and I caught a glimpse of Morlock, calmly shouldering his backpack, his sword back in his hand, the Baron a red smear on the dais steps behind him. He met my eye and saluted me gravely with the sword. Then the crowd pushed me out through the door and I lost sight of him.

The morning was warm; I was tired; my armor was heavy. It took me a long time to get from the Castle to the Riders Lodge, where I shed my armor with the help of one of the duty squires. I kept the sword, because I'd bought it with my own money, and I didn't expect to be back.

I went from the Riders Lodge to my house. It was mine, technically, but Naeli's older sons, Stador and Bann (already journeymen in their trades), were actually living there these days. Business is thin for any young man starting out, so I was paying for most of their groceries as well. Thend, the youngest, lived with Besk as his apprentice.

Stador and Bann, thank the Strange Gods (or whoever really runs the universe), were at home instead of work.

"We heard you were dead," Stador explained, embracing me, "and then that you weren't—"

"I need you to go to Besk's, right now," I interrupted. "Take whatever you would if you were never coming back. Because you're not. We're leaving Four Castles."

"Why?" Stador wanted to know.

It was a reasonable question, but what was a reasonable answer? *A stray I brought back from the woods killed the Baron of Caroc. The Baron of Caroc had no bones. The Whisperer in the Woods knows one of the Silent Words.* None of it sounded reasonable to me.

"Your mother," I said slowly, "if she were alive, would certainly wish it. Is that enough? Will you wait for the rest?"

"Sure," they said agreeably, and each of them got a small bundle of stuff.

I sent them on ahead to Besk's to get Thend started. "If I don't follow in an hour," I said, "start without me. Don't come back here; go west, into the woods. I'll follow as soon as I can." There were some tools I needed to gather if we were going to rough it in the woods until we got to the lands beyond. I found a lump of beeswax, as well, set aside to make candles, and brought it with. I thought it might afford us some protection against the magic Morlock had unknowingly given to the Enemy in the woods.

There was someone pounding on the front door by the time I was done, so I went out through a window in the back of the house and ran away up the alley. I heard someone following me almost immediately, but I ran on for a stretch, hoping to tire them out.

Finally, I heard whoever it was gaining on me, so I halted and turned, my face friendly, my hand near my sword.

It was Morlock. My face fell, but my hand dropped away from my sword.

"I can't tell you," I said as he ground to a halt beside me, "how not glad I am to see you."

Morlock shrugged his crooked shoulders, his white face impassive.

Maybe he was used to that kind of reaction. I could understand that, if he screwed up other people's lives as swiftly and as thoroughly as he had screwed up mine.

"You're leaving Caroc," he said, gesturing at my bundle. "Perhaps the entire, er—?"

"Four Castles, yes," I said. "I'm getting my sister's boys out of here, too. Somehow I don't figure my prospects in the Riders are what they were yesterday. What with me causing the Baron's death and all."

Morlock looked at me quizzically. "Would you want a career in the Riders," he asked, "knowing what you know now?"

"What *do* I know?" I said. I started walking again; I had to get to Besk's. Morlock fell in beside me. "So the Baron had a hard shell and no bones. It didn't mean he was a bad person."

"He certainly seemed like a pleasant fellow," Morlock replied solemnly, "for the little while I knew him."

I glared at him for a second, then had to turn away; I didn't want him to see me smile.

"Roble," he said to my back, "I need some help."

"Well, you certainly came to the right place," I said, turning toward him with renewed anger. "You certainly have a store of credit with me. There's nothing I wouldn't do for the man who wrecked my life."

"You've been cattle for these things," Morlock said, his face less impassive, his voice carrying an edge. "You and everyone you've ever known. Does that content you? Is it the life you'd wish for your sister's children? For your own?"

"I don't have any."

"Why not?"

"Because I don't want—" I bit my sentence off. I wasn't that crazy about women as women, but I had thought about having a family sometimes. But I didn't want the Boneless One in the woods to eat my children, the way it had eaten Fasra, and Naeli, and countless others. I didn't want them to live in fear of the woods, the Bargainers, the Riders, the dark. I didn't want them to live the life I'd lived.

"Okay," I conceded gruffly, "maybe it wasn't such a great life. It was the one I had. Now, for taking it from me, you want me to—"

"I want you to help me destroy the enemy in the woods."

"What's it to you?" I demanded. "You can walk away from here and never come back."

He shook his head. "When I was taught the Silent Words I swore never to pass their secret to someone who would use them for harm. Now, inadvertently, I have. There is only one way to redeem my word: to kill the thing that lives in the wood. I may not be able to do it alone. Will you help?"

"Urk." I thought about it—for about half a second. It was a chance to kill the thing that had killed Naeli. "All right. But I want to send my nephews on their way first, in case it doesn't work out. I don't want the Barons or whatever those things are after them." I paused for a moment, then asked, "What are they?"

"The Barons?" Morlock shrugged his crooked shoulders. "I'm not sure. At first I thought they might be segments of the Boneless One. But the Baron didn't know the Silent Word, or he would have used it to stop me from shelling him. Perhaps they were once Coranians, who fed on the Boneless One for so long that they became like it—"

"What do you mean?" I demanded. "Fed on it how?"

"That's how your society works, Roble. The aristocracy, the Coranians, meet in the Circles, and they are fed tal by the Boneless One. That's what gives them their extended lives."

"I thought all Coranians lived long lives."

"Not centuries-long lives. For that they need aid, some life-source beyond their own. This they get from the Boneless One—life-sustaining tal skimmed from his victims, or fresh corpses from the wood or the Road, and transmitted through foci of power hidden in their places of ceremony. In return, of course, they see that the Boneless One gets regular meals."

"They Bargained with the Enemy."

"Essentially," Morlock agreed. I guessed he hadn't heard my capital letters. To Bargain was the ultimate sin among my people, but that wouldn't mean anything to Morlock.

I walked in silence for a while, absorbing what he'd said. "Are you telling me," I said finally, "that the Enemy could attack us in the day as easily as in the night? That there are no lawless hours . . . or that days are as lawless as the nights?"

"I'm certain your Enemy could act during the day. It simply chose not to. The herd could not be culled too often or too deeply; there always had to be enough stock to ensure a supply of meals in the future. Hence the Riders, and other things to keep the people of Four Castles thriving, even though a steady stream of individual persons were sacrificed. During the day, you thrived. At night, your Enemy fed."

It was as if I was listening to someone breaking the law, knowing that it would never be unbroken again. My whole life had been turned inside out: I thought I'd been fighting the Enemy, and all the while I'd just been guarding its herd.

I glared at Morlock. To him, this was all just a puzzle, and not an especially challenging one. "You figured this out pretty quickly," I said trying (and failing) not to sound hostile.

"When you've lived as long as I have you've seen most things more than once. The hive-cities of the Anhikh, south of here, are not so very different. But when I ascended to rapture in the Baron's hall I could read the threads of tal-contact between the Coranians in the hall and the thing in the woods, with a great dark locus in the Baron. I saw his true form then, too, hiding within its shell."

"So what's the secret of *your* long life?" I demanded. "Something similar?"

Morlock looked away. I'd finally gotten under his skin somehow. "No," he said finally. "I was born in . . . a guarded land, far from here. Things are different there. I can never go there now. But whatever life I have is my own, not stolen from someone else."

I believed him, for some reason. Maybe because he seemed to have the usual complement of human bones. Which prompted me to ask, "Why does consuming someone else's tal make you boneless?"

"I'm not sure," he said. "My sister thinks there are two kinds of tal: one which unites spirit to flesh, and another which joins spirit to bone. The flesh-tal would be easier to extract while the victim is still alive. But if you consumed only flesh-tal then your flesh would continue to live, but your bones would wither and die over time."

This was a disturbing thought, but what really shocked me was his casual mention of his sister. When I thought about it I realized there was no reason he shouldn't have a sister. But he hadn't seemed that human to me.

We came to Besk's smithy, marked with a golden anvil painted on the door. I leapt up the stairs and entered without knocking; Morlock followed me in.

Besk wasn't there, but the boys were sitting in the middle of the shop with their bundles beside them. They rose to their feet and stared at Morlock.

"Stador. Bann. Thend. This is Morlock Ambrosius."

Morlock and the boys nodded at each other civilly. But then Thend said, "He looks like a Coranian."

"I'm not," Morlock said seriously.

"He's really not," I confirmed. "They hate his guts; believe me." I pulled the block of beeswax out of my bag. "Listen, Morlock, I was thinking—"

"An excellent idea," he said, nodding.

"Think there's enough wax here to stop all these big ugly ears?"

Morlock grinned one-sidedly. "Just barely. But I should tell them something about the way westward before we plug our ears. You might do well to hear it, too. Perhaps we should bolt the door so we are not interrupted."

"No." I was thinking that Besk would return; I didn't want to lock him out of his own place. Also, there was a question I wanted to ask him, outside of the boys' hearing. "You go back into the smithy and I'll hold the fort here. You can tell me about it later, if"—*we live*, I would have finished, but I noticed the boys staring at me with wide eyes—"it seems necessary."

Morlock nodded, and Thend led the way back to the smithy.

"Why do we have to have our ears plugged?" Bann asked.

"The Enemy has a new magic," Morlock answered seriously. "Wax in your ears will protect you from it." The door shut behind him, cutting off his voice.

I leaned back against the shop counter and waited. I suppose it was a long time, but it didn't seem so; I had a lot to think about. Presently I heard slow footfalls coming up the stairs; the door opened and Besk stepped through.

He didn't seem surprised or pleased to see me. "Roble."

"Besk. Does the Enemy feed you?"

Besk's face, not the cheeriest I'd ever seen it, fell even further. "I don't know," he said at last. "There is life in the Silver Stones; in a certain ritual of the Mysteries, we can share in it, be strengthened by it. I . . . I don't know where the life comes from."

"Did you ever ask? Do the Inner Circles know?"

"I don't know what they know," he said, but his eyes would not meet mine.

"So you ate Naeli," I said. "And Fasra. You and the other white-faces in the Circles."

He put his hand to his pale brown forehead, as if to check its color, and said haltingly, "I . . . I don't know. How would I know, if it were . . . if it were true? No, Roble, listen."

I nodded and motioned for him to continue.

"I learned something at the Mysteries, this morning. It's bad news from Rendel's, I'm afraid. Alev died this morning just after dawn."

Bring the stray out, Alev had screamed after the trap had closed on both his legs. *I'm done.*

But I'd pried the jaws of the trap open and brought him out.

I couldn't leave him there to die, but now he was dead anyway.

I couldn't conceive of it: Alev had been my partner for four years. I could imagine not being a Rider, not living in Four Castles, my own death. But I couldn't picture a world where Alev was dead.

There was another thing I didn't understand.

"Besk," I said, "how did you hear this? There hasn't been time for a baronial courier to ride from Rendel's to here since dawn. And no one would send a courier just to report a Rider's death, anyway."

"It's one of the secrets," Besk said slowly, "but I think you should know. Yes. It's necessary that you know. There is an interconsciousness in each Circle. We share things . . . Not wills. Each man makes his own choices. But knowledge. We know what the others know."

"Not sure I'd care for that," I said.

"We get used to it. It can be useful. I knew what happened at the Baron's court this morning because many of my Circle were there. But other knowledge came later. . . ."

"What do you mean?"

"It seemed like knowledge. It seemed so real. We learned that Morlock had used magic to delude the crowd, that you had helped him, that together you had murdered the Baron. I didn't believe it, even though . . . I don't believe it. But the Circles are looking for you now."

"If—Are you telling them where I am?"

"I would not have betrayed you by choice, Roble. Believe me. But the moment I saw you, *they knew*."

A shape flew between Besk and me—a darkly luminous green bird whose form would not quite come into focus, as if it were wrapped in a dark mist. It flew around Besk's head three times. With the first pass his eyes closed; with the second his head slumped; after the third he fell to the ground. The green bird flew back to where it came from: the door of the smithy. Morlock, standing there, caught it in a glass bottle and closed the bottle with a stopper.

"What is that?" I asked.

"Sleep," Morlock said. "Let's go."

I looked down at the unconscious face of the old man I had loved and trusted. I found I loved and trusted him still. I would have liked to tell him so, at least once, but you can't have everything you want. If I were Liskin, I'd say it was one of the rules.

As it was, we grabbed our stuff, plugged our ears, and got out of there, running up the Road westward past the end of town. I never saw Besk, or Liskin, or Four Castles ever again. But I dream about them sometimes.

The Road ends at the western edge of Caroc Town, which is the westernmost settlement of Four Castles, but we ran on into the woods. They are tame just there, by the town, and we kept on moving as fast as we could. If there were pursuers behind us we never heard them, thanks to our beeswax earplugs. We held a hard pace, going just south of due west, at Morlock's insistence.

"We don't want to end up in Tychar," he said, when I asked him about it. (We each unplugged one of our ears, so we could confer about our course.) "It's a nasty place."

"I never heard of it," I admitted.

"You wouldn't have got any travellers from that direction. People who go into the winterwood seldom live to tell about it."

"Why don't we head due south, then?"

Morlock walked awhile in silence. "We might do so," he said finally. "It would be less dangerous. But we would eventually end up in the Anhikh *kômos* of cities."

"*Kômos?*"

"The word means 'parade' or 'dance' or something like that. I suppose you might translate it as 'alliance.' But there is a leader, the Kômarkh, who has an authority something like that of the Ontilian Emperor."

I was going to ask why it would be so bad to end up there, when I remembered something Morlock had said earlier, about the Anhikh cities being like Four Castles. It was worth some risk to avoid being caught in another web like the one we were leaving behind us. We replugged our ears and went on.

An hour or two later, I had the oddest feeling—as if a voice that had been whispering at me all my life had just fallen silent. I stopped dead and looked at the others; they clearly felt it, too.

Morlock dropped his pack and pulled from it a short shovel with a pointed blade. He walked back and forth over the ground we had just passed a few times, and then started to dig down.

For a sorcerer, he wasn't afraid to get his hands dirty. I had a shovel among my things, so I pulled it out and started to dig as well. All of us unplugged our ears (we knew we were at the limit of the Enemy's influence) and we dug in shifts.

It took a couple hours to lay bare a trench only six feet long and four feet deep; the soil was interwoven with tree roots, living and dead, and we were cutting through wood as often as we were digging in dirt. Nor did we know exactly what we were looking for.

But we had no doubt when we actually found it. At first it looked like a heavy cable, thicker than a man's arm—the kind they use in the mines. Then it seemed more like a monstrous earthworm: it rippled as we looked at it in the afternoon sun. It passed from one end of the trench to the other.

"No doubt," Morlock said, "it runs all around Four Castles and the neighboring woods. This is the anchor of the Boneless One's influence."

"You knew it would be here," I said.

"I guessed something like it would be. The Boneless One is extremely powerful; its influence pervades the woods and even the towns. It must emit talic impulses in waves, constantly exerting itself. But even so, the influence would be intense at its center and increasingly vague and slight everywhere else until the talic waves dissipated in the wide world . . . unless there were some sort of wavebreak or wall which would rebound the waves back into the wood."

"So if we put a hole in the wall—"

"—its influence leaks away. Most of Four Castles, at any rate, will be free of it; I don't know about the Bargainers."

"Let's cut it, then," I said.

Morlock started to speak, hesitated, and shrugged his crooked shoulders. He picked up his sharp swordlike shovel and dug it into the wormlike cable, twisting and pushing until the thing was completely severed. Some blackish green fluid like blood poured out and began to fill the narrow trench.

"Yecch," said Thend (speaking for all of us, I'd say).

The torn ends writhed for a bit, and then pressed against each other like two ragged mouths in a passionate kiss. Presently the ragged ends began to merge.

"We need to take out a bigger section," I guessed.

Morlock nodded. He cut again with his shovel while I dug into the wormlike cable in the middle of the trench. When both cuts were through, we put the blades under the severed and suddenly still section of worm-cable and tossed it out of the trench.

Morlock looked bleakly at his ragged shoes, drenched with sticky cold worm blood. "I really need new shoes," he remarked.

"Look!" I said.

The two ragged ends of worm-cable stretched and thinned and crawled toward each other over the gap of bare mud. They met and began to merge.

"Bargain the thing," I muttered. "We need to take an even bigger section."

"I think so," Morlock said. "Roble, look at this." He gestured at the section of worm-cable we had tossed out of the trench. It lay still, turning gray in the green-gold light of afternoon.

"So? It's dead—hey!"

"Yes. If we cut the thing at two widely separate points—might not the stretch between die? We would want them to be widely separated. We want as big a hole as we can make in the Boneless One's wall."

"It might work."

"And if it doesn't, we can try something else. I think the time has come to go different paths. Do you think you can find the border line by yourself? I might be able to fashion you a detector."

I closed my eyes and stepped from one side of the trench to the other and back again. The whispering returned, then vanished again. "I can do it," I said. "It's obvious where the border is."

"Then. I'll travel north and east along the border for a day or so. You travel south and east the same length of time. This time tomorrow, we'll cut the worm, wherever we are on the border. If we're right, the wall will be broken and the dominion of the Boneless One will be over."

"Right!" It was another night without sleep, but I could handle that. There was a trickier issue at hand. I turned to the boys, who were staring solemnly at us.

I call them boys, but one was fully grown and the other two were almost men. All of them were used to fending for themselves, working long and hard, sticking by each other. I hated to send them alone into the wilderness, but I wanted them away from this in case something went wrong.

"Boys," I said, "Morlock is right: we part ways here. I want you to go on west and south for a day's journey. Wait there for three days. If neither Morlock nor I come to meet you there, I want you to head west to—" I looked at Morlock.

"Sarkunden," he said. "There's a man there who owes me a favor. I gave Stador a map and a letter of introduction."

"Good. Don't wait longer for us and don't come back; we'll catch up to you."

"What if you don't?" Stador said matter-of-factly.

"Then make your mother proud. I'm proud of you already."

I hugged each one of them as Morlock stood away, repacking his shovel.

"Then," Morlock said, waving to us all in farewell.

"See you back here in two days," I said, although I knew how doubtful that was, and, in fact, it didn't work out that way.

In a few moments we were headed in three different directions. I tried to not look after the boys, but it was hard.

There was worse stuff, both earlier and later, but for me that night journey was the most difficult part in the whole business. I kept seeing Naeli in the woods, walking on the Enemy's side of the invisible wall. The Naeli-thing kept trying to signal me, but I was wearing my wax earplugs and looked away whenever I saw her. It bothered me, partly because I figured it must mean that the Enemy knew where I was, and what I was trying to do. But mostly it bothered me the way thoughts of Naeli always bothered me: because I had failed her and Fasra when they needed me most.

Toward dawn the Boneless One gave up; or, anyway, I stopped seeing her. I was tempted to lie down and rest when day came, but I forced myself to go on at a steady clip. When I judged it something later than midafternoon I stopped walking and started digging.

I knew, before I was fairly well along, that the Enemy knew I was there and was worried. Because the Naeli-thing appeared again. Although I was standing on the far side of the invisible wall to do my digging, she tried to approach me. I swung at her with the shovel and she backed away.

I saw her lips move. She seemed to be saying, *They are coming; they are coming. Run, Roble, run.*

"Drop dead," I replied, and resumed my digging, working as fast as I could. Presently the Naeli-thing disappeared into the woods. I didn't doubt she had been telling the truth, in a way. The Enemy probably was sending Bargainers to stop me. I had to finish before they got there.

I did, but only just. I had exposed and severed an eight-foot-long section of the gigantic worm Morlock had called the anchor of the Boneless One's influence. The two frayed ends struggled desperately to meet and reunify, flopping about in the trench sloppy with muddy worm blood. But they couldn't extend so far. Then they stopped struggling and the wounds at their ends closed like mouths. They seemed to be healing even as I watched.

I saw this with a mixture of disgust and ruefulness. The eight-foot section of the worm I had removed was incontestably dead. But the two ends of the worm were clearly alive. Perhaps longer segments of the worm could live independently. If so, the task Morlock and I had set ourselves was doomed to failure. I was exhausted and depressed: all this work for nothing?

When I raised my head at last I saw them standing there: at least a dozen Bargainers, grinning at me with their needlelike teeth.

I raised the shovel—I'd left my sword with my pack, some distance away in the woods—and backed away. They stepped forward to follow . . . and stopped suddenly.

I laughed. "You can't come farther, can you?" I said. "You've hit the wall. You're bound within the Boneless One's shell!" I laughed again. Suddenly the situation seemed hilarious. But of course I was very tired.

A big shaggy man, who may have been the leader, stepped back from the wall. He pressed his hand against a medallion hanging around his neck. Then he nodded as if he had received instructions and stepped across the trench, the gap in the Boneless One's anchor-worm.

His face stretched in surprise as he stood there, on the free side of the trench.

"You didn't expect that, did you?" I said to him. "The voice has stopped. It can't run you anymore. You're free, if you want to be."

The shaggy man looked at me for a moment, seeming to waver, then glanced back at the other Bargainers, watching him solemnly from the other side of the trench. When he turned back to me, his face was resolute. He couldn't lose face before his followers. Being their leader meant more to him than being free. He leaped forward, lashing out with his truncheon. I did my best to ward him off with the shovel, but I'd been halfway to unconsciousness before these guys showed up. Pretty soon his truncheon connected with my head and finished the job.

I didn't really wake up until we came to the Bargainer village; at least, I didn't completely wake up. I remember hanging like fresh game from a pole carried by two burly Bargainers, and I remember seeing Naeli or the Naeli-thing again and again, but there are many lightless patches. When I came fully to myself I was on my own feet, being dragged along a narrow lane between high houses with narrow windows through which many eyes, some of them human, were peering.

There were times everyone fell to the ground, as if worshipping, and they dragged me down with them. I was too groggy to understand what was happening or make my escape at these times. Besides, my hands were bound and my legs hobbled.

They took me to a great open area in the center of the village and bound me to a stake. In the middle of the open area was a tree, tall and twisted like an oak. At the foot of the tree was a mouthlike opening.

No one had to explain to me what would happen next. I was past swearing, but if there were, in some fireproof lexicon, any word sulphurous enough to express my anger and dismay at the thought of being fed alive to the Boneless One, I would have used it.

It didn't cheer me at all to see a familiar, crook-shouldered figure slumping at a stake similar to my own on the other side of the clearing. They had got Morlock, too. What was it he'd said? *If this doesn't work, we'll try something else.*

"Hey!" I shouted. "Let's try something else! I don't think this is working!"

I don't suppose he heard me, if his earplugs were still in place; anyway, he gave no sign of it. I leaned back against my stake and tried to ready my mind for death.

But some part of me wouldn't give up, and when a young silver-haired Bargainer girl of twelve or thirteen years came toward me with a knife in her hand I feigned indifference, putting all my weight on the ropes that bound me to the stake. When she came within range I kicked out with my hobbled feet, knocking her over and sending the knife spinning from her hand.

This proved to be wasted effort, though, as a group of young men immediately surrounded me, slashing at my bonds. As soon as I was free they dragged me away; I stopped resisting when I realized that it was really *away*: away from the clearing, the tree, the mouthlike hole in the ground.

Then I recognized them. My nephews, Naeli's boys: Stador, Bann, and Thend.

"What the hell are you doing here?" I shouted, uselessly. We all still had wax plugging our ears.

They grinned recklessly and shrugged as they ran.

How mad was I, really? Not at all—as long as we got away.

They turned aside into one of the narrow houses, one with shutters drawn over the slitlike windows. I followed them in, and, turning around, I saw the Bargainer girl behind us.

Suddenly I feared a Bargainer's trap. But the door slammed shut and strong arms held mine prisoner as someone took the wax from my ears.

"Calm down, Roble," Stador said, his voice uncomfortably loud. (He obviously still had wax in *his* ears.) "We're safe, here, but we don't have much time."

"We sure as hell don't; that little Bargainer wench is in here!" I shouted.

Someone lit a lamp. I turned and saw the Bargainer girl holding the light. There was a pained expression on her beautiful dark face.

"Don't you know me, Uncle Roble?" the Bargainer girl said. "I'm Fasra."

I was still gaping, speechless, when the door of the house opened again and Naeli slipped in, slamming it shut immediately. She pulled two waxen plugs from her ears (using only her left hand; her right arm hung strangely limp) and grinned a needle-toothed grin at me.

"Roble, my dear, maybe you'll listen to me at last, eh? I feel like I've been chasing you all around the Whisperer's Wood. Man, if you were as smart as you are tough, you'd really be dangerous."

I stared at her teeth, filed to a carnivore grin, and knew this was no illusion. Because the Boneless One only shows you what you want to see, and I didn't want to see this.

"You Bargained," I said flatly.

Naeli looked surprised and offended. "Of course I did! How else could I save Fasra? What did you think I was going to do?"

"I didn't think you'd Bargain."

Now she was just scornful. "There's no difference between us and them," she said coldly. "It's just what side you happen to be on."

This chilled me, because by "us" I knew she meant *the Bargainers* and by "them" she meant *everyone in Four Castles*: Besk, Alev, me. I wanted to argue with her, but I couldn't. Wasn't that why I was leaving? Anyway, there never was a time I could get the better of Naeli in an argument.

"I'm not on either side, anymore, I guess," I said.

"That's why I want you to take Fasra and get out of here," Naeli said hastily. "She's not bound to the Whisperer yet—they wait until after puberty to do that—but they'll bind her soon. Take her away with you and the boys."

"Why can't you come?" I asked.

"The Whisperer has put a compulsion on me," she said, touching her chest. I saw, underneath her tunic, the outline of a medallion. "That was why I couldn't free you from the stake myself. I could only speak to you when he wasn't noticing me."

"And he isn't now?"

Naeli shook her head. "He hasn't often noticed me in the past day or so. It's almost as if there were two Whisperers now; the village is at war with itself and the Soundless Sound strikes often and often."

"Can't you—"

"I can't leave the woods while the compulsion binds me," she said, touching the medallion under her tunic again.

"Is that medallion the source of the compulsion?" I asked.

"Yes."

I approached her and looked at the cord securing the medallion around her neck. There seemed to be nothing unusual about it.

"Why don't you take it off?" I asked.

"I can't; that's part of the compulsion."

"Why don't you ask someone to take it off you?"

"I can't; that's part of the compulsion."

"If I take it off you, will you or I or anyone here be harmed?"

"No."

I reached out and took the cord with each hand and snapped it. The medallion dropped to the ground through Naeli's tunic. She turned and kissed me. I couldn't repress a shudder (I thought I could feel the razor teeth through her lips), but she didn't seem to notice, or perhaps didn't care.

"Now we can go together," she said, fierce and happy—strangely like the Naeli I once knew.

Naeli's boys chimed in, and Fasra, too. Stador explained how Naeli had met them in the woods and brought them to rescue me from the stake, which the compulsion prevented her from doing herself.

"*They* believed I was really me, anyway," Naeli said wryly.

I shrugged. "The Boneless One sent false images of you to me every night I rode through the lawless hours. I'd be long dead if I trusted everything I saw in the woods."

Naeli nodded slowly. "It's hard to say what the Whisperer knows . . . but he may have known I was thinking of you. I've been trying to figure out a way to get Fasra away from the Bargainers almost since we came here."

"So what's the plan now, or are we improvising?"

"A little of both," Naeli admitted, with her terrifying smile. "We'll be safe here from the Others; all of the fighting between Bargainers has been in the street. And the Soundless Sound can't reach us here, either. We'll wait until they send the stranger down to the Whisperer, and then we can escape while they're occupied."

"Tough luck on the stranger," I observed.

Naeli shrugged. She must have seen many people go that route, perhaps some she had known herself.

For me it was different. We always tried to bring the stray out, Alev and I. And only then (it wasn't my brightest day) did I realize who "the stranger" was. It was my stray, Morlock. Somehow the idea of Morlock and the idea of Alev were bound up together. I thought of Alev, his legs broken in the trap; I thought of Morlock falling down that mouthlike hole.

"Naeli," I said slowly. "Alev is dead."

"Who is Alev?" said this stranger who was my sister.

I shook my head. "Never mind. I have to bring the stray out, if I can. You guys can get away in the disturbance. Boys, wait for me a day at the meeting place we set; if I don't come, go on as planned." I plugged my ears, shutting out their protestations and good-byes, and ran out of the house, leaving the door open behind me.

Morlock's stake was empty and there was a crowd of people standing around the base of the crooked tree. It was possible I was already too late. I scooped up the knife I had kicked out of Fasra's hand and ran across the clearing. I plunged into the crowd, slashing with the knife in one hand and striking out randomly with my other fist.

I was like a lit candle applied to wood shavings; soon the Bargainers were all fighting with each other desperately. Some used only their right hand; their left arm swung useless at their sides. Others used only their left hand; their right arms seemed to be disabled. The left-handed people struck only the right-handed people and vice versa. I was careful to use both hands, baffling the Bargainers, who turned from me to attack the enemies they knew: each other.

I made it all the way to the center of the crowd, where Morlock, his lower body out of sight, was scrabbling desperately at the lip of the mouthlike hole, trying to pull himself out. His mouth was gagged and each of his wrists was looped with a twisted cord, as if they had been bound together.

I left the knife in a nearby Bargainer and bent down to grab with both hands at one of Morlock's arms.

Morlock's mouth was moving; it looked as if he was shouting some sort of warning. But the plugs in my ears kept me from hearing him, and the gag in his mouth kept me from reading his lips.

The ground crumbled under my feet. We fell with several Bargainers into the gaping earth.

My death grip on Morlock's arm saved me. When we had fallen several feet we jerked to a halt. Looking up through the shadows and the clots of dirt falling from the ragged edge of the hole, I saw Morlock had caught hold of a tree root. He didn't manage to hang on to it, but it slowed us down. He caught the next one and held it, but it bent ominously under our joint weight. There was another root protruding from the hole wall, not so far off, and I managed to pull myself onto it.

Both of us were so out of breath that talking would have been out of the question, even if we didn't have our ears plugged. While regaining my wind, I looked around at the questionable situation in which we found ourselves.

We were about midway down the gullet of earth, between the hole in the surface (still mouthlike, but more of a spreading grin now) and the bellylike chamber at the bottom. There was light coming from both directions—from the sky above and from a purplish luminescence emitted by a moss that grew thickly on the curving walls of the chamber below. Immediately under us was a pile of human bones, naked and fleshless with the fluted marks of chewing all over them.

Scattered around the floor were various Bargainers, flopping around like birds caught in a net. One or two were motionless, perhaps impaled on the sharp broken bones that were scattered over the floor of the chamber.

And there was something else. It was hard to tell exactly what it was. It looked like two bladders of unequal size, half filled with some sort of fluid, connected to each other by a thickish cord. One of the bladders was about as long as a man's arm; the other was less than half that long, and not as broad. There seemed to be some sort of hair or fur on part of the smaller bladder.

It was alive. It moved about the bone-paved floor by rolling, and as it rolled I could see it had some appendages—not arms and legs, really, but just floppy little things where arms and legs might be, or might once have been. I couldn't tell what sex it was, or if it had one, but I began to realize that some of the features on the less hairy side of the smaller bladder constituted a face. There was a slack half-open mouth, crusted with filth from the floor; above it a floppy boneless nose, two ear-flaps protruding from the surface of the bladder, and two dark glaring eyes. And across it all was a scar or seam, a dark purplish mark dividing the face almost in half. It passed between the eyes, to the left of the nose, and over the mouth, apparently sealing the lips together at the mouth where it crossed them, so it was almost as if the thing had two mouths.

The Boneless One (I didn't doubt that's what I was looking at) rolled over to one of the fallen Bargainers, a man who was struggling to regain his feet. Its two mouths pressed against his arm, as if in a kiss. The life went out of him in a moment and he fell dead to the ground.

After a while it rolled away, or started to, then paused. The appendages on one side of the body flapped uselessly. It was almost as if they were trying to hit the other side of the Boneless One's body. Finally the Boneless One rolled away toward another fallen Bargainer, a woman who was twitching limply, apparently unable to get up.

This time it looked as if one side of the Boneless One's face was trying to keep the other side from making contact with the victim. Again the useless appendages struggled, each set lashing out at the opposite side of the shapeless body. When the woman screamed, seeing the monster beside her, and began to edge away across the bone-strewn floor, the Boneless One gave up its pointless struggle against itself and rolled quickly over, locking its lips on the woman's left leg. She stopped moving instantly; her face became calm; her eyes closed. Her life was gone, her tal consumed. The Enemy moved on toward the next body.

It was weird, but I thought I knew what was happening when the Boneless One fought itself. I figured that we had done it, Morlock and I. If he had cut the anchor-worm as I did, it must have divided the Boneless One's influence into two unequal halves. In doing so, we had somehow divided the Boneless One itself, as if there was no difference between the Boneless One and the space where its influence ran. So now there were two Boneless Ones sharing the same body, and obviously each resented the other. I sort of hoped they would figure out some way to kill each other, but I didn't figure it would happen within the next few minutes.

Maybe, I thought, we should just drop down into the pit, seize some sharp broken bones for weapons, and try to poke the thing to death. It seemed like someone would have tried that, during the centuries the Boneless One had been eating human lives in this pit. But maybe they fell so far and hit so hard that they were stunned and the Boneless One got them before they could recover.

Then again, maybe that skin wouldn't be so easy to poke through. It could roll over the carpet of shattered bones without apparently taking any harm at all, not even a scratch. That brownish, pinkish, grayish surface was probably harder than leather. It would take more than a rotten bone to chew a hole in it . . .

Chew. I looked again at the bones. They had been *gnawed*; the toothmarks were clearly visible, even in the wretched purplish light. By what? If the Boneless One was truly boneless, it wouldn't have teeth. Besides, why should it gnaw flesh if it lived on the tal that sustained life itself?

Rats. There must be rats down there. Maybe a lot of rats. The rats would come in and clean up the meat after the Boneless One had drained the life. So why hadn't they appeared yet?

The Boneless One finished a third victim and paused, in midcareer toward a fourth. Its right pair of leathery lips wrinkled, as if it were saying something. The left pair of lips twisted in response, and my nerves were struck with the muted sound of the Silent Word. Then the left pair of lips seemed to say some-thing, and the right pair of lips responded with the Silent Word.

Was there something happening up above—some battle between the Bargainers controlled by the two warring segments of the Boneless One?

Maybe. Or maybe each side had called out to a cleanup crew of rats, and the other side had knocked them out. Because they were each afraid. Afraid of rats under the other's control . . . or under no control.

Rats! Morlock could summon the rats, if he only had his magic pipe with him. Then I realized he probably did: when I had last seen it he had been tucking it into his sleeve.

I looked toward Morlock, trying to catch his eye. He was hanging on to a root with his left hand, stripping the gag away from his mouth with his right hand. He stared bemusedly at the Boneless One as it drained the life from a fourth victim. I shouted, but he didn't hear me. I grabbed a clump of earth from the side of the pit and tossed it at him. Then he turned toward me, his eyebrows raised as if in inquiry.

"*Rats!*" I shouted. But either he didn't hear me (or couldn't read my lips) or he didn't see what I was driving at. Desperately, I tapped my left arm with my right hand, and then mimed playing a flute. All this activity caused my grip on the root to loosen and I almost fell. But by the time I had regained my perch Morlock was laughing (not at my acrobatics, I hope) and drawing the pipe from his sleeve-pocket.

He put the pipe in his mouth and began to play. I couldn't hear it, exactly, but somehow the feel of it penetrated the wax earplugs, almost like the Silent Word. It was a squeaky, spiky, chittering tune; it went on and on, never repeating but somehow always the same.

The rats began to appear, rising like a dark tide from the ground. The Boneless One seemed to try to halt them with the Silent Word, but its magic was masked by the endless chittering song from Morlock's pipe.

The Boneless One tried to eat the lives of the rats as they approached. Many died, but there were always more behind. The dark tide rose over the swollen shapeless form of the Boneless One and covered it.

The mindless whisper I always heard within me rose to an almost audible shriek and fell silent at last. The rats moved on to the other bodies scattered around the floor, leaving behind a bloody stain on the bone carpet and nothing else. The Boneless One was dead.

Morlock's pipe stuttered and shrieked. The living rats fled in terror. Morlock pocketed the pipe and tentatively unplugged one ear.

Both of my ears were already clear. The air was free of Silent Words; my mind was free of demonic whispers.

"Good idea about the rats," Morlock said laconically.

"I never liked rats before," I said, "but now I do. When I settle down, I'm going to keep tame ones, like birds."

Morlock grunted and climbed back up onto the root. "Up or down?" he asked.

I looked down at the bone-carpeted bellylike chamber, scattered with half-eaten motionless Bargainers. I looked upward to the light.

"Up," I said, and we went up.

We hadn't been at it long before Naeli's voice fell down to us from the light, followed by a rope. I swarmed up it and Morlock followed.

Naeli had tied it to the twisted tree standing above the mouthlike hole. The boys and Fasra were standing uneasily, with knives and clubs in their hands, at the edge of the hole. Further off, a ragged halo of Bargainers stood, glaring at us as we emerged from the pit.

"Let's get going," Naeli said to me crisply. "Some of these people don't seem to like what we're doing."

"I thought they'd scatter as soon as the Boneless One was dead," I muttered.

"Some did. But most of these guys were Bargainers because they wanted to be, and they suspect you of killing their god."

"That was Morlock," I said, gesturing at the bedraggled, crooked figure emerging from the hole.

"Roble's idea. Call it a mutual effort," he said. His gray gaze crossed Naeli's dark one; it was like swords clashing.

"Man, were you a lot of trouble," Naeli said. "I thought you were going to get us all killed. Morlock? I'm Naeli. This is Fasra. I guess you know my boys. Let's get out of here."

Morlock shook his head. "You go on," he said. "I have to find Tyrfing."

"A friend of yours?" demanded Naeli.

"My sword."

"Oh, that thing. The Whisperer had us bury it outside of town. I'll show you where it is." She turned and charged straight toward the crowd. We followed in a wedge behind. The Bargainers split up and ran as we approached, and soon we were out of town. We heard the Bargainers, although we didn't see them, gathering nearby in the woods as we dug down to recover Morlock's sword. So as soon as we had it we started moving westward as fast as our feet could take us.

That was days ago. We discussed going back to Four Castles, but rejected the idea. Naeli, with her filed teeth, would be an outcast there. And the thought of living among Coranians, who had fed on human lives to extend their own, was repugnant to me. Perhaps one of the three remaining Barons would pick up where the Boneless One had left off; perhaps they had already been stomped to bits by someone following Morlock's lead. Maybe Liskin would be the new power in Four Castles; he was already pretty boneless. It didn't matter. Four Castles was already far off and a little unreal to me, like somewhere you've read about in a book. It wasn't my place anymore. I don't have a place, at the moment; these days I have people instead.

Each day we move a little further west than I've ever been, camping at sunset. It's night, as I write this, but no one is sleeping. The boys and Fasra are sitting by the fire, swapping stories with each other and some jar from Morlock's backpack that thinks it's an old lady. Morlock is peering about inside Naeli's mouth; he says he can carve supplements for Naeli's teeth, so that she will have a slightly less wolflike smile.

I'm sitting here writing, not saying much—speaking aloud maybe one word for every thousand I scribble down. In a way, I think I miss the wordless whispering I have always heard in my head. It helped show me what I was by being what I was not: I was the enemy of the Enemy. But not now: in the last few days, I helped kill a Baron, the Enemy that lived in the woods, and (with them) my whole way of life. But here I am, somehow still alive. I don't feel like speaking much until I figure out who I am, now that the Enemy is dead.

This much I know. I will not live three hundred years. But, however long I live, I will wear no one else's uniform. I will swear loyalty to one person at a time. However long I live, my life will belong to me, and to those I know and care about. Except for that rule of love, all my hours are lawless now.

It's late; we had all better get some sleep. New lands, and new lives, tomorrow.

Fasra's Story

IX

Payment in Full

Who is the third who walks always beside
     you?
When I count, there are only you and I
     together
But when I look ahead up the white road
There is always another one walking
     beside you
Gliding wrapt in a brown mantle, hooded
I do not know whether a man or a woman
—But who is that on the other side of
     you?

—Eliot, *The Waste Land*

"The truth is my blood and breath, master: I cannot lie. I could sell either the youth or the maiden for six fingers of silver in Menebacikhukh, that benighted city of the Anhikh Komos where I was born. I will give you three silver fingers for either of them, seven for both."

We were crossing the marketplace in Sarkunden when the slave-trader put a long corpselike hand on one of Morlock Ambrosius's slightly uneven shoulders and made his pitch. Before that day I'd never so much as seen the walls of a city this big. From what I'd seen inside those walls, I didn't think I was going to like big cities much, even before the slaver spoke to Morlock. As the maiden under discussion, I waited for Morlock's response with real interest.

Morlock shot a cold gray glance at the Anhikh slave-trader and pointed out, "Buying or selling human beings has been illegal in the Ontilian Empire for more than two hundred years."

"The contract would be unofficial, of course. I would trust to the honor I see in your face, and perhaps, for form's sake, a guarantee placed in the hands of some mutually reliable person." He let his eyes linger on me, stroking his lips in an oddly salacious gesture.

"Is he a slaver or a con man, Thend?" Morlock asked my brother. "What do you say, Fasra?" he added, glancing at me.

"Whatever's creepier," I said flatly.

"I might go as high as eight fingers of silver," the Anhikh continued, "in spite of the unfashionably dark color of their skin and their lack of manners. The latter would soon be mended, yes indeed it would. What do you say, master? What is your response, your (shall we say) wholly unofficial response?"

"I am not your master," was the first part of Morlock's unofficial response. The second part left the slave-dealer on all fours, gasping with pain.

"Keeps," Thend muttered to Morlock. Following his glance, I saw a couple of armored figures approaching.

Morlock nodded and paused his unofficial responses while the soldiers made their way through the market crowd. They wore gear exactly like the city guards who stood at the gates, except they had the fist insignia on their shields: Keepers of the Peace.

"No fighting in the Market," the senior Keep said, as he came up. "You'll have to come along."

"This man is a slaver," Morlock said.

"So?"

"Slavery's illegal."

The senior Keep scratched his face and stared at Morlock for a while. "I guess it is," he finally admitted. "Technically. But this guy paid his market fee just like everyone else. What do you want me to do about it?"

"Let's check his wagon."

The senior Keep shrugged and gestured at the Anhikh. The junior Keep dragged him to his feet and checked the number on his market pass. We all trooped over to the matching wagon. On the outside brightly colored letters said (in two languages I knew, and probably others I didn't) that this was the roving headquarters of the Perambulations of Evanescent Joy and Portable Fun Company. Inside, the wagon was one big cage. When we dropped the back flap of the wagon and let in the light, dozens of eyes gleamed at us hopelessly through the bars. The wagon was half full of children of various ages, sizes, colorations (fashionable and unfashionable).

"They're orphans," the Anhikh slaver said sullenly.

"There's no orphan exception to the slavery law," Morlock pointed out.

As the senior Keep hesitated, Morlock forced the lock on the cage with something he had in his pocket and opened the door. The children, suddenly mobile, streamed out and vanished into the nearby alleys like water into sand.

The Anhikh muttered a few words that sounded like curses.

"Cool it," said the senior Keep. "Thanks to this gentleman you're a law-abiding citizen again. Keep it that way, or the girls'll be calling you 'Stumpy.'"

We left the Anhikh muttering imprecations over his broken lock. "Hey, pal," said the senior Keep to Morlock, "your face is sort of familiar. Didn't I cut your head off once?"

"It seems unlikely."

"It seemed that way at the time, let me tell you. But this guy whose head I cut off, or maybe didn't, he was an imperial outlaw. You'll still have to come with me; your young friends can go about their business."

Morlock silently handed the guard a piece of paper with a seal of dark blue wax on it.

The senior Keep whistled as he read it. "An immunity. Signed by the imperial commander at Sarkunden, Vennon himself. Only good for one day, but it must have been expensive."

"An associate acquired it for me."

"He must like you a lot."

"Not really."

The Keep tapped the seal with one finger. "This thing isn't actually valid, you know. Commander Vennon, may he lick his own elbow, can't suspend the Emperor's order of outlawry. I could still bring you in, or kill you on the spot."

"Could you?" Morlock wondered mildly.

"Uh." The Keep's face took on a remembering look. "Maybe not," he admitted. "Anyway, my skipper wouldn't half-bless me if I did. It'd bring down the market value for those temporary immunities, for one thing. My name's Thrennick—no, don't tell me yours, not when we're getting along so well. See you around sometime."

We continued across the marketplace until we came to a place that proclaimed itself, in a large banner, as CHARIS'S DISCOUNT EMPORIUM OF DELUXE WONDERS. A smaller sign burbled, *No job too large or too small! Satisfaction guaranteed! Charis and his team of expert thaumaturges will not rest until*—The rest was water-damaged and I couldn't read it, but I doubted I was missing much. A still smaller but more convincing sign said firmly, *No Credit.*

We pushed our way inside. As my eyes were still adjusting to the dimness, the shopkeeper rushed up to us, his blunt pale features stretched to display a somewhat oily professional friendliness.

"Honored sirs, young lady, what can we do for you?"

"You can bring me Charis," Morlock said.

I could see reasonably well by now—well enough to catch sight of a convincing replica of Morlock's head staring down at us from a tall, tomblike display case. I turned around to point it out to Thend, but he'd already noticed it.

"I am afraid that Charis sees no one, absolutely no one, unless it is absolutely necessary," the shopman purred. "It is one of his little ways. I am Stokkvenn, his chief assistant master thaumaturge-in-training, and I can almost certainly meet your needs. In all honesty, you might prefer to deal with me. Charis is a brilliant man, the greatest wonder-worker of our establishment, but his manners are a trifle—Excuse me, sir, but have we not met before? I'm almost sure of it."

Morlock pointed at the head glaring down at us. Stokkvenn looked at it, back at Morlock, and said, "Charis will be out to see you in a moment."

Stokkvenn disappeared into an inner room. Presently the same door opened and another man emerged. He was almost the opposite of Stokkvenn—tall, sharp-featured, somewhat distant in his manner. But he was pale—Death and Justice was he pale-skinned! At one time I'd thought Morlock was the whitest man in the world, but next to him this other fellow was practically translucent: ice white skin, yellow hair and eyebrows, green squinting eyes.

"Morlock Ambrosius," the newcomer said. "This is indeed a pleasure." If it really was a pleasure, his face didn't show it.

"Charis," Morlock said.

"I hope—At our last meeting—K-k-k-k-k. Or quasi-meeting, rather—" Charis's face hardly moved as he spoke, but from his strange disjointed speech I gathered he was terrified of Morlock.

"Do you have what I came for?" Morlock asked briskly. "If so, we need not consider the past."

"Er. K-k-k-k-k. I have. That is, I have some of the information you asked for."

"Paid for."

"K-k-k-k-k. Yes. Quite. Indeed, I got it right away. But months have passed since then, and I thought . . . K-k-k-k-k. Matters may have changed, you see. So I purchased an update, at great expense and for your personal convenience."

"Then?" Morlock replied, stepping closer and looking intently at Charis's face.

"The messenger from the guard captain is due. K-k-k-k-k. Is due any moment. Won't you wait, and—k-k-k-k-k—await him, as it were?"

"Hm," said Morlock. He reached over and tore out one of Charis's eyeballs.

All right—I admit it. I screamed. So did Thend, no matter what he says.

But the funny thing is: Charis *didn't* scream. No blood poured from the empty eye socket. He just stood there, squinting with one eye and saying, "K-k-k-k-k. I understand. K-k-k-k-k. Your impatience. K-k-k-k-k. Very understandable, even laudable, impatience. K-k-k-k-k—"

Morlock turned toward us, displaying the eyeball in his hand. Except, now that I brought myself to look at it, it didn't really look like an eyeball. More like a glassy imitation of one. The black glittering shreds hanging from the back of the eyeball didn't look like nerves, or anything that had grown inside a human body. Thend, obviously nerving himself up, stepped forward to take the thing and look closer at it.

"It's glazed clay," Morlock said with something like contempt in his voice. "The iris is painted on!" Apparently that was bad.

He turned back to the thing he had called Charis and, drawing his knife, split it open from collarbone to belly. I managed to keep from screaming this time, but only barely. It was babbling all the while about "—an investment—k-k-k-k-k—as it were, in time, to pay off royally—" but, increasingly, I couldn't look on the thing as human. It stopped speaking and moving when Morlock drew something out of the gap in its chest—a scroll of some sort.

"It's not Charis," he said. "It's a golem in Charis's image. Not Charis's own work, clearly."

"You can tell?" I asked faintly.

"I taught Charis how to make a decent eyeball," Morlock grumbled. He unrolled the sheet in his hand and glanced at it, adding, "The life-scroll isn't in his handwriting. And the stupid thing couldn't even speak properly. Not the product of the establishment's greatest wonder-worker."

"But maybe," I guessed, "the chief assistant master thaumaturge-in-training?"

"Exactly," Morlock approved. "Thend: get him."

Death and Justice, that annoyed me. Sure, Thend was big and strong for his age (almost fifteen). But I was about to point out that just because I was thirteen years old and a girl, it didn't mean I couldn't slap someone like Stokkvenn around and make him like it. Then I looked Morlock in the eye (those flaring gray irises were *not* painted on) and I decided it wasn't the strategic moment to say so.

"Fasra," he said to me, "drop the brass shutter over the window, bolt it, and stand by the door. Here." He tossed me the knife in his hand and said, "We may have company soon."

I was tempted to ask who'd died and made him God. On the other hand, I'd learned the hard way that sometimes it's smart to listen to someone who knows more than you do. I bit my tongue and did as he asked. He busied himself behind the counter, pulling things out of drawers and looking at them.

Pretty soon Thend appeared, dragging a squealing Stokkvenn behind him. "He was trying to go out the back door," Thend said to Morlock, and tossed the shopman up against the counter in front of Morlock.

"You bolted it?"

"Yes."

"We may have guests. Will it hold?"

Thend shrugged. "Not forever."

Morlock turned to Stokkvenn. "You wrote this," he said coolly, waving the life-scroll of the dead golem.

"No. I—"

"I'm not asking you; I'm telling you that I know. You keep the register here—the ink is still on your hands—and the life-scroll was written in the same handwriting. You made this golem of your employer. Why?"

Stokkvenn quacked wordlessly for a few moments and finally said, "The Sandboys made me do it."

If he'd said the Fluffy Puppies I couldn't have been more surprised. In my mind's eye I pictured a Sandboy as a friendly little figure made of sand, sitting on a beach somewhere.

"Who are the Sandboys?" Morlock asked.

"The Sandboys! The Sandboys!"

"Yes: them. Who are they?"

"They're the biggest water-gang in town, that's all! They wanted to take over Charis's business, but he wouldn't sell. It got pretty ugly. Then the big bucket of the Sandboys sent for me and he said they were moving in, whether Charis liked it or not. There was nothing I could do about it. If I went along with them, they'd keep me on to run the business for them. I was supposed to make the golem of Charis to keep up appearances. The gangs can't own businesses, you know—not legally."

"Fasra," said Morlock, "is there anyone outside?"

The shop was on the edge of a marketplace of a big city on market day. Of *course* there was someone outside, and I almost said so. But then I figured he meant someone in particular, so I had a look.

"Uh," I said. "A bunch of guys with metal sticking out of their faces. They've got swords and clubs and they're staring at the shop."

"The Sandboys," Stokkvenn said, shrugging. He was a little more at ease, looking Morlock in the eye now. Like he was thinking, *Maybe you have my number, but someone else has yours.*

"Stokkvenn," said Morlock, "your story doesn't work."

Stokkvenn instantly lost whatever ground he'd gained. "It's all I know!" he cried. "It's the truth!"

"It may be all you know, but it's not the truth. I was lured here with an authentic-looking message; either Charis or an excellent forger wrote it. It accompanied an immunity-pass which must have taken a great deal of expense or effort to acquire. Why would your Sandboys take the trouble?"

"I don't know! I can't tell you what I don't know!"

"Where is Charis, the real Charis, now?"

"I don't know. I think the Sandboys took him. He's probably dead."

"Unlikely. I think he's still alive, and someone wants me to lead them to him. Any thoughts, Stokkvenn?"

"None. I'm sorry. I've told you all I can."

"Hm," Morlock said. He dropped the life-scroll and vaulted over the counter. "Unfortunately, I believe you."

"Unfortunately?" Stokkvenn repeated faintly as Morlock took him by the shoulders.

"Unfortunate for me," Morlock said, "since all my questions are unanswered. Unfortunate for you, because you are now useless to me."

Morlock nodded at me, and I swung the shop door wide.

"No," Stokkvenn gasped.

"Coming out!" Morlock shouted, and threw Stokkvenn headfirst, stumbling into the street. There were some shouts, and meaty thumps, and I heard Stokkvenn's voice sobbing. A few moments later, when I peeked past Morlock out the door, Stokkvenn was gone. I never learned whether he lived or died.

"Not fair, Crookback!" someone shouted. "You said you were coming out!"

"I didn't mean me," Morlock called back. "Come in, if you like. I am Morlock Ambrosius; I await you."

There was some audible grumbling at this. They'd have had to come through the doorway one at a time, and apparently they'd heard some stories about Morlock that made them reluctant to try it. We'd only been travelling with Morlock a couple months, and I could have told them some stories myself.

"We'll burn the place down!" someone shouted.

"So what?" Morlock replied easily. "I'll walk away in the flames, and you will not follow me."

It was true that he could do that, but Thend and I couldn't. I hoped he was bluffing and looked anxiously at Thend. He shrugged and grinned nervously.

Morlock shut the shop door and barred it. He went over to the lifeless golem and ripped its ears off. He did something to them—I couldn't really see it in the shop's dim light, and what I saw I couldn't understand—and then he took one of them and fixed it to the doorpost with a long shining thing like a glass nail.

"Find the roof door," he said to Thend and me.

"Are you sure there is one?" I asked.

"I hope there is," he said and turned back to the golem ears, muttering a few words in a language I didn't know.

We found the roof door pretty quickly: it was a kind of a hatch in the ceiling of the back room. We called Morlock and he came back, one of the ears still in his hand. He handed it to me, thanks a lot, and climbed up the ladder to the roof hatch. He unbolted it quietly and tentatively peeked out. It was sort of funny, or would have been if I hadn't been holding a severed ear.

He lowered the hatch and dropped down to the floor. "Go on up to the roof," he said to us. "Stay low. I'll join you in a moment."

I was going to hand him his nasty ear back, but he'd already turned away. I followed Thend up to the roof and we crouched low, to keep out of sight of the Sandboys in the street before the shop (and, presumably, in the alley behind).

"Shut up," Thend whispered to me.

"I'm not doing anything," I whispered back.

"I heard you move and say something."

I'd heard the same thing, but it wasn't me. I held up the golem ear. Startled, he put his ear against the thing and then gestured that I should do the same from the other side.

We heard Morlock's voice as he moved around in the shop downstairs: "—'blood of Ambrose'—unlikely. *This really might be phlogopos juice, though. Yes. That'll do.*" After a few moments the severed ear emitted a crackling sound.

I realized that he had somehow enchanted the golem ears. We were hearing what the ear nailed to the shop door was hearing. This was what I thought, but what I said was, "He talks to himself when he's alone!"

Thend shrugged. "Sure. He's almost completely crazy: hadn't you noticed?"

I told Thend something I'd noticed about *him*, and he was hotly denying it when Morlock appeared through the hatch.

The crooked man pinned my brother with a single gray glance and Thend snapped his mouth shut.

"Can you jump across to that roof?" Morlock asked Thend, pointing at the nearest building.

Thend nodded.

"Do it, then. If you think anyone on the street saw you leap, keep on going and don't wait for us. We'll meet you back with Roble and Naeli. Got it?"

Thend nodded again.

"Then," said Morlock.

Thend ran, crouching, across the roof of Charis's shop, and leapt to the nearest roof. He waited there, crouching. No one called out; no one seemed to have seen him. He gestured that we should follow.

"Go," said Morlock.

"Why are you so sure I can?" I asked.

He looked at me, surprised. "You can run faster and jump farther than any of your brothers—except Stador, perhaps. If Thend can do it, you can do it. Go."

I was mad. "I'm not one of your stupid golems!" I hissed.

He looked at me more carefully. "Fasra, I'm sorry to seem abrupt. I set fire to Charis's shop after I sent you up here, and soon the gangsters will notice and risk breaking in. We should be well away by then. So: go. Now."

"Take your nasty ear!" I whispered furiously, shoving it at him. I ran across the roof and jumped to the next one. Morlock followed, holding the golem ear to one of his own, looking solemn and ridiculous.

We had crossed a few more roofs when Morlock abruptly dropped the golem ear, crushing it under his shoe. "They're breaking into Charis's shop," he said. "We'll try going down to street level here: they'll soon realize we escaped across the roofs."

He pulled up the roof hatch of the building we were on. He did it so casually, I thought the thing was unbolted . . . but then I saw the latch dangling from the undrawn bolt. He dropped down into the hatch and reached up to help us down.

As my eyes were still adjusting to the dimness within a big bulky guy approached us and shouted at Morlock, "Hey! Customers not allowed on roof! Get out of here! You two"—he gestured at Thend and me—"get back to rooms."

I saw now that the walls were covered in red velvet, and there were some pungent odors assaulting my nose—some sweet, some less so. I'd worked as a housekeeper—and that's all, by the way—at the village cathouse, so it was all pretty familiar.

"Uncle Morlock," I said, in a high-pitched little-girl falsetto, "what sort of place is this?"

The big bulky guy looked at me, puzzled, and then back to Morlock.

"I beg your pardon for the intrusion, and the damage to your roof door," Morlock said, presenting the big guy with a gold coin.

"Damage?" The big guy looked at the broken latch and said, "Oh, yeah."

He didn't seem too mad, though, and he was even less so when Morlock presented him with a second gold coin.

A third coin made the guy positively beam with welcome. "No problem!" he said. "Drop in any time! Stay as long as you like! What was name again?"

"Morlock Ambrosius. But we'll have to leave immediately," Morlock said. "We were escaping from a fire up the street and—"

"Fire?" said the big guy, not so friendly anymore. He shouldered past us and hauled himself halfway through the roof hatch. He must have seen the plume of smoke over Charis's shop right away because he dropped down and ran up the corridor shouting, "Fire! Fire! Fire up street! Everyone out! Fire up street!"

The corridor was suddenly full of screaming people in varying states of undress. Morlock drew me and my brother back against one wall and we waited for the riptide of frightened people to pass away.

"Why didn't you mention the fire before you gave him the money?" I asked Morlock, thinking that he could have saved himself three gold coins.

Morlock looked at me almost pityingly and said, "Then he wouldn't have waited to take the money."

Morlock's back was to Thend, who mouthed the word *crazy* to me. To emphasize the point he crossed his eyes, drew his upper lip above his teeth, and, after putting his wrists to either side of his forehead, waggled his hands gently. It was pretty funny, but I didn't react until Morlock glanced over at Thend and Thend's face froze in panic. *Then* I laughed.

The hallway was mostly clear by then, and we followed the tail end of the crowd down a rickety flight of stairs and into the street. It was full of people now, some panicking, some laughing, some screaming . . . and some who were cool and intent, their faces and their hands bristling with metal.

"Sandboys!" I hissed at Morlock.

He followed my gaze and said, "Both of you go. Get back to Naeli and Roble. I'll meet you."

Then he drew his dagger and long pointed sword. Somehow he was standing differently, too—sort of sideways, with his feet at right angles to each other. Then his sword flickered out and one of the Sandboys fell to the ground spewing blood. Morlock moved again—it was almost like dancing; I could not believe that crooked ugly man could move so gracefully—and another Sandboy was down, leaking blood onto the cobblestones. His sword and his dagger were dripping red now; several Sandboys were down, but more were approaching through the crowd.

"Come on!" Thend shouted in my ear.

I turned away and ran weeping through the hysterical crowd, heedless of whether Thend was following or not. It had all been sort of funny up to that point—even the worst parts with the golem-Charis and Stokkvenn. But it wasn't funny now. Those weren't golem bodies hitting the ground. Real men were trying to kill Morlock, and he would kill as many as he needed to escape. I wondered who would succeed and I wondered why I cared.

I don't want you to get the wrong idea about me. I'm not sure why I'm telling you about this at all: maybe because most of these people are lost to me now, and telling you about them almost brings them back. In any case, since I'm telling you about it, I want you to get the right idea.

I wasn't squeamish. I couldn't afford to be. From the time I was seven until just a few months ago I'd been living in a village where human sacrifice was a daily occurrence. Every night the adults of the village would go out into the woods and onto the Road and capture people to feed to the God in the Ground. I'd been taken that way myself, lost in the woods as a child. I'd only been saved because my mother went and pledged her service to the God in the Ground. In local slang, we became Bargainers, and we stayed in the Bargainer village until I was thirteen. Then Roble and Morlock killed the God in the Ground and freed my mother and we had to flee. I'd seen plenty of death, too much for a girl my age, too much for a person of any age, and it wasn't the deaths in the marketplace that disturbed me, exactly.

Part of it was the blood. The God in the Ground preferred to consume his victims alive in his pit under the Hungry Tree, so it was rare that any Bargainer had occasion to shed blood or see it. The sight of the blood sickened me and excited me in a way I can't explain.

Part of it was the thought that Morlock might die. My mother had condemned herself to years of horror for my sake. I loved her for it, and I was grateful, but there was no way I could ever pay her back. If Morlock died covering our escape, there would be another unpayable debt on my conscience, and I wanted no more of them.

All of which I offer as part-explanation for the fact that, as I ran, I sobbed, "Why won't they leave me *alone?*"

"I think they're after Morlock, not us," Thend gasped helpfully as he jogged beside me.

I told him to shut his piehole and ran weeping back to mother.

Our mother, Naeli, was sitting on the front steps of an abandoned house. When she saw us approaching without Morlock she stood and called out, "Roble."

Our uncle Roble and our two older brothers, Stador and Bann, came out of the house. All of the houses on this street were abandoned; nearly half the buildings within the city walls were empty. The city had once been much wealthier, much more populous. That was before the Khroi came, conquering the mountains and closing the pass to the north: the Kirach Kund, the River of Skulls—the place that was death to enter. (And which, for some reason, *we* were going to enter.) Since the north-south trade had been cut off there'd been less money to go around, less reason for anyone to live in Sarkunden, and the city was rotting away from inside. Maybe that was why everyone in Sarkunden was a money-hungry bastard. Or maybe they would have been money-hungry bastards wherever they happened to live.

Roble and Naeli waited until we were within speaking distance and then Naeli said, "Are you all right?"

"We're fine," Thend said.

"What about Morlock?" Roble said.

"Well, there were Sandboys—" I said.

"What's a Sandboy?" Roble and Naeli said, almost together.

I don't know how many people there are in your family. In mine it seemed like there were always twice as many people as there actually were, and every one of them was trying to interrupt me whenever I said something. I let Thend do most of the talking, only chiming in when he screwed something up, the way he does sometimes, or when someone was picking on him, the way Stador and Bann always were.

Thend's pretty determined, and he set out to tell the story from the beginning. There were a lot of interruptions, questions, and explanations and it took a long time, but he finally did it.

Naeli looked at Roble. "What do you think? Should we go and see what we can do?"

Roble scowled and shrugged. He looked at Thend: "What do you think?"

Thend opened his hands and said, "The fight's over by now. He's away or they caught him. Maybe they killed him, but Morlock thought they wanted him alive."

"They might have lost their tempers, though," Roble observed dryly. "He can be irritating."

"Tell me about it," Thend snorted.

Then the topic was whether we ought to go to the Sandboys and bribe them to release Morlock. I didn't know what we were going to bribe them with, as we'd left our homes with little more than the clothes on our backs, but nobody asked for my opinion anyway. I guess that's the price of not saying much: people assume you don't have much to say.

I finally did say something, though. "Hey!" I shouted, and pointed at the open doorway of the house. Morlock was standing there in the shadows of the entry hall.

Naeli and Roble wanted him to come out and tell his part of the story, but he gestured at them without speaking and backed into the house. Then we all realized that it was one thing for us to be standing talking in the street; it was another thing for him: an imperial outlaw who had a water-gang out after him. And we realized all this without him having to say a word, which was how he liked it. He didn't like to say two words if one or none would do.

We trooped inside. In the dusty entryway within, empty except for our gear, Roble said, "Well? What happened with the Sandboys?"

"Lost them," Morlock said. I saw Roble's face fall when he realized that was all we were going to hear about Morlock's big fight in the marketplace. Thinking back on those bloody bodies falling to the ground, I was just as pleased, but men look at these things differently, I've noticed. "Came in through the back door and heard you out there," Morlock added, in a burst of eloquence.

He sat down beside his big heavy backpack, a little abruptly.

"Are you wounded?" Naeli said sharply, going and kneeling beside him.

"Old wound in my leg," he explained. "It aches a little when I fight—or run."

My mother began to massage his leg.

Stador and Bann looked a little blank. Roble got this grin on his dark face. Like, *Bless you, my children.* Thend looked mad—he didn't like any of the signs that our mother and Morlock were getting close. Jealousy, I guess: he'd lost her for six years or more, had just gotten her back, and was in no mood to share her with a stranger whose skin made one think of mushrooms and dead fish. Personally, I was happy for her. She was younger then than I am now, a vigorous and beautiful woman in the last summery glory of her youth. But back then I thought of her as quite old, almost as old as Morlock, and I didn't see why two old people shouldn't be happy together. I wasn't surprised that she took to him either: the only other men she'd seen for the last six years had been either sacrifices to the God in the Ground, or the men of the Bargainer village, all of them pretty repulsive types. I actually don't think she'd been with anyone since my father died, and that was well before I was born, maybe fourteen years since.

The only two people who didn't seem to have any emotional reaction to what was going on were Morlock and Naeli themselves. Naeli was saying, in a matter-of-fact voice, "What are we going to do now?"

Morlock said flatly, "I think you should go to Ontil, the imperial capital. I still have some friends there and they can help you find a place to stand. I'll give you a letter."

"While you go north alone," Naeli said icily. "Into the Kirach Kund, without the information Charis was going to get for you."

That was what Morlock had been expecting from Charis: information from the imperial scouts on what the Khroic hordes in the mountains were up to. It might make the difference in surviving the trip through the deadly pass. He said he'd already paid for it and all he needed to do was pick it up. (He'd told us the whole story, but I've forgotten half of it, and I'm not sure I believe the half that I remember.) That was what had led to the fiasco in the Market today.

Morlock wasn't saying anything, as usual, but it was the way he wasn't saying it.

"Come on, Morlock," said Roble, a little impatiently. "If you're going to dump us here the least you owe us is an explanation."

I didn't see this at all. But apparently it convinced Morlock because he said, "All right. I'm going to try to find Charis. He's probably still alive—he's good at that sort of thing, and his enemies don't seem to have found him yet."

"And he may have your information."

"Um. Yes."

"Morlock! Spit it out!" Roble said it, but it might have been any of us.

The crooked man shrugged. "It's a question of who's really after him. The guard? He's been a goose laying golden eggs for them for years now. The Sandboys? I expect the same is true: he seemed to be greasing every palm in town when I was last here. No one has any motive to kill him."

"So there's someone else," Roble said. "Is it important who?"

"It might be," Morlock said.

"Why?"

"Charis would have attracted the hostile attention of this person shortly after he was fishing for information about the Kirach Kund—and the Khroi. It may be a mere coincidence, or the Khroi may have a powerful agent in this city. I want to know if this is true."

"Then we'll stay and help you find out," Roble said. "Afterward we can take up the question of who's going where."

"The hell we will!" Naeli said fiercely. "Morlock, you are *not* going to abandon us in this damnable place where everything and everybody is for sale."

"Ontil isn't like Sarkunden," Morlock said. "Nor do you know what the Kirach Kund is like."

"I know this much—"

"Let's table it," Roble said briskly. "I say we eat and sleep and start looking for Charis tonight when the Sandboys are in their little sandbeds."

Roble was pretty good at breaking up arguments. Maybe it was all those years of living with my mom. Anyway, that was what we did, but it didn't work exactly as he'd planned it.

We always kept watch at night, and we didn't see any reason to change that because we were camping in a house instead of an open field. (We didn't want to wake up and find the house surrounded by Keeps or Sandboys.) With seven of us no one had to stay up long, although it was a pain to stand watch in the middle of the night, so we rotated. That night, Morlock took the first watch and I took the second. Thend was third, and boy was he grumpy when I woke him. We argued about what time it was, and afterward I was too mad to sleep, so I wandered around the house to find someone awake to talk to. That was how I noticed that Morlock's room, on the second floor of the abandoned house, was empty, the unfastened shutters flapping gently in the night breeze.

It sort of looked like he'd climbed out the window, so I poked my head out and looked around. It took a while to spot him, but I finally saw a crooked silhouette right up at the end of the alley: Morlock.

I climbed out the window and followed him.

If you'd asked me why at the time, I couldn't have explained it. It certainly wasn't any echo of my mother's romantic feelings: I thought Morlock was repulsive. But I liked him and was mad at him in a way I didn't try to understand.

Now that I've seen my daughters with their father, I understand a little better. I never knew my father, and I was always latching on to older men in the Bargainer village—some of them pretty creepy. (It was only thanks to Naeli's vigilance that I was still a virgin at thirteen.) Morlock was another one of these stand-ins for my father, I think. In lots of ways he was a pretty bad fit, but in some he was a good one. My mother and he seemed to have something going on, or something about to begin, for one thing. For another, he had a wholly disinterested kindness for me and for Thend. In any case, I always felt *safe* with him—I knew he'd always stand between me and danger. The only other person I ever felt that way about was Naeli, and I knew there were some things she couldn't handle. I wasn't sure if that was true about Morlock. (Turns out there was plenty, but I didn't know that then.)

Anyway: I followed him. At first I tried to catch up, and then I realized that might not be too smart—if he noticed me while we were still close to the house, he might take me back and wake Naeli and Roble, and there would be screaming and shouting offensive to my sensitive spirit. So I started to sneak along, just near enough to keep him in sight.

After a while I realized something: I wasn't the only person following him. There was a furtive shadow slinking along among other shadows lining the street between Morlock and me. A Sandboy, I figured: maybe one of them had trailed Morlock to the house, in spite of what he'd thought, and was now following him to find out where Charis was (if Morlock was right about that).

I crept closer to the shadowy figure, very gradually and carefully so as to not give myself away. I wanted a closer look at him and, when I got one, I suddenly realized that I recognized the guy, even though (strictly speaking) I'd never seen him before. He was very dirty and bedraggled, but his greasy hair was a pale yellow and his sickly skin was white as a wax candle in dim ambient moonlight. His eyes, I bet, would be green. Charis—the original master wonder-worker of that nasty little establishment Morlock had burned down this afternoon.

I didn't like this. Maybe Morlock was wrong: maybe Charis himself had lured Morlock into town, hoping to kill him off and cancel his debts that way.

I waited until he had crept a little closer to Morlock and I had crept a little closer to him. Then, when he was crossing from one hiding place to another in the shadow-stitched street, I took him out, or tried to.

My brothers played this game called vinch-ball, and it is so stupid I could burst. I knew more about it than I wanted to, because I'd watched them play it so much, and because when they weren't playing it they were usually talking about it. Like most boys' games, it involved hitting people and knocking them over for no clearly defined reason. Well, I had a reason and, thanks to vinch-ball (I wish I'd never said that, but it's true), I knew how to tackle someone bigger than me and bring him down.

I hit Charis from behind, about the level of his knees. He gave a thin scream and fell backward. I scrambled out of the way and pounced on him. All that went according to plan.

Unfortunately I'd underestimated Charis. He was even thinner and weedier than his golem-figure, and his muscles were as soft as mud. But he was a grown man and he fought with the strength of desperation. I was starting to lose the fight when someone else joined the mix.

It was Thend. Between us, we managed to pin Charis's arms behind him as he wriggled, facedown on the street beneath us. He was still struggling and gasping, and I didn't know how long we could hold him, when suddenly he went limp.

I looked up. Morlock was standing over us.

"Charis," he said.

"Master Morlock," Charis replied, his voice muffled. "Would you please get your servants off me?"

"I am not your master," Morlock replied coldly, "nor theirs."

We let him go anyway and even helped him to his feet.

"How did you get here?" I demanded from Thend.

"Good thing I *did* get here," he sniffed.

"That's not an answer! Who's on guard back at"—I realized I shouldn't say too much in front of Charis—"back there?"

"Roble," Thend said. "He saw you go and sent me after you."

"He's asleep—"

"Roble's awake, or ought to be," Morlock said. "We agreed that I would go scout for Charis and he would wait for a message, in case I got into trouble."

"How are you going to send him a message?" Thend asked.

"If you need to know, I'll tell you," Morlock said, not like he was mad. He turned to Charis. "You don't look well," he observed.

"Thanks to you!" Charis snapped. "When I acquired your information, the Khroi became . . . interested in me. They ordered their man in the city to hunt me down."

"Who is he?" Morlock asked. "Perhaps I can defend you from him."

"No!" Charis seemed genuinely frightened. "Please don't . . . don't help. I wish no more obligations to you. No more to anyone. I'll find a way to destroy . . . the agent, or escape him . . . somehow. If I can pay you what I already owe, I will gladly close our account."

"Then?"

"If you're asking me where your information is—"

"I am."

"—it is under lock and key, safe in my house."

"Then we will go to your house."

"No!" Charis shouted. "I can't! They're watching for me there!"

"We will trust to your walls and your golems for the few moments we'll be there."

"I don't have any golems," Charis sobbed. "They won't obey me anymore. The Khroi's agent got to them somehow. I haven't set foot inside my house for three months. The last time I did the golems tried to kill me. Kill me!"

"Hm," said Morlock. "Didn't you write a stop-word into your golems' life-scrolls? Something that would bring them to a halt if they started to go astray?"

"Of course. What do you take me for?"

Morlock looked like he was about to tell him, then said, "Never mind that."

"Well, it didn't work anymore, that's all."

"I wrote stop-words into the golems I made for you a few months ago."

"Oh, I know all about that. I took the scrolls out and changed their safe-words to my own. And now that won't work. You look like you don't believe me, but it's perfectly true."

Morlock didn't answer this; he was silent for a moment, obviously thinking. "You obtained the information and secured it in your house?" he asked.

"Yes. I—"

"Was the place well hidden?"

"Yes. The—"

"Did you tell anyone the location? Did your golems see you hide it?"

"No. Whenever I—"

"Is it in a room with a window?"

"What?"

"You heard me."

Charis stared at Morlock for a moment and said, "Yes, there's a window. But it was shuttered when I hid the information; no one could see in, if that's what you're—"

"Then we will go to your house."

"But I *can't*—"

Morlock stopped him with a single glance. Oh, how I've tried to do that, but it never works, even with my daughters.

We went to Charis's house: a fortresslike palace of native blue-stone, not far from the western wall of the city. It was surrounded by a dry moat. There was no obvious way to cross the moat, but at one point in the wall there was a great bronze door; maybe that could be lowered like a bridge. Bow slits lined the walls above the moat; every now and then I caught the gleam of watching eyes.

We lurked in the shadows of a half-ruined building across the way from the bronze door while Charis pointed out to Morlock the window of the room where the information was hidden. "But we'll never reach it," Charis said despairingly, and I had to agree: the window was halfway up a smooth featureless wall. Even if we could get across the moat without being spotted we could never climb up. And, even if we could get in the front door (which we couldn't), I didn't like the thought of trying to sneak through a house of killer golems.

But Morlock, when Charis had made the layout clear to him, just nodded and took something out of a pocket sewn into his cloak. (His clothing was full of weird pockets.) It looked like a big feathery ball; he unfolded two winglike branches, revealing a glassy sphere hanging in the middle. It was like a bird with no head, black wings, and a glass body.

I had no idea what it was, but Charis did. "No!" he gasped. "Not—"

"Keep him quiet," Morlock said to us.

We did, enthusiastically.

Morlock held the bird-thing in his right hand. He struck flame with something he was holding in his left hand and applied it to the glass sphere. Nothing happened at first, but then something lit up inside the glass sphere. The wings stretched out and seemed almost to come alive.

Morlock said a couple of words I didn't understand and tossed the wing-thing into the air. It hovered above us for a moment, the glowing sphere casting a weird red light on our heads. Then it flew away toward the bluestone facing of Charis's house, its red heart trailing fire through the blue-black darkness. It hit the house exactly on the opposite side of where the information was hidden (if Charis was telling the truth). The wing-thing exploded when it hit the wall and flame splashed out, taking root even in the stone and continuing to burn.

"Wow!" Thend remarked brilliantly.

"Do it again!" I said.

Morlock grinned crookedly at us and gestured that we should let Charis go.

"My house!" he groaned.

"It's not your house right now," Morlock pointed out. "If we succeed tonight, it may be your house again."

"I don't see how."

"Then the fire loses you nothing. In any case, I'll pay you for the damage. We cross to the moat now."

"What about the watchers?" I asked.

"There won't be any. All his golems are instructed to fight fires when they occur. I noticed it when I was last here. He's terrified of fire."

"And why not?" Charis groaned.

Morlock did the shut-him-up-with-a-look thing again and we all ran across the open space and jumped down into the dry moat. Morlock led us around until we were just under the window of the room we wanted. He took something that looked like a big bean out of another pocket and, holding it up to his mouth, muttered some words to it. Then he put it down on the ground.

The bean burst like a hatching egg, and out of it crawled a vine with broad greenish black leaves. It crawled straight up the side of the moat and the wall above it.

"Wow!" said Thend. "That'll be handy in the mountains."

Morlock looked rueful. "I'm afraid it's my last one. I had four, but I traded three of them to this boy for his cow."

"That's crazy!"

"Well, I really needed the cow." The vine stopped growing. "I'll go first," Morlock said. "Send Charis after me. Then both of you come up; no one is to wait below."

"Morlock," I whispered, "I'm not sure I can climb all the way up to that window."

Morlock replied quietly, "Just take a firm grip on the vine and hold on." He did so, and vanished. I looked up and saw the vine was carrying him upward to the window. He fiddled with the shutters for a moment, then looked down to us and gestured. He disappeared into the now-open window.

"What a thief he could have been!" Thend whispered to me. "Robbery. Lock picking. House breaking. He can do it all."

"Tell him sometime," Charis said, with a pale unpleasant leer. "As long as I'm there to watch."

"Up the vine, you," I snapped.

His face got a mutinous look for a moment, but then he looked at ours. He turned and grabbed the vine. It carried him up the wall to the window and he climbed in.

Thend went next; I was last. It was like falling straight upward, and I nearly lost my grip at the top. But I didn't quite, and scrambled through the casement into the room I thought we'd never reach.

"Close the shutters," Morlock said, still quietly, but not whispering. There was a big commotion coming from other parts of the house; it looked like Morlock's plan was working so far. He struck a light and set it on a nearby table.

"What's that?" I asked in a quavering voice, just before it moved.

It: vaguely manlike, but half again as tall as a man, and broad in proportion, with thick trunklike limbs. Its huge hairless head had big batwing ears dangling on either side and one great blue eye occupying its whole face: no nose or mouth. I thought it was a statue, set with its back against the door to keep it shut, until it stepped forward, clenching one hand and raising a spear in the other.

Morlock's sword was strapped over his back and he drew it just as the creature moved, thanks to my warning, I think. He leaped forward and struck off the thing's head. The head went spinning off and bounced against the door . . . but there didn't seem to be any effect on the creature at all. It grabbed Morlock with its left hand and threw him like a rag doll against the far wall. Then it threw its spear, pinning Morlock's sword arm to the wall. It strode up to him and grabbed his left arm with its right. It clenched its left hand and began striking Morlock on the head and body with its great stone-like fist: heavy blows, killing blows.

Thend cursed and ran forward to grab the thing's left arm. It was the bravest thing I'd seen since Roble ran off to fight the whole Bargainer village and the God in the Ground with one thin knife (my knife, as it happens, and I never got it back, either, but maybe that's not important).

But it was perfectly useless. The headless thing kept on pummelling Morlock, dragging Thend back and forth with each blow. It didn't even seem to know he was there.

I looked around for Charis. He was crouched under a table across the room. Useless sack of quivering snot—but what good could he do? What could any of us do? The thing would kill Morlock and then each one of us. Unless I could make it to the window and the vine would take me down . . .

It was the only course that made any sense. I couldn't help Morlock or Thend. There was no use in my dying, too.

Glancing about wildly, I saw the thing's severed head, sitting on the floor in front of the door. The single blue eye, still alive, was intently watching its former body pummel Morlock. I thought about tossing the head out the window, but that wouldn't do any good; it could kill Morlock without seeing him, now. I shuddered, wondering what sort of monster could kill someone after its head had been cut off.

Then I knew, of course. It had to be a golem. That thing, that golem in Charis's shop today, it had gone on babbling after Morlock ripped its eye out and split open its chest. It had only stopped moving when he . . . when he . . .

"Oh, no," I whispered, as the idea struck me. "I can't do it. I *can't*."

But I had to.

"Aaaaa-aaaa-*aaaaaah*!" I screamed, running across the room and leaping onto the golem's back. Its shoulder was surging back and forth as it pounded

Morlock, and I almost got thrown off, but it didn't seem to know or care that I was on it, and I managed to hold on with my legs and left arm. I plunged my right arm down into the open neck of the golem.

The inside of the golem was sticky, like wet clay, and the nastiness of it nearly made me let go. But I held on and groped around inside the golem's chest until my right hand closed on something that felt like a scroll. I seized it and pulled it out through the open neck.

The headless golem was just throwing back its fist for another blow. It froze as I brought the scroll triumphantly out.

"Ha!" I shouted as it teetered there, and then added, "Uh-oh!"

The dead golem fell back to the floor with me under it.

"Owie," I complained, and passed out.

When I woke up I wasn't sure I had really been anywhere. It seemed like it was all a weird dream, and I was lying in my own sleeping cloak in the room of the abandoned house where Naeli and I slept.

Then I tried to sit up. "Be still, you stupid moron," said Thend, pushing me back down. I realized my head was in his lap. He bent down and kissed my forehead.

"Hey!" he said. "She's all right!"

I was about to correct him, because I ached all over. But then I realized that if I was all right I could sit up. I pointed this out, pushing his ugly face out of my way after patting his cheek, and struggled to my feet.

The room was suddenly full of people who were glad to see me. If you've ever had the experience, you can fill in the blanks here—I'm not going to describe everything that was said and done.

Eventually I noticed Morlock leaning against the doorway with a broad smile on his bruised face, watching me in the bosom of my family.

I glared at him. He was supposed to be invulnerable, protecting me from the bad people. And there he was grinning at me because, through sheer luck, his recklessness and the golem hadn't killed all four of us in Charis's house.

"Thanks for saving my life," he said, when the furor died down a bit.

"Yeah, well," I said huffily. "Watch your step. I might not be around to do it, next time."

He shrugged and opened his hands in a *well, you know* kind of gesture. This seemed pretty flippant, under the circumstances, so I clouded up and thundered at him for a while. I was pretty clear about what I expected from him and how he had so far failed to deliver. At least I tried to be, but the fact that my face was buried against his chest part of the time may have muffled some of my words, that and some of the weeping.

He patted my back awkwardly until I settled down, and then said, "Eh, what are you complaining about? You didn't even have to walk home."

Charis was standing nearby in the room beyond and he said, "I must say the young lady has a point. We all owe her a great deal. I would estimate—"

"It's not a business relationship," Morlock said. He wasn't smiling when he said it, but his tone wasn't really much different than when he'd been talking to me. Still, Charis crumpled like a moth who'd gotten too close to a candle flame.

I stood back and wiped my eyes. "So you got what you need from Charis's house? Now we go north?"

Charis's twisted face took on a panicky look, which Morlock ignored, saying, "Yes and no."

"Ugh. What a stupid thing to say! Which is it?"

"Yes, we got the information from Charis's house. No, we are not going north, at least not right away."

"Morlock thinks there's some threat to the city from outside," said Roble, coming up beside me. "He may be right."

"So what?" I said. If all Sarkunden sank into the ground it wouldn't ruin my day.

"Eh," Morlock said, "it's not my favorite city either. But it's the keystone of the Empire's defenses in the north. If it broke, the Khroi or the Anhikh could sweep in at will—possibly both."

"You're an imperial outlaw!" I said. "What do you care?"

He shrugged his wry shoulders. "I have friends in the Empire. If it collapses, they'll be in harm's way. I'm going to see about this."

"All right," I said grudgingly. "What do we have to do?"

"You," my mother said, with a calm that was just the thin icy coating on a deep dark lake of fury, "will do precisely *nothing.*"

I didn't feel like arguing with her. First because she obviously was one thumb's length away from crazy and I didn't want to push her in the wrong direction; second because I ached all over, especially in my belly. I didn't want to go anywhere.

"It's someone else's turn on the field anyway," Stador said, apparently thinking I was disappointed. "Come look at the map!"

The map was unrolled on the floor in the next room: a huge map of the city. Looking closely at it, I saw three tiny pieces of gold quivering on the map.

One was not far from the Great Market, where we'd had our run-in with the Sandboys. Another was moving down the twists of an alley toward the South Wall. One was firmly fixed on the citadel, where the Imperial Guards had their headquarters.

I looked at Morlock for an explanation, then decided it would be too much trouble to drag it out of him and turned to Thend.

"You remember those gold pieces Morlock gave the bullyboy in the whorehouse?" Thend asked. "They were ensorcelled. Those gold bits tell us where each one of those gold pieces are right now."

Well, I'd worked in a cathouse. I thought I could follow the reasoning. The Sandboys probably had their little sand-paws into every business on that street. The bullyboy had probably passed along what he knew, along with part of his loot. "So who's who?" I asked.

"If I had to guess," Roble said, "I'd guess the coin heading south is in the pocket of your friend from the cathouse. The one still near the cathouse is in the strongbox of the house's pimp or the Sandboys." He crouched down and tapped the gold fleck at the citadel. "This is the interesting one."

"I see," I said. "Someone in the Guards is slurping money from the Sandboys."

"The commander is my guess," Morlock said. "That immunity was the perfect bait to bring me into the city where the Sandboys are strongest. They're connected, somehow."

"But just because the commander's doing business with the water-gangs doesn't mean he's a traitor," Naeli objected. "The Sandboys wouldn't want a foreign conqueror in the city."

"Hard to say," Morlock replied. "They might be hoping for a better deal with the new rulers. Or maybe the commander is the agent of a foreign power, corrupting the local gangs. We'll go and find out."

"How?" I wondered.

Morlock shrugged, and I knew that was as much as he was going to say about it. He rolled up the map and stuck it under his arm. He and Roble spoke apart with Naeli for a few moments and then they were gone.

Then it was time to go back to bed, past time . . . but no one did. Bann went off to stand watch, and Naeli paced around in the entryway on the first floor, and Stador and Thend were playing a knife-throwing game in the map room. I was sitting on my bedroll, rocking back and forth, wondering why my gut hurt so much. I was wondering about that, and also wondering why Charis was standing just outside my doorway (as I could tell from his shadow on the floor).

"If you're waiting for me to put the light out," I called to him finally, "I'm not going to."

He appeared in the doorway then. "I'm sorry if I alarmed you," he said. "I'm in a bit of a quandary."

"And you think I can help?"

"I hope not. That is—you've done enough. Too much, I'd say. I owe you a very great debt and I don't see how I can repay it."

"It's on the house."

"Nothing is 'on the house,' if I understand what you mean. Everyone keeps track of these things, and debts have to be paid. Those are the principles by which I have lived my life."

"I can see you've made a big thing of it." This was a little icy, I admit, but my belly hurt and I didn't like the game he was playing (to the extent that I understood it).

His face twisted. "I was doing well enough—until I did business with Morlock."

"You shouldn't have tried to cheat him."

Charis sighed. "My troubles only really began when I stopped trying to 'cheat' him, as you put it."

"How would you put it?"

"I would say that no bargain justifies putting a man in danger of his life. No one can be fairly asked to trade away his life, because there is nothing of equal value he can receive for it. A bargain that puts my existence at stake is void." His voice was getting almost hysterical and he broke off, looking a little embarrassed.

"Then you shouldn't have struck the bargain in the first place."

Charis sighed. "That's true, of course. But I wanted what Morlock had to offer me. Now I've lost that, and nearly everything else as well, and I've contracted a new debt to you. You see my problem."

"Well, I didn't do it for you, if that helps any."

"It does, a little," he said, stepping into the room. "But—"

"That's close enough," I said. I wanted to have time to call out if he tried anything.

He stopped short, apparently not resenting my suspicion. "But I can't be sure," he said, "that you wouldn't have saved my life, even if others you cared about hadn't been in danger. I've learned a little bit about you, I think. And then there is the undoubted fact that you did save my life, at terrible risk to your own."

"I was saving my own life, too. I was in there in that room with the rest of you."

"Oh, no!" Charis said, shaking his head wisely. "Tell that to the others, if you like; I think it's safer for you that way, blunting the sharp edge of their gratitude. Gratitude can be a terrible burden to live with, day after day, and you're wise to give them the illusion that their debt is less than it really is. But *I saw you.* You looked at the window and knew you could escape with your life. Then you did the other thing."

For the first time I was sort of impressed by Charis. He did understand people a little bit. I thought about how I felt about Naeli and all that she'd done for me, and I knew he was right about gratitude, too, although I hoped there was more to it than Charis understood.

What had Morlock said? *It's not a business relationship.* Was there a way to live your life like that, not totalling up a balance sheet of benefits and obligations but instead . . . What? Morlock hadn't said what it was; he'd just said what it wasn't. Maybe Charis was right after all.

My head hurt, and not only my head. My stomach hurt, deep inside. I bent over myself gasping. My legs and the bedroll were all wet with blood. Glancing up I saw Charis was closer to me now.

"Get away from me!" I shrieked. I didn't want him cancelling his debts by getting rid of me.

Charis leaped back to the door. Stador and Thend rushed in, with Naeli and Bann only a few steps behind them.

My brothers pinned Charis to the wall while Naeli came over to me.

"I did nothing to her, Madam Naeli," Charis was babbling. "We were talking and she expressed pain. I'm afraid she is hurt from—"

"Don't call me 'madam,'" Naeli snapped. "I'm not some Coranian bimbo-herder." She bent over me and investigated briefly. "It's nothing to worry about, baby," she told me after a moment. "Just Aunt Ruby paying a visit."

"What?" asked Bann stupidly.

"Fasra will be flying the red flag for a few days, that's all."

"Huh?" said Thend.

"It's her time."

"Time for what?" Stador asked.

"Time for her period, you clowns. Will you get the hell out of here so I can take care of her?"

The boys herded Charis out of the room, and I started to sob.

"Look," Naeli said after we dealt with some of the practical issues, "it's nothing to be embarrassed about."

"I'm not embarrassed," I said, lying a little. I hadn't liked that horrified look all the males had given me before dragging their nonbleeding carcasses out of the room. "But it *hurts*. Is it always like this?"

"Um. Yes and no."

"Death and Justice, I hate it when people say that!"

"Calm down, honey. It won't usually be this bad, and your first one is hardly ever this bad. It's just that . . ."

"Mama, are you going to tell me about this or what?"

I hardly ever called Naeli "Mama," and it seemed to steady her a little.

"All right," she said. "Back in the Bargainer village, girls were always sealed to the service of the God in the Ground when they reached their menarche."

"Sure. But—Oh. You did something."

"Yes. There's a spell you can use to delay a girl's menarche."

"I didn't know you knew any magic."

"I don't know much. But every woman in that village knew this one. We all wanted our daughters free as long as possible. I always hoped I'd find a way to get you out before you were sealed to the Boneless One—and that's how it worked out, thanks to your uncle Roble."

"And Morlock."

"Yes. Him." I got the feeling Naeli wasn't so pleased with Morlock tonight. "Anyway, after we were freed, I stopped renewing the spell. I didn't realize that it would make your first period so severe, but that must be what's happening. I'm sorry, baby: I'm not much of a witch."

"Oh, you're all right, I guess." This was the point to say something mushy, and I was grateful to her. In a way, that was the problem. Did my pain at the moment pay for what she had done? Or had she paid some price I knew nothing of? Probably the latter. So my debt to her was increased by who-knows how much. That depressed me even further.

At some point, in spite of the depression and the pain, I slept. But not nearly long enough.

"Fasra, get up," Stador was saying.

I replied in the negative. That was the gist of it, anyway.

"This isn't a joke. The house is surrounded."

You know all those times you wonder whether you want to go on living? If something actually threatens you during one of those moments, you make your mind up in a hurry.

I sat up, told him to get out so I could change my rags, and got up before he was out of the door.

All the others were down on the first floor. I didn't get there much after Stador, with my pack on my back.

"Who's outside?" I asked Naeli.

"Imperial troops," she said. "They seem to be waiting for something, but they're all around the house."

"They're waiting for reinforcements," Charis guessed. "They're expecting

Morlock to be in here. And they have glass lizards. Glass lizards from Kaen. They're the best tracking animals in the world. We can never get away."

"So where do we go?" I asked.

"Exactly where they'll expect," Naeli said. "Down through the sewers."

"Why go where they expect us to go?"

"What's the alternative?" Naeli replied, and I had to admit she had a point.

We went down into the basement. I'd never been down there before; it was sort of creepy. But not so creepy as the big black hole Naeli uncovered, gesturing that we should go down in.

Thend obviously felt the same way as I did. "How far can we get in the sewer?" he grumbled. "If it's Charis they're after, I say we give him to them."

Charis jumped like a rabbit at that, and he didn't look very reassured when Naeli said, "We'll hold that in reserve. If we can get away clean, that's our first choice."

"Clean!" said Bann and gulped.

I growled and shouldered past all three of my big brothers. There were grips for hands and feet leading down into the dark pit. I jumped onto them and began climbing downward.

"Well?" said Naeli coldly, and the guys started to follow me, grumbling a little.

It wasn't really so bad. I mean, don't kid yourself, it wasn't like taking a walk in the hills after a spring rain. But I'd kind of expected it to niff like an outhouse that's been used by a hundred thousand people, and it wasn't anything like that.

When I got down to the bottom of the climbing grips, I was standing in a tunnel on a pretty wide ledge—wider than any sidewalk I remember in Four Castles. In the middle of the tunnel ran a stream of dark water several times as wide as the ledge, and on the far side of the tunnel there was another ledge. I could see all this because of a luminous green mold that grew in patches on the walls.

The tunnel seemed to go on forever in both directions. Other tunnels joined up with it at intervals, and the whole thing seemed to tilt slightly— so that everything could roll downhill, I realized, just like the proverb said.

"It's like a whole city under the city!" said Stador, when we were all down on the ledge.

"Yes," Charis said, with a certain amount of hometown pride, I thought. "The Old Ontilians built it, in ancient days. When Ambrosia rebuilt the city in the days of Uthar the Great, she could do nothing to better the sewers."

"Who's Ambrosia?" I asked.

Charis looked at me, his face slack with amazement—as if I'd asked, "What is the sun?" or "What is water?"

"Morlock's sister," Naeli answered. "Among other things, I gather."

"Other things," said Charis, as if he'd been punched, and shook his head.

"Go north," Naeli directed us. "Upstream. That's where Roble and Morlock will be looking for us, if we're not in the house. If need be, we go all the way to the Kirach Kund."

"Do the sewers reach all that way?" I asked.

"Yes and no," Naeli replied, and winked at me just before I exploded.

I turned around and started walking upstream.

We went as fast as we could; all too soon the clash of metal came echoing up the tunnel behind us. The Imperials were in the sewers.

"Quick and quiet," whispered Naeli, who led us up a tunnel leading northwest.

"They'll have glass lizards," Charis said. "They scent . . . they'll scent us."

He looked at me as he was speaking, and then away. All of a sudden I realized he meant, *They'll scent Fasra.*

I was furious. He didn't smell so delightfully fresh himself. And I'd saved his stupid life! Catch me making *that* mistake again.

I fell a little further behind, walking beside Thend at the back of the group. I was steamed at first, too mad to talk even if talking hadn't been too dangerous. But pretty soon I cooled off and, as I did, I realized something.

Charis, damn him, was right. If the imperial troops had hunting beasts, and if they had caught a scent in the house that they were trailing in the sewer, it was probably mine. Plus, I was shorter than everyone else. If it had been a matter of a short sprint, I probably could have left them all behind, but on a long walk I was inevitably going to slow the group down, even if I weren't feeling sick, which I was: the cramping had started again, as bad as ever.

I thought and thought and all my thinking came to one conclusion. I probably couldn't get away. But if I led the hunters astray, the others probably could.

It wasn't my first choice, believe me. I was going to bull my way to the front of the pack and argue with Naeli that now was the time to trade Charis for our lives and freedom. The trouble was, I soon realized what Naeli probably had realized back at the house: it wouldn't work.

Why were they after Charis, anyway? Because he knew something, or they thought he did. Probably the Khroic agent wanted him captured, because he was passing information on about the Khroi. Or maybe the Imperials wanted him because they thought he knew something about the Khroic agent. Either way, the trouble is, we had been traveling with Charis and protecting him—and knowledge is contagious. If the Imperials caught us they would take us all prisoner, and the Strange Gods only knew if we'd ever see the light of day again.

That left my fallback plan: that is, Fasra takes one for the team, like any good vinch-ball player. (I *hate* vinch-ball, but we've been through all that.)

Naeli was leading the group on a zigzag path through the interweaving tunnels: now northwest, now northeast, but always trending north. The ledges were a little narrower, and we were going single file. Naeli, at the head of the line, was often out of my sight around a corner. I dropped a little further back, and then further yet.

"What are you doing?" Thend whispered, looking over his shoulder at me.

I pointed over my shoulder, pointed at myself, and gestured wildly to the west. I hoped he'd get the idea and he did.

"No," he said, almost at his normal voice, and from the front of the line came an imperious whisper, "*Be quiet!*"

In a schoolroom whisper, I explained to Thend why it had to be this way.

He got it. There's nothing wrong with his wits, whatever you say about his manners.

"I'll come with you," he said quietly.

I shook my head. "You have to stay with the group—make like I'm always a little behind you. Otherwise . . ."

Otherwise Naeli would stop and come back for me. He knew it. His eyes looked tortured, and I hated the thought of the guilt I was inflicting on him. But I'd rather have him guilty and alive than have us all be guilt-free and dead in some imperial torture chamber. There are some occasions when family togetherness is overrated.

"I'm sorry," I whispered. "I'll catch up if I can," I added.

He shook his head, kissed me on the side of the face, and left me standing there. Soon he and the others were out of sight.

I stood for a moment where I was, and then backtracked a bit. There was an arched stone bridge passing over the stream westward. I reached under my tunic and unbelted the rags that had been absorbing (partially) my flow. I dragged it behind me as I crossed over the bridge. Then I waited at the tunnel junction until it sounded like the pursuers were almost about to come in sight. I left the rags behind on the ground and fled up the tunnel.

Soon I knew it was working: some, at least, of the pursuers were pursuing me. I couldn't run for very long, and soon I heard them behind me: the tramp of the soldiers' boots, muttered comments or orders (distorted into unintelligibility in the echoing tunnels), the sniffling of beasts (glass lizards?).

I turned northwest or southwest at the junctions, always trending westward. I doubted I'd escape them, but there was always the chance that they'd think I was unimportant to them, nothing to do with Charis, or Morlock, or their damn city. (I wished it were true.) And every moment they chased me was one Naeli and my brothers were using to get away. Or so I hoped.

How long it all lasted I really can't say. I'd had a long day and practically no sleep; a fog of weariness was settling over my mind. I found myself leaning against the entrance to one of these tunnels, my mind a blank, unsure what I was supposed to be doing.

Then, in the tunnel I had come out of, on the far side of the stream, I saw the glass lizards. They were on long leashes; I didn't see any of their keepers, though I could hear them. There were four or five of the lizards, about the size of large dogs or wolves, and, as they came out into the larger tunnel, their transparent forms caught the light from the walls, like jars of clouded glass and they turned bright translucent green. I could see what seemed to be a human hand in one of their stomachs.

I don't think they saw me: their eyes were sort of blank and squinty, and didn't look too useful. But they smelled me. Their heads weaved for a moment in the air as they stood before the bridge crossing the stream, and then they each pointed a blunt serpentine snout right at me.

I spun around, ran up the tunnel, and heard them following eagerly as I ran. That jolt of terror lasted for a long time, and I even left them behind for a while. But eventually I was stumbling and staggering again, slowing down, hearing them closing in on me again and unable to remember why I cared.

Presently I found myself staring, openmouthed, at a smooth-faced wall. There was no tunnel to westward: not northwest, not southwest. I couldn't understand it. How had they managed to block me off?

It was the end of the sewer system, of course, but I was too stupid with weariness to understand that. But I had just enough wit left to understand I had to turn right or left. At random I turned left and stumbled as fast as I could, leaning from time to time on the smooth wall running along with me on my right.

Except once, unaccountably, it wasn't there. I fell to my right through a dark hole and facefirst on a pile of stones.

Too tired even to feel pain, I crawled up the rockslide without thinking. At the top I staggered to my feet and looked blearily around. The place where I stood was much larger and more open than any part of the sewers I had seen; it was still underground, I guessed from the echoes.

Ahead was a dark river, clean and cold. I realized that this must be the river that fed the sewer systems. There was some source of red light across the river, but I couldn't see what it was. My first guess was torches, but that turned out to be wrong. To my right and left were rough walls of stone. Behind me in the sewers were the imperial soldiers with their glass lizards. If I was going to escape from them, it would be across the river.

I ran down to the bank of the river and was about to plunge in. I don't know why I didn't. I heard the soldiers shouting; I knew they had seen me. I could even hear the glass lizards snuffling behind me. I had every reason to risk leaping into the cold swift water—even if it killed me. But I didn't.

As I stood there, hesitating, a drop of my blood dripped off my shoe into the water. Instantly, a white light appeared in the dark water. Something like a glowing orchid leaped up from the river bottom and snapped at the drip of blood like a dog snapping at a bit of meat.

I stared, rooted with horror, as the glowing flower broke the glittering surface of the water. The skin of its petals was like human flesh, as white as Charis's, and they surrounded a dark mouthlike hole full of something like teeth. The hungry flower began to swing back and forth . . . seeking out the source of the tasty blood, I realized. Which was me, of course. As soon as I sorted this out I unrooted myself from the ground and ran up along the bank of the river.

Soon I heard a great hissing behind me, like a chorus of snakes. I turned my head as I ran and looked back. The glass lizards (their skins now translucently white like Charis's) had followed my trail to the edge of the river. There were half a dozen of them there, facing maybe twice as many of the hungry white flowers. The lizards and the flowers both seemed to be trying to eat each other.

I'd have cheered the flowers on, but just then something whacked me in the head as I ran. I bounced away and fell to the rocky ground, looking around groggily for what had hit me. It looked, at first, like a stone doorpost. Then I realized: it was the end of a stone railing for a bridge, covered with the same obscure (Old Ontilian?) carvings as the bridges in the sewer.

Bridge. River. Cross. I had just enough brains left in my head to connect those dots. I leapt to my feet again and raced across the bridge. As I glanced back at the lizards and the flowers, I saw that the soldiers had joined the fight on the side of their glass lizards.

Now, if ever, was my chance to get away. I ran off the far side of the bridge and away from the icy river as fast as I could. I don't know how fast this really was; I was nearly used up. But I kept going; that was the main thing.

But pretty soon I realized I wasn't going to get much farther. Not because I was all used up, though that was nearly true, but because of another obstacle in my path. It was another river, a river of fire. It was the color of blood and a good deal hotter. It was the fiery river's fierce red light that dimly lit the gloomy cave.

The fire was welcome at first: I felt my own blood pick up warmth from the heat; my shivering limbs took strength from it. But then it got hotter as I got closer. Long before I got to the fiery bank I had to turn away and run a parallel course.

I was beginning to think this was the end. I didn't know what was ahead, but if the soldiers and their glass lizards got across the icy river, they could probably trap me between the two streams.

I looked back to see what was happening. The soldiers had gotten away from the flowers, and they were now on the bridge. There were a lot of soldiers; more than I remembered. Only one glass lizard seemed to have survived the fight with flowers . . . but it was on my side of the river and coming up fast. It was the one with the human hand in its belly; it was translucently red, from the light of the blood-bright river.

You want to keep your eyes on the ground when you're running over rough terrain. I knew that, even then, but I was too stupid with weariness to remember it. I tripped and went down, of course, with the glass lizard right behind me. I rolled desperately to my right, toward the fiery river. I latched on to a loose rock and sat up, expecting the thing to be at my throat.

It nearly was, snapping and slavering at me with its glassy fangs. I bounced the rock off its blunt bright snout and it started back. Without getting up (no time for that) I crab-walked away from it toward the fiery river, its heat scorching my back. I reached out with my left hand, scrabbling for another rock.

The glass lizard sort of dodged in toward me . . . and then slid back to where it was, hissing. A mist, stinking like poison, came out of the blister-like sacs around its neck and drifted toward me. I scooted out of the stuff's way as soon as I caught a whiff of it, found my rock, and waited for the thing to attack again.

It didn't. As I crawled up along the fiery river it kept pace with me, but didn't move in toward me. Like I say, I was stupid with fatigue, so it took me a couple of minutes to figure this out. Then I realized: it was repelled by the heat of the blood-bright river. I could get closer to the fire than the lizard could.

"Hey!" I said. "Don't like the heat, do you?"

Recklessly, I threw my rock at the thing. The lizard wriggled out of its way, but didn't charge me, even though I was unarmed.

I chuckled, maybe a little crazily, and started to crawl closer to the fiery river. I couldn't have gotten to my feet if I'd tried, and I didn't feel like trying. My hazy idea, which looks even hazier as I recall it, was that what worked against the lizard might work against the soldiers—that I might be able to get closer to the fire than they could.

I inched closer to the fiery river. But it wasn't really fire: I could see that now. It was thicker than water, too—more viscous, somehow. It was like the streams of melted rock that come out of the Burning Mountains sometimes: "lava" they called it in Four Castles. It was beautiful and terrible; I felt like my eyes were burning out from staring at it. Hot tears streamed down my face, because I wanted to get nearer to it but I couldn't stand to.

There was life in the burning river. There were fiery flowers carpeting its banks, and little bright things flying from flower to flower, like bees made out of lava. I could see salamanders swimming in the stream. One of them looked at me with such a bright intelligent eye that I almost called out to it for help. But I couldn't speak, either; my throat was raw and choked from breathing in the burning air. I collapsed in a heap. The motion attracted some of the lava-bees. A cloud of them drifted toward me. I wondered what would happen if they landed on me, but there was nothing I could do to prevent it.

It didn't matter anyway. I heard the rapid footfalls of men coming up behind me. If this was the end, I'd just as soon be killed by the lava-bees as taken by the imperial troops and their glass lizard.

Then Morlock was there, his crooked form a dark silhouette against the bright red cloud of lava-bees. He snapped his cloak at them, scattering the cloud, and snatched one out of the air as they fled. He threw it straight over me and I heard a cracking sound behind me, like a heavy piece of glass breaking. I rolled over to see what had happened: the lava-bee had passed through the glass lizard, shattering its midsection. The glass lizard lay in pieces on the stones, opaque, inflexible, and dead.

Beyond it stood my uncle Roble, looking down at the dead lizard with a bemused expression. Behind him an imperial soldier was approaching. I gestured wildly, tried to speak, but couldn't.

The soldier came up and clapped Roble on the shoulder. "That Morlock!" he said. "Full of surprises! Did I tell you how I cut his head off, once?"

"Only about forty times," Roble replied. "But the day's young." He stepped over the dead lizard and bent down over me. "Fasra! Are you hurt?"

I croaked at him.

"She needs water," said Morlock, master of makers and of the obvious. "Let's get her out of this heat."

They dragged me to a cooler place in the wedge of land between the rivers, and the soldier handed me his water bottle to drink from. I recognized him then: he was Thrennick, the Keep we had met in the marketplace.

I drank, cleared my throat and spat, and drank again.

"How you find me?" I said when I could speak, in a manner of speaking.

"By accident," said Morlock wryly.

"We weren't looking for you, Fasra," Roble said. "Or rather, we thought you were with Naeli."

"I was. Only—"

"You don't have to explain a thing to me, you crazy little wench; you're just like your crazy mother. I'm just glad you're all right and I hope it did some good."

I drank in more water, and also the idea that I was, indeed, all right.

"Why soldiers our friends now?" I asked, after I caught a little more breath. "If are?"

Roble said, "Morlock showed Thrennick the map, as proof that Guards-Commander Vennon had been taking money from the Sandboys. Then Thrennick showed it to the second-in-command, and it was enough to get him to arrest his boss. Then he gave Thrennick a commission to take command of all the parties searching for Charis. He was furious at Vennon."

"Oh?" I said.

"Well, the poor guy hadn't been cut in," Thrennick explained. "Commander Vennon never was very bright that way. And when we searched his quarters we found letters proving he and another man had been acting as the Khroi's agents in the city."

"Who's the other man?"

"Well, the fellow didn't sign his name, and Vennon claims he doesn't know it, but Morlock said he recognized the handwriting."

"Who?"

"It was Charis," Morlock said.

I felt stupider than ever. Morlock had gone to Charis for information on the Khroi. Charis had tried to cheat him, and when that failed he had gotten the information. This had brought him under the hostile attention of the agent of the Khroi in Sarkunden . . . who was Charis, apparently.

"Charis is trying to kill *himself*?" I said stupidly.

Morlock shrugged and didn't otherwise answer.

"Not exactly, miss," Thrennick said patiently. "You have to understand, Vennon was a spy and a traitor, but an honest one. When Charis bribed him to get information about the Khroi, he sold Charis the information. But then he reported to the Khroi through their agent that Charis was collecting information about them for someone else. The agent told Vennon to pick Charis up and interrogate him and Vennon tried to do it, first with the Sandboys (who'd been in his pocket for years, or vice versa) and then with the imperial troops."

Something about this explanation didn't satisfy me, although Roble was nodding sagely as Thrennick spoke. Morlock wasn't nodding or making any other sign that he agreed, so I asked him, "What do *you* think?"

Reluctantly Morlock said, "Thrennick may be right, as far as he goes. But the writing in the agent's messages to Vennon *is* Charis's. I think Charis wrote the message which lured us into the city, also. And I read the life-scroll of the watch-golem in Charis's house, the one you stopped. It was instructed to kill any human who entered the house; there was no exception specified for Charis himself. He wrote that, too."

"Maybe it was just an accident?"

"Eh. Charis doesn't make mistakes with golems. If he made that golem, and presumably the other golems in the house, a danger to himself, it must have been deliberate in some way."

"*Why?*"

I thought he was just going to shrug again, and if he had I swear I would have gotten up on my feet and beaten the snot out of him. But what he said was, "Charis sold off little bits of himself until there was nothing left but the bargains he had made, and the fear of breaking them."

"*So?*"

"Death ends fear. Maybe you can't understand that."

I tried to tell him that I did understand, and that I wasn't sure he was right about Charis, and how Charis had understood how I felt about Naeli and being grateful, and that was why I had done what I'd done, but I wasn't sure it was enough—

"No," said Morlock interrupting me.

"No?" I asked, a little angry. Who was he to tell me how I felt?

"You owe Naeli nothing. She owes you nothing. That's not why you risked everything to save her. You are not debts on each other's balance sheets."

"What is it then?" Roble asked.

Morlock shrugged. "The bond of blood. Blood has no price! You don't buy it or sell it. When the need arises you shed your own to protect your own, and you don't count the cost."

I was appalled. Charis's balance sheets of debt and obligation I could understand. The fierce credo of blood-loyalty announced by this cold-eyed white-faced man was too irrational. I couldn't believe it any more than I could have reached the river of fire running behind us: it was completely impractical. Suppose you didn't like someone you were related to? What about people you weren't related to: what did you owe them?

Roble seemed to be thinking along these lines. He said to Morlock, "What about you and us? We're not your blood."

"Aren't you?" Morlock asked.

"*Are* we?"

Morlock looked away toward the burning river. After a moment he said, "My people—the people who raised me—said there were two kinds of blood: given and chosen. The blood you're born into is given. The kinship you choose is no less binding."

"Makes sense," said Roble casually, and turned to Thrennick, who was standing nearby with a few of his soldiers, all of whom wore rather blank looks. "You've caught up with Vennon's troops and cancelled their orders," he said, "so what happens next?"

"Officially," Thrennick said, "I'm to take you all into custody and bring you back for questioning."

"And unofficially?" Roble asked.

"Unofficially, I'm supposed to slip a knife into Morlock here and bring his head back to the new commander as proof he's dead."

"And actually?"

"Oh, I suppose you all will have gotten away while I wasn't looking. I'd like to bring Charis back, though. It might mean a promotion for me; the new commander would like to know what kind of information he was selling to the Khroi, and for how long."

"He'll be with Naeli at our rendezvous point," Morlock said.

"Let me send my men with these trackers back to their barracks; me and one of my soldiers will tag along with you."

He must have gone to do that, because the next thing I remember was someone whining with a Sarkunden accent, "Why do I always get picked for these rotten jobs?"

"Because," Thrennick replied, "I like to know who's behind me and, whenever there's a fight, there you are behind me. You and my butt, Tervin."

I tried to get to my feet, but Roble just picked me up and started to carry me. I tried to tell him I was still bleeding and he'd get stuff all over him, but he just told me to shut my piehole. My piehole, like the rest of me, was pretty damn tired by then, so I did as he suggested and pretty soon fell asleep.

"I don't like the sound of it," Thrennick was saying when I woke up.

We were still underground, not too far from the fiery river; I could tell by the red gloom in the air. We were standing at the foot of a steep black cliff. The men were all staring upward with listening looks, so I tried to listen, too. What I thought I heard, from high above in the red gloom, was the clash of metal on metal.

"If your people are fighting someone," Thrennick was saying to Roble, "I don't think they're our soldiers."

"Then," said Morlock, and gestured at either side of the cliff. Following his gesture, I saw there were two narrow paths climbing upward.

"Huh?" said Thrennick, and then, "Oh, I get it. We go this way, you go that way. All right, why not?"

"Uncle Roble," I said as the two soldiers turned to the left and started scaling the narrow path, "I can walk."

"Good," said my uncle grimly. "I think I'm going to have to use my hands."

He meant he'd need to fight, of course, but we used both hands and feet to scramble that steep crooked rockslide pretending to be a path. I was thinking about asking Roble whether he wanted to give his favorite niece a piggyback ride when I noticed the clashing had gotten a lot louder.

"This is it," Roble said to Morlock, who nodded. They both looked back at me. "Stay out of this," Roble said firmly, and Morlock said the same thing without saying anything.

"Hey!" I said. "As if I want to get my head cut off after everything I've been through."

That wasn't really an answer, of course, but what did they think . . . that I *wanted* to get my head cut off, after everything I'd been through?

Morlock, who was in the lead, drew his sword. It was weird looking, more like dark glass than metal, with pale veins of lighter crystal running through it. Roble drew his shorter, broader blade and leaped up to stand by Morlock on the narrow ledge. They stood there for a second and I almost caught up with them, poking my head up over the level of the ledge. Between their legs I could just see what was going on, but I didn't understand it at first.

This is what I saw, or thought I saw: my mother and my brothers and Charis, surrounded by a bunch of little men all wearing the same weird costume. It was a funny dark purplish color and shiny, like the shell of a beetle. They had knobby armored legs, and each costume had three legs and three arms. And on their heads they wore buglike pyramidal masks with one eye on each face of the pyramids. The ends of their arms were covered by metallic sheaths with long clawlike protrusions. They could stab with the points like foils, or slash with the edges like sabers.

Then I realized the obvious: they weren't men, and those weren't costumes. But they were attacking my mother and brothers. There were so many of them—I'm not sure how many, but a lot. Only the narrowness of the ledge was working in my family's favor. But, Death and Justice, they looked desperate, and my mother and Thend had blood on their faces. They were facing us, with these beasties facing them. Beyond them Stador and Bann were fighting against another crowd of monsters on the other side of the ledge. In the middle sat Charis, doing nothing for anybody, even himself. It wasn't clear if the bug-things were trying to capture him or rescue him from Naeli and company, but he couldn't have been more indifferent either way.

"Khroi," Morlock muttered to Roble. "Watch out: they have three arms."

"Noticed," Roble replied, obviously pleased to be more taciturn than Morlock for once.

"Eh," Morlock replied wittily, and they charged into the battle.

There were at least five ranks of the buglike Khroi between Roble and Morlock and the rest of my family. The men took out the first rank almost before the Khroi knew they were there.

What, you think they should have announced themselves and cried out a challenge, all orderly and sportsmanlike? Try it when your family's life is at stake. Personally I was glad those sneaky bastards were on our side.

I was glad, but I wanted to do something. The joy on Naeli's wounded face when she saw Roble and Morlock was a beautiful and painful thing to see. I wanted to earn a piece of that, honestly; I was always pretty jealous where my mama was concerned, I guess. But it was more than that: Naeli was fighting for her life, for my brother's lives, and what was I supposed to do, just stand there on a pile of rocks?

Then it occurred to me: *I was standing on a pile of rocks.*

I wasn't reckless about it; I realized that a bunch of ill-thrown missiles could hurt my people more than the buglike Khroi. But some well-thrown ones . . . they might at least have some surprise effect.

There was a long heavy pointed rock digging into my knee. I grabbed it and lifted myself up onto the ledge. Picking my time, I hurled the stone at the Khroi who was fighting Naeli. The blunt end struck the Khroi on one of its eyes. It swung half around, its three arms waving. Naeli stabbed low, just above its tripod legs, and it crumpled.

"Hey!" I shouted, and added a suggestion the Khroi probably would have found impossible, even if their reproductive system were like ours. (It isn't, I found out later.)

Now instead of looking happy Naeli looked worried. That made me mad, and I took it out on some more Khroi. I didn't feel like I could reach the Khroi on the far side of the ledge (not without risking a strike on Stador and Bann) but I kept the rocks flying at the narrowing field of Khroi on the near side of the ledge.

Then Roble hewed one in half, and the fight on our side of the ledge was over: the Khroi had been reduced to severed bug-parts scattered over the stone.

Roble and Morlock charged past Naeli, Thend, and Charis without so much as a *Hi, how are you?*

"Bann, give way!" Roble shouted. I knew he wanted to take Bann's place in the front line, probably have Morlock take Stador's. The ledge wasn't wide enough for the men to shoulder past the boys.

But Bann didn't fall back and he didn't answer. Maybe he didn't hear—it was pretty hard to hear anything over the clashing metal. Maybe he felt like he couldn't risk stepping back. Anyway, he wasn't moving. And he was bleeding; so was Stador: I could see it staining their shirts.

Here's where it gets a little weird. Morlock takes his sword and stabs it into the ground. Then he runs up and launches himself over Stador's shoulder, like he's playing leapfrog. In midair he shouts, "Tyrfing!" and the sword flies out of the ground and into his hand as he lands. And he hits like a boulder and takes down a couple of the Khroi as he lands. Then he grips the sword (it is called Tyrfing, but I have no idea how he gets it to come when he calls) with both hands and starts swinging it like a reaper harvesting wheat.

Stador was on the ground, now, and Bann was slumping beside him. Roble shook his head and jumped over them shouting, "Behind you!" (So, like, Morlock wouldn't cut his head off.) Morlock shifted back to a single grip as Roble took a stand beside him, and they settled down to the business of clearing all the Khroi off the other side of the ledge.

There were more Khroi over there than there had been on the near side of the ledge, but pretty soon they had help: the imperial soldiers, Thrennick and Tervin, were attacking the Khroi from the other side.

I cheered them on with a few more obscenities I'd learned while working in the cathouse, and then decided to help out with a few well-thrown rocks. I was bending over, scrabbling for a good missile, when something grabbed me by the ankle.

I was bent over, so I looked through my own bloodstained legs at the thing. It was one of the Khroi who'd been cut almost in half. It had lost the metal sheath from the ends of its arm (it only had one left, and no legs at all). There were six or seven snaky things, like boneless fingers sprouting out of the end of its arm, and it was gripping my ankle with those.

I tried to shake loose, but it was terribly strong. It dragged me down to the ground and started to pull me toward the edge of the cliff.

I screamed, of course. Who wouldn't? The trouble was, my scream wasn't terribly loud. The fall had knocked my breath out of me, and the battle noise was reaching a crescendo just then. I could see Naeli bending over Stador and binding up one of his wounds. Bann and Thend were sitting nearby, gasping for breath and staring at nothing. Nobody seemed to hear me or see me. It was as if my death were taking place in some secret place worlds away from these people who had been my family.

Then somebody landed on top of the Khroi, making its carapace crunch horribly. It was Charis. The Khroi released my ankle to pound feebly at Charis, who rolled with it over to the cliff's edge and pushed it off.

But it had caught hold of him just long enough to keep his momentum going. His feet tumbled over the edge and his body began to follow as he clutched desperately for a hold on the bare dirt and rock of the ledge.

This, I guess, was the moment for a Charis-like calculation of who owed what to whom. Should I have tried to figure out if Charis was still in my debt? (I had, after all, saved his life twice, and he'd only saved mine once— but I hadn't acted *in order* to save his life whereas he . . .) Well, I didn't. I didn't even think about Thrennick wanting Charis alive. There was a roaring in my ears like a river of fire, and I rolled over to seize the arm of this evil icy man who was, apparently, one of my blood—chosen, if not given.

He was saying something. I didn't pay any attention; I was trying to dig my feet into the ground. I hoped my weight, pressing down on the rough surface of the ledge, would be enough to anchor his.

The trouble was: it wasn't. In a silence that seemed to fill the whole world I heard the most horrible sound I've ever heard: my body scraping over the stones of the ledge.

"Help here!" I shrieked, into the sudden silence, and slipped a little further toward the gulf. *I really should let go now*, I told myself. *Can't do this, can't go over the edge with him.* But I clung even harder to his arm, so hard that my fingers sank deep into the flesh. That seemed weird, even then, but I didn't have time to think why.

Then Naeli grabbed on to my feet, arresting my slide toward the cliff. I sobbed gratefully and hung on to Charis's arm.

But he was still sliding away from me. I didn't understand it. I wasn't moving, but he was still sliding off the edge of the cliff.

Then his arm ripped away from his body. I was left with it and, no doubt, a dopey look on my face. I'll never forget Charis's expression as he slipped, one-armed, away from me into the abyss.

Morlock was abruptly there. One leg thrown forward so that his foot was at the brink, he bent over and seized Charis by the neck. As Charis gasped and choked Morlock lifted him out of the brink and tossed him beside me on the ledge.

I was still gripping the severed arm tensely. When I realized this I let it go, kicked Naeli away hysterically, and jumped to my feet. I didn't know what Charis was, but I didn't want to be near him.

Morlock, however, had no such qualms. He was kneeling down beside Charis. At first I thought that he was holding Charis's one remaining hand: a pretty sentimental act for a man like Morlock, but you never know. Then I realized: he was feeling for a pulse.

And not finding one, apparently. "Remarkable!" he said to Charis's tormented face. "The skin temperature is lifelike. If there were a heartbeat, the likeness would be perfect."

"I was working on that," Charis said sullenly. "It's a minor issue."

"You still have a heart, though?" Morlock inquired, with an air of polite interest.

"Oh, yes," Charis replied. "I couldn't dispense with it. The entire torso is essentially intact."

"May I?" asked Morlock.

"If—Oh, I suppose it doesn't matter," Charis said gloomily.

Morlock reached into the horrible man's open shirt and felt around a little.

"That's not human skin," he said flatly, withdrawing his hand.

"Well, I decided to venture on a clay integument for my torso," Charis admitted, "but the organs are still functioning. They have less to do now, of course."

"You anticipate an extended lifespan?" Morlock asked. "Less wear and tear on the organs? You may be right. Anyway, this is an admirable achievement. Really remarkable."

That was when I started to laugh quietly to myself. An admirable achievement! That thing!

"What's wrong?" Bann said to me. "What's happening?"

"Don't you see?" I said, or shrieked, I'm not sure which. "He's turned himself into a golem."

Morlock looked over at me. "Not entirely," he said mildly. "Charis's limbs and skin may be golemic but the rest of him, his core, is as it was. Do you," he said to Charis, "get full sensation from your clay skin?"

Charis shuddered. "No, thank God Avenger. Really, Morlock the Maker!" he said, drawing himself up. "I don't think you fully appreciate what you call my achievement."

"Explain it, then," Morlock suggested.

"Do you suppose that I myself did these delicate operations on my own frame? I had to have golems do it. For each operation I created a team of golem-surgeons with careful and elaborately written life-scrolls. The slightest error in any golem's composition and I would not have survived a single operation."

"What makes you think you *did* survive?" I shouted. Then I put my hand over my mouth and sat down. I didn't feel that great; I don't suppose any of us did. Naeli and Thend both came and sat down on either side of me, each one putting an arm around me. That made me feel a little better.

Charis droned on wearily, "My face became so many masks. It wasn't mine anymore. As the Khroi's agent, I spied on the city. As your debtor, I spied on the Khroi. As the Khroi's agent, I had to hunt down the man spying on them. If my plans had succeeded, all my debts would be paid. I would have given you your information, surrendered you to the Khroi, and destroyed the spy in the city. But now all my bargains are broken."

"You would have destroyed yourself to fulfill a bargain?" Morlock asked.

"My crowning deed as a maker," Charis replied, smiling faintly. "When this . . . business interrupted me, I was writing the life-scroll of a golem which could replace my entire face."

"Oh."

Charis seemed to think Morlock was insufficiently impressed. "Don't you see? The delicacy of the operation—the need to inculcate the golem with my every skill so that the new face would be such a masterwork of artifice that no one would realize it was artificial!"

"Why?"

Charis glared at the crooked man as if insulted by so obvious a question. "All of you!" he shouted, waving his remaining arm. "The Khroi. The guards. Vennon. The water-gangs. *You*. All of you, everywhere, surrounding me with open mouths like baby birds squawking, 'I want this, I want that, Do this, Don't do that, Tell me this, Don't tell him that, Give this to me, Take this from me.' Everyone screaming *me me me* and none of them *me*."

Morlock opened his hands and waited: he still didn't understand.

"It was my chance to escape," Charis said wearily. "The new face didn't have to look like my old face. Everyone knew who I was, but if I succeeded no one would know who I was. I wouldn't owe anybody anything; nobody would owe me anything. I could have been anyone. *Anyone*."

"Who is it you want to be?" Morlock asked patiently.

Charis thought for a moment. "No one," he said finally. He pushed himself over with his remaining arm, spun off the edge, and was lost in the red gloom. We heard his body make wet solid impact with the cliff several times as he fell.

"There goes my chance at a promotion," said Thrennick wistfully after a few moments of silence. "Master Morlock—"

"I am not your master."

"Fine; I just want you to do me a favor."

"What?"

"If you ever come back to Sarkunden—"

"Yes?"

"Please don't look me up. I mean, I still have nightmares about the *last* time."

The soldiers went back to the city through the sewers, but we took another narrow rocky passage up into the light. I couldn't believe how good the fresh air tasted and felt in my lungs, and my eyes drank down the light till I could feel it in my toes. Then I looked at the others and I noticed they were all bleeding as much as I was, if not more. This seemed to me very funny and terribly sad, more or less at the same time, but Naeli said a little hysteria under the circumstances wasn't unreasonable.

We were in a cave facing the north. Outside there were mountains piercing the horizon like pale thorns. Through them led the Kirach Kund, the River of Skulls—as dangerous as its name sounded or more. But as long as there was no one there who would try to buy or sell me or himself, I wouldn't complain.

THEND'S STORY

X

DESTROYER

AND NIGHT WAS MOTHER TO HATEFUL DOOM
AND THE DARK DESTROYER; SHE GAVE BIRTH
TO DEATH AND SLEEP AND THE TRIBE OF
DREAMS.

—HESIOD, *THEOGONY*

t was the bones again: Thend rarely dreamed about anything else anymore. They were climbing the slope toward a rift in the high horizon: the Kirach Kund, the pass leading north through the mountains. And Thend slipped and fell in a slope of scree. He slid downhill for a while, and a bunch of the oddly shaped stones slid down after him. It was embarrassing, but not dangerous, and he wasn't concerned until he noticed something about the nature of the "rocks" around him.

"Hey!" he shouted, his voice ragged from panic. "These are bones!"

He had fallen face-to-face with an unmistakable skull; there were many others scattered about. Some of the skulls were shattered; others had holes bored in them. All were gray as stone, and they were not quite human-shaped. The skulls were, if anything, larger than human, but the arm bones and leg bones were shorter and thicker.

Morlock slid expertly down the edge of the scree and offered Thend a fish-pale hand, pulling him out of the pile of gray bones.

"What were they?" Thend asked. "Where did they come from?"

"They were dwarves," Morlock replied. "There was a great kingdom of the dwarves under these mountains once. Now they are all dead or fled, unless a few hide under the earth so deep their enemies can't find them."

"Their enemies?"

"The Khroi."

The Khroi: the insectlike warriors who ruled the mountain range they were daring to cross.

"They killed them long ago," Morlock said, a strange elegiac tone in his voice. "Now the bones are turning back into the rock from which they grew." He said a word or two in a language Thend didn't know and turned away.

All that was as it had really happened. But when, in his dream, Thend turned around, his mother, Naeli, was standing behind him. There was a large horn or tusk spiking out of her mouth and he was afraid of it. With a quick birdlike motion she bobbed her head and put a hole in his head, just like the holes in the skulls scattered thickly around him.

He woke up with a scream trying to work its way out of his throat. In the end he didn't scream—but it didn't help that Naeli was the person shaking him awake. "Your watch," she said briefly. "And there's trouble."

Thend rolled to his feet and looked around. Everyone was awake, even though it was the middle of the day. (They travelled by night and slept during the day.) His uncle Roble was standing over there by Morlock; Thend's two brothers, Stador and Bann, were with them. Even Thend's younger sister, Fasra, was sitting up in her sleeping cloak. But apart from her, who was usually trouble, Thend didn't see anything that looked like a problem.

Morlock said, "Trouble?" and lifted his wry shoulders in a shrug. When he saw this wasn't enough information for his audience he added, "I saw something that bears a closer look."

"I'll go with you," Roble said.

"No you won't," Naeli disagreed. "You're our two best fighters; one of you has got to stay with the group."

Thend noticed that Stador and Bann were annoyed by this. But it was impossible to argue with the fact: they all remembered how Roble and Morlock had swept away a company of warrior Khroi.

"Well, he'll have to take someone with him," Roble said, conceding Naeli's point. "We decided no one should travel alone."

Morlock's eyebrows raised a little at this. He hadn't realized that the group's rule would be applied to him, obviously. But he was adaptable, and he remarked with his usual eloquence, "Eh."

"I suppose you mean me," Thend's little sister, Fasra, said, a bragging tone in her voice. She could be insufferable, but Thend decided she was right. If you counted toughness as anything other than the ability to lift weight, she was the genuine article. And she wasn't absolutely stupid, Thend reluctantly admitted.

"Thend," Morlock decided.

"But—" Naeli said and stopped. She put her hand on Morlock's arm. His gray eyes met her brown ones. Then she released him and stepped back.

Everything, just everything, annoyed Thend these days, but that annoyed him the most of all: how his mother and Morlock could communicate without words. Also, how she touched this pale-skinned stranger just as unselfconsciously as she did her children or her brother.

Morlock turned away from the group without speaking. Thend followed suit and they went side by side over a ridge to the northwest.

"What was it you saw?" Thend asked finally.

Morlock grunted. "Aside from your face, you mean? You haven't smiled since we left Sarkunden."

"That's not your business!" Thend said fiercely.

Morlock shrugged his crooked shoulders and said nothing. They walked on a while in silence.

"I'm having bad dreams," Thend admitted finally.

"Tell me," Morlock said.

Thend did, and Morlock said nothing for a while. Then he remarked, "You may have the Sight."

"I don't know what you mean," Thend said, afraid that he did.

"The Sight," Morlock said didactically, "is a talent for receiving sensory or mental impressions through tal, the phase of being which links living spirit to dead matter. Most people see only with their eyes, hear only with their ears, think only with their brains. A seer can gain impressions of things he never saw nor heard, and to some extent think outside material limits, knowing segments of the future and past."

"Then my dreams are *true*?" Thend asked in horror.

"Dreams are dreams," Morlock said firmly. "They come from many sources: things you have seen or done or heard of, sense impressions, fears, and hopes. Dreams are neither false nor true, but they may contain truths and yours contains one that cannot have come from your own knowledge."

"What? Where did it come from?" Thend asked wildly.

"It may be the shadow of a future event. I hope not, though."

"How do I get rid of it? I can't stand these dreams anymore, Morlock. Every time I look at Naeli I want to vomit."

"The Sight? You can't get rid of it. I'll teach you about it, though. The more your awareness is trained in the use of the Sight, the less it will trouble you."

Thend sighed. "Okay. Should we start now, or just go back to the group?"

"We should look at that, first," Morlock said, pointing.

Thend had been assuming that Morlock pulled him away from the group just to talk to him. Now he glanced ahead and saw what Morlock had seen, but he didn't understand it.

They were walking down from the crest of the ridge into a little rift in the mountain's side, too narrow to be called a valley. The rift was carpeted with the tall green-gold grass that looked soft as cotton but would slash bare feet and legs like finely honed razors. At the bottom of the rift was a stand of trees, a mix of dark-needled pines and fluttering aspens. (They were too high in the mountains for anything Thend considered a proper tree; there were no elms or oaks or stoneleaf majors.)

Two of the pine trees had been stripped, except for a couple of branches each—it was hard to see them, as they stood behind a curtain of aspen leaves. But as he gazed, Thend became surer: those weren't branches; there was something hanging suspended between the stripped pines.

"What is it?" he asked Morlock.

"A Khroi, I think," the crooked man replied.

They went on down among the trees and long before they stood in front of the stripped-bare pine trunks, Thend saw that Morlock was right.

The buglike Khroi's flexible arms were bound to its chest and its three legs were wound over and over with the same silken substance. It hung from the surface of a great spiderweb woven between the two naked pines.

"Is it dead?" Thend wondered.

"He," Morlock corrected.

"How do you know? What do the females look like?"

Morlock grunted. "Hope you never find out," he added after a moment.

He crouched down to examine the ground as Thend looked up to find that one of the Khroi's three eyes was open and watching them. The iris was the same dull purplish color as the carapace, but it was still an oddly human eye to peer out of so strange a face and Thend was troubled by it.

"Well," said Morlock, standing up, "I am no tracker, to read a story from bent pine needles. But clearly the spiderfolk have done this. If we are travelling over their territory it is bad, in a way, but also good. That is why we are clinging to the western edge of the pass; the Khroi avoid it, for they fear the spiderfolk."

"Shouldn't we, too?" Thend asked.

Morlock spread his hands, which meant nothing to Thend.

"Why did they put it—*him* up here?"

Morlock shrugged. "They do it sometimes. It may have a ripening effect. Also—"

"They're going to *eat* him?"

"Of course. Spiderfolk will eat any kind of motile life, including each other, if nothing better is available."

"Shouldn't we let him go?"

Thend always found Morlock's face hard to read, but it seemed he was surprised. "A Khroi? No."

That made Thend mad. "Why? Just because he's a Khroi?"

Morlock shrugged his crooked shoulders. "The spiders kill the Khroi. The Khroi kill the spiders. I see no reason to interfere: either will prey on humankind, given a chance."

Now Thend was madder. "To you, the Khroi are just the monsters who killed the dwarves." He pointed at the Khroi hanging in the spiderweb. "Do you see him? Have you even looked at him? Have you never known a Khroi as an individual, as a person?"

Morlock's cold gray eyes fixed on Thend. "I travelled extensively with one, once."

"And? When the journey was done did he kill *you*? Did he leave *you* to die?"

"He killed himself."

"He—Arrrgh!" Conversations with Morlock were always taking these abrupt left turns. Thend never had never gotten used to it, but at least by now he knew when there was no more point in talking. He turned away, drew his knife, and started slashing away at the web-stuff.

Morlock didn't help, but he didn't interfere either. When Thend had severed enough strands of the web the bound Khroi fell to the earth with a wheezing sound that might have been a cry of distress or relief. Thend cut his narrow boneless legs free of the sticky silken stuff and then, more cautiously, freed the Khroi's arms. At last he stood back, waiting to see what would happen. If the Khroi was too ill to move, what would they do? It was possible the Khroi was past saving.

The Khroi slowly rose to the ped-clusters his kind used for feet. He flexed each of his arms and legs all along their length, an eerie sight. There were a few wounds on his head and arms that were leaking the dark fluid the Khroi used for blood, but none of the wounds appeared to be disabling. He turned so that one of his three eyes faced Morlock and another faced Thend. The Khroi had needle-toothed mouths at the three corners along the base of their pyramidal heads, and this one clacked his mandibles once or twice, a mannerism Thend thought might be like clearing his throat. But then, instead of speaking, he jumped over and bit Thend on the shoulder, right through his jacket and shirt into the flesh below.

"Hey!" screamed Thend, and Morlock was there, kicking the Khroi in the midsection. The Khroi flew through the air and rolled a few feet on the ground, slamming into the base of a tree. He leapt back on his legs with unbelievable swiftness, gripping a sharp rock in one of its stringy palp-clusters, so unlike hands.

Morlock drew his sword, Tyrfing. Sunlight glittered along its black-and-white, strangely crystalline blade. "You have your weapon," he observed ironically. "I have mine."

The Khroi lifted the sharp rock and marred himself with it, scraping it savagely along his purplish carapace by the neck. He kept pounding with the rock until the point broke off, stuck in his shell like a tooth. He dropped the rock, looked at the two of them with two of his eyes, and then fled away through the trees.

"How's that wound?" Morlock asked, turning away and sheathing his sword.

"It's the best kind," Thend snapped. "Hurts and everything."

"Well," Morlock said, smiling a little, "it's not too deep." He tore a strip from the hem of Thend's jacket and said, "Hold this on it. When we get back to camp I'll whomp up a poultice to keep off infection."

"Whomp," Thend muttered as he pressed the cloth against his wound. He felt as if the world was whomping him. "He didn't have to bite me."

"I think he was marking you," Morlock said. "So he would know you again, if he saw you."

"He meant it as a *favor*?" Thend demanded, pointing at his wound with his free hand.

"He did the same thing to himself," Morlock pointed out.

"So that I'd recognize *him*?"

The crooked man nodded.

"I hope I never have to."

The crooked man nodded again.

They climbed back up out of the rift, each wrapped in silence and his own thoughts.

"What was it?" Roble asked, when they returned to the little camp. No one had gone to sleep yet; they were all standing there, waiting.

"A Khroi, bound by the spiderfolk," Morlock replied. "When he got loose, he bit Thend," he added, as Naeli's eyes strayed to the bloody rag Thend was pressing against his neck.

"Whenever my children go somewhere with you, they get hurt," Naeli snarled at Morlock.

Thend dreaded what would come next. Morlock would explain what had really happened and Naeli would focus her rage on Thend. When he was no more than nine she had run off into the woods to save her daughter from the Bargainers and the Whisperer in the Woods, and he hadn't seen her for more than six years. Now the Whisperer was dead, they had been reunited and Naeli apparently intended to take up where they had left off: with Thend as a nine-year-old. He resented her long absence; he resented her assumption that he hadn't grown or matured during the time when she'd abandoned him. But no matter what he thought about her, there was something in his mother's black burning eyes that could turn his knees to jelly. He braced himself for the worst.

Morlock shrugged and said, "What's that smell?"

"If you think you can shrug *this* off—" Naeli began threateningly.

"Shut up, you stupid moron," Thend shrieked. "I cut the thing loose and it bit me. Morlock got it off me. It's my damn fault, now leave me alone! I mean him," he ended lamely.

Naeli looked again at Morlock, then moved over by Thend. She moved his hand from the wound and examined it. "It's not serious," she conceded. "But it might have been. He should have stopped you."

"He said not to," Thend whispered. Thinking back, he wasn't sure that was true, but it was close enough.

"He should have stopped you," his mother repeated in a voice that was loud enough to be heard by everyone there. "Part of taking care of a child is telling him no and making it stick."

This was so fearfully unjust to everyone, just everyone in the world, that Thend couldn't even speak. And Thend wasn't a child, even if he wasn't a man yet. If he never made any of his own decisions, how would he ever become a man? He felt he would have been in a better position to make this case if his face wasn't covered with tears and snot, so he let his mother lead him off to have his wound cleaned and bandaged, but he was seething inside with unshed fury. And his skin crawled whenever she touched him.

"What's that smell?" Morlock asked again.

"You really want to know?" Roble asked. "I thought you were just putting Naeli off."

"I really want to know."

"A sort of cat-beast attacked us while you were over the hill. Actually, there was a regular pack of them, but when Bann speared one they all seemed to be frightened of its blood: it's got a pretty pungent stink, as you noticed. Anyhow, then they ran away."

"Where's the corpse?" Morlock said.

Roble pointed at the west end of the camp. Morlock didn't stir from where he was standing but, looking over at the body, said, "A snake-leopard. We must move at once."

"They're not so fearsome," Roble protested. "And if—"

"Why, Morlock?" Naeli called over, interrupting.

"They are the skirmishers of the spiderfolk. Look!"

Naeli and Thend went together toward the dead snake-leopard. It was hardly leopard-sized, somewhat larger than the predatory tree-cats in the woods surrounding Four Castles. But it wasn't really a cat: instead of fur it had the mottled scaly skin of a lizard, and its mouth hanging open displayed the forked tongue of a snake as well. Its slashed throat dripped greenish yellow blood. Wading in the blood were pale bugs, eight-legged like spiders, lapping up the still-warm fluid with long dark tongues.

"Those are newborns," Morlock said. "They grow taller than Roble. And they prefer red blood. The adults will be here soon, led by the snake-leopards."

"We'll put a pad under your backpack's strap," Naeli said to Thend. "That'll be a better bandage than anything we can tie on."

Moments later, they were on the move, headed east.

The Kirach Kund: a trench dividing the longest mountain range in the world into two unequal halves. The Whitethorn Range lay to the west, running all the way through the Wardlands to the perilous seas off the Broken Coast. The Blackthorn Range lay to the east, running beyond knowledge—some said it went to the eastern edge of the world. At the heart of the Blackthorns lay a kingdom ruled by the dragon-taming Khroi.

Everyone feared the Khroi, and when they decided they had to cross the mountains (Thend was never sure when they had decided that, or why) Morlock recommended that they follow the western edge of the Kirach Kund. The Khroi feared the spiderfolk, and something about the mountains themselves, though Morlock never said what.

Now they were fleeing from the spiders toward the Khroic side of the pass, and Thend knew they were nearing it when they topped a rise and saw, smoking in the valley below, the outstretched form of a dragon.

This was alarming at first; even Fasra, who hadn't a lick of ordinary sense, looked concerned. But the dragon was obviously dead: a big steaming trench had been eaten out of its side; most of the smoke came not from the dragon itself, but from a smoldering fire its blood had started in the valley's thick grayish grass.

There were no Khroi in sight, but lurking in the fire was a great wolflike beast, and surrounding it were a group of full-grown spiderfolk, attempting to drag it out of the fire with their silken threads. The fire withered the threads and the spiders dared not approach closer. But they, and their pack of snake-leopards, surrounded the fire: the wolf couldn't easily escape.

"Maybe we should turn east again, " suggested Stador uneasily.

"I don't think so," Roble said, looking at Morlock. "You know what I'm thinking?"

Morlock grunted. "My enemy's enemy . . ."

". . . is a fine distraction for my enemy," Roble finished.

"If you guys are planning on doing something," Naeli pointed out, "we need to know what it is."

"Look," Roble said, "suppose we go down there, drive off the spider-folk—"

"That may be too much to hope for," Morlock observed. "If they're alone, they may stand and fight and we should be prepared to flee. But if others are coming, and they know it, they'll likely retreat and attack together in force."

"But by then," Roble said, nodding concessively to Morlock, "we'll be gone. And if there are any spiderfolk on our trail, when they come this far, they'll become occupied by that wolf-thing down there. And if it's gone by the time they return, they'll have a split trail: ours and the wolf's."

"Werewolf's," Morlock said.

"Oh? I wondered how it could stand to be in the fire."

"Why do you have to run around killing things all the time?" Thend shouted at Morlock.

This was hardly fair, but Morlock took the question seriously. After a moment's thought he said, "I suppose I'd rather see them dead than you."

"But—" Thend noticed his mother glaring at him and he shut up.

Naeli turned to Roble and Morlock. "All right, if we're going to do this thing let's have some sort of plan. We'll all go into the valley, but Thend, Bann, Fasra, and I will hold back; you two and Stador will attack the spiderfolk and their snake-leopards. The rest of us will intervene only if necessary to help you escape. Agreed?"

Stador looked flattered to have his life put at risk, Bann annoyed that his wasn't. Roble said, "Right!" and Morlock nodded indifferently.

They ran together down into the valley; but at a certain point Naeli gestured, and Stador, Roble, and Morlock ran on alone.

"What's so special about them?" Fasra muttered, angry at being left behind.

"They're expendable," Naeli said dryly. Bann laughed at this, and even Fasra smiled, but Thend didn't think it was funny. His uncle Roble was the closest thing he'd ever had to a father. If Thend wanted any one thing in life it was to be more like Roble: handsome, fearless, never at a loss for words or actions. Should someone like that be thrown away just so that someone like Thend could live a little while longer? Thend couldn't see why.

Thend's feelings about Stador were mixed, but Morlock was another matter. If *he* wanted to lay down his life for Thend's sake, that was his business.

The crooked man ran, just as he walked, with an odd loping stride. He clapped Roble on the shoulder and said something to him, then veered off straight toward the fire while Roble and Stador swung to the right and rushed the spiderfolk there.

Morlock's monochrome sword glittered in his hand as he plunged into the line of snake-leopards and spiderfolk, kicking and stabbing. The snake-leopards yowled with dismay and the spiderfolk leapt aside: they had been intent on the werewolf hiding in the fire. Morlock ran straight to the border of the flames, where a stunted tree had partly collapsed into sullen embers. Morlock scooped up a fistful of live coals and scattered them among the spiderfolk nearest him.

Thend had been appalled the first time he saw Morlock reach into a campfire for a handful of coals that he proceeded to juggle for their somewhat-horrified amusement. Even though he understood that fire didn't affect the crooked man the way it affected other people, it was still hard to watch.

The spiderfolk screamed; one of them fell to the earth with a gooey sort of thump that was sickening to hear. The others retreated a ways, gathering their clouds of snake-leopards about them with wordlike hisses. Roble and Stador fell back and stood beside Morlock.

"Looks like they're going to stand and fight," Roble observed.

Morlock shrugged and waited.

The snake-leopards spread out in two wings, one of them charging straight toward each of the two groups.

"Get back with the others," Morlock snapped, and stepped into the fire beside the werewolf.

Roble and Stador ran back and joined their family. They formed themselves in a ragged line with blades drawn, waiting for the snake-leopards to mass and attack. Thend held his sword grip with both hands to keep from trembling, and he was glad to see he wasn't the only one doing that.

The snake-leopards massed together, but their attack never arrived. As they leapt toward the quivering line of blades, there came from behind the screaming hiss of the spiderfolk. Morlock and the werewolf were attacking them with fire, Morlock hurling fistfuls of live coals and the werewolf kicking up a steady stream of sparks and burning grass with its back legs.

The snake-leopards went back to protect their spidery masters, and the whole group fled south and west over the ridge.

Morlock and the werewolf stepped out of the fire on different sides. They said a few things to each other that Thend didn't catch. Then the werewolf stood there, a black smoldering wolf-shape with fire-red eyes, as Morlock turned and walked away.

"So you speak Wolf, too, Morlock?" Naeli said as the crooked man rejoined the group. Thend admired her nerve in being able to talk to him. But then, there was something of the monster in Naeli too. (And in himself? He was her son. But he didn't like to think about that.)

"Not really," Morlock said. "My sister knows more. I think he offered me part of his kill." Morlock gestured behind him at the fallen dragon. "I'm not sure if he was just boasting. He says he killed it last night while it was sleeping, and the spiderfolk took its rider: that would be your friend, I think," he said, glancing at Thend, who flinched.

To cover up his fear Thend said, "I'm surprised you didn't take any. I bet dragon meat is mighty tasty."

"Dragons think so," replied that horrible old man and turned away.

They went on out of the valley, north and east.

The march went on and on. During one of their rare and brief halts the adults were discussing whether they should find a place to sleep for the night. Morlock didn't think it was safe to strike the lights they would need to travel after dark, but Naeli argued it was still more dangerous to settle in a place where their enemies might come upon them. But they were well toward the eastern side of the pass now, nearer the Khroi than the spiderfolk, and Morlock was saying it was a good risk to stop and rest.

Thend stared away into the eastern sky, still hot and red with sunset.[1] There was a cloud of strange birds over there. It was as if their eyes were reflecting the sun, even though they were facing toward the night-dark western sky. After a while, as they got bigger and Thend was more sure that the evening light wasn't playing tricks with his own eyes, he pointed at them and asked, "What kind of birds are those?"

Morlock glanced over and swore, "Sustainer!"

"They're sustainer birds?" Stador asked, not understanding.

"It is the dragon cavalry of a Khroic horde," said Morlock, in something nearer his ordinary speaking voice. "My friends, I have led you astray. We must part company here. I will do my best to draw them away from you. Bear north as straight as you can and God Sustainer be with you."

"But they can't have seen us yet," Roble protested. "Let's take cover and talk it over."

"We have no time to debate," Morlock said. "If we can see them, they have seen us. It was my fault we didn't turn west after we left the werewolf. Save yourselves and go!" He shouldered his pack and ran off eastward, toward the dragons.

Roble turned away from the fiery eastern sky, his dark face twisted with a dark emotion. "Let's go, then," he said, "and *save ourselves*." He said it like a curse.

They went as fast as they could, but it felt like crawling. Whenever possible they kept to the shadows, hiding from those fiery eyes in the eastern sky. But they stumbled over stones in the dark, and they had to feel their way

---

1. In Morlock's world the sun rises in the west and sets in the east. See the appendix on astronomy and the calendar. (JE)

carefully over the broken ground, lest they fall into a pit or a ravine. They didn't dare strike a light.

Soon they heard Morlock's voice shouting, *"Khai, gradara!"* Rising like a swift distorted moon over the line of rocks to the east, they saw a dim blue dragon fly upward, lit by its own smoky red eyes, snarling in triumph. The struggling shadow of a man was gripped in its right foreclaw. But the man still carried a glittering crystalline sword and, dealing it deftly, he cut the claw from the dragon's foreleg at its joint. The man fell out of sight, still gripped by the severed claw; the dragon screamed in pain and wrath and plunged upward, vomiting fire and smoke. Other fire-eyed, bat-winged, serpentine shapes followed the course of the fallen man to earth.

Thend clung to the side of the rock face, stunned with the thought that Morlock was dead, or soon would be. He hadn't known it would hit him so hard. He felt somebody sneak her hand into his, and looked down to see Fasra looking up at him with a tear-streaked face. She shrugged as if to say, *What can we do?*

There was nothing they could do except try to get away, and that was what they did, creeping along the dark side of every rock they could find to cover them.

But it was all for nothing. The dragon cavalry flew over them and dropped nets and, when they were trapped, the Khroic soldiers came and knocked them out one by one.

Thend struggled as best he could, but it was no use. He noticed, too, that the Khroi who clubbed him into unconsciousness had a purplish carapace marked by savage scraping near the neck. The point of a rock was stuck there in the Khroi's shell like a tooth.

"I should have left you for the spiders!" Thend shouted; then the Khroi's club descended and darkness with it.

Thend dreamed he was flying, and then when he woke up he found it wasn't a dream. He was hanging facedown in a wire net, hundreds or thousands of feet over the moons-lit broken ground of the Kirach Kund. Twisting around, he saw the net was gripped in the claws of a dragon. He wanted to shout something defiant and insulting, but fear kept a grip on his throat: he had never been so high in his life and he didn't like it. He closed his eyes and pretended he was somewhere else, anywhere else.

He must have slept or passed out. When he awoke he could hear the adults talking to each other in low voices. But he could hear other, inhuman voices, too, so he was spared the terrible, tempting illusion that their captivity was only a dream.

Thend opened his eyes to see Fasra's frightened face in profile. If she was scared, then things were pretty bad. Beyond her Thend saw his brothers. On the other side he saw his mother and her brother, and beyond them Morlock looking rather beat up.

Roble and Naeli avoided meeting Thend's eye, but Morlock looked him straight in the face, smiling sadly. "We meet again!" said the crooked man.

"Unfortunately," Thend said rudely, because he didn't know what else to say, and Morlock nodded in agreement.

Things were unfortunate indeed. They were all sitting there in a valley, bound hand and foot with leathery rope. Even the werewolf was there, hogtied and snarling. Standing over them were huge Khroi warriors, of a type Thend had never seen. On one slope of the valley, rank on rank, sat a whole horde or tribe of Khroi. Facing them, on the other side of the valley, were dozens of fiery, bat-winged, serpentine forms in various dark colors: an irregular burning rainbow of dragons.

Thend looked up to the sky. Chariot, the major moon, was eastering; and Horseman, the second moon, was high in the sky. Thend looked up at it, thinking that this was the last sky he would ever see. The thought was convincing but cold; he felt nothing about it. He wondered if this were part of dying: giving up interest in anything as the jaws of death clamped down.

He looked at the valley. He saw the Khroi were of many different types. There were the strange gigantic warriors who stood over them, guarding them with spears. Nearby were the warriors, wearing spiked blades on their palp-clusters; they wore white ceremonial tabards with some kind of writing on them. Above them were ranks of Khroi wearing black surcoats. It struck Thend that they might be elders, Khroi who had aged out of the warrior class. Above them on the slope was a milling crowd of Khroi dressed in black and white rags. Some were dancing, others were lying on the ground, waving their palp-clusters and ped-clusters in the air. Highest of all was a lone figure who sat on the steps of an empty gigantic throne. He wore a tabard of white embroidered with red and black in a chaotic pattern.

The dragons all spoke only to this Khroi who sat before the empty throne, never to the others, and all the other Khroi also spoke to him; he alone spoke to the dragons.

There was some sort of discussion or negotiation going on; Thend didn't know if it was all about them, although some of it clearly was. He had thought that the dragons were merely animals that the Khroi rode, like a man riding a horse, but he saw now that he was wrong. There was some sort of alliance between the two races.

The discussion appeared to be coming to some kind of conclusion when it was interrupted. Morlock interrupted it, rising to his feet (he must have untied the rope around his ankles), and, turning away from the Khroi, he spoke directly to the dragons in something that sounded a great deal like the language they had been using.

The dragons responded heatedly, and a few edged closer to Morlock when the Khroi leader interrupted them with a harsh word.

"If you have anything to say," the Khroi leader called down the slope in Coranian, "you will speak to me, Morlock Ambrosius. I am both *kharum* to this guile of dragons and *marh* to this horde of Khroi. They speak to me, and I speak for them. But I tell you now, Destroyer: there is nothing you might say that I would wish to hear."

Morlock looked once down the line of dragons, left to right. Thend thought there was a smile on his face as he met the dragons' burning eyes. Then he slowly turned his back on them and many snarled in anger as he did so.

Morlock called up the slope to the Marh, saying, "Your name? It seems you know mine."

"I have many names," the Khroi leader said. "I was called one thing by the gods-who-hate-me in their thoughts before my first birth. That is ever my true name and I will learn it only in death at my final damnation. The Virgin Sisters called me another name after my second birth, when I ate my way clear from my dying host. As warrior-in-training I had a third name; as warrior-in-deed I won a fourth. In my time I became an elder and a seer, and I had names in both those avatars. Now I am Marh Valone, marh of deathless Valona's horde. Work your magic on my name at your peril, Destroyer: it has Valona's strength in it."

"I don't use binding magic," Morlock observed, "or fear it. I greet you, Marh Valone. You call me Destroyer, but if you spare our lives we will spare yours."

Marh Valone fixed one of his three eyes on Morlock. He left his seat before the vacant throne and walked down the slope, never looking away. The dancing figures in black and white tried to restrain him, but he kicked them out of his way and continued down the slope, where the elders and warriors made a lane for him. He stood at last before Morlock, just beyond the hulking spear-carrying guards, and said, "What did you say?"

"Perhaps I wasn't clear. I—"

"I speak and understand this language better than you," Marh Valone interrupted him. "I use it because most of you understand it. That's Dwarvish law, as you learned from your foster kin under Thrymhaiam. If I had chosen I could have addressed you in Dwarvish, in Brythonic or Latin: in any language you know. No one-face language is difficult for us; our young invent more complicated ones before they lose their quadrilimbs. You can have no vowels-in-harmony, no consonant-rhythms. Each of you has but one mouth, only one! And you are barely able to use that, in song or speech. No, *Destroyer*, I ask you to repeat what you said simply because I desire to hear you say it again."

Morlock calmly repeated, "If you spare our lives, we will spare yours. Blood for blood: that is Dwarvish law as I learned it under Thrymhaiam."

Marh Valone lifted all three of his boneless arms, and each of his three mouths emitted a different musical sound. Behind him on the slope many of the warriors and elders mimicked him. The dancing figures in black and white covered their eyes with their palp-clusters and moaned.

Marh Valone crooked each of his arms at an alarmingly sharp angle and silence fell. "Oh gods-who-hate-us," he said at last, "I thank you. Oh Ancestors who cast us out and revile us, I thank you. Though we have earned your loathing, though we are sunk and stained with the evil of wandering through these evil lands, you have sent us this gift. We have heard the Destroyer beg for his life, *and be refused*."

"I am a maker," Morlock said, "not a destroyer, except to defend myself or those of my blood. If you do not choose to harm us, you need fear nothing from me. Your seers will have ways to test these words, as sure as any oath."

"No oath sworn to us can ever be binding, Destroyer, as well you know," Marh Valone said. "We are the accursed. Your lies will not deceive us, either: we are the servants of the Great Lie. It is the Great Lie who tells us all these truths, who guides our visions of the future, who makes us unclean. We know who you are, even if you don't. You are the Destroyer."

"Your seers have had some vision?" Morlock guessed. "But the future is not fixed, like the past. The future is the sum of our decisions; we can change our minds in the present and save ourselves in the future."

"I tell you again, *do not lie*. Some parts of the future can be chosen; some come at us like an avalanche, choose what we will. I was a seer and I know this. I have walked in the future and the past, as I know you can. Do you know me, Destroyer? Did you never see me in your dreams? I am your enemy. I have dedicated my life to defeating you so that Valona's horde might be saved."

"Waste of a good life," the crooked man observed.

"*You* would think so. The dreams first came to haunt Valona's seers before my second birth. When the host died and I lived, they became darker and more definite. As a warrior I fought to make Valona's horde strong so that we could resist you when you came. As I became a seer at last, I walked through the dreams of terror you sent against us from the future and I made maps of the things-that-would-be so that our elders could guide the horde away from the death you designed for us. But always the shadows of future danger changed: you changed them to defeat our plans! And when I became an elder, I continued to plan for the day you would arrive.

"Because I alone truly understood your threat against us, the other elders raised me to be their chief, marh of Valona's horde. Then I set my plans in motion. I purchased human agents in the city to the south. When you corrupted and defeated them, I knew the Destroyer's hour had struck and you were coming to attack us. I sent a troop of warriors to capture you and the agent you had corrupted, but you killed them all. The dreams of our seers grew dark to the point of madness; even now they rave and scream that all is over. But now, at last, it is our fear which is over. We have you! We have you!

How does it feel to know that you have failed, Destroyer? How does it feel to know *you* will be destroyed? Will you say nothing? Is it mute, that one drooling mouth given you by the gods-we-hate?"

"I have a thing to say, if you will listen."

"Say it. I find I have a great hunger to hear you plead and whine and beg."

"Once there was a man who knew the future," Morlock said quietly. "He lived by the sea, and an oracle told him he would drown in saltwater. So he fled inland from the seacoast. When he was crossing a bridge over a river in flood, the arch collapsed and the falling stones carried him down to the water and he drowned there, in a flooded salt lick by the side of the river. His fear drove him to the fate he feared. So it is with you, Marh Valone."

"There is no fate," Marh Valone cried. "That is the lie you told before, and it is true. We have defeated our fate and your hate."

"Put aside your fear. I don't hate you, but if you harm me or mine, if you threaten to do so, you will suffer for it. Blood for blood: that is the only law I know."

Suddenly the Marh was surrounded by the dancing Khroi in black-and-white rags. They reached out their palp-clusters toward him imploringly, and their triple mouths sang a song Thend did not understand.

The Marh's eyes widened in anger or surprise. He gestured with all three of his arms, pointing back up the slope. The dancing Khroi grew silent and still; they bowed down and laid their carapaces on the ground before their leader. But they still stretched out their arms imploringly to him.

"Your presence has poisoned our seers," he said accusingly to Morlock. "I have gloated over you too long, perhaps. Now, because you are *rokhlan*, a dragonkiller, the guile of dragons wish to have you for their prize, and as their kharum and as marh of Valona's horde, I grant that wish. You and your property will be taken from here to the Giving Field, where the guile may dispose of you for their sport. The werewolf has also killed a dragon, although by mere treachery and stealth, and he too will be given to the dragons, as, of course, our Lost One must be. This blood will seal the bond between guile and horde. These others will go and give their lives for our future in the Vale of the Mother. At the next gathering we will pray their names to the gods-who-hate-us. I have spoken; let others obey."

Morlock asked, "What do you mean 'seal the bond'? Aren't these dragons your servants? Don't you ride them like animals?"

The crooked row of dragons erupted in fire and noise. For a while nothing could be heard except their fiery words, meaningless to Thend. He wondered if a fight was going to break out between the dragons and the Khroi then and there, if that was what Morlock was trying to provoke.

Marh Valone fixed Morlock with one eye and stared at him. Then, when the uproar had gone on for a while, he lifted all three of his arms and called out, with all three of his mouths singing at a different tone, a word Thend did not recognize. It sounded as loud as any dragon from where Thend sat, and the row of angry dragons subsided into something like order. Marh Valone spoke a short sentence in the same language, at a slightly lower tone of voices. Thend turned to see the dragons wordlessly lowering their heads in submission. But all of them were glaring at Morlock's shoulders: he had not deigned to turn and look at them while they were shouting and he did not do so now.

"That was quite a good try," Marh Valone said to Morlock confidentially. "Pride is what binds them to us: they are exiles from the greater guiles to the south and east, ashamed to live as solitaries. If you stayed among us for a time you would no doubt find a way to use that pride and turn them against us. But you will die tonight, a free gift from horde to guile, and their pride and gratitude will bind them to us closer than ever."

Marh Valone would have turned away then, but another Khroi voice, discordant and clashing, forestalled him. Thend looked and saw standing nearby the Khroi whose carapace was marked, the Khroi he had rescued from the spiders.

The Marh stopped moving away and looked with one eye, then another, at the marked Khroi as he spoke. (Did the Marh's gesture indicate surprise? Attentiveness? Some emotion a man could never feel? Thend wasn't sure.) A moment of silence followed, and then Marh Valone turned to Thend. "Our Lost One has requested that you also be given to the dragons. It is a sin against our future, but no one has ever done for one of us what you dared to do, and I grant this favor to the Lost One. I will not pray for you to the gods-who-hate-us, and so they may forgive you. I have spoken; let others obey."

"No!" shouted Fasra. "Leave him with us!"

But each of them was firmly held by three of the giant Khroi-guards; there was nothing any of them could do.

"I'm sorry," Morlock muttered. "You chose your guide unwisely. Good-bye."

The guile of dragons rose into the air and flew away southward like a storm. The noise of their passage made further speech useless, and Thend could have said nothing anyway: that fist of fear was gripping his throat again. He looked at his mother, whom he had loved and feared, and at Roble, the man who was closer to him than his long-dead father, the man he had wished he could be, and all he wanted was to die with them. But the Marh's cruel kindness had denied him even that.

The others watched without words as Thend and Morlock were dragged away. The werewolf was picked up and carried, too, and the Khroi that Thend had saved, "the Lost One" as Marh Valone had called him, walked slowly alongside them.

"Why is it a favor to be given to the dragons?" Thend called to Morlock after they had been dragged for a while. (The dragons had long gone on ahead and they could hear each other now.) "Won't they—?"

"They'll kill us and eat us," Morlock said. "The others will die too, as hosts for the Khroi young, in the Vale of the Mother. It is slower, more painful, more horrible."

"And this is all *your* fault somehow?"

"No!" said Morlock.

Thend wished he could say something to comfort the crooked man. Not that there *was* anything to say. So he said nothing.

Suddenly they were surrounded by a faster-moving group. Thend had a crazy hope that the others had gotten away and come to rescue them—but it was only the dancing Khroi in black-and-white rags. They spoke to the gigantic Khroi guards in birdlike harmonious voices, and the guards (looking nervously at each other) stopped dragging the captives along.

The dancing Khroi stretched out their arms imploringly and sang at Morlock, just as they had to the Khroic marh before, but this time Thend could understand them, as they sang in the language Thend thought of as Coranian.

"Spare us," the Khroi sang, "spare us, Destroyer. You are a seer, like ourselves, although you do not walk always in the tal-realm as we do. Spare us, have mercy on us, do not destroy us, and we will not pray for you to the gods-who-hate-us and they may forgive you."

"I will spare you," Morlock agreed, "if you spare me and my friends. I will give mercy for mercy, blood for blood."

"We cannot spare you," the Khroic seers sang. "The warriors act; we advise; the Sisters and the elders, led by the Marh, decide. His word is our law; we cannot break it. But only your word is your law. You can spare us, even if we destroy you. Please, please, let us kill you in peace."

"Is it horde law for you to plead with prisoners like this?" Morlock said. "Did you not defy the marh's command to return to your place on the slope? You pick and choose the laws you will obey. You choose the destruction before you, just as he does. Spare me and my friends or I *will* destroy you. Blood for blood: that is my law."

The Khroic seers put their palp-clusters over their eyes and moaned. The gigantic guards took this as a sign that the interview was over and they dragged Morlock and Thend onward.

"How can you destroy them?" Thend called when the wailing seers had passed out of earshot.

"Why would I want to?" Morlock replied glumly. "Death is their dream, not mine. If only I could understand why! I took care to not explore this journey with visions, for I knew the Khroi had seers and one seer's vision can encompass another's. I wanted to pass under their notice, but they were waiting for me all along. It is strange. . . ."

Presently they came to a wide flat area where a dozen or so posts of maijarra wood had been driven deeply into the stony ground: the Giving Field. A faded blue dragon was waiting there. The claw had been severed from his right forelimb and the fresh wound was still oozing blood or pus that smoked sullenly on the ground. His dim red eyes watched glumly as the Khroi guards lifted up their prisoners and hung them from hooks driven into the maijarra wood high above the ground. The Khroi whom Thend had saved from the spiders was bound and hung there, too. Then, without ceremony, the guards left them alone with the dragon.

"Is this it?" Thend called over to Morlock. The prisoners were hung in a line, with Thend and Morlock on either end. The werewolf was next to Morlock and the Khroi was next to Thend.

"No," Morlock said. "I suppose the dragons are settling which one of them gets which one of us, along with our stuff." At this, Thend noticed that their packs and weapons had been brought along by the guards and left off to the side of the Giving Field.

There was a long period while Thend wondered how the dragons would decide these important issues. A fight? A contest? A vote? Some combination of these? Should he hope that it would take a long time or no time at all?

Meanwhile Morlock was looking at the leather thong binding his hands, at the packs, at the Dragon who watched him grimly without ever looking away.

"Do you think you can unhook yourself from that thing?" Thend called over.

"No," said the crooked man. "Not with our friend watching. And listening."

This last was a mild rebuke, Thend realized. The dragon was not an animal; it might be able to understand them. If Thend had a good idea, he should probably keep it to himself and hope that Morlock had it, too. Unfortunately, Thend had no more ideas, good or bad.

"Thend," Morlock said presently, "I'm sorry."

Thend was embarrassed. He should never have blamed Morlock, even as a stupid joke. "It's all right," he said. "I know it's not really your fault."

"Not about that," Morlock said, but he didn't say what he *was* apologizing about. Which meant he couldn't. Which meant it was an Idea. And he was apologizing because it might end up getting Thend killed, even if it got Morlock free.

Thend thought carefully about his response. He didn't want to die, but if Morlock got away maybe there was something he could do to save Thend's family. That was tough luck for Thend, of course, but it wasn't like his chances looked good at the moment anyway. He couldn't say anything to discourage Morlock from whatever crazy plan he'd come up with, and he couldn't say anything to suggest to the dragon that there *was* a crazy plan.

"It's still all right," Thend said at last. "I understand." And he hoped

Morlock had understood him as well as he had understood Morlock. (If he had.)

Morlock said something, but not to Thend and not anything Thend understood. He looked straight into the dragon's dimly burning eyes and said it: in Dragonish, Thend guessed, or some language the dragon understood.

Thend was right. What Morlock said was, *"Hey, Smoky! What's taking your masters so long?"*

The dragon snarled, a long low rumbling, like stones grinding together under the earth, and said, "I have no master but Marh Valone, kharum of my guile."

"You actually answer to that insect?" Morlock asked. "He told you to stay here and keep your murky eyes on us?"

"No!" the dragon snapped. After some long bitter moments of silence he added, "My guile-mates asked me to wait here and watch you."

"Oh," said Morlock distantly. "I see. I think."

The dragon lashed his tail in a catlike gesture of irritation and looked with glowing disfavor at Morlock.

"It is a position of considerable trust," the dragon insisted.

"I'm sure they can trust you, Smoky," the crooked man replied generously. "I'm sure you'd never *even think* of *taking* something that was *theirs*."

There were several barbs to this insult: that the dragon wouldn't have the courage or cunning to steal from his guile-mates, that the prizes were unequivocally theirs not his, and "Smoky," which implied that the dragon's fire was not as bright and hot as a dragon's fire should be.

"Don't call me 'Smoky'!" the dragon snarled.

"Do you prefer 'Three-Claw'?" the hanging man asked, with an appearance of civility. "Your leg might grow back in time, but I see that you're a dragon of, well, of a certain age and perhaps you don't expect to live much—"

"My name is Gjyrning," the dragon hissed. "Use it when you address me or die."

"I'll die anyway," Morlock pointed out. "But I'm not worried: you can be . . . trusted. Remember, Smoky?"

The dragon smiled—not a gesture of amusement or friendliness in a dragon—and said nothing. Venomous dark smoke leaked out between the terrible green-black teeth.

"Gjyrning . . . Gjyrning . . ." the crooked man said, as if thinking aloud. "Doesn't that mean 'puff of lightly warm steam'? I seem to remember—"

The dragon barked, "It means 'mourning—suffering—death'!"

"So you knew how your career would end from the beginning," the crooked man said, almost as if he were impressed. "I wish more dragons would pick suitable names. I captured a dragon once outside of Thrymhaiam whose name meant, so he claimed, 'World-shaking-conflagration-of-eternal-flames,' but his fire wasn't hot enough to kindle dry leaves. It was too much trouble to kill him, so I gave him to the Elder of Theorn Clan as a gift. The dwarves used him as a beast of burden. They could 'trust' him, too, because every time he tried to steal something they would beat him with sticks and he'd squeak out some smoke at either end. He soon learned his place. They called him Squeaky. That's a fine name for an elderly blue dragon whose fire is not as hot as he thinks it is, don't you think?"

Gjyrning, an elderly blue dragon whose fire was not as hot as it had been, lumbered across the open field, his jaws streaming fire and smoke. But his stump was clearly troubling him; he kept putting his weight on it, as if the right claw-foot were there, and stumbling. He halted about twenty (human) paces from the stakes and visibly brought himself under control.

"That's right!" said the horrible crooked man with the offensive manner. "They've trained you well; you can be trusted. No one can say you don't know when your fire's faded, when it's time to give up fighting and blowing flame rings and just settle down and call yourself Squeaky—"

The dragon lurched forward, his narrow chest doubling in size.

Thend couldn't understand what Morlock and the dragon were saying to each other, but he could tell from Morlock's harsh jeering tone that he was baiting the dragon, trying to provoke a rage. When he saw the dragon swell up he knew he should close his eyes and hold his breath: dragons breathe venom as well as fire. But if these were the last few minutes of his life he decided he didn't want to spend them staring at the inside of his eyelids. (He had tried that without much success earlier, anyway.)

The dragon roared out a blast of flame at Morlock. The red torrent carried him backward and Thend could see him dimly, a crooked darkness in a sheath of flames. Then he disappeared and the dragon stopped roaring.

There was a dark fog of smoke and steam and venom about the post where Morlock had been hanging. The dragon peered through it with his dimly glowing eyes, trying to find Morlock's body.

The crooked man had rolled off to one side after the flames burned through his bonds, and he wasn't dead yet, Thend was relieved to see. He knew that Morlock's strange blood protected him from fire, but he hadn't been sure the crooked man could suffer the roar of an angry dragon and live.

Morlock called out hoarsely, *"Tyrfing!"*

The accursed blade flew from its sheath bound to Morlock's pack; glittering, it shot through the smoke-laden air to the hand of the man who had made it. The dim blue dragon leapt back in surprise as it flew past. Then he lunged forward at Morlock, his one remaining foreclaw stretched out.

Morlock was already running forward. He dodged under the dragon's wolflike jaw as it descended and ran on past the dragon's left foreleg. The dragon turned to swipe at him with his right foreclaw—and missed, forgetting that his right foreleg was a stump. Morlock dashed on, raising the monochrome crystalline blade over his head with both hands.

Thend wondered where Morlock would strike. He had heard, in songs and tales, that dragons had numerous weak spots and hollows in their chests where a determined warrior might strike a deathblow, could he only get near enough.

But Morlock didn't strike at the dragon's body, as such, at all. The blade caught the dragon's left wing, folded batlike along his side. Tyrfing severed the joint and passed through much of the leathery flesh before the dragon screamed and rolled over. He was trying to crush Morlock, but the pinions of the dragon's wings gave the man space to scrabble through between the mass of the dragon's serpentine body and the stony earth.

Rather than roll again, as Thend expected, the dragon leapt to his feet and backed away lumberingly from Morlock.

As he watched the dragon's movement, slowed by his wounded foreleg, Thend realized why Morlock had attacked the dragon's wing. Now the dragon could neither fly away, with his broken wing, nor run away, with his wounded foot. There was no escape for him.

Abruptly, surprisingly, Thend felt sorry for the dim blue dragon: mutilated, mocked, mutilated again, and now trapped with that terrible crooked man in this narrow field hedged in with steep slopes. He pushed the feeling down as hard as he could. Morlock might be sort of a bastard, but he was *their* bastard, fighting desperately for Thend and his family. But the feeling didn't quite go away.

The dragon meanwhile lunged forward on his unwounded foot and made as if to snap at Morlock with his teeth. Morlock dodged to the dragon's right—and was struck end over end by the dragon's mutilated foreleg.

That might have been the end of the battle right then, if the dragon had still possessed raptor claws to catch and kill his enemy. And it nearly was: Morlock ended up slumped against the base of the post where he had been hanging; there was no sword in his hand. The dragon leapt at him with a happy roar and he had to crawl, rather than walk, away from the post; there was something wrong with one of his legs.

The dragon himself was wounded, in wing and foot, and he obviously tried to outthink his opponent. Morlock had only one place to retreat: behind the row of maijarra-wood posts. It turned right to lumber toward the nearer end of the row, attempting to get around them before Morlock retreated through them.

But Morlock, scrabbling along on all fours, was not attempting to retreat. He crawled toward something gleaming among the fire-blackened stones of the Giving Field: his sword, Tyrfing. Thend wondered why he didn't just call it to him, but then reflected that this trick might be something Morlock might have to set up in advance. In any case, his fingers had closed on the grip of the sword before the dragon realized what was happening.

The dragon turned to face him, and Morlock lurched to his feet with a harsh crowlike call that might have been a battle cry or a scream of pain for all that Thend knew. Then the crooked man, crookeder than ever now, loped forward, his sword raised high.

The dragon flinched backward toward the maijarra-wood posts, then turned again to fight.

But it was already too late. Morlock ran up on the dragon's wounded wing, trailing on the ground, and climbed it like a ladder. The dragon bucked and writhed, but Morlock stabbed down between the spikes protecting the dragon's backbone, and the dragon's back legs collapsed. He ran forward along the dragon's back and stabbed again: the dragon's forelegs gave way and the serpentine body fell wholly to the ground.

Morlock staggered forward toward the dragon's neck and what Thend guessed would be the killing blow. But he paused and spoke, although Thend couldn't hear what he said and would not have understood it if he had.

In his native language, which was also the dragon's, Morlock was saying, "I regret my words to you, Gjyrning. Need drove me; I meant none of it."

The dragon chuckled smokily and whispered, "You didn't fool me, rokhlan! At least . . . not entirely. I am old; most of my hoard has been stolen by others; the guile have been sizing me up for fodder. I thought . . . this way . . . if I killed you in battle, stole their prize . . . I could at least die in glory."

"Then," Morlock said.

"Wait!" Gjyrning gasped.

"Only a moment, Gjyrning. More deeds await me this dark night."

"Morlock . . . what will you tell them of me . . . the ones who live under Thrymhaiam?"

"I can never go there now," Morlock said, and slid the blade of his sword between the dragon's neck-plates into his skull, killing him. He jumped down and limped away as the dim red eyes grew dark behind him.

The scene was strangely dark with the dragon dead. Where the dragon had bled there was a sullen glow among the bare blackened stones of the Giving Field, and Thend saw that Morlock's blood, too, lit smoldering fires among what little there was to burn. Most of the light came from the cold bitter moons overhead.

Morlock limped down the line of posts until he reached Thend. Reaching up his sword, he slashed the thongs holding Thend on the hook. Thend fell to his feet and gasped. "Thanks!" he said, inadequately but sincerely, and then added, "Ouch!" His arms hurt suddenly.

He looked guiltily at the crooked man, who had suffered far more, but Morlock just said, "Stretching the limbs hurts worse when it stops than when it's happening. Can you use your arms?"

Thend flapped them around a bit. "Yes," he said.

"Then we'll deal with them later. We have things to do."

"Right."

Thend ran over to where his property was. He found a knife strapped to his pack and came back with it. As Morlock watched, resting on his sword, Thend shinnied up the pole where the Lost One was hanging and slashed the rope that bound him to the hook. The Khroi took the fall on his carapace and slowly rose to stand on his ped-clusters, flexing his boneless arms and turning his head slowly to look at Thend several times with each of the eyes on his pyramidal face.

"You're welcome," Thend said pointedly. After what Marh Valone had said, he was sure that the Khroi could understand him and speak if he chose. The Khroi didn't, though, at least not then. Thend glanced at the werewolf hanging on the next post over.

But Morlock was already limping there. He put one hand under the hog-tied werewolf's back and said politely, "Snap at me and I'll cut you in half." The werewolf didn't snap at him. Morlock reached up, slashing the bonds holding the werewolf, and carefully put the beast on his own four feet.

The werewolf spun about and snarled.

Morlock held Tyrfing at guard and waited.

The werewolf glanced over at the dark hulk of the slain dragon, then back at Morlock. He backed away a pace, then another, and his gaze dropped.

"Then," said Morlock and turned away.

The werewolf took a long look at Morlock's back, and eventually trotted after him.

Morlock walked (if that was the right word) straight up to the Khroi and rapped on his pyramidal head as if it were a door.

"Anyone there?" he asked.

The Khroi backed away, as if threatened. "Warriors may not speak to outsiders," said the Khroi at last, speaking through only one of his mouths in a buzzing unclear voice very unlike Marh Valone's. "But I am not a warrior now. I am nothing. Yes, I am here. I see you."

"What's your name?" Morlock asked.

"I have no name," the Khroi said, "except my true one, which the gods-who-hate-me know but I do not."

"What do your horde-mates call you?" Thend asked.

"That does not matter," the Khroi said. "I am lost. The gods have remembered me, to my doom, and now I have no horde, lest my doom become theirs."

"What do you think you owe Thend, here?" Morlock asked.

The Lost One looked at Thend with one of his eyes. "Nothing," he said. "Everything."

"I see your point," said Morlock. (Thend wished he did.) "Does your debt extend to a willingness to act? Will you do something for the chance to go untethered to the gods-who-hate-you?"

"What?" the Lost One asked reasonably.

"Thend's mother—"

Both the Khroi and Thend started a bit at this.

"—yes, his *mother*," Morlock continued, "was one of the captives taken to the Vale of the Mother. Of your mother, of Valona. Will you take us there?"

"You are the Destroyer," the Lost One said in his expressionless buzzing voice. "You will slay Valona. You will slay the horde."

"No," Morlock said. "We seek only to rescue our friends. Besides, what is it to you? You have no horde any longer. They cast you out, for their own good, not yours. The only horde-mate you have now, as far as I can see, is Thend. He is not one of the damned; he is not one of the lost. How will it be if you cross into the realm of the gods with one such as him for your horde-mate? Perhaps it will ease the gods' anger."

One of the Lost One's eyes still rested unblinkingly on Thend. He did his best to look unlost and undamned, since that seemed necessary to Morlock's plan.

"Very well," the Lost One buzzed. "But there must be no killing."

"I don't promise that," Morlock said. "We may need to kill some Khroi to rescue our friends. If need be, we will die fighting. You must join us, join our horde and stand beside us. If not, we leave you here to go your own way. By yourself."

The Lost One covered his eyes with his palp-clusters. Then he lowered them and pointed one longer stringy palp like a finger at Thend.

"He does not know what I am, why I am lost," the Lost Khroi said. "But you know. He is not our enemy, as you are. And you say this to me. You ask this of me."

"If you were my enemy, I would have killed you already," said the crooked man. "Join us, be one of us, or stay here alone. And you must choose now."

The Lost One closed all of his eyes for a long moment, then opened them. "May the gods forget me," he said. "I go with you to the Vale of the Mother. Follow me; it is not far."

Nor was it, as the crow flies, but none of them were crows. Each of them had lived through a long and dreadful day. The werewolf slunk along the ground, dragging his tail. The Lost One was given to fits of stumbling and shuffling; all his limbs would stiffen abruptly, as if from pain or maybe, Thend thought, some sensation the Khroi didn't share with other people. Morlock was perhaps the worst off. Every time the crooked man took a step his whole body twisted, reminding Thend of a millworks he had once seen where something had come askew and the interlocking machinery slowly destroyed itself. But Morlock moved as fast as any of them, never complaining, ripping strips from his clothing as he went to staunch the flow of burning blood from his various wounds. So Thend clenched his teeth and didn't complain about how much his feet and arms hurt.

The Giving Field was just across a ridge from the Vale of Council, where Thend had first awakened. The Vale of the Mother was on the north side of the Vale of Council, past the long sloping shoulder of a mountain. The journey down into the now-empty Vale of Council was not too bad, but the climb up the far slope tested Thend's resolution not to whine. Fear helped: fear for himself and for his family. There were strange sounds coming from over the far slope.

They finally came to the crest of the slope, crawling up the last stretch to keep from being seen. That is, Thend and Morlock did; the werewolf and the Lost One would not approach the crest.

The Vale of the Mother was formed by two shoulders of a mountain (one of which they lay upon). Across the vale was a steep shelving cliff of dark broken stone. Together the barriers formed an irregular triangle with a meadow running down its long narrow center. Thend guessed part of the far mountain had collapsed in older times to form the flattish floor of the valley.

In the valley itself there was a torchlit swarm of Khroi, male Khroi. They wore the black of elders, the white of warriors; Thend thought he even glimpsed the black, white, and red tabard of the Marh. They were dancing or running an irregular course that looped back on itself twice.

Where the loops joined lay a massive Khroi: Valona the Mother; Thend was sure of it. She crawled, lengthwise on the ground, too massive and ungainly to stand. Unlike the other Khroi, she had a fourth limb extruding from her upper carapace and another from her lower carapace, so she swayed about on six legs, with two waving like arms above her.

Behind her she dragged a massive sac full of bulbous objects: an egg-sac, Thend realized. It hung from her thick writhing neck. When the dance reached a certain point she trundled forward. Her pyramidal head split open in three parts and out of the horrifying gap came a horn or spike. The horn stabbed toward certain shadowy figures struggling on the ground, backlit by the torchlit dance. The Mother stabbed one, two, three, four times. And each stab was accompanied by a scream in the mother's voice. Thend's mother's voice. Naeli, not Valona.

Thend would have screamed himself, but he could not speak; his throat was knotted tight with horror. Shuddering, he got to his feet, not knowing what he would do, but Morlock pulled him down, off his feet and back under the crest of the ridge.

"We're too late," Thend hissed, when he found he could speak. "There's nothing we can do!"

"Shut up," Morlock said, and turned to the Lost One, who was sitting, rocking in a circle with his palp-clusters over his eyes. "You: listen to me. There are no seers in the Vale of the Mother. Where did they go?"

Thend, thinking back, realized this was true. He had seen none of the ragged black-and-white streaming cloaks of the seers.

"They should be there," the Lost One said after a long pause. "All males of the Horde should be there, to blend their seed with the Mother's eggs and father the next generation."

"What about the guards?" Thend asked. "They're not dancing around. If they leave the prisoners at some point—" He choked himself off. He had been thinking that would give them a chance to rescue his family, but then he remembered it was already too late.

The Lost One lowered his palp-clusters and peered through the shadows at Thend, first with one eye, then with another. "The guards are not males," he said finally. "They are the Virgin Sisters, the might-have-been-Mothers. They were denied the Royal Chrism and grew up sterile. They will never leave the prisoners until tomorrow's children eat their way clear of the host-bodies. Then the Sisters will tend the twice-born."

"The prisoners may leave the Sisters, though," Morlock said. "Listen, Thend. No, listen to me."

"You don't understand," Thend whispered. "It—she—no chance—we—"

"No," said the horrible old man, "it's you who don't understand. There is a thing we can do, but it depends on you. Will the werewolf go and rescue your blood-kin? The Lost One? No. The hardest part of this task will fall on you. If you won't, if you can't do it, we had best leave now and get away while we can."

"Do what?"

"I am going to go into deep vision," Morlock explained. "I may be able to create an illusion that will baffle the Khroi. Their seers would certainly see through the trick if they were here, but they are not. It may work."

"What can I do?" Thend asked.

"Stay clear of my vision. Wait until the prisoners disappear. They will still be where they were, but you won't see them; no one will. Go to them, then, and free them. Beware the Sisters. Do you understand now? Time is short."

I'm just a boy. No, I don't understand. Let's run away, run away now. It's too late. We can't help them and I don't care if we can help them.

"Yes," said Thend.

Morlock drew Tyrfing. The white branches in the black crystalline blade were glowing bright. Morlock's gray eyes, too, emitted a faint light. Then they closed and Morlock fell like a stone and slid some distance down the slope.

The long silence under the shadow of the crest was seasoned by the bird-like song of the celebrating Khroi, the occasional screams of a victim. Thend looked at the Lost One and at the werewolf, both of whom declined to meet his eye. He crept up to the crest and peered over. If there was some sort of illusion forming anywhere down there, Thend couldn't see what it was.

He slid down the slope and whispered to Morlock's supine form, "Hey, Morlock. It's not working. Hey!" He reached out and jostled the older man's shoulder.

The world fell away. He was standing above his own body. But he was not himself, as he had always thought of himself: he was a sort of cloud of bright bronze-colored motes as sharp as knives. It was strange, but as he looked/thought his way around himself, he realized that this was his true form, had always been.

He looked through the hill at the valley below. Matter was practically invisible to his talic vision: he could see the shapes of his family lying like a row of colored fires in the Vale of the Mother. One fire was fading down, like the coals of a neglected campfire. Within it lurked bright fishlike forms of alien life.

He found the fire that was the silver network of his mother's life and saw that she had, as he feared, been sown with Khroic eggs. This was grievous and he grieved for it, but emotions and thoughts were strangely altered in the visionary state. It was like the unreality of a dream.

Or the reality of a dream. As he looked at his mother, he realized that he was also looking at himself, looking at his mother. He was *here*, in this place/time, but he was also *there*, in another place/time. In fact, there was a whole line of Thend-clouds, proceeding from here-now away into a direction that was neither up nor down nor front nor back. The direction, Thend knew intuitively, was *past*. How often he had come forward in a dream that was partly a vision, to dwell for a while in this moment of the future and mis-understand it?

He saw the line of Thend-clouds move, whenever the Khroic Mother moved. The Thends-that-were stood peering through the silver network of Naeli's life toward the Khroic mother in her lumbering dance of life and death. That was the source of his terrible dreams. He had been seeing one mother through the mask of another. Now, knowing what he knew, he could separate the mother from the monster.

He wanted to say this to someone, to put it into words so that he could understand it himself, and he thought of Morlock.

Morlock's body was a heap of nearly invisible matter, hardly distinguishable from the mountainside it lay upon. Morlock himself, the real Morlock, stood below in the Vale, a pillar of monochrome flames, transfixed by varicolored streams of dim light. He was drawing the light toward him, and directing it away from him at the almost-invisible cliff face that towered over the vale. Not far away was a lumbering web of many-spiculed fire that could only be the Khroi Mother, in the middle of the double-looped dance of burning souls.

Beyond them all stood the seers.

Thend was aghast. There were so many of them—only a few talic imprints were sharp and clear, but there were many, many others, rank on rank, proceeding away in a direction that was neither right nor left nor up nor down nor front nor back. They were here but not now, Thend realized: the *placeness* was the same but the *timeness* was different. These seers had come to this moment in their vision, as Thend had. But all the past-Thends were as definite and real as he was himself: these were different, more indefinite as they were further away in time. They were from the future, from times that didn't fully exist yet, coming back to witness this moment.

Why? Thend wondered. What importance did it have for them? Then he realized that he might be able to find out. If he let his mind drift in the not-direction that was not-past, he might see something of the near future. He attempted it, and his mind filled with fire and death and falling stones.

Thend! he not-heard Morlock not-say. *Get out!*

The vision abruptly left him and he found himself shivering on the dark mountainside, crouching over Morlock's unconscious form.

He had a horrible sense that time had passed, too much time. He leaped up the slope to peer down at his family. They were still there, some of them were still moving. He couldn't tell if any more of them had been sown with eggs; he wished he had thought to look while he was in rapture.

Whatever Morlock had planned didn't seem to be working. The Khroi Mother was lurching forward to implant more eggs. Thend glanced down behind him: the werewolf was lying like a dog at Morlock's feet; the Lost Khroi was crouching with his boneless arms wrapped around his carapace, as if he were suffering from cold or pain. Thend shook his head: there was no help to be expected from either of them. He slipped over the crest and into the Vale of the Mother.

He crept along from one patch of brush to another, hoping their shadows would hide him. Evidently they did, but in the end he had to leave them and burrow his way through a long swathe of mountain grass that tore at his face and hands. After he had been at this a while he felt himself lifted off the ground by a terribly strong grip on his neck. He was caught in the palp-clusters of a Virgin Sister.

Her grip was painful without making it impossible to breathe. He saw over her carapace how the grass he had crawled through had been pressed down, creating a dark line in the firelight that pointed straight at him. Brilliant, Thend, he said sourly to himself. Really cunning.

Even the Virgin Sister who had captured him appeared astonished by his ineptitude. She looked at him with one eye, then another, and opened her mouths to speak, probably to call out to the other Sisters. But she had lost her chance: a blue-eyed gray shadow fixed its jaws around her narrow neck. Its weight bore them together to the ground.

The werewolf! He bit through the Sister's narrow neck and the suddenly lifeless head rolled away downslope to rest in deep grass. Air whistled through the ragged oozing end of the Sister's neck: she wasn't dead yet. Her palp-clusters tightened around Thend's throat. He grabbed one of the arm-blades thrust into a hilt hanging from her belt. He shoved the knifelike point deep into the neck hole of the carapace and twisted it about, hoping blindly to strike a vital organ and kill her before she killed him. She convulsed and her palp-clusters loosened, nerveless in death.

The werewolf had already rolled to his feet and was running downhill toward the captives. Thend shrugged: the time for stealth had obviously passed. He suddenly realized he had lost his knife somewhere, so he kept his grip on the dead Sister's armblade and ran after the werewolf. The other Sisters hadn't seen them yet; it wasn't clear that anyone had. But someone would soon. Their only chance, and it wasn't much of one, was to run down to the prisoners, free them, and fight their way clear.

That was what Thend was thinking when his family disappeared. He was looking right at them when it happened. They were half sitting, slumped against stakes to which they were bound. Some of them were bleeding. There were garlands of mountain flowers on their heads. Fasra was looking around wildly, perhaps she had heard something behind her; she turned and looked straight into Thend's eye. Then they were gone: the prisoners, the stakes they were tied to, everything; there remained in their place an odd patch of shadow in the firelight.

Meanwhile the bonfires flared up, light passing from one to the other in an arc like a red rainbow. Khroic voices called out in astonishment, and when the light faded many cried out again. They all were pointing and staring at the cliff wall above the valley.

Thend, looking there too, was astonished to see his family on a rock shelf at the base of the cliff wall. Not only them: Thend himself was there, with a ragged crown of flowers, and Morlock, and the werewolf (the wreath around his gray neck), and even the Lost Khroi.

An illusion, Morlock had said. He was going to make an illusion. This was it. So his family was still there, where they had been. The Khroi Mother, the Virgin Sisters, the warriors, and the elders all turned toward the cliff wall. Thend and the werewolf raced down to the patch of shadow and Thend whispered, "Where are you? I can't see you."

Unfortunately, half a dozen of the Virgin Sisters heard this remark, and turned suddenly back toward Thend and the patch of shadow. They plunged their palp-clusters in the shafts of their armblades and drew them, running straight at Thend and the werewolf.

Thend stood straight and hefted his rather awkward weapon. If he'd only had a moment to free some of his kin, the odds would have been better. But he would do what he could, and hoped the werewolf would fight with him. He hoped that right up to the moment he heard the rustle of the werewolf's feet as it ran away uphill through the deep grass. Then he had no hope at all.

The Lost One stepped between the Virgin Sisters and Thend.

His motions were stiff and awkward: it was as if all flexibility were gone from those boneless limbs. He was not armed; Thend had no idea what he intended to do. But his presence obviously shocked and appalled the Virgin Sisters: they stopped short and stared at him, turning their heads to look at him with one eye, then another, then a third.

The Lost One gripped his carapace around the neck hole in three places. His boneless arms strained and the carapace ripped apart as if it were rotting from within.

Something, something white and milky-looking dripped down off his inner torso. Thend had never seen a Khroi without his shell before, but somehow the lost Khroi looked wrong, unbalanced, as if part of him were eaten away . . .

Eaten away. That fluid: some of it was moving upward, not dripping down. As he watched in increasing horror, as the Lost One fell to the ground and ceased moving, Thend realized the white "fluid" was made of very small particular elements, each one with many legs, eight tiny little legs.

"No!" Thend screamed. "You get out of him!"

He ran over and started stomping on the spiderfolk who had grown in and fed upon his friend, his horde-mate, the Lost One. He was weeping and cursing as he did: the Lost One was obviously dead, had been dead since before Thend had seen him. The spiderfolk had seeded him with eggs and had left them to grow and grow within him. There was no point, but he kept on stomping anyway until he remembered the Virgin Sisters.

They stood some way off. Each one was staring at him intently with a single eye. Long moments passed. They sheathed their armblades and walked away. Trembling, not sure what had just happened, Thend turned back to the patch of shadows that concealed his family.

"Death and Justice," his mother's voice hissed out of the empty air. "Get away from here, Thend, before they come back!"

"I don't think they're coming back," he said, his voice (and his legs) a little wobbly. "Keep talking so I can find you."

So his mother told him he was a deranged maniac who ought not to be allowed loose and that she hadn't raised her children to be bug food, and would he *please* go away *now*, and he followed her voice to find the stake she was bound to. He found the ropes by feel and slashed them with the edge of the armblade. Once freed she stopped protesting but took the armblade from him and set about freeing the others: apparently she could still see them within this strange patch of shadow Morlock had made. The most terrible moment came when Stador's body slumped to the earth, half out of the zone of shadow, and Thend saw that his face was slack and lifeless, the wreath of sacrificial flowers falling from his head. He was dead, unmistakably dead. The others emerged, tearing the wreaths from their heads, alive but bleeding.

No, Fasra wasn't bleeding. He had saved at least one of his family, at least one, if they could get away.

Meanwhile the Khroic horde was swarming about the base of the cliff, just below where the illusion-prisoners were. Someone was bound to look back here sooner or later. So Thend's heart fell when his mother stooped down to pick up Stador's dead body.

"Leave him," Roble said, his voice harsh with the horror of what he was saying. "He's dead."

Naeli looked up, her dark eyes blazing. "With those *things* in him? No!"

Thend knew exactly what she meant. The eggs would hatch; the hatchlings would eat their way through Stador's dead flesh, the way the spiderfolk had eaten the Lost One. If they brought the corpse away they could burn it or something, deny their enemies a future from Stador's death. He grabbed Stador's legs. Roble muttered under his breath and helped him and so did Bann, weeping silently. Together they hustled the corpse up the slope toward the crest. If they could only make it that far, Thend thought, they would be safe. He didn't know why he felt that way, but he did.

But they didn't make it that far. Suddenly there was a roaring that drowned out even the chaos of Khroic voices, and the sky was filled with a fiery light that made the bonfires look dim. The guile of dragons had come. Now the dragons would hunt them down, just like before. There was no escape. There never had been a chance of it, just a false hope. He stumbled and nearly fell as he continued to run, burdened by Stador's dead body. He noted without understanding that they were casting no shadows on the ground, that they were moving within a patch of shadow. Then he did understand.

The others were now muttering with despair, echoing his own, and Roble was saying, "If we have to die, I'd rather try to fight—"

"Listen, I don't think they can see us," Thend said hurriedly. "It's something Morlock is doing."

"I saw us on the cliff," Fasra said quietly, in a dim lost way that made Thend want to weep; he wasn't sure why.

Shockingly, Roble snickered. "That sneaky bastard," he said. "How did you get away from the dragons, Thend? Another one of Morlock's tricks?"

Thend remembered the mutilated blue dragon, its red eyes fading as its corpse cooled in the moonlight. "Sort of," he said. "Tell you later."

"They're killing them," Fasra said, in that same vague oh-look-at-that tone. "They're killing all of them. Us, too."

They were at the crest, but they turned then to see what she was talking about.

The Khroi and the dragons were fighting. Many of the Khroi were already dead, and one of the dragons lay smoldering between the bonfires. Several dragons were smashing the base of the cliff with their tails, burying the illusion-prisoners in shattered stone.

"Why?" gasped Naeli.

Thend thought he knew. Another one of Morlock's tricks, indeed: why else had he put up images of himself, of Thend, of the Lost Khroi and the werewolf? They were the dragons' prizes, but Morlock had made it look as if the horde had stolen them from the guile. He must have known how the fiercely greedy dragons would react. . . .

Then the cliff gave way and the mountainside fell into the narrow valley, nearly filling it. The shock blew Thend and his family off their feet, and when they arose they saw that the horde had been completely destroyed. Several of the dragons had been caught in the collapse and struggled feebly in the smoking rubble, but their former compatriots left them there and flew away: north, west, south, east, alone.

Choking from the dust, they hauled Stador's corpse over the crest of the (now very shallow) valley and put him down not far from Morlock.

The crooked man was returning from his vision, the werewolf standing over him. His sword was dark, and presently he opened his eyes. He sheathed his sword and struggled to his feet.

The werewolf, backing away, snarled at him.

"Probably," Morlock replied. "I thank you, though."

The werewolf disappeared into the moonlit, dust-choked night.

"He thinks he's safer travelling alone," Morlock remarked. "Poor old Stador," he said, his eyes falling on the dead body. "It was a grim death."

"Maybe you can think of a better one for the rest of us," Naeli whispered. "Except for Fasra and Thend. Take care of them, please."

"I'm not a deviser of comfortable deaths," Morlock rasped. "If Thend helps me, we can cut those eggs from you before they hatch. The Khroi aren't like the spiderfolk; there may only be three or four eggs in each of you. It will hurt worse than death, and then you may die anyway . . ."

"Of course!" Thend said. "Mother, we can do this. I'll go into deep vision, and I can tell Morlock where to cut."

Both Naeli and Morlock turned to look at him. Then they looked at each other. "Something like that," Morlock said.

"Well," Naeli said wearily, "as long as he isn't a miner . . ."

So the long night after the long day was followed by another long day. They found a cave where Morlock and he faced the terrible task of cutting open his kin to save their lives, then sewing them up like old clothes with thread and patches. Then they faced the easier, but somehow even more ghoulish task of extracting the Khroi eggs from Stador's dead body. At last they buried Stador in a cairn of stones.

Naeli started to weep then, and she wept until she fell asleep, and even then she sobbed from time to time. Thend sat by her until she slept, wishing he could do something to ease her pain, sorry for her, tired of her. Tired of everything, really. That was the problem with surviving: you had so much work to do!

He pointed this out to Morlock, when all the others were asleep, and Morlock said, "Rest then. I'll watch."

Thend shook his head wearily, although he knew he would sleep soon no matter what. He said to Morlock, "So you did destroy them, in the end. They were right about you."

"No," Morlock replied.

Thend knew he was on dangerous ground. He was too stupid to think of shrewd questions, but he needed Morlock to say something more than this. He tried to express this all by opening his hands and grumbling a bit.

Morlock looked at him with a one-sided smile for a time and said, "Should I have lain down and died for Marh Valone's convenience? Should I have let him kill you, your whole family, simply to settle his fears? He would have found something else to be afraid of, Thend. Those who rule by fear will always be ruled by it, until they are destroyed by it. Now, at last, Marh Valone need fear no more."

"So that's why you did it? A sort of mercy killing?"

"I did not kill Marh Valone. He turned a blade on himself when the dragons appeared over the Vale of the Mother. You should sleep."

"I can't stand the thought of sleeping," Thend admitted. "I'm afraid of the visions."

"It won't be so bad," said Morlock, and unstoppered a green bottle he held in his hand. A green bird flew out and circled round Thend's head, and before he knew it he was dreaming.

His dream was a vision, but in truth it wasn't as bad as he had feared. He saw the seers of Valona's horde, fleeing into the eastern mountains, along with a few of the Virgin Sisters. They carried with them an infant girl-Khroi they had anointed with Royal Chrism. They were already calling her Valona: the horde would go on.

They saw him, too, for the Khroic seers always walk in vision, and one seer's vision encompasses another.

We will remember you, Horde Mate of the Lost One, they said, not with words.

All right, Thend replied in the same fashion. *Remember the Lost One, too. He was better than any of you.*

Thend turned away from them in a direction that was neither up, nor down, nor any side. It was still a little frightening, but he wouldn't let the fear rule him. Turning away from the past, he looked straight into the future.

NAELI'S STORY

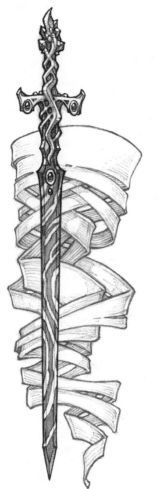

XI

WHISPER STREET

AN OLD MAN STIRS THE FIRE TO A BLAZE,
IN THE HOUSE OF A CHILD, OF A FRIEND, OF A
    BROTHER.
HE HAS OVER-LINGERED HIS WELCOME; THE
    DAYS,
GROWN DESOLATE, WHISPER AND SIGH TO
    EACH OTHER.
           —YEATS, *WANDERINGS OF OISIN*

admit it: I liked him at first. That's partly due to the kind of men I'd been buried in for more than a dozen years: half-witted townies who thought a youngish widow was anybody's meat; needle-toothed Bargainers who thought of anybody as meat for their God in the Ground. Morlock wasn't much to look at, maybe, but he wasn't like that. Plus he had very impressive hands: strong and many-skilled. I remember the first time I saw him lacing up both his shoes simultaneously, one hand per shoe, while keeping up his side of a conversation (as much as he ever did, anyway). Or the time my fifteen-year-old Thend bent his knife, using it as a prybar. Morlock took the blade, a steel blade mind you, in his hands and bent it back. It wasn't quite straight, but at least it would fit into the scabbard. Then that night, when we made camp, he set up a kind of portable forge full of flames that talked back to him, and he remade the blade better than before—all without a word of recrimination. And anytime a crow came by he would have a conversation with it, tossing it grain from his pocket for bits of semi-useless information. And he did this stuff like someone buying a pound of cheese: it was perfectly ordinary. How can you not like a man like that?

Well: I learned. It started the first time one of my children came back from one of his crazy expeditions bruised, bleeding, and unconscious. This is not the way to win a mother's heart. The world is full of dangers, and one of them is going to kill every one of us eventually: as a reasonable person, I accept this. As a mother, I don't and never will; I refuse to be reasonable about risks to my children, and the risks seemed to increase any time Morlock was in the neighborhood.

By the time we reached Narkunden, north of the Kirach Kund, one of my children was actually dead: Stador, my oldest boy, had been killed by the Khroi in the mountains. I don't want to talk about it except—no, I don't want to talk about it at all. It's enough to say that we were there because of Morlock and I blamed him for it. I still do.

I was the only one, it seemed. My brother Roble thought the world of Morlock, and so did my children, my surviving children. He would do the most remarkable things. For instance, we settled in Narkunden for a while to heal up (most of us were wounded by the Khroi—yes, those are the scars you've noticed on me). Morlock and my sons built a weird crooked little house on the edge of town, right by the river, and he set up a workshop on the top floor and he started to make things for sale in the city; that's what we mostly lived on, before we opened up the Mystery Zone.

The Mystery Zone was a hallway that ran around one corner of the house, and Morlock had fixed it somehow that you could walk up the wall and stand on the ceiling. It began as a nuisance-distraction. People knew Morlock lived in the crooked house, and they were always trying to bribe us to let them into his workshop when they thought he wasn't around. Actually, he didn't care, but we were sick of it, so he built the Zone onto the house and suggested we run them through there instead. My daughter, Fasra, dreamed up a line of patter to go with it—how a magical experiment had shattered the law of gravity locally, and how the place was somewhat dangerous to enter. We made them sign a contract not to sue us if they were maimed or killed by the wild magic of the Mystery Zone. That made them wild to get in; pretty soon we were making more money from the Mystery Zone than anything else.

"Why not just make a bucketful of gold and save all the footwork?" I asked Morlock once. He could literally do that; I'd seen him. (Yes, it seems like an awfully convenient skill to have, but, no, I don't know his recipe.)

"Against the law," he answered. Apparently Narkunden didn't like having their markets flooded with artificial gold and they'd passed a law, so that any sorcerer who wanted to spend money in the city had to show proof he'd earned the stuff, not made it. I didn't believe this until one of these guys actually showed up at the door one day and demanded to go through our books, and even then I couldn't quite believe it. I mean, I had lived most of my life under the dictatorship of a monster who fed on human souls, but at least he didn't send agents to root around in your cash box.

"So why stay here?" I asked Morlock after the first of these regular visits.

He grunted at me. He actually does that: you say something to him like a person, and he just makes a sort of noise.

Anyway, his latest gimmick was glass. He'd noticed that some types of glass seemed to slow down light, so he made glass that slowed it down even more—incredibly slow. There were chunks of it scattered around the house, still holding the luminous image of a leaf or a sunset or a face that had been trapped in them days ago. Bann, my eldest (surviving), was excited by this and got Morlock to teach him how to do it: his idea was that you could create a block of glass that would slow down the light passing through it to a full stop, creating perfect and permanent images of things.

Meanwhile Morlock's mind was moving in a different direction. One morning he appeared at breakfast holding a big lens of gray glass and wearing a half smile that, for him, was a shout of triumph.

"Um," my brother Roble said, peering through the lens. "This is maybe the murkiest piece of glass I've ever seen."

"Keep an eye on Naeli," Morlock suggested.

Roble swivelled to face me and I saw his brown eye quite clearly through the glass.

"Naeli, would you wave your hand?" Morlock said.

Exasperated, I flipped him a gesture I'd learned among the Bargainers.

"Wait a second!" Roble said. "She moved before you asked her! This thing sees into the future!"

"Yes."

My sons, Bann and Thend, and even my daughter, Fasra (who hadn't been showing much interest in anything since that terrible night when Stador died), looked intrigued and swarmed behind Roble, peering at the glass over his shoulder.

"It's so murky—I can hardly see anything," Bann complained.

By now Roble was holding the lens up high so they could peer through it. I caught a glimpse of my children, my surviving children, a corsage of expectant quizzical looks in the bright glass.

"I don't know what you mean," I said. "I can see you all clearly."

"Your mouth moved before you spoke!" Thend called. I heard his voice before I saw his lips move. Then I understood the glass worked two ways, and I was seeing a few seconds into the past. I wondered if a lens could be built for me to somehow see Stador again, alive and well and happy. And I wondered if I would dare to look through it if I held it in my hand.

"How does it work?" Bann asked.

If you want to get Morlock to run his mouth, ask him a question like that. They started talking about a bunch of things I neither understood nor wanted to. But in the end Bann said, "But why is the glass so cloudy?"

"The future hasn't happened yet," I said impatiently. "The odds of you seeing any particular event are very low."

Silence. If you want to shock your children, show them you have a little intelligence. "Flip the glass," I suggested. "The other side looks into the past and everything is very clear. All those events are fixed."

They did, and now I was looking into the lens of the future. Seen through the glass, my children's healthy brown skins wore the grayish sheen of death. Their eyes were almost invisible, shadowed by uncertainty. I looked away. Someday, they would die, and I would die, and everyone would die, and I couldn't blame it all on Morlock. But somehow, just then, I wanted to.

Now Bann was holding the glass and walking around the room. "I see furniture clearer than people," he said, "but the walls and floor and ceiling are clearer than the furniture. Is that because their positions are more certain in the future?"

"Exactly," Morlock said approvingly.

Bann passed the glass to Thend and stared off at nothing. After a moment or two he turned to Morlock and said, "Would the positions of some people be more certain than others? A watchman who has a fixed route at a fixed time, or . . . ?"

Morlock shrugged and opened his hands. He seemed to expect we would know what that meant.

"Let's go down to the street and check!" Thend shouted, and ran out the door. We all trailed after him.

The street was full of passersby. We were on the edge of the city of Narkunden, but Narkunden's sister city Aflraun was right across the nearby Nar River, and when the city-states weren't actually at war, there was a brisk traffic back and forth across the bridges. I didn't enter into the discussion about whether some people were easier to see than others, because I really didn't give a damn. I'd only followed the others out to make sure that Morlock didn't kill one of my children by accident in the street.

Oh, you think I'm exaggerating? All right: so I'm in the street standing next to Morlock as he holds the lens. And he's flipping it back and forth to get the contrast between a-few-seconds-past and a-few-seconds-future. While he's gazing through the past lens I look idly past him and see someone standing behind him. In the real world, this other guy's just standing there, making a kind of shrugging motion. In the future glass, he's stabbing Morlock in the neck.

I punched him. No, not Morlock, though I kind of wanted to: the other guy, the guy about to stab him. I hit him hard, right on an eye, and the eye burst like a rotten grape, and some kind of darkish foul fluid that wasn't blood poured out.

Roble had seen it too, and Morlock instantly figured out what was happening (whatever he is, he isn't stupid), and they each grabbed one of the guy's arms. He had a knife in each hand, and I shouted to the children to get back in the house. They looked at me uncertainly, as if they were about to refuse, but then they looked at me closer and decided there might be something scarier in the street than a guy with two knives and they ran back inside. I didn't need any glass to see the future: the next time I gave them an order like that they might not obey it. But that was tomorrow's problem; I turned back to today's, which, like most of my problems, involved Morlock.

He and Roble each had one of the assassin's arms in both of their hands. I stood free, ready to help if needed or take the guy down if he wriggled loose (as he was struggling to do).

Suddenly the assassin stood still. Maybe he realized that he just wasn't going to get away. There was something weird about his face, apart from the rotten-smelling goo leaking over it. It was totally expressionless, even when he was fighting, like he wasn't really there somehow. The pale features had a blue-green cast, like a corpse.

"Let me go," he said in a voice as dead as his face. "I will self-bind not to harm you or yours."

"No," said Morlock.

"I can buy my freedom with knowledge," said the man with the smashed eye. "I can tell you so many things, so many secrets."

"I know who sent you," Morlock said coldly. "Shall I tell you a secret? Demons are not immortal."

The man with the broken eye screamed. Except, I guess, maybe he wasn't a man. He screamed and screamed. Then he fell limp to the ground, and the knives clattered on the stones of the street.

"Street-killings, even in self-defense, are an implicit violation of your residency contract," a scandalized voice remarked.

I groaned. Of course! The city government sent this weedy pale fellow, Glemmurn, once a month to inspect our books and make sure that we weren't spending more money than we actually earned in the city. And today, of all days, was the date for our inspection.

"We didn't kill him," Roble observed. "All we did was defend ourselves when he attacked us. And in fact—this body's been dead for some time: give it a niff."

Glemmurn, his pale face greenish with horror, stepped toward the corpse with the broken eye, took one whiff of the air surrounding it, and staggered backward. "Savage Triumphator!" he groaned. "An unregistered zombie!"

"Don't worry," I said. (The poor thrept seemed really horrified.) "It's dead, or dezombied, or whatever you call it."

"You don't understand!" he wailed. "That just creates more paperwork: unauthorized deactivization of an unregistered zombie is itself a code violation—there will be incident reports and witness affidavits and second-death certificates and tax assessments on the labor of the zombie and tax-penalty assessments on the unpaid labor taxes. . . . I'll be in the office all night long. And I promised to take my nonobligated semipartner Zaria to the election rally this evening out at Remer Fields."

"Well, there'll be other election rallies," I said.

He looked at me as if he suspected I might be an unregistered zombie myself. "Of course there will," he said sadly, "but she won't need to wait for one. My meta-cousin Vestavion will be all too willing to escort her tonight. That serial monogamist, that man-of-many-contented-partners, that winsome glib glad-footer! After all: you know the effect election rallies have on women. The speeches! The chanting! The policy presentations! It makes them crazy. I might as well start saving up now for their wedding morsel: they're as good as preengaged."

"Look—" I said, hoping to stop him before he confided in me again.

"I've warned her about him," he said confidingly. "But he's an accountant with a private banking firm, and I think she's swept up in the glamour of all that—"

"This was not a zombie," Morlock observed.

"I could have been a banker, but I like to work in the open—What did you say?"

Morlock said it again.

"What is it then? Or what was it, rather?"

"A harthrang," Morlock said, and stopped. As if, you know, that explained everything.

"Don't keep us waiting, Morlock," Roble said after a second or two. "What's a harthrang?"

"A demon possessing a corpse," said Morlock, as if he were saying, *We've run out of onions.*

"Impossible," quacked Glemmurn. "The municipal demon-shields are—"

"—flawed," Morlock interrupted, and gestured at the corpse with the smashed eye.

"Ur. Well. I'll still need a certificate of second death from a physician. And I suppose I'll have to write up a brief incident report and a crematorium deposit-slip. But," he added, brightening up as he went on, "I won't need any witness affidavits, and there won't be any tax forms at all to file. If I postpone a couple of visits until tomorrow, I could be out of the office before sunset, and rally here we come. Hm. Yes. Yes indeed. Oh, Zaria, Zaria, grant me the blessings of your sweet franchise—That is. Yes. I think I'll make an official determination that this was a harthrang, not an unregistered zombie. If, of course, you'll submit a letter of support addressed to my board of advisors, describing the harthrang phenomenon and the steps you took to neutralize the demon—How did you neutralize it, by the way?"

"He scared it away," said Roble.

Poor pasty-faced Glemmurn looked at my brother (what a study in contrasts!), looked at the corpse with the smashed eye, looked at grim crooked Morlock and said, "Yes, the board will accept that, I think."

I went back into the crooked house and sent Thend to fetch the physician next door, a red-haired bundle of self-regard who went by the modest moniker of Reijka Kingheart.

"I'll go!" hollered Fasra, when she heard me talking to Thend.

"You won't," I said. "Glemmurn is out there, and he'll be in here in a minute to look at the books. You're the only one who understands them—"

"Oh, come on!"

"—and you're going to explain them to him. Thend: go." Thend looked at me, not angry, almost sad. Of all of us who survived, I think Thend was the one who'd been changed the most by our trip through the mountains. He was only fifteen, but he was getting the poise and the patience of a grown man, and his deep brown eyes seemed to see deeply into everything they looked at. I often had the uncomfortable sense that he was humoring me, going along with this farce of a parent-child relationship because it was important to me. But he went and did as I told him; that was the main thing.

"Stupid old Glemmurn," Fasra grumbled, approximately. "I wish he were in a sewer somewhere. I *like* Reijka, Mama."

I sort of hated Reijka's guts, but I didn't say so. "She'll be over here in a minute," I said, "and she'll probably want to have a look at our wounds before she goes. She always does."

Fasra quietly slammed open the cash drawer and demurely yanked out the bound volume where we kept track of our accounts and gently smashed it down on the counter.

"Don't tear any pages," I said as she flipped open the account book.

"I have *my* emotions well under control, thank you," she said, with a searing glance from her bright black eyes. "Now, let's see: when was that *stupid, greasy, dough-faced* bucket of *dumbness* last here?"

I told her and stepped back out into the street.

Reijka Kingheart was there, examining the twice-dead corpse and somehow simultaneously giving Roble the eye. I could have told her it was a waste of time—Roble isn't much for the ladies—but why do her any favors? For one thing, she was a Coranian. I'm not a bigot; I just hate all those pasty-faced shifty bastards.

If you can stand to look at someone whose skin is the color of spilled milk, I guess she wasn't bad. And whatever charms she had, the whole street knew about them. Personally, I don't care whether a woman shows her arms and legs on the street, if they can bear the examination, but I think that the design she tattoos on her sagging middle-aged nipples should be a secret shared with a range of acquaintance narrow enough to exclude me. But the sheer fabric Reijka used for her body-wrap made the whole world her close personal friend.

Glemmurn was obviously impressed, and as she rose from where she had been crouching beside the dead body I thought he was going to ask for the bounty of her franchise, and to hell with nonobligated semipartner Zaria. But then she told him she wasn't going to fill out his stupid paperwork and his face turned to stone.

"This body has been dead for several days; decomposition is well established. I found several symbols carved into the flesh that appear to be the anchors for some sort of reanimating spell. I attest it to you in the presence of these gentlemen—and this lady," she said, nodding companionably toward me. I'd have corrected her about my status (and theirs) except that in Narkunden everyone is a gentleperson, even noncitizens like us. "But I'm not going to go to your office and swear out a statement in front of a justiciar. Not unless you're going to pay me for my time."

"Citizen Kingheart, my department's budget—"

"Listen, I have the same budget as you: thirty hours a day, no more or less. If you want a significant amount of my time, compensate me. You know as well as I do that you can put all our names and statements in your report and that will be as good as an affidavit, since agents have field-justiciar status for the purpose of taking testimony."

"Yes, but I don't like to use it unless it's necessary."

"Great weeping walnuts: be a man. Don't do any paperwork for him, gentlemen. He only wants it to bulk up his files. They weigh it all at the end of the year, and the bureaucrat with the heaviest stack gets some sort of promotion. That's what my ex-obligated full-partner used to say, anyway."

"Citizen Kingheart, I must caution you not to encourage resident contractees to shirk—"

"I *am* a citizen, and I know my rights and theirs. Anyway, don't you have a date tonight? Zaria was telling me about it. You want to stand here all day talking?"

Glemmurn jumped like he'd been stung by a queck-bug and looked anxiously up at the sun. "All right," he said. "I'd better check the books inside before I leave. Just pin your second-death certificate to the corpse."

"Done."

"Er. Someone should—"

"I'll take it to the body dump," Morlock said.

"Hurry back, Ambrosius," Reijka said. "I've got a proposition for you. Not the one you've been dreaming of either."

"Eh," said Morlock, but I didn't like the way he said it—a little more cordial than his usual grunt. I was worried that he too might be susceptible to her autumnal charms. (The woman was seven years older than me at least. Not that it's any big deal; I'm just saying.) He stuffed a rag in the body's broken eye and tossed it over his shoulder as he walked away up the street.

"I like a man who's not afraid to get his hands dirty," Reijka said, which was so much like what I was thinking that it made me mad. "I'd better go inside, too—see how you all are healing up," she added.

"Any excuse to get my clothes off, is that it?" Roble bantered at her.

"They are rotten clothes," she agreed smoothly. "Though looking at skin as hairy as yours won't be much of an improvement. Don't you ever shave your shoulders?"

"No. Do you?"

I turned away. Again, I could have told her that Roble didn't care for girls much, but she was a big enough girl to find that out for herself.

Reijka examined Roble and Bann first while I hovered nervously nearby and Glemmurn looked over our books with Fasra. Presently I heard Fasra's voice rising, and I reluctantly abandoned my post to see what was happening.

Fasra was not actually upset. She was explaining with some enthusiasm the biggest source of income showing in our books, the Mystery Zone. Glemmurn was looking more skeptical by the second.

"I don't understand," he was saying as I came up to them. "How can anyone stand on a wall? And how can that result in money coming into your cashbox? I'm afraid—"

"The money's easy," I interrupted. "People give it to us. For the rest, I'd better show you. Fasra, we'd better tell Glemmurn all we know about this."

I was telling her it was time to baffle him with brilliance. Fasra smiled gently and nodded. We left the books and the cash box in Thend's care and together we led Glemmurn to the Mystery Zone part of the house.

"What we tell the rubes," Fasra explained, "is that an uncontrolled outburst of Morlock's magic shattered the laws of gravity locally."

"Name of a nameless name!" Glemmurn gasped in shock.

"Oh, that's just nonsense," I reassured the pasty little man. "Really, Morlock and Bann built the thing. We don't know how it works, but no laws were broken—'natural or local,' as Morlock says."

We led Glemmurn through the Gate of Shadows (a dimly lit anteroom) and into the Mystery Zone (a sort of hallway that ran around one corner of the crooked house). He watched solemnly as Fasra walked up a wall and poured herself a cup of water, and the water flowed uphill from where he was standing. She went through the elaborate patter we give the rubes, and then explained the actual situation as best we understood it. She really was dazzling: that girl could talk a landfish into a kettle of boiling water. And then, because he still wasn't saying anything, she did the same thing again.

He still hadn't said anything when we led him back out of the Mystery Zone, but he was shaking his head slowly. Reijka, Roble, and the boys were sitting around the counter where we kept the cashbox and the books, deep in conversation about something, but they broke off and looked up as we approached. At that point, Glemmurn realized it was his turn to say something.

"I am deeply concerned," he said.

That was when I knew we were screwed.

"Not only are you earning money through magical means," he continued, "but you are also engaging in deliberate deception. When you tell visitors—"

"Oh, that's just for entertainment purposes," Reijka interrupted. "No one really believes it. They just started giving tours in the Mystery Zone because everyone was sneaking up to the back door and trying to bribe their way into Morlock's workshop."

I felt I could grow to love this woman.

"Nevertheless," Glemmurn said doggedly, "I find that these noncitizen residents have been conducting business in a magical structure nonapproved by city regulating authorities. I appreciate the fact that Morlock Ambrosius may be reluctant to reveal the, er, sorcerous secrets of this, er, 'Mystery Zone,' but I must insist—"

"It's a four-dimensional polytope," Morlock's voice said.

We all jumped a little. For a guy with a bad leg, he moves pretty sneakily: no one heard him come in.

"A what?" Glemmurn asked.

"It's a four-dimensional polytope—a structure which exists in four dimensions. There's a fifth-dimensional sheath, also. Gravity is more malleable in the fifth dimension."

"I don't wish to be party to your, er, sorcerous knowledge—"

"Eh. I never know what people mean by 'sorcerous.'" Morlock seemed miffed, possibly because he had been tempted into saying more than three words in a row, and looking around the room afterward, he realized he might as well have kept his mouth shut for all the good it had done. Bann might have understood him; the rest of us didn't. He added gruffly, "Consult the mathematicians in your Lyceum. There used to be a pretty good geometer on the faculty."

"But still, the deception involved—"

Of course it was hopeless. When somebody says "but still" they mean, *You may be right but I'll never change my mind no matter what you say.*

He didn't, either. When Reijka threatened him with her semipartner the professional litigator, he agreed to take the case to his superiors, but in the meantime we were embargoed from spending any money in the city of Narkunden.

"If that's all you can say," Reijka concluded, "you might as well get out of here and spread your peculiar brand of joy in someone else's life. And I hope Zaria takes up exclusive full-partnership with Vestavion. He may be a bit of an oily fledge, but at least he isn't a dusty old droop with his cranny full of queck-bugs."

It takes a person with a certain amount of character to stand up in the face of unanimous disapproval from a roomful of people, and Glemmurn wasn't made that way. He babbled something about "just doing the job," then fled before any of us could give him our opinion of his job.

"Well," Reijka said, breaking the dismal silence that Glemmurn left behind him, "if his bosses don't reverse him, I'll take the matter up with the borough syndic. But for the time being you'll have to shop across the river in Aflraun, I guess."

"Why didn't we settle in Aflraun in the first place?" Fasra wondered. "It's a lot more wide open there."

Roble looked at Morlock and, when it was clear the crooked man was not going to say anything, said, "We needed a place to heal up, after the mountains. And it's safer here."

"Except for harthrangs," Morlock added thoughtfully. "There might be a few more around town: bodies have been disappearing from the graveyards. That's what they were saying at the body dump. I'll place a demon-sconce around the house."

"You'll want Bann and Thend to help with that, I guess," I said. (He always did: Thend for Seeing, Bann for Making.) "I'll go across the river and buy us a couple days' worth of food. Roble, why don't you and Fasra hold the fort here?"

"Holding the fort is boring," Fasra grumbled. "I'll never get any interesting scars that way."

When I realized she was referring to our nightmare among the Khroi, I was speechless for a moment. I had been on the verge of suggesting that Stador come along with me and do the heavy lifting, and suddenly I remembered that Stador was dead and rotting in a hole in the mountains. And here she was making a joke about it. On the other hand, Fasra's jokes were rare and fragile things these days. I wanted to cloud up and storm at her, but in the end I just said lightly, "You could get a scar. Sooner than you think."

"I think she means it, kid," Reijka said, grinning at me. "Never mind. I'll stick around and we'll write an angry letter to the syndic and a friendly one to my litigator."

"Why not the other way around?"

"The litigators are the ones who run this town. The syndics and bureaucrats just think they do . . ."

I grabbed a bag of money off the counter and walked out the door. It was a little brusque, but I wanted to get out of hearing range before I started snuffling. In fact, I made it almost all the way to the Aresion Bridge over the River Nar when suddenly for some reason I remembered how Stador had looked in the green-and-gold shirt he had worn to his first Castleday when he was six years old. It wasn't like I was trying to remember it; the image forced its way into my mind. It was followed by a wave of others and I had to stand there in the middle of the street, clutching my bag of coins and weeping, until the tide of memories receded and I could think about something else again. That's how grief works for me. It's always there, but you can almost forget about it for a while; you think you might be over it. Then it drags you down and drowns you in itself.

What can I say? I don't know if you have kids. If you do, I suggest you die before they do. It'll save you a lot of trouble.

Eventually, I made it to the bridge. The Narkundenside guards gave me kind of a funny look; maybe they'd been watching me weep. But they didn't say anything about it: they just asked to see my proof-of-residence. By the time I'd crossed the bridge to Aflraunside, my eyes were dry (if somewhat sore) and the guards there didn't even glance at my card; they just wanted their bridge toll.

Aflraun is a lot livelier than Narkunden. If you want a banker, a bookkeeper, an academic, you go to Narkunden. If you want to buy or sell something, if you want to fight with somebody, if you want to become famous (or at least notorious), you go to Aflraun.

For one thing, the towns are run very differently. Narkunden has a democratic charter where the syndics go to the people for reelection every year, and any important law has to be passed by a citizen assembly, and all citizens get the same vote. Aflraun, on the other hand, is a democratic timocracy. All citizens get a vote, but your vote counts more depending on how important you are. You can acquire importance (the technical term is "gradient") through money, or other achievements, but one of the most common ways to achieve it is through dueling, as the victor in a duel automatically inherits the timocratic gradient of the person he kills.

Noncitizens aren't exempt from the constant duelling, but noncombatants are: duellists actually lose gradient if they are seen challenging or provoking someone not carrying unconcealed weapons.

More people prefer to live in Narkunden: it's safe, quiet, law abiding. But they swarm over the bridges to spend money and time in Aflraun. Commercial magic is not illegal there; neither is prostitution (another way to gain gradient, but apparently only if you do it right) nor public brawling nor most other things.

Then there is Whisper Street. I find it hard to explain Whisper Street; you'll have to bear with me for a moment. It is a place where, for a fee, you can become invisible and say anything you want. Physical contact is forbidden (not that it doesn't happen sometimes), but no speech of any sort is regulated. You can be anyone or anything that you want, as long as you can convince someone else of it. Apparently it is the city's great moneymaker, greater than people coming to watch the duels or engage in the gray-market activities banned in Narkunden and elsewhere. Whisper Street gets a little longer every year, to accommodate all the people who want to participate. Morlock said to me once that someday the whole city will be inside Whisper Street, and I'm not sure he was joking.

I'm not a fan of Whisper Street. If you'd ever been a widowed mother in Four Castles, you would have had your fill of being invisible. That's one thing. Then, after that, I was a Bargainer, kidnapping people on the Road, robbing them and carrying them away to the God in the Ground. I did it because I had to do it to save my daughter. I'll tell you the whole story sometime if you're in the mood to listen. But the point was that I was always doing things I hated. "This isn't me," I had to keep saying. "This isn't me."

But you are what you do. It *was* me, doing all those terrible things. I escaped when I could. But while I was there, that's what I did and that's what I was. What was I, now that I had escaped? I still wasn't sure. But, in any case, I didn't want to take my face off and pretend to be somebody else. I wasn't that sure I could ever find myself again. Maybe this doesn't make any sense: it was how I felt.

The point is, I had to cross Whisper Street to get to the main market of Aflraun, but I didn't want to participate. You have to pay to become invisible on Whisper Street, but you pay a little more to not become invisible: they give you a little wreath to wear that exempts you from the spell. I paid my fee, got my wreath, and started to make my way across the broad empty avenue, jostled by whispering people who didn't seem to be there.

It can be pretty icky, and it was that time. I passed by a group of people who were discussing in low tones their sexual practices involving overripe fruit. A couple others were shrieking at each other a set of accusations involving serial murder, treason, and genocide. The argument seemed to have started over a difference of opinion about some athlete or politician, but even that wasn't clear.

I was about halfway across when a voice spoke insinuatingly in my ear, "Why do you travel with the man who killed your son?"

I didn't think the comment was addressed to me. Crossing Whisper Street you're apt to hear almost anything, and you'll go crazy if you try to take even half of it half seriously. Still, the voice had struck a particularly raw nerve. "Drop dead," I muttered, and would have passed on.

"It's Stador who's dead, and Morlock who killed him," the voice said, keeping up with me.

I stopped in my tracks and snatched at the direction the voice had come from. Of course he (I was sure it was a he) avoided me easily. "Who are you, you coward?" I snarled.

"I'll wait for you in the portico by the Badonhill Hostel," said the voice. "Ask for Aurelius: that's who I am."

"I've got more important business than interviewing liars—"

"Then do it. I said I'll wait for you. Good-bye, Naeli the Cat."

That really frightened me. Naeli does mean "the cat" in the homespeech my mother and father used to speak. I never learned much of it: they wanted me to speak Coranian and Castellan (the language they call Ontilian in the Empire of Ontil). In the north a few people knew Coranian, and many spoke dialects of Castellan/Ontilian. But I had never met anyone outside of Four Castles who knew the homespeech of my parents. It gave me this weird feeling that the speaker knew more about me than I knew myself. I didn't like it, so I shouted at him for a while, but he didn't speak again.

I bought the food, and I sent it back to the crooked house in Narkunden by way of a chartered porter. When my hands were free I asked my way to the Badonhill Hostel. It was northward, not too far from the Camlann Bridge, more than two miles downriver. With all the walking I had already done, it didn't sound appealing. But by then I already knew I was going to go confront Aurelius, so I went.

The Badonhill Hostel looked like the oldest building in the city, but it was in extremely good repair. It towered over a small market area, but there wasn't much business going on that day. In the portico outside the hostel there were tables, and at one of them a man was sitting who looked even older than the building, if possible, but also in extremely good repair. He wore a white cloak over blue clothes; he was reading a book sewn into a blue binding with a white star on the cover. He looked up as I approached: dark blue eyes under white bristling eyebrows.

"You're Aurelius, I bet," I said.

"You win the bet," he said. He didn't rise but gestured at a chair and said, "Won't you sit down? My people will bring you something."

"Your—" I said, sitting across from him.

He rapped his knuckles, and a blue-and-white-clad servant appeared from a door I hadn't noticed in the wall of the hostel behind Aurelius.

"Would you like something to eat? Something to drink?"

"Not until I know what this is about."

He laughed and said, "Tea for me, Zyrn. Bring two cups, in case she changes her mind." The servant stepped back into the doorway and disappeared.

"What's your interest in Morlock?" I asked. "And why are you bothering me about it?"

He didn't answer. He looked at me assessingly and after a moment said, "I suppose I can see it. You resemble Morlock's wife somewhat: a crude copy of a more sophisticated original—"

"His *wife?*" I snapped, nearly jumping out of my chair. I'd had no idea Morlock was married. It seemed as odd as a tree stump or a broken boulder being married.

"Well, ex-wife," Aurelius conceded. "His exile from the Wardlands technically dissolved the union. But I'm a little old-fashioned, and I don't think these bonds are so easily broken. I see he didn't tell you about her. Well, maybe that's not significant. He doesn't *talk* much, does he?"

"What's this about?" I demanded. "What are you getting at?"

"I'd rather go at this slower," Aurelius admitted, "but I realize you don't have all day. I am interested, as you put it, in Morlock for a number of reasons, but the most urgent one is that he's trying to kill my wife. I'm bothering you about it because he's already killed one of your sons and may succeed in destroying your entire family."

What he said about my family was so like what I feared that I froze for a moment. But I didn't want to give him a single clue how close to my heart he had struck, so I said, as calmly as I could, "My son was killed by the Khroi. Morlock wasn't even present at the time. I was, though, and there was nothing I could do about it. Thanks for reminding me, you heartless bastard."

"I'm sorry," he said, with every appearance of regret. "Really I am. I'm trying to appeal to you through your wounded heart because we have a common interest, a desperately serious one. I ask you to think about this painful subject only to avoid more pain for yourself and your family. Of course the Khroi killed Stador, but who was really responsible? The Khroi aren't much more than animals. Why were you in that mountain pass? Would you ever have gone there but for him? And now your son is dead."

"You don't give a damn about my son. About any of us."

"That's true, in a way," he admitted cheerfully. "You're nothing to me. But my wife is. We can help each other. We must help each other. We must save what we can of the people we love."

I met his blue eyes and, Strange Gods forgive me, he looked earnest. More than that: honest. Like I could trust him. And I wanted to believe him. It let me off the hook, you see. Morlock had warned us and warned us that the Kirach Kund was dangerous, and we hadn't listened to him. Of course, he hadn't given us all the details. If he had, we would have chosen differently, of course. Of course we would have. That made it his fault, not ours. It had to be that way. It had to be that way, because if Morlock wasn't responsible, then we were. Or, more precisely, I was. I had killed my son.

I said nothing as all of this was chewing through my brains. Zyrn, the blue-and-white-clad servant, brought the tea and vanished again, without Aurelius so much as looking at him. The old man poured us each a cup of tea, sweetening his own with honey and milk from jars on the table and leaving mine black. We both drank. The cups emptied and Aurelius refilled them.

"How did you know I didn't take honey or milk?" I asked. It wasn't important to me; I just felt the silence had to be broken.

He bent forward eagerly. "The same way I knew you would ask that. The same way I knew you would have to shop in Aflraun today. I read it in my map of the future."

"Oh?" I said faintly.

"Yes, indeed." He reached inside his heavy white cloak and drew forth a rolled-up sheet of some kind of heavy paper. He reminded me a little of Morlock at that moment: the crooked man's clothes were full of odd pockets and things.

Aurelius moved the teapot aside and spread the sheet out on the table. It was filled with odd lines of different colors. The lines were in motion, tangling with each other, untangling. I realized suddenly that they were sinking deeper into the paper, as if it were a box, and rising out of it. I blinked a few times and looked away, feeling dizzy.

"It's a little unsettling at first, isn't it?" Aurelius said eagerly. "It's all due to my new scholium of teleomancy. What is the future, except the actions we will take in the future? And we will take those actions because of certain intentions; nobody does anything for no reason. And all those future intentions are rooted in our present concerns. If we could sample the intentions of a significant number of people in a community and trace how they would interact, we could foretell the future with a certain amount of accuracy."

"Without using the Sight," I said.

"Yes." He seemed not to want to talk about that, but he went so far as to add, "The visions of two seers can overlap, you see, and one will know what the other knows. Where's the advantage in that?"

A knowledge-hoarder. I knew the type: almost everyone who has a little magical knowledge hides it in his gown until he can spring it on someone and get something for it. Aurelius all of a sudden seemed less like Morlock. If you expressed the slightest interest in Morlock's latest wonder-working, he would tell you about it until your ears got sore; it was the one thing that made him verbose.

That meant Aurelius was telling me because he expected to get something out of it. I considered the possibilities and finally said, "You're telling me this to impress me. You can do something Morlock can't."

"Oh, so many things!" Aurelius cried out, his wrinkled face filled with a boyish enthusiasm. I wondered how old he was, really.

"And you want me to help you against Morlock," I added.

"I do," he agreed. "For my sake, and for the sake of my beloved wife. And I think you will, too, for the sake of your family. It's suffered so much. Why need it suffer any more?"

It was a strong argument with me. I pick my loyalties carefully, and anyone outside the line has to look out for themselves. There was definitely a line between Morlock and my children. But there was a line between Morlock and Aurelius, too: I didn't know Aurelius, except that he frankly wanted something from me. I had no real reason to trust him.

"No," said Aurelius deliberately. "You don't."

I looked up. His eyes were on the squirming lines of his map. He raised his gaze slowly and smiled at me.

"You've sampled me," I said. "You have a window into my intentions."

"Yes, Naeli, I took that liberty the last time you crossed Whisper Street to get to the marketplace."

"But you haven't sampled Morlock's."

"Oh, but I *have*. I did it some months ago, before you knew him, I believe." His face fell as he continued, "I almost had him in my grip, then. But he . . . he had help and got away."

"Good for him."

"Yes," Aurelius replied wearily, "good for him. I am an evil old man who wants his wife to outlive him, and Morlock is the shining sacred hero who would make that impossible. Have it as you would like. The question is what you will do, what you are willing to do, to protect what remains of your family. You could have saved Stador: not in the Vale of the Mother, indeed, but by keeping him away from there, by taking another path. The powers surrounding you are immense, Naeli: I show you this"—he gestured negligently at the strange map that he was so proud of—"merely to give you a sense of that. You must use foresight to walk between the dangers safely, to protect yourself and the people you care about."

"You haven't told me what you want me to do."

"And I'm not going to, not today. You're not sure of your own mind yet, and so there's no way I can be sure of you, either. Find some way to decide, some grounds for your decision."

"I can hardly do that without knowing what the decision will be about."

"It will involve a break with Morlock, an absolute break: I can tell you that."

"Suppose I ask Morlock about you?"

"Then you will have made your decision. I can tell you this: he has not told you everything about himself. Has he mentioned the old lady he keeps in a jar?"

"What?" Every other thing the old man said seemed to knock me off my feet. It was a good thing I was sitting down.

"He keeps a crazy old lady in a jar. God Creator knows why; I don't. The jar should be somewhere in his workshop, if you can get in there."

I pushed my cup away from me and my chair away from the table. "Thanks for the tea," I said, and stood. "I'll let you know about the other thing."

"If I'm not here," Aurelius said, still not standing, "leave a message with Zyrn, or anyone who works in the hostel. 'Yes' or 'No' will do."

"Won't you know my decision from your crazy map?"

"Probably," said the old man, and smiled a crooked smile.

It was a long walk home, and I had a lot to think about. I went straight to Whisper Street and paid the lower fee to become invisible with the rest. I felt like someone was watching me, and for once I looked on the invisibility of the street as a comfort. That was probably a mistake: the trip was especially unpleasant, with passersby whispering at me and jostling me, especially a strange troupe of people who said nothing and smelled very bad doing a strange shuffling dance that blocked almost the entire street. I finally made my way past, groggy with the reek, and exited from Whisper Street near the Aresion Bridge. In fact, I was very groggy, for some reason, and I don't even remember most of the walk.

It was late afternoon by the time I found myself back at the crooked house in Narkunden. Thend and Morlock were working in the front room when I entered the house—I don't think they heard me. They were replacing the window frames: something to do with the "demon-sconce" Morlock thought we needed now, no doubt. They worked together companionably, speaking little except, "Hand me that hammer," and that sort of thing. I listened to them, trying to decide how I felt about Morlock—and Thend, too, as he was almost a stranger to me.

Never stranger than when he said abruptly, "The future is split in two. I feel like I'm split in two."

I wanted to rush in and hug him. I had no idea what he meant, but I knew he was hurting. But I stood there in the shadows, listening.

"You worry too much about the future," I heard Morlock say. "Don't let your Sight block out the things you can see with your eyes, hear with your ears, feel with your hands. All these things are real, too. Don't let your gift become a curse; it needn't be. And if you don't watch where you're hammering you're going to lose a finger."

If there was one right thing to say, this was clearly it. Thend laughed; it eased my heart to hear him.

I wish I'd turned away then, because he next said, in a low voice I almost couldn't hear, "*She* tears me in two. She thinks I'm just a boy, but I'm already almost a man."

My fears about who "she" was were unfortunately confirmed when Morlock said, "I'm no expert on mothers. I only met my own quite recently. Or one-third of her, anyway."

"Death and Justice, you are weird."

I could almost hear Morlock shrug. "Eh."

They started hammering again and I sneaked off.

I drifted away, lost in dark thoughts. Without planning it, I ended up in the hallway outside Morlock's workshop. The lock on the door glanced at me with a coppery eye and released its long bronze fingers from the door handle. I pulled it open and entered.

There was always a lot going on in Morlock's workshop, whether he was there or not. Today I saw his snarky little flames crawling like fiery ants over a couple of blue glazed jars. I thought of what Aurelius had said, and I wondered if Morlock was planning to make a collection of old ladies in jars.

"Hi, Naeli!" the flames said to me, among other things I won't repeat. They just get more irresponsible if you encourage them, so I didn't, not too much, and proceeded to look around the room.

At the end of a long worktable was a blue glazed jar, not so very different from the ones the flames were working on. Next to it on the table lay its lid. Next to that was a book lying open, face up. The text seemed to be about some kind of gnome, although dragons or mandragons came into it, too (for reasons that weren't clear; I didn't want to flip pages to find out). A sound of humming or singing was coming from the jar.

I approached it cautiously, but not so much that the person humming didn't hear me. "Who is that?" a quavering voice asked. "Is that you . . . whatever-your-name-is?"

"It's me," I said, going closer.

"Who's 'me'?" said the voice irritably. It was obviously coming from the jar.

I went closer and looked in the mouth of the jar, and was startled by what seemed to be a watery gray eye peering out.

"Oh!" said the voice. "I know you. Wait a minute. Wait a minute. I know you. Fasra!"

"No, I—"

"Shut up, won't you dear? Let's see. Aloê?"

"No."

"Voin?"

"No."

"Reijka?"

"No! Give up?"

"My dear. Oh, my dear. If you only knew me, you would know that I never . . . I never . . . Let's see, who were you again?"

"Naeli."

"No, don't be ridiculous. She's dead."

"You may be thinking of someone else—"

"—or not well. Not at all well. They were in here talking about it."

"Were they really?"

"Well, I don't know, truthfully, my dear. I'm not well myself. I'm almost completely crazy, as a matter of fact, so you'll have to forgive me if I wander a bit. Could you get me a bit of water, Fasra dear?"

"Naeli."

"Is Fasra there?"

"No."

"Oh. I thought she was. Could you get me a bit of water, Voin dear?"

I looked around and saw a glass pitcher full of clear water nearby.

"I hope this is safe," I said, picking up the pitcher. "How do I . . . ?"

"Just pour it through the mouth of the jar like last time," the old woman's voice said. "Thank you, dear."

I poured a little water through the mouth of the jar, and after a moment the old woman said, "That's fine! That's enough! Thank you so very much, dear little, um what's-your-name."

"Are you thirsty?" I asked. "Can I help you out of the jar somehow?"

"Oh, I never drink or eat—that's a function of the antideath spell. I just needed a little water for a focus. Morlock is not very strong on the water-magics, poor fellow, and I'm trying to teach him a little, but I have the damndest time trying to remember them myself."

"Should you be doing magic if your memory is failing?" I asked, a little alarmed.

She laughed wheezily and said, "Oh dear! Oh my dear! Who said my memory was failing?"

"You did."

"You made that up!" she said accusingly. "You are always making things up! I've had occasion to warn you about that before, young lady!"

"We just met," I pointed out hopelessly.

Silence. Then, wearily: "I'm sorry. Most of me is missing, you see, and my memory is really not very good. It comes and it goes."

"I don't suppose—" I began, and broke off. It had occurred to me that she might be Aurelius's wife, the one he claimed Morlock was trying to kill. But there didn't seem to be any use in asking her a question I was having trouble even putting into words.

"Never suppose, my dear. Supposing makes a *sup* of *pos* and *ing*."

"What?"

"Did I say it wrong? It was supposed to be funny. I must have said it wrong. Anyway, you can only ask, my dear. If I know, and can remember, I'll answer. I've become very fond of you, Fasra dear, in my way."

I was going to ask her how she knew Fasra, then, but I decided I had more chance of a straight answer from Fasra herself. "Do you know an old man named Aurelius?" I asked.

"Aurelius? Aurelius Ambrosius?"

"Maybe," I said slowly. "His surname might be Ambrosius."

"Oh my dear! Oh my dear! I may not be the freshest buzzard in the flock, but I'm not old enough to have known Aurelius Ambrosius! He died fighting against the Saxons before I was born! At least," her quavering voice lost its brief burst of confidence, "I think he did."

"Maybe it was someone else?"

"Maybe *who* was someone else? I'm not following you, dear. Anyway, now that Fasra has finally brought me some water, I think I'll try fashioning my water-focus. Is Morlock there?"

"No."

"That's right. That's right. They were going to go somewhere and talk about poor Naeli without that silly old woman interrupting them. How I wish she would shut up, sometimes! Because so often it turns out I'm the only one in the room."

"Um. Good-bye, then."

"What?" the old woman's voice squawked. "Who's there? Oh, thank God, they brought me a little water. Maybe I should try making a water-focus. . . ."

I sneaked away, shushed the flames as they tried to banter with me, and fled the workshop.

I was feeling kind of light-headed—had since I left Aurelius, in fact, and I wandered around the house a little without thinking of anything in particular. When I looked up I was in the big room we had made our refectory. Fasra and Reijka were sitting at the table, looking at me solemnly.

"Hello there," I said, a little bolder than I felt. "How goes the letter writing?"

"Oh, Mama," said Fasra, and she got up and ran to me. "Oh, Mama," she said weepily, burying her face in my chest as she wrapped her arms around me.

"What is all this?" I asked, amazed. "What's wrong, honey?"

"Nothing," she said, raising her wet, darkly luminous eyes to meet mine. "Nothing. Oh, Mama."

Reijka had risen, too, and her cool green eyes seemed to measure me. "Maybe we'd better have a look at you, Naeli," she said. "I never really got a chance to examine you. The other day," she added significantly.

"The other—" I choked off what I was about to say. I didn't like the way this sounded. "All right," I added, finally. "Let's go to my room. Fasra—"

"No—I've got to—I'm going to tell the boys."

"Tell them *what* exactly?"

"Oh—nothing!" She flashed me a grin and fled out the far door of the room.

Reijka walked in easy silence alongside me until we were in my room.

"I'd like to know what this is all about," I said.

"I'd like to look you over before I answer," the physician replied.

I pulled off my gown. I noted sourly that my wounds were somewhat more healed than they had been when I last looked at them—this morning, or so it seemed to me.

Reijka looked me over and spent an unusually long stretch of time staring into my eyes. Then she said, "All right, sit down on the bed and tell me something."

"I want someone to tell *me* something."

"Oblige your healer."

"What is it?"

She held up the gown I had been wearing. "Was this the dress you put on this morning?"

"It—no."

"Show me the dress you last remember wearing."

I got up and moved around the room. There was a russet thing with gold trim I wore on days when Glemmurn was due. "This one."

"All right. Are you ready to hear this?"

"I think so."

"You haven't had that dress on for several days. You've been in some kind of haze, and we had to dress you, Fasra and I. Since the day Glemmurn was here and that rarth-thing—"

"Harthrang."

"Whatever. Do you remember anything that happened in the intervening time?"

"Some." I wasn't going to tell her everything. "Not much."

"All right. Be that way. I may not be the master of all fricking makers, but I know a binding spell when I see one, and what to do about it."

"A binding spell." The hospitable Aurelius and his kindness in pouring me a cup of tea. Or maybe it had been something about the chair. They say you should never accept anything from a sorcerer without finding out what it will cost you.

"Yes," Reijka was saying. "They don't really work on someone who doesn't engage in binding magic herself, and that's what kept it from being effective. But the residue was afflicting you, somehow. I dosed you with Voin's Reflective Purifier—"

"Voin?"

"Um. Yes. Do you know her work?"

"I've heard of her," I said, a little imprecisely. I pulled on my gown, the one they had put on me today. "Thanks, Reijka. We owe you, and not just money. I'll—"

"Savage Triumphator, will you slow down a moment?" she wailed, hanging onto my arm as I tried to get out the door.

"I'm not sure how many moments I've got at the moment," I said.

"You say you owe me, not just in money. Pay me off in time. Just a little of your time, Naeli."

I was reluctant, but she had my word. "All right." I shook her hold off but turned back to face her.

She seemed a little unready. "Mother of stones," she muttered, "why do I always get interested in women like you?"

Women like me. I goggled. So much for my insight into the minds of others. I'd been sure it was Roble she was after. Thend must have gotten his Sight from my husband's blood, if it's one of those hereditary things.

"If that's what you wanted to tell me," I said, "I have to tell you—"

"No, no. I just wanted to shock you a bit, I guess. You're always being such a bitch to me. Very unprofessional: I'm sorry. But: look, Naeli. This place isn't safe for you anymore, you or your family. The harthing, or whatever it was. The binding spell. It's not safe."

"I know."

"I don't know what's going on—"

"Neither do I. Not really."

"Sure, Resident Naeli, sure. You were tearing out of here because you had no idea where you were going. No, I'm not asking you to tell me; I imagine you have some sort of reason for not doing that. And Morlock—"

I hadn't decided what to do about Morlock, yet. I shook my head.

"Then what are you going to do about it? No; never mind. You wouldn't tell me anyway. I'm telling you: I'm planning a business venture that will take me out of the city and on tour through the towns of the north for some time. I think you and your family could profit by the change of scenery. You should think about coming along with me. That's all."

"Hm." It *was* worth thinking about. But it sort of depended on whether I sided with Morlock or Aurelius, and I wasn't sure what I was going to do about that yet. "Have you talked to the others?"

She threw up her hands. "Of course! But what's the use in that without also talking to you?"

I closed my eyes. I could almost see it. Maybe I had seen it, while in the haze of Aurelius's binding spell.

"You're exaggerating, I think," I said, opening my eyes. "Roble's his own man, and Bann and Thend are getting there. And Fasra might be as tough as any of them."

"So I exaggerate. It's one way to tell a kind of truth."

I didn't really agree with that, but it wasn't worth pursuing just then.

"I'll have to think about it." I could hear other people moving around the house. "And I have to go now."

"Think," she said. "Go. I hope you come back next time better off than you came back last time."

"Me too. I . . . I still owe you, Reijka."

"Stop flirting with me," she snapped, and I turned and left before I could tell if she was joking.

I went down the back stairs and out the back door. Fortunately, my gown had a few stray coins tucked away in pockets. I used them to pay the toll on the Camlann Bridge and to cross Whisper Street so I could get to the Badonhill Hostel. Aurelius and I were going to have a little conversation.

The streets of Aflraun were even busier that day. Whisper Street was packed with those ill-smelling louts doing their shuffling dance; I decided it must be some kind of cult.

There were more duels, too, all over the place: I was splashed with blood three different times by the time I reached my destination. Disgusting. Narkunden might be as dull as dishwater, but at least it was clean dishwater: you could go about your business without swaggering bravoes waving their blood-soaked swords at passersby.

The marketplace outside the Badonhill Hostel was bustling with buyers and sellers, and the tables of the portico were full of people cooling their heels and slurping down Zyrn's special mind-wiping tea, or perhaps brews even more delightful.

One table near the hostel wall was occupied by only one person, an elderly fellow dressed in blue and white, quietly reading a book.

I sat down across from him and said, "I could learn to hate you, old man."

Aurelius put down the book he was reading—a different one than last time; this was bound in some kind of gray leather—and said, "I know. You wouldn't be the first, believe me. But I had to try it. It was the most efficient way to get what I want, and what I want is fearfully important to my wife's safety."

"What is it?"

"I want unrestricted access to that crooked house Morlock has built in

Narkunden. There are protections placed around it so that only certain people may enter, or allow others to enter."

"Can't you break through his protections?"

"The path of least resistance is almost always the wisest one, my dear."

"I never found it so."

Aurelius spread his hands in a disturbingly familiar gesture. "A philosophical difference. But you should be glad I don't want to put your family on the front lines of a magical war. They tend to take a fearful toll on innocent bystanders."

"Not that you care."

"Of course I don't. You see how frank I am with you. In a very few years, as I or Morlock count them, you will all be dead anyway. But I know that *you* care and, as it happens, that gives us a common interest."

"If I could get my family away—"

"No. I must ask you not to do that. Anything like that would surely give Morlock notice I am coming. I must be allowed to enter the house at a time he does not expect. That means you, your brother, and your children must all be there."

"So that you can use us as human shields. To limit the severity of Morlock's counterattack."

"No. I just want access. I would let you and yours flee before I went in to confront Morlock. If I can find some way to assure you of that, I'd like to do so."

I sort of believed him. It made a certain amount of sense. Whatever sort of force he was planning to bring with him, Roble and my boys could probably make trouble for them. I wouldn't rule Fasra out of any action, either: what she lacks in muscle she makes up for in moxie.

"I'm not agreeing to anything," I said.

"I don't expect you to."

"But how will I reach you if I decide to go along with you? Because I'm never setting foot in this hellhole of a city again if I can help it."

"What? Aflraun?" The old man smiled broadly. "I like it. The place has flavor."

"So does henbane," I said. "Don't waste time with me, Aurelius. You either read this possibility in your little map of the future, or you can't do half of what you say."

His smile became even broader. He drew his map of the future from his heavy cloak and unrolled it. Inside the map was a crooked coin; it looked as if it had been bent somehow. He handed it to me.

"If you decide to help me," Aurelius said, "break the coin. You can do it with your fingers with a little effort, as long as you do it intentionally; it won't break by accident. When you break it, I will know and I will come to the crooked house so that you can let me in."

"How long will it take you to get there?" I pocketed the coin.

"As soon as I can," he said composedly. "It may depend on circumstances. You understand."

I understood. He probably had it figured to the splintered half-heartbeat, but he wasn't going to tell me. A knowledge-hoarder. Well, I already knew that about him.

"Is your name also Ambrosius?" I asked, trying to knock him off his game a little.

He laughed pleasantly, but after a few moments it became clear that he wasn't going to say anything.

"Is the old woman in the jar your wife?" I asked. "She said she didn't know you. Assuming you are who you say you are."

"I am," the old man replied, "but I am more than that. You'll have to get used to this, if we are to have an acceptable alliance, Naeli. I tend to tell the truth, but I will always know more than I say."

A crooked shadow fell over the table. I looked up to see Morlock standing beside me. "Good day to you both," he said.

I said a faint hello. Aurelius muttered something, and his fingers twitched toward his open map with the moving multicolored squiggles. Then he froze as Morlock put down on the table a blue glazed jar, much like the one I had seen in his workshop. Morlock unhooked his sword belt (thrown over his shoulder as a baldric) and hung it on the back of a chair. He sat down without waiting for an invitation.

"The Badonhill Hostel," Morlock said, stretching out his legs comfortably. "I suppose you call yourself Aurelius around here."

Aurelius had been watching Morlock with his mouth partly open. Now his mouth snapped shut, and I was almost sure his pale cheeks were flushing slightly. "I have a perfect right to that name," he said after a moment.

Morlock laughed raspingly.

Now I was sure about the blush. Aurelius's jaw clenched twice. Then his face relaxed and he said, "May I offer you something, my boy? A glass of wine, or perhaps something stronger? I taught them how to use a still, here, and they make the most remarkable beverage out of potatoes. I'm sure you'd enjoy it."

"No, thanks."

I had no idea what that exchange meant, but Aurelius obviously felt he had scored a point. "If you change your mind," he said kindly, "let me know. I always keep a little nearby. Very nearby."

Morlock reached out and tapped the open map. "Teleomancy?" he asked.

"Yes," Aurelius said curtly.

"It won't work."

"Won't it? Won't it, indeed? Why not, pray tell? Listen closely, Naeli. We are to be favored with a lecture by the master of all makers. Do try to pay attention."

"Intentions are not actions. And not all events are intentional acts."

Aurelius laughed now. His laugh was more musical than Morlock's (everyone's is), but somehow it was more unpleasant. He rolled up his map of the future and said, with a polite smile lighting his face, "Well, I must make the best of what poor talents I have. Corrected, whenever possible, by your enormous wisdom."

Morlock opened his hands, closed them.

"A daring retort," Aurelius said to me. "With conversation like that, it's a wonder his wife left him."

"Hey," I said, "leave me out of your pissing match."

Aurelius's features wrinkled more deeply with distaste. "A delightfully urbane image. Yes, Morlock, by all means let us leave Naeli out of our *pissing match*. Was there something else you came here to say? Or was it just to give your aged father a few pointers on teleomancy and other forms of urination?"

Aged father. That certainly explained a lot.

"My true father has been dead these three hundred years or more," Morlock said somewhat heatedly.

"Ah, yes," Aurelius drawled. "Old Father Tyr, gone through the Gate in the West, to sit in judgement with Those-Who-Watch until the end of time. That's the story they tell under Thrymhaiam, isn't it? Trust a dwarf to invent a tedious afterlife. Just *sitting*, you know, and *judging*. What a pity he isn't sitting here now. To judge what became of the man he raised. But his dead hand lives, doesn't it, Morlock—his grip from beyond the grave?" Aurelius gestured at the sheath hanging from the empty chair. "Tyrfing: 'Tyr's grip.' That's what the name of your deadly sword means, doesn't it?"

"Maybe I should have called it 'Merlin's tongue,'" Morlock replied.

"Good God, how unkind," Aurelius said, now very much at ease. "What would Old Father Tyr say if he heard you talking that way to your *ruthen* father?" He snapped his fingers, and Zyrn appeared from the half-hidden doorway. "Are you sure you won't have something to wet your throat? I can see this is going to be a long conversation."

Morlock looked at Zyrn's face, which Aurelius (or Merlin?) had yet to do in my presence. Morlock said to his father (*ruthen* father: I think that means natural father, as opposed to *harven*—the foster father who raises you), "The conversation needn't be long. I just came to see that Naeli wasn't poisoned again."

Aurelius/Merlin shook his head irritably. "We've been over that, and we're friends now—I think I can say that, Naeli?"

"You may," I said. "I won't."

"Well," the old man said, "I myself feel the need of a little something. Zyrn—"

"Zyrn," Morlock interrupted, "would you be free?"

The waiter's flat pebble-like eyes fixed on Morlock's. "Master?"

"I am not your master," said the crooked man. "Would you be free?"

The pebble-like eyes flicked from Morlock to Aurelius to Morlock again. "Master. Yes, master."

Morlock stood and, reaching his fingers into Zyrn's tightly bound hair, ripped something loose. A little blood came with it, and Zyrn fell sobbing to his knees. Morlock dropped the thing in his hand on the ground and crushed it with his heel. Zyrn leaped to his feet and ran away laughing hysterically into the marketplace crowd.

"You insolent little prick," the old man said, all pretence of civility dropped. He clapped his hands and the table was all of a sudden surrounded by armed men.

"This man offends me," the old man said. "I'll pay the usual fee."

"We fight," said one of the armed men, tapping Morlock on the chest. "Get me? Bring your sword. No need to be splashing your greasy gut-stuff on everyone's table."

"I am Morlock Ambrosius."

Five or six of the armed men looked at Morlock, looked at Aurelius, and walked away from the table.

But the one who had challenged Morlock wasn't fazed.

"I figure it is you," the challenger said. "The old man, he is always complaining about you. You are a bad fellow, I think, very greasy. Besides, I see your painting down to the Mainmarket Justiciar's House. I know it is you. Kreck, you are even uglier in person. I spit on your ugly face. I spit on your ugly mother. She krecks with dogs, I think. Ugly ones, the only ones that will take her. You get me? We fight. My name—"

"I don't care what your name is."

"My name soon to be famous, dripping with moist gradient. Also, the old man will pay me good. Money and gradient! Yoy and yur!"

"Eh," said Morlock, which I guess was his valuation of money and gradient, if not yoy and yur (whatever they are). He reached for the sword belt hanging from the chair.

"That is a magical weapon, not to be used in a formal duel," old Aurelius said sharply.

"You hear?" said Morlock's challenger, tapping him on the chest. "This formal duel, not informal, like that night when the swineherds taught you how bittersweet love can be, ha ha. I always kill in the formal way, for the juicier gradient. I am very correct, unlike your moldy flea-bitten sister who cools her feverish oft-travelled rump in muddy swamps."

"You win duels with that abuse?" Morlock asked, apparently with real interest.

"Some," said the challenger. "More than a few. People get mad and I get them. Others think I'm stupid and I get them. Shik! Shik! I always win, because people think me stupid."

"Eh. I think you're stupid, too," Morlock admitted. "Can someone loan me a sword?" he said to the crowd of bravoes standing around. "I'll gift them with whatever gradient I earn by killing Shik-Shik here."

The armed men—I saw two or three of them were women, actually—all looked a little nervous. One of them reluctantly offered Morlock a short single-edged blade.

Morlock checked its balance and weight, shrugged, and said, "Thanks."

The combatants moved out to the cool red sunlight of the open market-place to conduct their highly formal duel. The bravoes who weren't fighting formed a ring: this would be a well-witnessed fight, anyway. Marketeers with nearby carts irritably tossed canvas tarps over their goods to protect them from the inevitable blood.

I turned back to the old man who was watching with cool amusement. "Do you really think Shik-Shik is going to kill Morlock?" I asked.

"It's too much to hope for," said Morlock's father. "But you know what? I killed Stador."

"What do you mean?" I whispered.

"I need you to be a little quicker than that, Naeli, because we don't have much time. We talked about responsibility once. I am responsible for your son Stador's death. I wasn't trying to kill him, of course—I was trying to kill Morlock."

"You weren't even there."

"That's the genius of it! I don't think you truly appreciate my genius, Naeli. I didn't need to be there. I didn't even need to be alive. For over a generation I sent nightmares about Morlock to that poor insect who eventually became Marh Valone. I fashioned him, and through him Valona's Horde, to be a weapon to strike down Morlock should he pass through the Kirach Kund on a mission which displeased me. When he did so, the trap snapped shut. Morlock, unfortunately, got away, but you and your family were caught and mauled in it. Stador was killed; you and others were mutilated; no one escaped unscathed, not even that delightful young girl whom you have labored so long to protect and who now suffers from such horrible night-mares. For all this, I am responsible. Do you believe me? It is important that you believe me."

"It seems . . . possible."

"That's enough, I think. Do you imagine that we have grown so close, in the two or three conversations we have had, that I will hesitate to do the same thing again, if ever I get the chance?"

"No. I don't suppose you will."

"Right! Exactly! Your family is nothing to me! As long as you travel with Morlock, as long as you are on terms with him, you and your family are in danger. I will destroy them, not out of malice, but simply to get at Mor-lock. The only way clear is to make a clean break. Help me, and you are out of the danger zone. He won't want to have anything to do with you, even if he does live, and you won't be in danger from me anymore."

"So everything you said before was a lie."

"Not everything," said the old man cheerfully. "I really am trying to save my dear wife's life. This Shik-Shik is doing better than I had imagined."

I turned to look at the duel. Shik-Shik had the longer blade and he was trying to make the most of it with showy cuts and stabs. Morlock kept retreating in a fairly narrow circle, his pale eyes cool and concentrated. I had seen my share of life-and-death battles, and in my view Morlock was taking the measure of his opponent.

I turned back to the old man who had risen to his feet and was holding the blue-glazed jar. It was capped, and he was shaking it gently.

"Remember what I've said, Naeli," the old man said. "I don't ask you to blame Morlock, although some people would look askance on a son trying to kill his mother. The point is that danger surrounds him and he can't help it. *I* can help it, but I won't. You'll have to make a choice about what's more important to you, your family or Morlock. And we already know what that choice will be."

He tossed the jar on the ground and it shattered. It was just a broken jar; there were no old ladies inside.

"I thought that was probably a ruse," he said. "At least I'll have Tyrfing. . . ."

He moved around the table to lift Morlock's sword belt from the chair. As I watched him move, I realized something. His shoulders were as crooked as Morlock's, if not more so. But he stood, and wore his heavy cloak, to disguise it.

He put his hand on the sword grip and drew the blade. His expression went blank.

It wasn't Morlock's sword, Tyrfing. The blade was only about four inches long, and on the bright steel surface was etched a name: PSEUDO-EXCALIBUR. The word or name meant nothing to me, but it obviously did to the old man: his pale wrinkled features grew bloodred with rage.

With a cry of frustration the old man threw the blade down on the ground by the broken jar. "Unbelievable! He walks with this useless toy on his back through the fightingest city in Laent! The man should be locked up for his own safety!"

The old man looked at me, but it wasn't as if he saw me there. "I don't like this," he whispered. "He's up to something. Better drum up a few reinforcements." He walked away and disappeared into the half-hidden door in the hostel walls.

I got up and walked away from the table, into the dim red light of the autumnal evening. Shik-Shik was lying on his side, gasping through a red-bubbling grin that had been sliced in his throat. Then: he didn't gasp anymore and the bubbles grew still.

The bravo who had loaned Morlock his sword was unhappy.

"So you kill him," the bravo was saying. "You're Morlock Ambrosius. For you, this is a kill with very low gradient, if any. You could *lose* gradient by this killing. That travels with the sword, by our deal."

"What do you want?" Morlock asked. "Money?"

The bravo drew himself up proudly. A moment passed. "How much money?" he said.

Morlock handed him a few coins from one of his pockets. The bravo accepted the coins without looking at them, nodded curtly, and walked away.

"We'd better get out of here," I said to Morlock. "The old man was muttering about reinforcements. What is his name, anyway?"

"Merlin Ambrosius."

"Is he really your father?"

"My *ruthen* father."

"Are you really trying to kill his wife?"

"No, but I am setting about something that will probably result in her death."

"I don't see the difference."

"Neither does he."

We left the little marketplace and headed toward Whisper Street.

"Isn't this the route he'll expect us to take?" I asked.

"Yes. Unfortunately, that's because it's the only route we can take. We have to get back across the river."

"What about his reinforcements?"

"We have some, too."

The day, already getting cold and dark, suddenly got a lot colder. "What in the ground are you talking about?"

Then I saw Roble walking toward us up the crowded street. He was carrying a couple of things in his arms.

As I caught sight of him, a tall thin man dressed in red velvet stepped out of the shadows. He tapped Roble on the chest and said something.

"Not another stupid duel," I muttered.

Morlock sped up and I followed him.

"I . . . I knew a fellow with a brown face once," Red-Velvet-Pants was saying. "He . . . he was a foincher. You heard me. I think . . . I think you may—may be a foincher. Also. I mean, as far as I know, you may be."

Roble was taking this in with equal amounts of amusement and pity.

"If you're not a foincher, you ought to fight me and prove it," Velvet-pants was explaining carefully. "And if you are a foincher, I should fight you. Would you like me to . . . to elucidate further, or may we . . . that is—"

Morlock grabbed Velvet-Pants by the back of his neck. The long, terribly strong fingers of the maker's left hand wrapped nearly all the way around Master Velvet-Pants's skinny throat.

"Drop your sword belt or I'll break your neck," said Morlock.

"You—can't," rasped the startled yet velvety one though his constricted throat. "Mere assassin. Ation. Lose gradient!"

"Me and my partner don't care about gradient," Roble told him kindly. "But we are in a hurry, and we will have to kill you if you don't get out of our way. So drop your sword belt and get lost, hey?"

Velvet-Pants thought about it for a second, then undid his sword belt and let it fall clattering to the ground. Morlock let him go. Velvet-Pants gave a resentful glance over his shoulder. His eyes widened as he seemed to recognize Morlock. (From his painting in the Justiciar's House maybe. No, I have no idea why there was a painting of him there.) He scuttled off.

"Thanks," said Roble. He handed Morlock one of the things in his arms: a sword belt with a sword grip protruding from it: his real sword, or so I hoped.

"Thanks," said Morlock, and slung the belt across his shoulders.

Roble wordlessly handed Morlock a blue-glazed jar, twin to the one Merlin had smashed in the portico. Morlock received it, nodded.

That's what those guys call a conversation.

Grinning, my brother handed me the other thing he'd been carrying: a quarterstaff. "Your usual, I believe."

It was true I was pretty handy with any sort of blunt instrument: you had to be, among the Bargainers. But this was practically the only time Roble had come close to mentioning my life with them in the months we'd been travelling together. It was sort of a warm family moment, in a weird way—with, you know, weaponry.

"Thanks," I said. And I have to admit, in a town full of bloodthirsty idiots, it did feel good to have the quarterstaff in my hands. Technically, this put me in the ranks of those who could be challenged, but only by other bravoes (or bravas) who were carrying staves, which they mostly didn't.

The warmth vanished when I saw my daughter's face in the crowd ahead. "Trouble behind you," she sang out. "Oh, hurry *up*!"

I'd have hit Morlock with the stave as hard as I could if I didn't think he was as necessary to get my children out of this mess as he had been instrumental to getting them into it. I think that was the moment I really made my decision about the old man and his crooked coin, although I only became aware of it later.

Glancing back as we ran, I saw there was a body of armed men moving up the street from the Camlann Market. They didn't look like soldiers, but they did look like trouble. We caught up with Fasra and she said, "The way is still clear to Thend's station. He's halfway to Whisper Street. If that's still where we are going."

"Have to," Morlock said.

We ran up the road, ignoring catcalls and challenges. We picked up Thend as we went. Thank the Strange Gods: he was not carrying a visible weapon. He said as he jogged alongside us, "The way is still clear back to Whisper Street. You are being followed, though."

"That's 'we are,' honey," I pointed out to him, and he grinned. Like it was a holiday. Well, it was better than moping, under the circumstances.

Bann was waiting for us by the Whisper Street gate. He also was not visibly armed, but in his arms he carried an apparently heavy object under a cloak.

His face was sweaty and marked with worry. "The gate guards say they won't let this through," he said. "They say this looks like a weapon and weapons aren't allowed."

"You didn't ask them right," Roble said reassuringly, pulling out a fistful of gold coins.

We stepped as a group through the outer gate. One of the guards (toll-takers, really) looked up, saw Bann, started to say, "I told you . . . ," and stopped abruptly. He'd seen the gold in Roble's hands.

"We really, truly, urgently need to get across Whisper Street," Fasra said sweetly. "We promise not to hurt anyone. Unless you get in our way."

The guards looked at the gold, looked at our faces, took the money, and waved us through.

"This is just like Sarkunden," Fasra said as we stepped into Whisper Street. She disappeared. "Except everyone is a Sandboy," her disembodied voice added.

"Grab hands or something," I said. "No one gets lost."

"No need," Morlock said. "Go south, past the dancers. Hurry."

I didn't like anyone overriding me when I gave my kids an order, but we were in the middle of a situation, so I had to roll with it.

We shouldered and elbowed our way through the sightless crowd of

Whisper Street. It was almost dark, but the street was dense with people whispering about the things they had to say when they thought no one was looking.

There were more of the dancers, as Morlock called them, than ever; they blocked almost the whole street, the scratching sound of their many feet louder than all but the nearest voices. We had to force our way through them one by one. I heard Fasra gasping, and somebody retched.

They didn't just smell bad. They smelled . . . dead. I held my breath and tried to stay close to the others. Eventually we seemed to be on the other side of them; ahead of me I could hear a fervent conversation amongst the Overripe Fruit Society. I wanted to tell Fasra to cover her ears. It's true she had worked (as a maid—nothing else) in the village whorehouse. But Whisper Street was full of people creepier than you would meet in the average brothel.

"Bann," said Morlock's voice.

"Here," said my son's.

"Have you got a firemaker?"

"Yes."

"Set it off."

There was a thumping sound as Bann set down the thing he was carrying, and I heard the cloak being cast aside. I saw the flame my son suddenly held in his hand, although I couldn't see the hand.

Then there was a stream of sparks and a deep vibrating sound, like a tuning fork as big as a house. The stream of sparks became a pillar of fire stretching up toward the dark blue sky. Then, when it was twenty or thirty feet above us, it burst.

Glowing dust showered down from whatever-it-was, all along the length of Whisper Street. The dust didn't seem to be affected by the invisibility spell on the Street, so that whatever it fell on suddenly became visible, a ghostly glowing shadow of itself.

Chaos erupted. People did not come to Whisper Street to see and be seen. Many of them had quietly slipped off their clothes, the better to conduct their conversations, and these people in particular panicked. A man and a woman in the Overripe Fruit Society suddenly realized they were married, and the sound of their happy reunion rose in fell shrieks above the cries of dismay that filled the once-whispering street.

I saw dusty simulacra of my children and brother standing nearby, and a dusty glowing statue of Morlock, holding a jar in his hands.

"Do you hear me?" he was saying. "Do you see me?"

The dancers were still dancing, unbemused by their sudden visibility. They were dressed in their funeral finest, but their flesh was wearing away; for many of them it was already in rags, or oozing out through the seams of their shrouds. But at the sound of Morlock's voice they turned and looked at him. (I say looked, even though many of their eyes were gone, the empty sockets gaping like tiny dark mouths.)

"Nimue Viviana," said Morlock. "Listen to me. I am Morlock Ambrosius. I can take you back to yourself. I can give you rest. Follow me."

The still dancers stood still a moment longer. Then they took a step toward Morlock.

Beyond them I saw the dusty glowing shapes of many armed men.

"Morlock," I said.

"Now!" he cried. "Follow me!" He turned and ran. They followed, their dead feet resounding like thunder along the street.

"I'm a step or two ahead of you, I think," I said.

"Stay that way," he said. "Go down to the Aresion Gate and take the bridge across the river. If I fall behind, don't wait for me."

"Who's Nimue Viviana?" I asked.

"My mother."

"Oh. I thought she was the crazy lady in the jar."

"She is."

"What . . . ?"

"Merlin split her in three parts to try to keep her from dying. Part of her is in the jar. Part is possessing these corpses. Part is elsewhere."

"The antideath spell."

Morlock's glowing dusty face turned to me as he ran and nodded. "Did she tell you of that? Good."

"So you'll break the antideath spell?"

"If I can."

"And she'll die?"

"Probably."

"So he wasn't lying."

"Merlin?" Morlock shrugged as he ran. "Don't count on that. He lies when it suits him."

"But not this time."

"Seems not."

The disorderly troop of corpses that followed us—followed Morlock, more precisely—shoved people out of their way and trampled them if they would not go. There were screams of pain and anger behind us, screams of fear before us, on every side the despairing shrieks of those who had tried to feed some obsession of Whisper Street and hide it from the world. For some reason it all reminded me very much of life as a Bargainer. Maybe it was the night work, or the corpses.

We finally reached the Aresion Gate and ran through it, stampeding the panicky toll-takers before us. The glow of the dust faded in the ordinary unwhispering street; in the red irregular light from house windows and the rare streetlamps, we all looked as if we had just come out of a hay barn or an attic.

Many of those windows slammed shut as he passed. By now we constituted a full-fledged riot, and as we ran through the dark streets of western Aflraun, already filling with evening mist from the river, I heard the whistles and horns of the night guard being summoned. There were no guards on Aflraunside of the bridge, though, so we thundered past and across the foggy river.

Most of us did, anyway. The others were almost on the far side when I turned and saw that Morlock had slowed almost to a halt in the middle of the bridge.

"Morlock, come on!" I shouted. A bunch of people were entering the bridge from Aflraunside. Some wore uniforms; some didn't. I didn't want words with any of them. The shuffling corpses formed a pretty effective traffic block, even for each other, but I supposed the soldiers could force their way through if they really wanted to.

But now Morlock absolutely stopped, and the rout of corpses stopped, too, staring at him and his blue jar.

A guard from Narkundenside came up beside me. "You can't bring that many zombies into the city," he said. "I don't care what paper you've got on them."

"I don't think they're zombies," I said.

"What are they then?"

"Arrrgh!" If a harthrang was a demon possessing a corpse, what was one-third of an old lady possessing a herd of corpses? Possibly those-who-know have a technical term for it, but I didn't and don't know it.

"'Arrrgh,' huh?" The guard shook his head. "I don't think there's anything about it in the regulations. To hell with them, anyway."

"To hell with regulations?" I asked, amazed. I'd never heard anyone from Narkunden say something like that, not even Reijka, who seemed to be a free spirit.

"Straight to hell!" he said, grinning around the words. "You know what we got going on, past your zombies or arrrgh or whatever they are?" He gestured at the crowd of armed, torch-bearing men filling up the far side of the bridge.

"A lynch mob?"

"A war!" He said it cheerfully. "I already sent messages to the other bridges and the watch commander about it. There hasn't been a war with Aflraun for more than *two years*. About time. No promotions in peacetime, no hazard pay, no overtime except on holidays and elections. No excitement. A war is good for morale, and they do say it's good for the economy, too. We ought to have a war at least once a year, right after the election."

Morlock was doing something. He had put the jar behind him and he was kneeling on the midpoint of the bridge. With his right index finger he traced something—a letter, a rune, or something—on the cornerstone and leaped back.

The bridge between Morlock and the crowd of corpses fell away, dropping through the dark misty air to the dark water below. Morlock picked up the jar and leaped back again, and more fell away.

"Hey!" cried the war-loving guard beside me. I wasn't sure if he approved or not; I was having trouble understanding him in general.

Morlock uncapped the blue jar. I caught a glimpse of a large, distorted gray eye through the mouth of the thing. Then he turned the open end of the jar toward the other side of the broken bridge.

"Speak to them, Nimue," Morlock was saying. "They are you. They can't reach you unless they let those other bodies go. Speak to them, Nimue. Speak to yourself."

A quavering voice uttering a language I didn't know came out of the uncapped jar. It seemed to be singing a kind of song. In a moment the song was taken up by the hoarse, whistling voices of the corpses across the broken bridge.

A couple of the corpses shuffled forward and fell away into the misty darkness, splashing in the water below.

"You must let the bodies go and cross over," Morlock was whispering. "You have no hope in that flesh; it is not yours. You must let it go and cross over to yourself."

A few more bodies fell forward into the water. Then they all fell over where they stood.

In the misty gap between the two sides of the broken bridge, I saw some kind of shape. The shape itself had no color I could see, but it left strange imprints on the midair mist. Was it a spinning wheel? A monstrous head with hair coiling like snakes? A woman striding through a cloud? None of these things, I think, but *something* had left those corpses and was coming toward us though the middle of the dark air.

"I did not know the bridge fell away like that," marvelled the helmeted blork standing next to me. "Would've been handy a few years ago when they came at us with crank-driven siege breakers. That was the war I made Special Task Co-Leader."

The shifting figure outlined in mist reached our side of the broken bridge. Morlock put down the jar and stepped back. A funnel of mist appeared above the jar, dissipated. Morlock waited a moment, then stepped forth and capped the jar.

"Doesn't she need air?" I asked him, stepping forward.

"No." He tucked the jar under his arm and didn't seem to want to say any more.

So I tried to get him to say more. As we walked down to Narkundenside, the guard tagging along behind us, I asked, "So will she die now? Is the anti-death spell broken?"

"No," he said. Then, maybe to forestall another question, he added, "There is a third part of her: her core-self. If it is reunited with her shell and her impulse-cloud, she will be herself again."

"Impulse-cloud?"

"Part of the mind under the mind. If it thinks, the thinking has little to do with words."

"It looked like a ghost or something, when it was crossing over."

Morlock nodded. "An impulse-cloud that survives the death of a body may become a ghost."

"A ghost." I laughed. Morlock looked curiously at me and I explained, "Give credit where it's due. Whisper Street was a perfect place to hide a ghost."

"Yes. Except for the bodies."

"The bodies?"

"The bodies missing from the graveyards. An impulse-cloud has a great hunger to be reunited with its body, and then it will settle for any body. Nimue was drawing body after body to her from the graveyards. That's how I found her."

"And when you find her final part, her—"

"Core-self."

"—her core, and she's reunified, what will happen then? Can she go on living?"

"The antideath spell will fail if she becomes unified, probably. That's why Merlin cut her up in the first place."

"Why are you doing it, then? I thought you weren't a deviser of . . . of comfortable deaths."

He gave me a crooked smile. "I foresee nothing comfortable about this death, from first to last."

We were up with the others now at the Narkunden side of the broken bridge. They said nothing, but eyed the blue jar and listened solemnly. They probably knew more about it than I did; they must have talked about it when I wasn't around (physically or perhaps just mentally).

"That's no answer. You should be keeping her alive. She's your mother."

Morlock lowered his head. I think his expression was pained or angry, but he's hard to read at the best of times and now it was getting on for full night. "She's suffering," he said after a moment. "She is divided, not herself. How can I make you understand?"

"Is this what she wants?" Roble asked. "This self-union?"

Morlock shrugged and spread the fingers of his free hand. "She seems to. Of course, she is not sane. If she were, she would not be suffering this way."

There was a silence for a moment and then the bridge guard said, "I don't mean to interrupt, but the city government is going to want someone to pay for the bridge."

"Have someone from the Guild of Pontifices stop by my residence. I'll pay them."

"I don't know how much it'll cost—"

"It doesn't matter."

The bridge guard took down Morlock's address to give to the guild. As Morlock was about to turn away, he reached out and grabbed the sleeve of Morlock's free arm. "Listen, honorable sir," he said.

"I'm listening."

"How'd you know the bridge falls away like that? I worked as guard here twenty years, and my dad before that, and I never knew. I'll bet a month's bonus pay that no one who works here knows. How did you know the bridge could do that?"

"I built it."

Different versions of the same smile appeared briefly on the face of my daughter, my brother, my two sons (my surviving sons). I felt it tugging at my own mouth. A proprietary pride. He was one of us, and he had done this thing.

He was one of us—and Stador had died because of that. He was one of us—and my remaining children and my brother had run past the snapping jaws of death because of that. He was one of us—and we were all in danger because of that.

And so I knew. I almost feel like I decided before—did I tell you about this? I guess I'm getting tired. But that was when I knew what I had to do. I *had* to do it. I felt terrible about it, and I still feel bad about it. I knew they would hate me for it, and I guess maybe they do hate me for it.

But, when the time was right, I was going to have to break that crooked coin and summon Merlin. Events would have to take their course. We were all in danger because Morlock was one of us, and that meant that he could not be, any more.

That night, after the crooked house was quiet at last, I stood outside in the street door, holding the crooked coin. I let the intent take shape, clear in my mind, and snapped the coin with my thumb and first two fingers.

The coin clicked as it broke, and then the pieces sagged, as if they were made of rotten flesh. I tossed them into the gutter and lost sight of them. By the time I looked up, Merlin and about twenty slippered thugs were already sneaking around the corner toward me.

"I hoped you'd do the clever thing, Naeli," Merlin said, his smarmy sincerity heating up the cold night air.

I hissed a well-chosen obscenity at him, but he just laughed, then added, "Where's your family?"

"Asleep in the front two rooms," I said. "I wanted them to be ready to get out of here."

"Fesco," said the old wizard to one of his thugs, "check that. Go silently and wake no one, or I'll kill you."

I held the door open and Fesco shouldered past me.

"What's your story?" Merlin asked, climbing the steps to stand beside me. "They won't go willingly without my son, or so I guess."

"So you know. You sampled them, you white-faced lizard!"

"All but Fasra," Merlin admitted good-humoredly. "She scares me a little. There's more there than meets the eye."

"There's plenty there that meets the eye!" I snapped.

"You never heard me say otherwise, madam."

"Don't—" I bit off the rest of my usual comeback. *Don't call me "madam"; I'm not some Coranian bimbo-herder.* Maybe I wasn't, but I didn't feel like bragging about it tonight.

He smiled unpleasantly at me, his teeth gleaming through the night shadows. Him and his map of the future. How I hated him. How I feared him.

Our friendly thug Fesco appeared at the doorway and nodded.

Merlin looked at his other thugs and gestured at me.

Suddenly there were several thugs on each side of me, and some in front of Merlin, and some behind the rest of us. It was like a military formation. It was awfully crowded on the stairs of the crooked house.

"I thought you were going to let us go."

"Shut up," he replied briefly. He looked at the thugs surrounding me. "If she doesn't shut up, you make her shut up. Don't kill her, though, unless I tell you to."

"Liar," I whispered hopelessly.

In his way, Merlin was as hard to irritate as Morlock. Morlock could irritate him, naturally—Morlock can irritate anyone . . . the master of all irritants, that's what they should call him—but I had never been able to. Until now. What I said then got deeply under his skin. His face turned toward me and I saw his features working strangely in the light of the major moons.

"I don't intend to betray you, Naeli," he said. "I simply wish to verify that you have not betrayed me. I keep my word. I suppose Morlock told you differently?"

I didn't say anything, because he seemed like he was about to do something crazy. Eventually he calmed down and we went, a slippered platoon, into the crooked house.

In the front room the forms of my brother and two (surviving) sons could be seen in the moonlight from the open window. Merlin eyed them from a distance; then he waved his thugs away and stepped closer to the sleeping forms. He drew a dagger and plunged it into Roble's face. Roble's chest continued to rise and fall, as if he were sleeping. Merlin turned away to stab Thend and Bann. None of them reacted.

"Damnation," he said sincerely. He turned to one of his thugs and said, "Fesco. Take Elnun there. Go find the thing in the next room that looks like a girl. Rip it to pieces and come back to me."

Appalled, Fesco whispered, "But what if—"

"You can speak normally," the wizard interrupted. "Light a lamp or two while you're about it. No need for secrecy. They're long gone. Aren't they, Naeli?"

"Yes," I said, since it was now obvious.

"I wanted so badly for you to do the clever thing," Merlin complained. "I hoped against hope. You won't say where they went, I suppose?"

"No."

"You may change your mind about that," said Merlin, "or I may change it for you. What a lot of work that would be, though! I think we'll just search the house, first."

"You—" *will be wasting your time*, I was going to say, but thought twice about it. If he wanted to waste his time, it was fine with me.

"You!" Merlin repeated mockingly. "You!"

"Drop dead."

"Someday I will. Long after you have died and been forgotten, of course."

Fesco returned alone. "It wasn't a girl. Something in its belly bit Elnun when he stabbed it and he's dead."

"I told you to make some light," Merlin complained. "Do it now, and—"

"Aurelius," Fesco interrupted, "unless you tell me more about this job, I'm leaving and taking my men with me."

"We're here to capture someone," Merlin said. "That's all you need know."

I remembered how some of the bravoes had reacted to Morlock's name in Aflraun, so I decided this might be the time to speak up. "It's Morlock Ambrosius," I said. "That's who he's sending you after. Heard of him, have you?"

Fesco was appalled, but skeptical. "Can't be. He'd be centuries old."

"He was in Aflraun tonight," one of the thugs said. "He killed a man and burned down Whisper Street and smashed the keystone of the Aresion Bridge—*bam!*—with his fist, like this: *bam*. I heard about it from—I heard about it from—This guy told me."

Fesco turned to Merlin. "What about this, Master Aurelius?"

"His name's not Aurelius, either," I said. "He's been lying to you about everything."

Merlin looked at me for a moment, smiled gently, and said, "I've not been lying, but it is true that I have not told you all that I know. I seldom do. Fesco, my true name is Merlin Ambrosius."

Every one, and I mean *every one*, of those dirty soft-shoe cutthroats went down on one knee.

"Great Master," Fesco said, bowing his head reverently, "forgive us and command us."

"Get back on your feet and do as I direct," Merlin said kindly. "You'll still be paid. I don't expect anything from gratitude."

"We do not forget. We will never forget."

"That's good to know," Merlin said. "I, too, have a long memory: for good and evil, Naeli. For good and evil."

His threat meant nothing to me; I was just trying to fill up time. I wondered what Merlin had done in the past to receive the instant devotion of these alley-bashers.

The thugs got lamps and divided up into various groups to search the house. Merlin had the now-docile Fesco pick five thugs to accompany him, and me, into the Mystery Zone.

"The fame of it has reached even across the great river of the north," Merlin told me slyly. "So I naturally take this chance to visit it without the usual admission price."

They went very carefully. Fesco and two thugs preceded us through the Gate of Shadows (the dark room we used to disorient visitors), searching it carefully before Merlin and I entered, followed by the thug rearguard. They tried the same thing with the zone itself, but their formation broke when a couple of the thugs tripped and fell up a wall.

Merlin waved me through and followed along, an expression of wonder lighting his pale cold features. The two thugs were standing on the wall, disoriented. One of them made it back to the floor, but the other staggered like a drunk and ended up standing on the ceiling.

"Well," said Merlin to me, "I won't lie to you, Naeli. I find this remarkable. At times like these, I almost wish Morlock and I were on better terms. I don't suppose you can tell me anything about this?"

"What's it worth to you?"

"How mercenary. Or are you talking about your family?"

"I'm not talking about money, anyway."

"Well, if you put it like that, I don't think anything you tell me will be worth any concessions for your family's safety. As long as they are levers I can use to apply pressure on Morlock, I'll use them. When they are not, they've nothing to fear from me. You see how honest I am with you, Naeli."

I was honest with him about something.

He laughed and said, "You're not the first to say so, though others had more elegant ways of putting it. Well, I think what we have here in your Mystery Zone is some sort of four-dimensional polytope."

"It is," I conceded.

"Well, that much is obvious, isn't it? But I'm having a little trouble working out the geometry. Is it regular, do you know? Did he ever show you a three-dimensional map of the thing?"

"No."

"He may not have one. He can do multidimensional calculations in his head. God Creator knows where he learned it—not from the dwarves; all the math they know is bookkeeping. He stayed at New Moorhope for a time; perhaps they taught him there." He shook his head. "No, I just can't work it out. Unless he knows a way to bend gravity?"

"He says gravity is more malleable in the fifth dimension," I remembered.

"Is it?" Merlin said thoughtfully. "Is it really? The four-space polytope must be nested in some sort of fifth-dimensional structure then. Interesting. I'll have to give that notion some serious study, one of these days. I'm indebted to you, Naeli."

"Then—" I broke off.

"Ask your question. I know you've been dying to."

"Why are you wasting your time in the one place in Laent where you know Morlock is *not?*"

"Of course Morlock is here, Naeli, or will be soon."

"Does your map of the future tell you that?"

"As a matter of fact, it does. Not that I needed it. Yours were the actions I had trouble predicting."

"And you never did."

"Oh, of course I did. I *hoped* you'd do the sensible thing, but I rather thought you wouldn't. Shall I outline it for you? Morlock made those simulacra and you sent your family and him away somewhere—possibly with someone you came to know in Narkunden. If necessary, I'll look into that. You told them you'd catch up with them later, after decoying me off their trail. When they were safely away, you summoned me. You have no intention of ever seeing them again and are quite prepared to die. Is that about it?"

He was exactly correct, so I told him he was wrong.

He ignored me. "You don't really know Morlock, though, it seems. Once the family is well away, or on its way, he'll be back."

"Why?"

"Are you being modest? The oldest reason in the world."

I laughed.

"You may overestimate the number of women who have looked on him without some mixture of fear and disgust."

"Who says I don't?"

Merlin looked at me almost sadly. "I'm being honest with you. Why can't you be honest with me?"

I really think he thought I was being unfair. He admitted to causing the death of one of my sons, and was willing to kill everyone I cared about as a secondary effect of his schemes. But I disappointed him because I wasn't more forthcoming about who might or might not have been the recipient of my girlish laughter. Death and Justice, what a mirror-kisser he was.

In the uncomfortable silence that stretched out between us, we suddenly heard, faint and far off, the harsh sound of men screaming in the last extremity of pain or fear.

"He's here," Merlin said in a businesslike tone. "Fesco—"

He never finished. There was an earthquake, or something—the floor started to shift under our feet. The ground was pretty lively in Four Castles; we lived just south of the Burning Range and we were always suffering earthquakes. (My husband died in one, when a quake collapsed the mine he was working in.) So I knew what I had to do: get out.

But as I turned on my heel and the floor writhed like a snake beneath me, I saw the door at the end of the hall slide out of sight. Then the shaking threw me off my feet: we were all of us tossed in a heap, including the guy who had been on the ceiling, and I had to concentrate on not getting impaled by their drawn blades.

I was successful, but a couple of them weren't. When the rest of us shook loose from each other and stood up, two of Merlin's thugs didn't. One was Fesco: he was coughing up blood and seemed unlikely to be doing much else for the rest of the time he had left. The other was the guy who had been on the ceiling: he had fallen straight on somebody's sword. He wasn't moving at all.

"Two down," I said. "Five to go."

Merlin glanced at me sharply, and then his withered face bent in a sneer. "You're an optimist, young woman. Still, it was clever of him to build this toy to trap me with. The ingenuity of its making is relatively trivial, you understand; one expects that of him. It's his cunning use of it that really impresses me. He's learning, old as he is. If he had Ambrosia's unsparing ruthlessness or Hope's steady devotion, he might really become dangerous someday."

He looked up and down the Mystery Zone. The hallway had changed shape. It was now longer, with a sharp turn at either end.

"Two of you," Merlin said, "lead off. The other two, follow. Let's see what the other side of this place looks like."

The four surviving thugs (Fesco had stopped breathing) all looked as if they had to think once or twice before deciding to accept Merlin's orders. But they did, falling into place without a word to him or each other, and we moved up the corridor. When they reached the turn, one of the lead thugs shouted, "They're down there!" and ran on ahead around the turn.

We heard boots thundering up the corridor behind us.

"Penned in!" Merlin hissed. "Can he have brought allies?" He grabbed my arm and hustled me around the bend.

Allies. I was terrified that this meant Roble and my children—what other allies did Morlock have? I glimpsed back as Merlin dragged me around the turn in the hallway. There were armed men approaching up the hallway behind us—not anyone related to me, I thanked the Strange Gods: the sweating frightened faces were pale as fish-bellies. They did seem a little familiar, though.

Merlin stopped as soon as he had dragged me around the bend. He turned around. There were sounds of fighting from both ends of the corridor. I looked down and saw the lead thugs fighting with someone just around the bend. Turning back, I saw our rearguard thugs fighting with someone just around the corner.

"Stop it!" shouted Merlin. "Stop it, you idiots! You'll kill each other!"

All the fighting stopped. I saw two bodies lying on the corridor floor ahead of us. They looked awfully familiar also: one of them was certainly Fesco.

"There's only one turn in the corridor," Merlin muttered. "It's bent back on itself. Then—wait a moment—"

He didn't have a moment. A hatch opened in the ceiling in the middle of the hallway and Morlock dropped out of it. He held a sword in one hand, not Tyrfing, and a dagger in the other. He raised the sword to guard as his boots struck the floor. The hatch shut by itself; you couldn't even see a line where its edges were.

The four surviving thugs figured they knew what to do. The two behind us rushed past to engage Morlock. So did the two at the other end of the corridor.

"Wait!" shouted Merlin. "Oh, hell and damnation. There they go."

Morlock turned sidewise and dodged down the corridor. He threw the dagger, and one of the thugs caught it in his left eye, stumbled, fell, and was motionless. Meanwhile, Morlock was efficiently passing his sword through the other thug's midsection. He ran on down the corridor (we could hear his footfalls growing closer around the corner behind us) with the remaining two thugs in close pursuit. Suddenly he swerved to one side and scrabbled at the right-hand wall. Another hatch opened up and he dove inside. It swung shut behind him and disappeared. There was some smoke hanging in the air.

"Wonderful! Excellent!" shouted Merlin. He turned about and, passing by me, stepped around the corner. He simultaneously appeared at the far end of the corridor. He looked up at me and said, "Join me, won't you, Naeli?"

I didn't take the same route he did, because it bothered me, but walked straight down past dead Fesco and the other cold thug beside him, the still living thug trying desperately to staunch the bleeding in his abdomen, the motionless thug with the dagger in his eye.

"Four down," I said. "Three to go."

"Oh, shut up and have a look at this!" Merlin said impatiently.

This was a trail of fire guttering along the corridor. It disappeared next to the wall where Morlock had disappeared.

"What is it?" I asked.

"Blood!" Merlin crowed. "The blood of an Ambrosius. One of our men must have wounded him."

"Your men," I said.

"Have it your way, you fool," Merlin said tersely. He turned toward the wall and gently felt about with his hands, so long and clever, so much like Morlock's, but even paler and acrawl with stark blue veins.

"Got it!" he whispered, and the hatch swung open.

We all crowded forward to look.

Through the hatch there was a narrow side corridor. No door was visible and the hallway dead-ended in a blank wall, but there was a window on the left-hand wall through which part of a moon and some stars were visible.

"That's our exit, I think," Merlin said smugly.

The two thugs tried to shoulder through, but Merlin stopped them. "No! One ahead, one behind. He may have many ways in and out of this corridor. We must still be vigilant."

The thugs argued for a while who should go first; then they decided to flip a coin for it. The winner smiled, tossed the coin to the loser, and stepped through the hatch.

It all happened in a moment, but here's what I think I saw.

As he stepped through the hatch he stumbled. As he fell face forward, his hair and beard suddenly streamed out in front of him. His nose even got longer, pointing upward, and his face seemed to slide upward on his skull. He made a small quacking sound of surprise and then he fell, straight up the hallway, and hit the blank wall at the end of the short hallway so hard that he splashed, like a bag full of red jelly.

"I really must pay more attention to fifth-dimensional gravity effects," remarked Merlin coolly, as he threw the hatch shut.

"But—" said the surviving thug.

"Ware!" shouted Merlin.

Morlock had exited another hatch in the wall and was coming toward us, bloody sword in hand.

"Five down," I said to the last thug. "Two to go."

"Shut *up*!" he groaned.

Fiery blood was dripping from one of Morlock's hands, but somehow that only made him seem more sinister as he limped toward us.

"I don't want this," the thug said to Morlock in a pleading tone. "I never wanted this. They never told me I would have to do this."

"Then put your sword down," Morlock rasped. "Do it now."

"You do and you'll face *my* wrath," Merlin called.

"Mother of stones," the thug hissed, "how I hate you both!" He raised his sword and leaped at Morlock. The crooked man flipped burning blood in his eyes. The thug clawed at his face and Morlock stabbed him through the chest. Moments later he was dead on the corridor floor.

"You used to gather a better group of swordsmen," Morlock remarked.

"I was in a hurry," Merlin replied. "Anyway," the thrifty necromancer added as he drew something from his left sleeve, "at least I don't have to pay them now."

He threw the thing in his hand—it looked a little like a stick—and said something. I didn't quite hear it, but I felt the shock: it had to be the activating word of a magic spell. Then the stick didn't look like a stick anymore: instead it was something like a narrow silver bird with a long sharp beak. It flew under Morlock's guard and through his side, appearing on the far side scattering fire and blood from its razor-sharp feathers.

Morlock gasped. Maybe I'm going to sound stupid here, but: that was shocking to me. I'd seen all sorts of things happen to Morlock in the time I'd known him, but I'd never heard him make a sound like that. Worse, the thing spun about in midair and came back at him through the fiery cloud that had begun to envelope him. He tried to block it with his sword, but it spun low and passed through his right leg. He sobbed with pain, but managed to catch the thing between his sword and the floor. He snapped it somehow—I could hardly see him because of the wall of fire rising from his blood on the floorboards—and it seemed to go dark, just a stick again, a broken one now. Then he slumped to his knees, and bloody fire rose like a curtain in front of him.

I turned to look at Merlin. There was a sad contemplative look on the old man's face. But he was taking another of these flying sticks from his other sleeve. He was going to throw it. There was nothing Morlock would be able to do about it, even if he was still conscious. (It was hard to tell. I couldn't see much of him.) This one would kill him for sure. Merlin raised the stick to throw it.

I moved at the same time, and as he let go the stick and started to say the magic word to activate its deadly spell, I punched him in the throat.

His face rippled, as if I were seeing it reflected in troubled water. His dark blue eyes looked at me with shock and an unspoken accusation. (Mirror-kisser! He couldn't believe everyone wasn't on his side, somehow.) The silvery thing fell back toward him as I jumped away. It didn't look like a stick, or a bird. Instead it was more like a long narrow-lipped mouth full of narrow pointy little teeth—a Bargainer's mouth. Breaking the spell as Merlin uttered it had caused the weapon to recoil on the old man somehow. It was more than I had planned, but I admit I felt a certain satisfaction as the mouth-thing landed on Merlin's neck and chest and began to gnaw at him.

I turned away toward Morlock and was horrified to see how much worse he was, now supine on the burning floor in a pool of his own burning blood. Then the floorboards gave way and he fell from sight.

I jumped after him. It was the stupidest thing I'd ever done—I think it holds the record to this day, in fact. What if we'd ended up in a hallway like the one that had killed Merlin's penultimate thug? I would have ended up in a red smear next to Morlock, that's all. But in the moment of emergency I had some crazy idea I could help—grab him before he fell too far. (And maybe I just wanted out of that horrible one-turn trap, even if it killed me.)

We fell, but not with the deadly speed that had killed Merlin's unwary thug. It was more the way snow falls: we drifted amid glowing debris down a long shaft with dark walls. At the bottom was a floor with a door set into it.

The door was locked with one of Morlock's own devices. The crystalline eye looked at him and released the hold its long bronze fingers had on the door.

"Go through," Morlock whispered through the ember-lit darkness. It was the first clear sign I had that he was still alive.

I kicked aside some burning debris and swung the door open wide.

The street outside the crooked house beckoned to me. Only the ground fell away at right angles to the threshold of the door. It looked as if I were about to fall straight through a hole into the moonlit sky. A wave of vertigo swept over me.

"Hurry," hissed the bleeding, burning, crooked man.

I sat down on the threshold of the doorway and swung my legs into it. Gravity on the far side grabbed them and dragged them toward the ground. I inched my way out and found myself on my back, staring upward at the sky.

I rolled aside as Morlock jumped out the door and landed on his feet. He landed with a pronounced wobble and started staggering down the street, no less wobbly as he went, still trailing gouts of burning blood.

I hopped to my feet and caught up with him. "Hey, wait a moment," I said, reaching out for him.

"Keep away," he snarled. "Don't wait. Move. Merlin. After us."

"Morlock, he has to be dead. Did you see what that thing was doing to him?"

"Unlikely!" That was all he said. He actually pulled a needle and thread out of his pockets and started sewing himself up as he hobbled along. It was pretty horrible, but just stumbling along watching was even worse, so I said, "Can I help?"

"No. Blood. Burn you."

"Your clothes don't burn," I pointed out.

"Dephlogistonated."

"Deef—what does that mean?"

"My clothes don't burn."

"Have you got some gloves that have been dephloginated, or whatever you call it?"

He didn't stop walking (if you could call it that) or using the needle to sew up the terrible gash in his side. But his face became more thoughtful, less a mask of pain. "Hm," he said at last. "Dephlogistonated gloves. Excellent idea, really."

"Then you have some?"

"No." The pain clamped down on his features again.

When he was done sewing up his side he settled on a curb for a moment to wrap bandages torn from his cloak around his wounded leg.

"Morlock," I said, as he rose to move again, "we have to talk."

He grimaced. "No doubt. Walk, too. I go south."

"Back through the Kirach Kund?" I said. "Is that where you sent them? You—"

"Can't go meet them!" he interrupted.

I relaxed a little. That was the hardest part of the conversation I'd anticipated: telling Morlock we had come to a parting of ways. Then I thought a little about what he'd said.

"Do you mean you can't, or I can't?" I asked.

"I can't," he said. "You shouldn't. Think it through."

I would have much preferred that he explain it to me: both because he knew more than I did, and so that I could argue with him. But getting words out of Morlock was like uprooting tree stumps, even at the best of times—which this wasn't.

Anyway, I could see what he meant clearly enough. If Merlin had some way of tracing us or following us, we would lead him straight to Roble and the children. Then we'd be back in the same situation: all of us at risk because of this duel between Morlock and Merlin.

"Do they know?" I asked finally.

"No," Morlock admitted. "They expect us."

"Why—?" I started to ask, then broke off.

Morlock snarled at me, and sounded like nothing so much as the werewolf we had met in the mountains. I waited, but he didn't say anything else.

Anyway, maybe it was clear enough. He was fond of Roble and the children. Maybe even of that milky wench, Reijka Kingheart. And he'd had to walk away from them, his last words to them a lie: "I'll see you soon," or something like that. Otherwise they would have come with, or followed after, and he couldn't have that. Maybe that was it. Something was bothering him, anyway.

Abruptly, he stopped. It was as emphatic as shouting: I knew he had something important to say. His pale eyes, lit strangely by moonlight, stabbed through the shadows at me.

"I go south, then east over the Nar," he said. He swallowed painfully and continued. "You: north maybe. Northside of Narkunden, maybe Semendar or Aithonford—places to work, hide, be safe."

"All right," I said. "When do you think I can see my children? Where will they be?"

He shrugged. "Spring or summer maybe."

"That's half a year or more!"

He shrugged again. "By then, eh. By then this thing between me and Merlin. It will be over. I think. I think he. He won't care about you then."

Merlin might not care about my family, but . . . I suddenly thought of that look of betrayal he had fixed on me. He might be interested in looking me up to settle a score. It might be better for my family if I didn't come near them for a while, a long while.

It tore my heart, but I knew they would deal with it better than I would. And every mother knows that time of parting will come eventually: I just hadn't expected it to come that suddenly, to lose all my children at once. All my surviving children. I thought of Stador rotting in that hole in the mountains and sighed.

"How will I find them when it's time?" I asked at last.

I guess I expected him to pull some magical whatsit out of his pocket, but what he said was, "Look for Kingheart's Cavalcade of Wonders."

"What?"

"It's a carnival. A travelling show that goes from town to town."

"*That's* the business proposition Reijka had for me?"

"Yes. Her parents ran a carnival, but they wanted a settled life for her. They bought her a citizenship in Narkunden, a prenticeship with a physician. But she hates it and now she's starting her own show."

"A carnival." I thought about it, and some icy pain deep within me eased a little. Not tied to any town with its stupid rules and laws. I'd known some travelling players in Four Castles and had always admired their camaraderie and freedom. "Not a bad life."

"Eh."

"Did you travel with them?" I asked. "With Reijka's parents? Is that how you know her?"

"Yes, Lonijka Kingheart and her husband took me in once." He looked away; there seemed to be some painful memory hidden behind the words. "That was around the time Reijka was born."

"Huh."

"Good fortune to you," he muttered, and turned away.

Wait, was what I did not say. Maybe I should have. Whatever I should have said, I didn't say it. I didn't say anything, but just stood there with my jaw clamped shut as he hobbled away and disappeared around a corner.

I did like him at first, and a little bit toward the end, too. But not enough to die in that stupid vendetta between his father and him—and not enough to forget that my son had died in it. I waited until he was gone, and then I walked away in exactly the opposite direction.

That was quite a while ago. I suppose by now one of them has killed the other, or maybe they're both dead. I never did hear how it played out. I sort of wish I knew, but more importantly I wish I knew if it was safe to see my family again. I've been working on a farm north of Narkunden for the past two years, and the farmer just came in and told me to knock off work for the night.

A carnival is coming to town.

XII

Interlude: The Anointing

The trees went forth on a time to anoint a king over them; and they said unto the olive tree, "Reign thou over us." But the olive tree said unto them, "Should I leave my fatness, wherewith by me they honour God and man, and go to be promoted over the trees?" And the trees said to the fig tree, "Come thou, and reign over us." But the fig tree said unto them, "Should I forsake my sweetness, and my good fruit, and go to be promoted over the trees?" Then said the trees unto the vine, "Come thou, and reign over us." And the vine said unto them, "Should I leave my wine, which cheereth God and man, and go to be promoted over the trees?"

—Judges

The day of anointing is a proud day in the life of a Gathenavalona. So the elders say; but the Sisters are silent. Gathenavalona did feel proud, a little, as she watched the ceremonies. The carapace and face-shell of her charge were peeled carefully away, and the royal jelly applied directly to her purplish pulsating flesh. Old Valona was there, wearing the Wreath of Parting, and Marh Valone crowned the new Valona with a Wreath of Becoming. There was a dance, which the Sisters partook in, since it involved no mating. There were speeches and ceremonies and stories and feasting from dawn nearly to dusk. This would be a very special season of Motherdeath, some said the best kind of all.

Gathenavalona tried to be happy, but her heart wasn't in it. At her former charge's insistence, she went along to the new Mother's Nest and settled in for the night together.

"The place is too big for me," said young Valona (Dhyrvalona no more since her anointing). The jelly gleamed all over her exposed skin.

"You'll grow into it," Gathenavalona predicted. "The Mother is the greatest of all the Khroi."

"When will my egg-sac grow in?" Valona asked sleepily.

"Soon."

"Will you still sleep in my nest when I'm big?" Valona asked, sounding sleepier yet.

Gathenavalona closed her eyes. "If you wish it," she whispered at last.

Young Valona sang:

"Gathenavalona! Speak up!"
"Gathenavalona! Stand tall!"
"Gathenavalona! No one hears what you don't say."

It was the sort of thing a nurse says to a young Khroi after her Second Birth. Gathenavalona laboriously blinked one eye. Her former charge was making a joke, and she felt obliged to register amusement.

Two of Valona's half-open eyes opened wide, and she was clearly concerned; her soft gleaming head was somehow more expressive without its chitinous shell.

"Would you like to hear a story?" Gathenavalona asked, with feigned gaiety, before Valona asked her a question she would have to answer.

Young Valona's eyes went half shut again. "Yes," she said thickly, with just one of her mouths. "Tell stories. Am tired. Feel strange." She rolled over and lay at ease in the Mother's Nest.

Gathenavalona sat down beside her and told her stories until long after she was sure the new horde mother had fallen asleep. She did not weep, because Khroi do not weep.

XIII

TRAVELLER'S DREAM

. . . THOU ART STILL
THE SON OF MORN IN WEARY NIGHT'S DECLINE
THE LOST TRAVELLER'S DREAM UNDER THE HILL.
—BLAKE, "TO THE ACCUSER"

I t's a long way from Aflraun to the eastern reaches of the Lost Woods, long even as the proverbial crow flies. And Morlock Ambrosius, despite certain legends to the contrary, was not a crow: he had to walk on, not fly over, the mazelike paths meandering through the foothills of the Blackthorn Range. Seven kinds of danger would walk those paths with him: thieves, earthquakes, volcanic outbursts, dark-gnomes, werewolves, dragons, and (most terrible of all, perhaps) the dragon-taming Khroi.

He was prepared for a bad journey. In fact, he counted on one. (There was some chance he would be followed, or at least observed.) But the journey was far from over before he realized that he hadn't prepared enough. This reflection struck him most forcibly on the journey's forty-second night: he was being stalked by a pack of werewolves and he had run out of both silver and wolfbane.

So he ran. Werewolves, in their nocturnal form, are like other wolves: if they flush a quarry who is determined and able to elude them, they usually give up and seek easier game (the very young, the very old, the gullible, and the morbid). But with his dark unruly hair, slightly crooked shoulders, and loping irregular stride, Morlock had a rather wolfish look about him. It wasn't impossible that they thought him a werewolf incapable of making the nocturnal change. There were such, Morlock knew, and these imperfect monsters (more *were* than *wolf*) were persecuted ruthlessly by their more perfectly ambiguous brethren.

He came to the verge of an unexpectedly bowl-like valley with a high toothlike hill in its center. He didn't like the looks of the place. He would have turned back or gone along the verge—except for his pursuers. Listening carefully, he thought they had broken from single file and were fanning out behind him. Whichever way he turned he would meet them. His only chance lay ahead. It would be better to confront them, if he had to, on a hill, with his back to the slope.

Leaping over the verge, he dashed down into the valley. Here he actually began to gain on them, and on the valley's level floor he held his own. The high hill loomed over him, black against the night-blue darkness of the sky, the silver drifts of stars, the blank unequal eyes of the major moons setting in the east.

Then: the chase was over. He stumbled and fell across a low hedge trimmed with flowers, planted at the base of the hill. But even as he leapt to his feet to defend himself from the imminent predators, he laughed. There was no mistaking the sweet clear scent of aconite rising from the broken leaves.

Wolfbane! He laughed again as he drew his sword and cut a pile of loose stalks with a single stroke. He thrust the sword into the earth and reached over one shoulder to draw a jar of fire-wylm from his pack. He scattered some wylm on the branches and they burst into flame. Swiftly he corked the jar and thrust it in a pocket.

Lifting a cluster of burning stems as a makeshift torch, he saw his pursuers: seven dark wolf-shapes, still as stones, watching the light with green glittering eyes.

After recovering his sword, he whirled the torch in the air, to feed the flame and spread the smoke, both deadly to his pursuers. He barked at them, the short staccato barks of an aggressor, and moved forward to the edge of the wolfbane and then beyond it, sweeping the burning stalks from side to side before him.

If he had challenged them earlier, they would have done their best to tear him to bits. But the werewolves were now far from anything they considered their territory; the intruder had made no claim on it, properly running when challenged; and since he dared to handle wolfbane, he was clearly no kin of theirs.

There was a brief but unhurried consultation as Morlock slowly advanced against them. They touched each other's noses and wagged their tails. Then, without a glance in Morlock's direction, they vanished one after another into the arc of shadows beyond the dying flames. When he was sure they were gone, he dropped the burning stems and ground them under his feet, turning then to stomp out the lingering flames in the wolfbane-lined hedge. Finally he moved back behind the hedge to catch his breath in relative safety.

But glancing up, he realized he wasn't alone. A tall robed figure stood farther up the hill, its features invisible in the shadows.

"Why have you trespassed on my hill?" the figure demanded, in a harsh deep voice. "You have stolen my herbs and wantonly cut and burned a hole in my hedge."

"I was defending my life," Morlock said sharply. Then he continued more slowly, "Still, I regret having harmed something you value. I'm willing to recompense you, within reason."

"What could *you* have that *I* would want?" the other demanded scornfully. "A dwarvish hoard in your peddler's pack? Or merely a map to find one, which you will reluctantly part with, for a nominal fee?"

"I am Morlock Ambrosius. Many a dwarvish hoard has been spent to buy the things my hands have made. If you reject my offer, I won't insist. Thanks for the wolfbane." He turned to go.

"Wait!" said the other.

"I'll wait," Morlock said, turning back, "but not for long."

There was a brief pause, and then the figure spoke again, in a light hesitating voice. It was hard to believe the same person was speaking. "I apologize, Morlock Traveller, for my harsh words. Your offer is generous, but . . . It raises a difficult question. Will you accept hospitality while we discuss it?"

Morlock stood with his weight on his good leg and thought for a moment. He didn't like or trust this person. But the thought of walking away from an unpaid debt nagged at him. He had been raised with too much respect for property, or so he had often been told. But that was the way he was. He nodded reluctantly.

The robed figure turned and walked up the steep hill. Morlock followed.

They came at last to a cave entrance on the west side of the hill. There was no door, but the entrance had once been sealed by a wall of mortared stone—the edges were ragged, if weathered, and Morlock noticed the stones that had been the wall in a grass-covered heap nearby. The opening was radiant with firelight.

The fire was in the center of the chamber within; a pot of herbs was boiling over above it. The infusion stank like poison. A ring of flat stones encircled the fire, blackened through long use. There were some other signs the cave had long been occupied: the pallet of rotting straw along the wall, the dust that covered some of the crude bowls and cups. Yet . . . the place had the air of a temporary camp, as if the tenant had stopped here briefly some years ago and had never happened to leave.

Morlock glanced at his host, who seemed to be waiting for him to say something. At first Morlock thought the man (it was clearly a man) was standing so that a shadow fell over part of his face. But there was no obstruction between the man and the fire, and the shadow was too dark for any such mundane cause. It was not as if the man's skin were dark, either—the features on the left side, including the eye, were invisible, wholly concealed under the layer of shadow.

"Half of your face appears to be missing," Morlock said then. He was not famous for his tact, but in a situation like this tact was hard to define.

"My face is still there," the other replied, in the light wavering tone Morlock thought of as his second voice. "The darkness simply . . . overlays it."

"You want me to remove the darkness," Morlock said flatly.

"Yes . . . that is . . . most of it. I need some of it to help me hear." In fact, the other seemed uncertain whether he wanted to be rid of the darkness or not; the half of his face which Morlock could see was round and almost expressionless, marked only by confusion.

"I don't understand," Morlock replied finally.

The other nodded. "I realize that. How could you? Perhaps if . . . or . . . Follow me," he directed abruptly in his first voice, the deeper more commanding one.

Morlock shrugged the pack off his crooked shoulders. He took a water bottle out of it and had several long drinks, rinsing away the dust and dry phlegm of his long run. Then he corked the bottle, repacked it, and joined the other who stood fidgeting at the back of the cave.

The man ducked down his head as Morlock approached, and scurried into a low passage that opened up at the back of the cave. More deliberately, but not actually lagging, Morlock followed him.

The passage ended at the verge of a pit. Pausing there the other said, "Do you hear anything? Listen!"

After a moment of listening to echoes, Morlock said, "The pit is deep, but there's no breeze. I guess this is the only entrance."

The other hissed in irritation, just long enough to sound faintly beast-like. "Not that! Do you hear nothing else?"

"No."

"Then we must go down," the other said. Somehow he sounded both pleased and disturbed—perhaps faintly jealous.

"Not without light."

The other immediately began to protest. "But a torch will simply muddy the air, which is stale enough. Besides, you will hear better in the dark." He continued for awhile in this vein.

Morlock said nothing. After the other had completed his cycle of protests and repeated a few of them he finally fell silent, expecting a rebuttal that never came. Morlock waited. Eventually the other went and fetched a lit lamp from his dwelling area.

The light revealed that the pit was about forty feet across. Broad stone steps spiralled downward along the wall of the pit. Sulkily the two-voiced, shadow-faced man handed Morlock the lamp and led him downward.

If nothing else, the lamplight helped Morlock avoid a kind of fungus that sprouted all along the dank stone wall. The fungus grew a cap, like a mushroom or a toadstool, but each cap had as many as seven stalks under-neath it, giving them a sinister spiderish look. Each cap, too, had a slash across it like a lipless mouth, and some of these emitted chirping cries of protest as the circle of lamplight passed over them.

At the bottom of the pit was a rough stone floor at a fairly steep slope. The lower part of the slope was hidden by a darkness that the light of the lamp did not dispel. In the rough stone of the floor was a smooth hollow in the shape of a man lying prone. The head of the shape was eclipsed by the tidepool of darkness at the lowest part of the pit.

Morlock knelt and traced the unclear outlines of the shape. His maker's instincts told him that it had not been made, but worn into stone by long use, like cart tracks in the cobblestones of a busy street. He wondered how many times someone had lain there to wear away that template form, how many years, how many someones it had taken to make that shape.

Looking up, he caught the eye of the other, who was watching him eagerly. "Do you hear it now?" the other asked.

Morlock rose to his feet and concentrated. "I hear a sort of murmuring. I can make no sense of it."

The other sighed. "I first heard that voice . . . well, some years ago, I suppose. Difficult to say how many . . . I was travelling south to . . . to look for treasure in the mountains," he said, with a sudden blurt of boyish enthusiasm. "I hardly knew what real treasure awaited me," he said more slowly.

Morlock refrained from comment.

"I camped in the cave at the top of the hill—others had been there before me. I explored the passage, thinking the dwarves might have made it when they ruled these lands. It was there that I first heard the voice in the darkness. It guided me down the stairs and spoke to me as I sat here. Finally . . . after a while . . ."

"You put your face in it," Morlock said flatly, since the other seemed to be unable to come to the point.

"I listened to it," the other said defensively. "The pattern"—he gestured at the smooth form at Morlock's feet—"was here even then. Many people have sought wisdom here."

"Where have they gone, I wonder?" Morlock asked dryly.

"Not everyone has the passion for . . . for true knowledge," the listener said complacently. "It"—he gestured at the pool of shadow—"tells me I have lasted longer than many listeners."

"Impressive," Morlock acknowledged.

"After a while . . . I forget how long it was . . . it, the voice, it suggested that it leave a part of itself inside me, so that I could hear it better. I resisted for a long time, but . . . I finally agreed to let it . . . do it. There was just a little darkness at first; you hardly noticed it. And I did hear the voice better . . . much more clearly. I didn't realize the darkness would spread. . . ."

Morlock waited for him to continue, but he seemed to be finished.

"What does the darkness tell you?" Morlock asked.

The listener fidgeted uneasily. "It told me you were coming," he said after a lengthy silence. "But usually it tells me . . . secrets. Ways of looking at . . . at things."

"Hm." Morlock wondered if the listener was hiding his hard-won secrets or hiding, even from himself, that they didn't exist.

"After all," the listener said in a rush of enthusiasm, "what you see is simply a vein or artery in a vast network of darkness that stretches far beyond the mountains and down into the heart of the earth. It is older than time and knows more."

Morlock doubted all this, although he didn't say so. He was beginning to have more definite, more local ideas about this darkness. He asked, "Why do you think the darkness tells you its secrets?"

The listener looked pleased but confused, as if the question had never occurred to him before. "Well . . . I'm not sure . . . Perhaps it was lonely."

The ringing naiveté of this suggestion struck Morlock unpleasantly. He glanced at the mouth of darkness open in the lowest corner of the room. Lonely? Hungry was nearer the mark, he guessed.

"I can't breathe here," Morlock said then, and turned away to walk up the winding stairs. After a moment's hesitation the listener followed him upward.

When they had returned to the listener's squalid living quarters, Morlock put down the lamp and said, "I want to examine the darkness on your face. Sit down."

The listener obeyed him, a look of alarm on his visible features. Tentatively, Morlock put the fingers of his right hand into the darkness on the listener's face. The darkness formed no barrier; it was less substantial than fog. Almost immediately Morlock's fingers touched the surface of the listener's cheek. There were long gouges in the otherwise unlined skin of the listener's face.

"You have clawed at the darkness," Morlock observed.

The listener nodded, a little guiltily. "I was . . . frustrated. Frightened. I didn't think it would spread. I didn't know what would happen if it would spread further . . . I still don't. Did I hurt myself?"

The wounds felt swollen and hot to Morlock's touch. "Can't you tell?" he asked.

The listener shrugged. "It is . . . a little numb, under the darkness. I can't move that side of my face very well, either."

"Can you see from your left eye?"

"Sometimes," the listener replied truculently, and Morlock knew he was lying.

Morlock withdrew his hand and looked at his fingertips. No darkness adhered to them; he would have been surprised if it had. He rubbed his two sets of fingertips against each other meditatively, checking for any numbness. There was none. There had been almost no sensation at all as his fingers had entered the darkness, only a kind of feeling that was hard to define, because it was not felt by the fingers at all. Few could define that feeling or recognize what it implied, but Morlock was one of them.

"Do you know what tal is?" he asked.

"No," the listener replied.

Morlock nodded, unsurprised. "It is a medium," he explained, "nonphysical in nature, but capable of physical effects. It is the means by which consciousness works its will through the body. All conscious beings possess tal; some, like elementals, have no physical bodies at all, only tal-schemata which respond to the various elements."

"Ah," said the listener vaguely, clearly considering the point irrelevant.

"The darkness on your face is tal," Morlock explained. "But it is not your own, at least not originally. It is a sort of colony from an alien awareness, and it serves the ends of that awareness."

"How?" the listener demanded. His visible features displayed both alarm and skepticism.

Morlock had some ideas on that subject, but he did not intend to discuss them. Anything he told the listener he would also tell the darkness. "That is not germane. If you want the darkness removed from your face, I will undertake to do it."

The listener looked both hopeful and anxious. "Would you . . . If you could leave part of it? Say, under the ear, or . . . or even on the temple—"

"I am not a barber," Morlock interrupted sharply. "Nor do I undertake half-works or not-quite-accomplishments. I do a thing or I don't. Choose."

The choice was clearly far from easy. The struggle on the listener's visible features lasted for some time. But finally he muttered in the hesitant "second" voice, "Yes. Remove it."

Morlock did not hesitate. He clasped his hands and summoned the rapture of vision, forcing his consciousness from his body and into the tal-world.

The listener burst into a quiet green-gold fire. Morlock himself became a monochrome torrent of black-and-white flames. The stone and dirt about them, having no tal, sank away almost to invisibility in Morlock's vision. But he felt the warm many-centered glow from a nest of mice in the wall of the cave, and through the stones he caught the brief flash of a passing night-bird, like the streak of a meteor in the lifeless sky.

The darkness lay across the green flickering fire of the listener's face. Morlock reached out with the black-and-white flames of his hands and laid hold of it.

In fact, Morlock did not move. But he commanded his tal-self to move, without his body (which it normally overlaid). To his awareness, it was as if he had laid his hands on the darkness.

And the darkness was alien. He knew that as soon as he came into contact with it. And it knew him. Not by name, perhaps (though it did not say what it knew, it can be difficult to tell what such darknesses may know). But it knew his kind. It had been lured here and trapped by a master maker of the dwarvish race, after the darkness had attacked and devoured several members of the maker's family. This all happened millennia before Morlock was born.

The dwarvish maker, after his great victory over the darkness, became its next victim. He had been the first of many who had lain on the stone and put his face in the darkness: listening there for the voices of his lost beloved ones. He had lain there until his life was drained away. Morlock heard his voice, among many others, whispering in the dark. But the only secret he learned was the untellable sorrow of their eternal agony.

This he learned as the darkness confronted him through the medium of Morlock's vision. Then Morlock seized hold of the darkness that had implanted itself in the listener's face and tried to tear it loose.

The listener screamed. Morlock heard it dimly through his ears. He heard it, more directly and more terribly, through his unmasked awareness. The green fire that was the listener's talic self writhed like a serpent and seemed to grow dim, as if he were dying.

After a moment's hesitation, Morlock redoubled his efforts. But the resistance was too great: he saw that the sessile darkness had deep barbed roots in the light of the listener's being. As he strained, his inner vision perceived that many of the green flames of the listener's tal had dark centers, reminding him of the myriad staring eyes in a peacock's tail.

He let his grip relax, and the nauseating rapport with the darkness was broken. The green flames of the listener's being leapt up again. It seemed to Morlock, though, that they were not as bright as they had been before.

He reimposed his talic self upon his body, and his awareness inhabited his flesh again. He came out of the trance like a swimmer surfacing after a dive through deep water. His face was clammy with sweat, and his clenched hands were shaking.

The listener lay unconscious on the floor of the cave, his visible features twisted in convulsive agony. The darkness seemed to cover more of his face than it had. Morlock made sure he was still breathing (and likely to go on doing so). Then he carried the listener to his pallet and put him to bed.

Morlock didn't like the feeling in the cave, so he laid his bedroll outside on the hill. From the time that he withdrew from the vision until he fell asleep, and afterward, his thoughts were unrelievedly dark.

It was not just that he had failed. He had actually made matters worse. And he had no idea what he should do next.

The next day dawned, chill and bloodless: the new sun was hidden by high clouds. Morlock rose, stretched his sore muscles, and took a meditative walk around the listener's hill, which was planted with an alarming variety of poisonous herbs.

Returning finally to the cave entrance, he found the listener standing

there, smiling with the right side of his face. "So," he said in the commanding voice with which he had first addressed Morlock, "how do you like
my garden?"

"It seems to run to poisons."

The listener, stung, replied hotly, "It is all 'poisons' as you call them.
But, to those-who-know, a handful of the right 'poisons' can bring life out of
death. You found my wolfbane useful enough last night, didn't you?"

Morlock did not reply. It occurred to him again that the listener's two
voices were not merely manners of speech, but two almost totally different
personalities. The matter had an obvious explanation: one voice expressed the
listener's true personality; one voice spoke for the invading shadow. He wondered if the explanation was true.

"Would you care for some breakfast?" the listener asked diffidently, in his
second voice.

"Yes, indeed," Morlock replied. "Thank you." He was suddenly quite
hungry.

He was less hungry when he saw that "breakfast" was a squirming
bowlful of seven-legged mushrooms from the deeper cave. The listener took
a wriggling mushroom from the bowl and, ignoring its chirp of protest,
spitted it on a pointed stick and held it in the fire until it stopped moving
or screaming. Then he offered it to Morlock.

"No, thank you," Morlock said. "Some water perhaps."

The listener shrugged indifferently and tossed the blackened mushroom
into the flames. He handed Morlock a warm drinking jar and drew a live
mushroom from the bowl. He pulled its writhing stalks off and ate them one
by one as its chirps of pain subsided into silence.

The water in the jar was dark; an oily substance rode the surface and he
could see dark leaves drifting in the fluid below. There was a bitter, familiar
reek: the nightleaf plant, he thought—used by the Anhikh mind-sculptors
to prepare their victims.

"I asked you for water," he said to the listener, who paused in his mushroom dismembering. "This appears to be an infusion of nightleaf."

"The water from the well is poisonous," the listener explained, in his overly
ingenuous second voice. "The darkness told me how to purify it with herbs."

"Why don't you seek out another source?" Morlock asked.

"There is none on the hill."

Morlock saw the way things were drifting, but (to see what reaction he would get) asked, "Why not look further? There must be some nearby."

"It is not safe to leave the hill!" stated the listener in the first voice's harshest tones.

Morlock put the jar of drugged water down like a gavel, ending the discussion. "I'm going to find water," he told the listener. "I should be back by nightfall. Good day."

The listener gave vent to a chirping protest, not unlike one of his own mushrooms. Morlock paid it no heed, pausing only to gather the empty water bottles from his pack before walking down the hill.

Morlock found a clear mountain stream running northward about a hundred paces east of the listener's hill. He filled his water bottles, washed himself thoroughly, and sat down to a light breakfast of water, flatbread, and dried meat, not materially different from the forty-odd breakfasts that had preceded it.

This, he reflected gloomily, was not his sort of task. The subtleties of deep healing were beyond him, and they were clearly what was needed here. Oh, he knew enough of the art to keep himself in one piece during his dangerous and mostly solitary wanderings through the unguarded lands. But a higher kind of healer was called for, here: an Illion, a Noreê, a Merlin. (He considered consulting Nimue, or at least as much of her as was available. But he was reluctant to loose her impulse-cloud anywhere near that hungry darkness under the hill.)

Anyway, what would they have told him, if they had been there to advise him? *Walk away!* Yes, he was sure of it. They would have known that Morlock, for all his intelligence about things and ideas, saw people in fairly simple terms, and they would have told him that this was not simple.

Now that he had committed himself to something that was probably beyond him, he felt he understood something of the complexities. The problem? A darkness on a man's face. The solution? Remove it. Very easy. Except . . .

Except: the man had cooperated in the placing of the darkness. It partook of his life and grew, entwined itself through him, became part of him. It was not a sort of blemish on his face that could be removed; it was rooted in the man's consenting soul. The listener might object to the darkness' propensity to spread, but he did not object to the darkness itself, to its nature, to its presence in him. Perhaps he could not; perhaps the choice, once made, was irrevocable.

Morlock shook his head. That sort of thinking was useless. He would not accomplish his task by moaning about how difficult it was.

He thought about the darkness infesting the man, about what it was. A sort of mouth, really, feeding upon the listener's vitality. It would steal the man's tal and therefore drain off his physical energy (although the thing in the pit needed only the former). In that case, there must be a "throat"—a channel to carry the stolen tal down the darkness in the pit. It should have been visible when Morlock had ascended to tal-rapture, and perhaps it had been, but he had not thought to look for it. That, at least, was an error he could correct.

Errors . . . The listener believed, or said, that the darkness was a natural part of the underworld, older than time. But Morlock had been raised, quite literally, underground, and he knew different. He knew, too, from his violent rapport with the darkness last night that it was not sessile in nature, nor was it native to the hill.

I have lasted longer than many listeners, the listener had said. This was possibly true, but it implied he could not last much longer. And: *It told me you were coming.* How had it known that? Why had it told the listener?

In the old days, before it was trapped, it had been able to travel from place to place to find its victims. Now it had to lure them into coming to it. Had the darkness selected Morlock as the listener's successor? He could always refuse to be seduced by the voice in the darkness . . . but its ability to persuade was proven by its survival for such an unthinkable length of time in such a Creator-forsaken wasteland. It would be safest simply to leave, to walk away, to make his given word into a lie.

Morlock gloomily eyed the mouth of his water bottle, but found no answer there.

He returned to the hill from the south, just for the change. There, at the base of the hill, just inside the wolfbane hedge, he found the listener's well.

Moved by curiosity, he lowered the metal bucket by its chain into the well and drew up some water. It was clear and cold; Morlock's intuition detected no spiritual taint. He took some in his hand and prepared to taste it.

"It's poisoned!" he heard the listener's first voice say. He looked up and saw the other standing on the hillside above him.

"How do you know?"

"The darkness told me."

Morlock shrugged and tasted the water. It had the faint metallic tang of the best well water.

"If you have no ideas," the listener suggested brightly (in the second voice), "you could go down and consult the voice in the dark."

"I have two ideas," Morlock said sharply. It was true, although he had been unaware of it until that moment. That was the way his mind worked.

The listener's half-face fell, as if he were disappointed. "But suppose they don't work?" he asked.

"Then I will think of two more," said Morlock Ambrosius, and drank the water in his hand.

Creation takes place in a sacred silence or an untamed ecstatic cacophony. It needn't be solitary, but those present tend to be initiates: creators, or assisting the creation, if only with their attention.

Healing was different, Morlock had found, and he didn't like it.

"What is that?" asked the listener, in the shrillest weakest tones of his second voice.

"It is a focus of power," Morlock said curtly.

They were in the living area of the listener's cave. The listener eyed the focus fearfully and said, "It looks like a sword."

Morlock refrained from replying; the focus obviously was a sword, its blade a crystalline black interwoven with veins of white.

"Is that Tyrfing?" the listener asked. "Doesn't it have a curse on it?"

"That's a story," was Morlock's careful reply. It was true, and sounded like a denial.

"Couldn't you have killed the werewolves with that?" the listener asked, a little less hysterically.

"I was intending to," Morlock said, "when I ran into your hedge of wolf-bane. It seemed like a lucky chance at the time." He paused, then continued more slowly, "Like any focus, Tyrfing can be used as a weapon. But the psychic penalty of using a focus to destroy a life is . . . extreme. It amounts to experiencing your opponent's death yourself. I would take many a risk before I chose to do that."

Before the listener could ask another question Morlock summoned the rapture of vision. The listener's physical form vanished behind a screen of dim green flames, themselves obscured and interwoven with the alien darkness. Morlock looked down at his tal-pattern of black-and-white flames. Concentrating, he forced himself to reach out and take hold of the sword, Tyrfing.

Tyrfing's dark crystalline blade became alive with Morlock's distinctive tal-pattern: a black fire seen through white branches.

Few seers could move their bodies once they had summoned the rapture of vision, but Morlock had trained himself to it. And once he took up Tyrfing, whose nature reflected and amplified his own ability, he could move without difficulty.

Stand by the door! he said to the listener, who started, and then backed carefully away to the cave entrance.

As soon as he looked for it, Morlock saw the dark umbilical cord extending from the clot of darkness infecting the listener. The other end disappeared into the passage leading to the darkness under the hill.

Morlock was pleased. So far his guess had proven right. The colony of darkness infecting the listener was sending nourishment of a spectral kind back to the darkness imprisoned underground.

The cord did not recede from him as he approached; he wondered whether it could perceive him. There was probably a limit to how much it could move, at any rate. The hill and its cave were woven with magic intended to bind the darkness and make it helpless.

Morlock lifted his blazing sword and severed the connecting darkness.

He was successful, but the success was momentary. As he watched, the two severed ends of the dark cord, wriggling like snakes, lifted up and rejoined seamlessly above his sword. He swung the blade again; the cord of darkness again parted and re-formed almost instantly.

Morlock turned away and shook off the rapture like an irritating acquaintance. The world of matter and energy loomed up; the world of the spirit receded. The black-and-white flames sank down; Tyrfing became a blade of black, white-veined crystal. Glancing over, he saw the listener had taken on his mundane appearance also.

The listener's mouth was wide open, his visible eye was closed, his half-face clenched in the grip of a powerful emotion. His body was shaking. In the confusion and weariness that follows rapture, Morlock did not immediately understand what was happening. He speculated gloomily that this attempt had been as pointlessly agonizing to the listener as the last one.

Then, slowly, he understood. The listener was *laughing*—in relief, uncontrollable amusement, contempt.

Morlock reflected that he was holding a sword. The listener had none, was quite unprepared. A single swift motion of his arm and the listener's laughter would be quelled forever. And it would fulfill his agreement: he would sever the listener from his darkness and his life in one gesture. Simple, elegant, direct. Morlock could bury the body and be on his way, all promises kept.

Morlock's internal struggle was intense, but brief. What decided for him, in the end, was the rule of fair bargaining that had been taught him in childhood by the dwarvish clan who fostered him. "A bargain is more than words," his *harven*-father, Tyrtheorn, used to say. "A bargain is a trust. Keep the bargain. Keep the trust."

It was the rule that kept him from killing the listener, only the rule. He had seen too much death to suppose that anyone had a right to life, and he did not believe that the listener would ever do enough good to justify his own life, even to himself. Morlock himself would certainly prefer to be murdered rather than live with an alien darkness poisoning his spirit. And just coincidentally, he found that he hated the listener enough to kill him. Everything pointed in one direction, a river of darkness urging him toward what he really wanted to do anyway. . . . Only the rule stood in the way: "Keep the bargain. Keep the trust."

Morlock sighed and sheathed his sword. It occurred to him that he was not going to kill anybody at the moment. He would have liked to speak with his *harven*-father, but Tyrtheorn had been dead these three hundred years.

The listener was silent at last, watching him carefully. There was an air almost of disappointment in the cave. Perhaps the darkness longed to be free of the listener even as he longed to be free of it. What would have happened if Morlock had killed the man in unguarded rage? Would the mouth of darkness have been free to settle on Morlock before he was aware of it? It may, at least, have hoped so, and directed the listener to provoke Morlock to murderous rage. He wondered if he had ever seen the listener behave naturally—had ever seen him act except at the prompting of the darkness that owned him.

"Are you out of ideas?" the listener asked finally.

"No," Morlock said. "I have one more. I think you should leave the hill."

"What?" shouted the listener, in the first voice.

"The darkness under the hill is feeding on you. The farther you get from it, the less easily it can do this; it is bound to this location by a magical trap. I think if you got far enough away, and stayed away long enough, the darkness on your face would be forced to withdraw."

The listener laughed again, more curtly and dismissively than before. "You don't know!" he said in his second voice. "The darkness is . . . everywhere. If I left it would refuse to teach me any more secrets. But it could . . . Don't you understand? Darkness is everywhere. It . . . No one can escape it."

Morlock shrugged his crooked shoulders. "There is darkness and darkness. I assure you, the one under this hill is quite local."

"You don't know!"

"I do."

"I won't leave!" cried the listener shrilly. "I won't! I *won't!*"

Morlock looked at him wearily. Something inside him, some intuitive voice of his own, told him that this was the true solution. This was where a great healer, like Illion or Noreê, would throw his or her whole weight. They would marshal arguments, talk all night, wear away the listener's reluctance (the source of which was painfully obvious). They would display patience; they would comfort the listener's fears, foster his strengths.

But Morlock knew his own limits. He shrugged again and said, "Then."

"You have no more ideas?"

"Not at the moment."

"Oh." The listener paused, then observed slyly, "Perhaps you should go down and ask the voice in the darkness. It knows more secrets than you can imagine."

"Most people do," Morlock replied absently. He had no great thirst for secret knowledge. He walked out of the cave, saying "Good night" as he passed the listener.

Night had risen long ago. Morlock stood for a moment by the cave entrance and breathed in the strange poison-scented air that lay over the hill. His thoughts were somber. True to his boast, he had already thought of two more ideas. He might close up the passage to the darkness, or simply abduct the listener and carry him far from the hill. They were good enough ideas, but (separately or together) they were obviously doomed to failure.

No scheme to remove the darkness from the listener could be successful without the consent of the listener, and that clearly would not be forthcoming. The listener was wholly subject to the darkness; probably he had bargained with Morlock only because the darkness itself had prompted him to detain Morlock from his journey westward.

Morlock lay down and wrapped himself in his sleeping cloak, hoping some revelation would come in the night. And, in a way, one did.

Morlock awoke when the side of his head struck the edge of a stone surface. He awoke instantly and completely; his eyes gaped wide, hungry for light. There was none. The lightless air was dense and close, woven with subtle sounds: the labored breathing of the listener (who was struggling to haul Morlock by the shoulders), the chirrups of seven-legged mushrooms . . . They were under the hill. The listener was dragging him down to forcibly put him into the darkness.

He braced his feet and pushed. The listener squawked and went down. Morlock rolled over him and sprang to his feet on the winding stairs. He seized the listener and slammed him against the wall of the pit. It took all his willpower to keep from strangling the life out of the treacherous listener.

"I'm sorry!" the listener squeaked, in his second voice. "It said it would let me go if I gave you to it. It said . . . It said it wouldn't harm you. . . ."

Then all his willpower was not enough. He found his powerful skilled hands had wrapped themselves around the listener's throat, choking off his protestations as they would soon choke off his life. Morlock trembled in anticipation of the listener's death. It didn't seem like murder. In that instant he thought of the listener's death as a great work of art he would create, by blind impulse out of improvised materials, guided by intuitions born of the embracing darkness.

Darkness?

The murmurs from below had reached an almost deafening crescendo.

He opened his hands and drew in a long calming breath. "No," he said: to the listener, to the voice in the darkness, to himself. "It won't work."

The listener whimpered unintelligibly and fell at his feet.

Morlock stepped over him and climbed the winding stairway out of the pit. The darkness was, indeed, persuasive—now he could attest to that himself. He could hardly believe that his actions were really his own until he stepped out into the open and the light of the three moons sheared away the shadows like a knife.

That was when the answer came to him.

After drawing a bucket of water from the well, Morlock broke the chain and carried the bucket to the top of the hill. He left it there to collect moonlight for the rest of the night.

Walking back down the slope, he numbered the things he'd need: two clay jars, a sheet of sealing wax, a lump of twilight, a rock, a fire.

The fire he could make later; the twilight-shadow he could collect around dawn. He had a wax tablet, for making notes, in his backpack; that would do for a seal. He also had a Perfect Occlusion in his pack: it established a zone that no light could enter or leave, unless the light source was physically carried in or out. (It was a little tricky to set one up so that the inside remained perfectly dark, but of course he didn't mind a little ambient moonlight for the project he had in mind.) The stone he could get anywhere; it need have no special properties except a certain shape and size.

He set up the occlusion by the wolfbane-lined hedge, laying it out in a flat space and staking down its seven corners with spikes of native rock. Then he went off to see about jars.

The ones the listener had been using in his living area were irretrievably contaminated and useless for Morlock's purposes. He decided to make his own, and searched out the listener's clay pit. There, to his surprise, he found several clay pots and jars, finished and set out to dry. They were rather weathered (as if the listener had made them some time ago and forgotten about them) but perfectly sound. Morlock trudged with them to the stream and back (there being no spare bucket for the well).

When he returned, long before dawn, the occlusion had established itself. He had found a good stone at the stream, too: about the size of his fist and approximately the same shape, but smooth from long years in the streambed. He dropped it beside the occlusion and climbed the hill to collect the bucket of water, now drenched with implicit moonlight.

He covered the bucket with the wax tablet (he had nothing else that would do), brought it down, and set it by the occlusion. Then he dug a pit in the turf and started a fire. Once the fire was going well, he planted three stones around it and settled the bucket on them, over the fire.

Morlock watched the bucket closely, waiting for the water to boil. Once it did, steam would upset the cover and that was bad. Moonlight would escape and, worse, firelight might enter. Fire destroys moonlight whenever they make contact, as does any light (except starlight, the most fragile and subtle of lights).

As intently as he watched, he almost missed the moment. The bucket, after muttering and shaking itself from the heat, suddenly grew quiet. A moment later, a puff of boiling steam shot forth from between the metal rim and the melting wax of the tablet. It was irradiated by a bolt of white-hot moonlight. Morlock slapped the tablet down against the bucket rim and snatched the bucket from the fire with his free hand. (It was hot, but it took a considerable fire to annoy Morlock; that was the destiny of his blood.) He leapt into the zone of Perfect Occlusion.

Water was still bubbling through the semiliquid surface of the wax tablet, but no light accompanied it. Morlock took the wax tablet away and was pleased to see a considerable mass of cooling but still white-hot moonlight slumped in the bottom of the bucket. It looked almost dense enough to work it with his fingers.

Morlock, of course, did not risk this. He set the bucket down, sat down himself, and, clasping his hands, summoned the rapture of vision.

He reached out with the monochrome flames of his tal-self and worked the white-hot cooling moonlight into a sheet. Then he creased the sheet and folded it. He creased it again and folded it. And again and again: more than thirty times, until the sheet had become a long, thin dense strip of moonlight, narrowing to a point. It was still malleable, the hot orange color of a setting moon. In a perfect world he would have preferred to reheat it, but Morlock was a realist. He picked up the strip of moonlight and plunged it into a jar of cool water, where its radiance instantly became a brittle wintry blue.

Leaving it there, Morlock drew Tyrfing and stepped out of the Perfect Occlusion. The time was just before dawn. Morlock cut himself a suitable lump of twilight shadow from the hill's silhouette just before the sun rose on the opposite horizon. Quickly hiding the shadow under his cloak to protect it from daylight, Morlock sheathed Tyrfing and dismissed the rapture.

The weight of the world fell across his crooked shoulders. He had been in the visionary state for hours. And the worst of it was, he knew he had many hours to go before he could sleep.

When Morlock lifted his head he saw the listener standing not far away. The darkness, once symmetrical, now seemed to be sending out shoots or pseudopods into the right side of the listener's face. His nose had wholly disappeared, and this (along with the pinched fleshless character of his visible features) gave his face a skull-like appearance—not even a whole skull: a skull drenched in quicklime so that part of it was eaten away. The listener, Morlock guessed, hadn't long to live.

"Didn't you hear me?" the listener's second voice was demanding. He sounded peevish, like a sick weary child.

"No," Morlock admitted.

"I said that . . . I'm sorry about last night. The darkness . . . that is, the voice explained—"

Morlock waved him to silence. "Tell me later," he said. "I'm busy." He turned away and walked back to the Perfect Occlusion, bright blue in reflection of the morning sky. Glancing back, he found the listener had followed him.

"What is that?" the listener asked, eyeing the occlusion.

"Part of what I'm doing."

"Is it . . . ?" the listener said, both eager and anxious, "Is it . . . another idea?"

"I'll tell you if it works," Morlock replied sharply.

The listener's less-than-half-face looked hurt. Morlock was angry at the listener for being so oppressively weak, but he was also angry at himself for giving way to his irritation.

"Look," he said finally, "you seem tired. Why don't you go to sleep?"

The listener nodded slowly, with his skull-like less-than-a-face. He turned away and stumbled wearily up the hill.

Morlock stepped into the Perfect Occlusion, now lit within by brittle blue light. He drew the chunk of twilight from under his cloak and the strip of moonlight from the jar of cool water. He spent the rest of the day sharpening its edge on the lump of shadow.

Just after sunset, Morlock carried two jars of water up to the listener's cave. One was hot—just off the fire, in fact. One was cold, just drawn from the well (with the restored bucket and chain). Under one arm was the wax tablet.

The listener was still sleeping. Morlock put the two jars of water by the listener's pallet and dropped the wax tablet in the hot water to soften it. Then he returned to the Perfect Occlusion.

When he reentered the cave, he held the blade of moonlight in his right hand, the stone in the left. Dropping the stone next to the jars, he lifted the shining insubstantial blade and cut open the listener's chest.

He could hardly see the listener's heart, tangled about as it was with tendrils of invading darkness. The heart is the source or entry point of human tal; it would naturally be the focus of the darkness' attack, but would hold out until the end.

The end was dreadfully near. The listener's insides were rotten with darkness. Morlock clenched his teeth and reached through the tendrils of darkness until his fingers closed on the breathing fist-sized heart. He drew it out between the pale slats of the listener's ribs.

The listener stopped breathing.

Morlock moved with cautious speed. Until now the only danger had been that the listener would wake up. Now it was possible he never would. Morlock literally held the man's life in his hands.

He placed the heart in the jar of cold water. It quickly sank to the bottom, heavy with unshed blood and tal, pulsing futilely like a fish without fins. Water ran over the rim. He drew the wax tablet from the hot water and pressed it over the mouth of the cold jar, sealing the heart inside.

Now he picked up the fist-sized stone and (bending aside the pale ribs) placed it on the heart's dark pedestal.

The listener drew a long shuddering breath.

Morlock carefully folded back the listener's flesh, and it rejoined seamlessly. The filthy robe, too, healed like the second skin it was.

The listener choked out something in his sleep. Morlock couldn't tell what it was. He gathered up the jars and carried them away, along with the shining insubstantial blade.

Morlock was eating flatbread and dried meat, sitting between his fire and the Perfect Occlusion, when the listener came down the hill.

"Good evening," Morlock said. "How are you?"

"I feel strange," the listener said, in a rather hollow version of the second voice.

"Would you like some bread and meat?"

The listener shook his head impatiently. "Food is horrible," he declared, in a slightly tinny version of the imperious first voice. "Flesh is nasty. Life is unclean."

Morlock was in no position to disagree. He ate some more meat instead.

"Something has changed," the listener said insistently.

Morlock said nothing. He wasn't ready to tell the truth, and would not lie.

"I'll go ask the voice in the darkness," said the listener.

"If you do," Morlock replied, "it will kill you."

The listener looked at him for a moment, a single eye peering out of a mostly eaten face. He turned away and walked up the hill. Morlock watched him go into the cave and disappear. Then he followed the other, going up the hill and entering the listener's living quarters.

He was alone; the listener had gone on down the pit where the voice whispered in the darkness.

Morlock sat down and waited.

The night passed quickly. Morlock dozed on and off. The listener did not return until just before sunrise.

Morlock heard some scrabbling in the passage at the back of the cave. He looked over and saw the listener's hand clenching and unclenching on the threshold.

Morlock leaped to his feet and ran over. He drew the listener out of the passage and carried him over to the pallet.

Darkness had spread across the listener's face and throat, leaving only one frightened blue eye. His body jerked convulsively; he seemed only to control his right arm. The skin on his other arm was sallow, with poisonously dark veins woven into the slack muscle.

Morlock understood, of course. In fact, he had been expecting this. The darkness had devoured all of the listener's tal . . . or at least enough of it that he could no longer control his own body, or even make it breathe.

Pity bit Morlock like a snake. He knelt down by the convulsing listener and took his living hand. The listener turned his remaining eye to look at him. But Morlock could say no word of comfort. What was there to say?

The listener screamed. It came out as a mere gasp, since his vocal cords no longer knew how to respond, but Morlock understood. Some moments later, the listener's fingers relaxed in the nervelessness of death. Morlock let them go and the hand fell to the ground with a conclusive thud.

Immediately the darkness began to rise from the listener's corpse. Tendril after tendril lifted, forming a complex drifting cloud in midair. Morlock stood up and watched it warily, prepared to draw Tyrfing if it moved toward him. But it didn't. When the last tendril lifted from the listener's corpse, the whole cloud drifted slowly, almost reluctantly, into the passage leading to the pit. It merged with the mundane darkness there and disappeared.

Morlock nodded. Without its anchor in the listener's psyche the darkness was dragged back to its trap under the hill.

He reached down and picked up the withered corpse, as light as a straw man or a rag doll. He carried it out of the cave and down the hill, laying it beside the Perfect Occlusion in which were hidden the moonlight blade and the dead man's heart.

Then he took a mallet out of his pack and returned to the cave.

The passageway down to the pit was easy to destroy. It had been built; its maker had deliberately balanced stress with counterstress. Morlock simply had to unbalance them.

Unpleasant work (he hated wrecking things), but nothing compared to what he had already done. The dwarvish maker who had made this passage and the demon-trap at the bottom of yonder pit had undoubtedly been a genius. But also a fool: if he had only had the presence of mind to perform this selfsame act, his own life and that of countless others would have been bettered, if not saved.

"Better late than never," observed Morlock, who was fond of a proverb. He shattered the keystone of the last arch and it collapsed in ruin.

When the last sunlight had faded from the sky, Morlock brought out the sealed jar and the moonlight blade. He opened up the corpse's chest with the shining insubstantial blade, then laid the instrument aside. He reached under the dry slats of the ribs and pulled out the fist-sized stone.

Breaking the seal on the jar, Morlock reached in and drew forth the live struggling heart. He forced it under the ribs and watched as it wriggled into its accustomed place.

The corpse gurgled and convulsed. Morlock held it down as he carefully folded back the severed flesh. It rejoined seamlessly, and the dirty robe likewise, like a second skin. Morlock let the corpse go and stood back as it gurgled and convulsed its way into life.

In time the body stopped writhing and lay still, breathing heavily as it stared up into the night sky. Presently he lifted his head and looked over at Morlock.

"What's your name?" Morlock asked. It was something he'd long wondered.

"Trannon," the other replied in a light tenor, very unlike either the first or the second voice.

"Trannon, I am Morlock Ambrosius."

They greeted each other solemnly.

"I am headed east from here," Morlock said after telling Trannon the whole story for the third time. "The nearest town, though, is Heath Harbor, somewhat north of here. I can take you there—"

Trannon refused. "I know Heath Harbor well. I can reach there easily enough, if that's what I decide to do."

Morlock pondered this comment as he finished folding up the disestablished Perfect Occlusion. When he had packed it away and tied the water bottles to his pack, he turned back to Trannon.

"What do you intend to do?" he asked bluntly.

Trannon looked thoughtful—at least, as thoughtful as he could. (Except for the reddish brown gouges on the left side of his face, the experience had left him looking rather unmarked and ingenuous.) "Perhaps I'll stay," he said. "I can serve to warn people away from this spot—" He stopped short when he saw the expression on Morlock's face.

"That seems to me to be habit speaking," Morlock said carefully. "If there's one thing you must do, it's get away from here. Travellers don't pass by twice in a generation, and there is no danger of one stumbling across the darkness by accident; that passage is closed.

"Still—suppose—"

Morlock shook his head. "The decision is yours to make, but consider: if there is danger for anyone in this place, there is double for you. No, I will not debate this. The decision is yours."

Trannon nodded solemnly and said nothing.

Morlock gave him a few blocks of dried meat and flatbread, over

Trannon's protests. "You can't get to your mushrooms now," he pointed out, "and you won't find game very plentiful unless you go further north." He also gave Trannon the moonlight blade. "I don't know if it will be any use to you, but it is well made and will last for some time, if you keep it out of sunlight and firelight. If nothing else, you can sell it in Heath Harbor."

Trannon accepted the blade without protest. Possibly, Morlock thought, he felt he had earned it.

Morlock threw his pack over his crooked shoulders. "Well, Trannon," he said. "We may meet again, or not. Either way, good fortune to you."

"Good-bye, Morlock Traveller," the other said. "Thank you."

Morlock walked away quickly. He had the feeling that Trannon was intent on doing something that would wreck everything Morlock had done. That was his choice; Morlock had discharged his own obligations, and they in no way included being Trannon's nursemaid forever. But the thought still bothered him.

He looked back when he reached the far side of the valley, and saw Trannon motionless in the moonlight beneath the toothlike hill.

Morlock set himself to climb the slope before him. When he reached the crest he looked back again. The other had disappeared. Morlock shrugged and walked on eastward.

When he finally got to sleep, late the next morning, Morlock's rest was broken by a nightmare. He dreamed that he had opened his own chest with a moonlight blade, intent on replacing his heart with a stone. But when he reached in to remove the heart, he found neither heart, nor stone, nor anything.

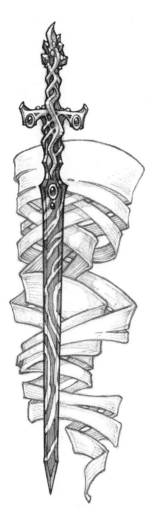

XIV

WHERE NURGNATZ DWELLS

"ANYONE HERE?" HE ASKED, AND ECHO
ANSWERED, "HERE!"

—OVID, *METAMORPHOSES*

The storm was getting thicker and the day was getting darker—if you could even call it day anymore. Rhabia was having second thoughts about her decision to walk alone from Thyrb's Retreat to the town of Seven Stones. On a good day she could have almost made the trip by now, but she hadn't anticipated how much the snow would slow her down. This was a bad road to travel at night; there were gnomes and werewolves living nearby. Unfortunately, it was too late to turn back: for all she knew the danger lay behind her. She'd have to trust to luck and keep going.

For a moment it looked as if her luck had deserted her: she saw a silhouette even darker than the sky, looming in the snow ahead on the road. Then she recognized the crooked form and laughed: it was just that odd wry-shouldered man who had been staying at Thyrb's. She ran on to join him. He was no particular favorite of hers—she didn't even know his name—but there was safety in numbers on this haunted road.

"Hey!" she shouted over the hissing of the wind-driven snow. She wanted him to know she was coming up behind him: he was probably as nervous as she was.

He turned to face her . . . sort of. There was just a dark patch where his face ought to be, with a slash for the mouth and two holes for eyes. A large dark hump loomed behind the featureless head. . . . She stopped, stricken by a sudden panic. But then one of his hands tugged at the dark patch and it came down around his neck; it was just a mask against the snow and the freezing wind. The face revealed was the one she expected to see: dark weather-beaten skin with a crooked smile and gray searching eyes that peered at her through the murk. The hump, she now saw, was just his rather large backpack.

"I don't know if you remember me," she said, almost apologetically. "I'm Rhabia. We sort of met back at Thyrb's."

He nodded.

"I thought we could walk together, at least as far as Seven Stones," she forged on.

He nodded again and gestured at the road beside him, as if it was his to give. When she was level with him he began to trudge forward through the snow again.

"It'll probably be safer for both of us," she explained. "There are were-wolves nearby. Gnomes, too."

He nodded a third time, and said, "Werewolves are certainly less likely to attack two than one."

"Cowardly beasts," she agreed.

"Just careful," he disagreed, and pulled his mask back up.

"Do you have to wear that thing?" she complained. "It gave me a turn when I saw it."

"I'm wearing it."

"Oh," she said, shrugging. It wasn't like his face was that much more attractive.

"I had to cut off somebody's nose once."

"Oh?" she said, a little alarmed again.

"Frostbite. Now I wear this thing when it's cold."

"Oh."

"You have just said, 'Oh,' three times."

"So what if I have? You think your conversation is winning any prizes, with all this talk of nose-cutting and frostbite? What are you, some sort of surgeon?"

"No. I make things. And you?"

"A little of this, a little of that. Right now I'm taking a message from Thyrb to a goldsmith in Seven Stones." The message was a letter of credit for a large sum of money, but Rhabia thought she'd keep that to herself. Not that she anticipated any trouble from this guy, but you never could tell. "He told me he'd pay me double if I got it to the addressee before tomorrow morning, so I headed out in spite of the snowstorm. Now it'll be midnight before I get to Seven Stones and I'll never find the goldsmith before morning, unless he lives above his shop. So here I am freezing my ass off and Thyrb will keep my bonus after all, may Morlock eat his liver."

Her companion turned to look at her and then looked back at the road. She supposed he was offended by her swearing in Morlock's name. Lots of people didn't like it, especially at or near dark, but she thought that was nonsense. It was one thing to be afraid of gnomes and werewolves, which everyone knew were real. But had anyone ever really seen Morlock Ambrosius? Even if he'd ever really lived, that was hundreds of years ago; he wasn't likely to show up here and now.

"I doubt he would," her companion remarked, sounding more amused than offended.

"Who would? Would what?" Her train of thought had distracted her from the conversation.

"I doubt Morlock would chew on Thyrb's liver."

"How would you know?"

"Eh. Who eats liver by choice?"

"There is that, of course," she admitted. "Even on Thyrb there must be more attractive cuts of meat. His heart, for instance, for a very light snack."

"You loathe Thyrb, but you work for him," her companion observed.

"I'll take his money to do a job I'm willing to do, but I don't work for him. I work for myself. You must understand that, being a journeyman . . . what is it you make, exactly?"

"Many things."

"All right, so you're a journeyman tinker. Someone pays you to mend his kettle, but is he your boss? I ask you."

"I see your point."

"Say, what is your name, anyway?"

Her companion trudged on for a few steps through the knee-high snow without saying anything. Rhabia began to think he might not have heard her (the wind was blowing something fierce) and was about to repeat herself when he said, "As a matter of fact, it's Morlock."

A qualm of fear gripped Rhabia's heart. Here she was, alone in the middle of a howling blizzard, surrounded by werewolves and gnomes, taking a stroll with Morlock Ambrosius. . . . But, no. It *couldn't* be him. Her fear receded.

"Isn't that *funny?*" she said, a trace of nervousness still present in her laugh. "I suppose it causes you a lot of trouble."

"Now and then," Morlock admitted.

"You should change it."

"My name is my name. I don't trust people who go by pseudonyms."

"I suppose some people even think you're Morlock Ambrosius."

"It has happened. What makes you so sure I'm not?"

He's trying to scare me, Rhabia thought, and laughed again, more confidently. "I've seen you by daylight, Morlock. Yesterday, at Thyrb's Retreat."

"So?"

"Everybody knows that Morlock Ambrosius will turn to stone if he stands in the light of day."

"I didn't know it," Morlock admitted, "and I thought I'd heard all the Morlock stories. Gnomes will turn to stone in sunlight, or so I'm told by those-who-know."

"Well, maybe Morlock is, or was, a gnome? Morlock Ambrosius, I mean, not you."

"No, gnomes, as I understand it, begin as worms living in the intestines of dragons."

"Eww."

"Eh. Neither birth nor death is ever a nice business."

"Wise. Very wise. Get back to the worms."

Morlock made a two-handed gesture that seemed to mean something, and continued, "When the dragon dies, they eat their way out of the corpse and dig into the ground, spinning a chrysalis around them. In due time two gnomes will be born from the chrysalis."

"Two?"

"Yes, the gut-worm of the dragon has both male and female ends. So a male and a female gnome will be born from the chrysalis. Although I'm not sure how they reproduce, if at all."

"Weird. You know a lot about gnomes."

"Never seen one. When I knew I was going to travel through these mountains I asked around about them."

"But everyone says Morlock grew up with the gnomes—"

"Not gnomes. Dwarves. He was raised by the dwarves as a fosterling, after his parents went into exile from the Wardlands."

"Wow. You know a lot about Morlock, too."

"That's more or less inevitable," he pointed out, and she had to concede the point.

"Who was the great mind that named you Morlock, anyway?" she asked.

"It was my mother's idea, I believe. There were a lot of Mor- names in her family: Morgan, Morgause, Mordred, Morholt. Morlock sounded good to her."

"She can't have liked you much. Letting you in for all this confusion with Morlock Ambrosius."

"Well, we never really knew each other. I was raised by foster parents. Dwarves, in fact."

"Screw you," she said amiably, and they walked on for a while without speaking, leaning into the bitter white wind.

Hours later the storm was getting worse, and the day was long gone. If it weren't for the trees lining the road, much of the time they wouldn't even have known where to walk, the snow was so thick. The wind blew it in deep drifts, almost impossible to cross. Then beyond there would be a stretch where the snow hardly covered their toes.

They were struggling through an especially rough patch, now. The snow had been packed into a drift higher than Rhabia's hips. Morlock got a short pointed shovel from his pack and began to clear a narrow way through the drift; Rhabia followed.

"We've got to get to town!" she shouted. "This storm will kill us!"

"We could make some sort of shelter in the woods!" he called back. "But . . ."

He didn't need to finish. It was no good saving yourself from the storm, only to offer yourself to passing werewolves and gnomes. Damn Thyrb and his letter of credit, anyway, Rhabia thought sourly.

"What brings you out in this mess, anyway?" she shouted. "I've got money riding on this, but you . . ."

"Going to visit my mother," he shouted back. This was so unexpected an answer that it hardly seemed stranger when he added, "Or one-third of her, anyway."

After an appalled moment Rhabia decided it was just another one of his sick jokes. She pounded on the left and lower shoulder and shouted, "Hey! Better let me shovel for awhile. You can follow along and work on a better class of witticism."

He surrendered the shovel without a word and stepped aside. She led for a while then and he followed.

At last they came to a place where the road was almost clear, all the way to the next bend.

"Whooo!" cried Rhabia gratefully, and would have stepped forward.

Morlock pulled her back beside him. "Wait," he said.

"Why? Take your hands off me, pal."

"How did this stretch of road get so clear?"

"How did the last stretch get so packed? The wind, Morlock."

"Look at the edges of the road. The drifts are squared off. Somebody cleared this patch of road deliberately."

"So? We can thank them when we see them."

"I think we'd rather not see them."

He reached back over his left shoulder and grabbed a handle which she had thought was just part of the framework of his backpack. In fact, it was the grip of a sword, slung across his back in a shoulder-scabbard.

It was a pretty weird-looking sword. The blade glittered darkly in the dim light, like polished basalt. But there were veins of white crystal in the black. As she watched, flabbergasted, the white veins began to glow and flicker. The blade was soon like a strip of black-and-white flames, and Morlock's gray eyes glowed with their own light behind his dark mask.

The light in the sword and in Morlock's eyes faded.

"Have you got anything that will burn?" he asked her.

Wordlessly she felt through her pockets. She found the note Thyrb had sent her this afternoon, asking her to come see him, and she held it out to Morlock.

He shucked off one of his gloves and stuffed it in his belt. Then he drew the edge of his blade across his palm. Blood, black in the dim light, sprang forth. He reached out with the wounded hand and took the note.

As soon as the paper came in contact with his blood it began to burn. When it was well lit, he dropped the burning note onto the strangely clear stretch of road.

It fell to the snowy ground . . . and through it. Somehow Rhabia could still see the note as it was ten feet or more under the surface. Eventually it was lost: extinguished by the snow or burned out.

"What the hell is that?" snapped Rhabia, gesturing broadly at the road, Morlock himself, the sword.

Morlock pulled his mask down and met her eye. "This is my sword: Tyrfing."

Tyrfing. It was a name from the legends . . . the legends that spoke of a crook-backed monster whose blood was a fiery poison. . . .

"Who are you?" she shouted. "Who are you really?"

"I told you, but you kept talking yourself out of believing it. I'm Morlock Ambrosius."

"Screw you!" she shouted, and continued to curse him violently to his face. It didn't mean anything, except to show him she wasn't scared. Which she was, of course.

He sheathed the sword, pulled on his glove, and put his left hand on her right arm. "Rhabia," he said urgently, interrupting her torrent of obscenity, "despite whatever stories you've heard, I'm not here to feast on your internal organs, or haul you off to hell." He took the shovel from her nerveless hands and turned back to the road. He crouched down and swung the shovel firmly down onto the patch of open road. The road disappeared, revealing a yawning dark pit below. Morlock withdrew the shovel and the road reappeared.

"This appears to be a trap set by a gnome," Morlock said. "We were meant to leap forward in relief onto the clear road and fall into the pit."

"Screw you!"

"You're not my type," Morlock replied sharply, a little annoyed for the first time.

"Why? Too strong? Too independent? Too—"

"Too stupid. Listen, won't you? This is life or death for us."

Rhabia settled down. Wordlessly, she motioned him to continue.

"The gnome will be nearby, and he will have set more traps. We had better leave the road, and we had better split up. I'll go south of the road; you go north. If you run into trouble, call out and I'll do what I can for you."

"Fine. Except *I'll* go south and *you'll* go north. And if you get in trouble, be sure to call out. Someone might give a damn."

Morlock shrugged and stowed the shovel in his pack. Rhabia stormed off into the woods on the south side of the road and began to make her way toward Seven Stones.

She hadn't gone very far when she heard some sort of noise from the woods on the north side of the road. She wasn't sure what it was, but it had to have been pretty loud, or she wouldn't have heard anything over the howling wind.

"Morlock!" she hollered, peering through the snow-swept darkness.

There was a small light, there, on the other side of the road. And there was something that looked a little like Morlock, only it was several feet off the ground, struggling in the limbs of a tree. Only the tree limbs were pre-hensile, like a monkey's tail, and the more she looked at it, the less it looked like a tree.

And down by the light . . . *holding* the light: what was that? Shorter than most men, with a flat head, covered with yellowish woolly fur, with ears pointing toward the horizon . . . a gnome? It was fussing with something bulky that lay on the ground. Morlock's pack?

This was clearly her chance to escape. The road-pit was between her and them. Even if the gnome saw her, what could he do about it? This *was* clearly her chance to escape. Too bad for Morlock, of course, but so what? The trouble was . . . there was something about some poor fool trapped in a situation that was his own damn fault that brought out the maternal in her. Usually her good sense trumped any impulse to intervene between the fool and his fate. But she was uneasily aware that, had she not snappishly overruled Morlock, that might be her struggling over there in the not-tree. Plus there was something he'd said. . . .

. . . call out and I'll do what I can for you. . . .

But the shoe was on the other foot, apparently, and it was up to her to do something for him, if she could. Rhabia swore silently but sincerely and drew her long knife, the one balanced for throwing. The gnome, or whatever it was, had a tendency to dance around a bit, but eventually he grew still again. She took aim and threw.

It was a good throw. In that light, at that distance, in that weather, she had no hope it would be a fatal blow. (Where were the internal organs in a gnome, anyway?) But at least it might hurt him; at best it might seriously trouble him.

At the last minute, though, the dagger slid aside and the point buried itself in snow. It might have been a gust of wind, but Rhabia didn't think so. The gnome dove and grabbed the dagger. He seemed to sniff it, and then he looked directly, searingly intently at *her*.

"Damn." Morlock—if it was Morlock (she thought it was)—was no longer struggling in the tree . . . if it was a tree (she didn't think it was). That gnome had nothing else to do now but come after her. She would have run off into the woods, but she found she couldn't move.

The gnome tossed what looked like a coil of rope across the road. It tied itself to a nearby tree. The gnome leapt up on the rope and skated nimbly across.

"Oh ho!" it said in a scratchy repellent voice as it looked up at her with the dark beautiful eyes of an evil kitten. "I'll have fresh meat for breakfast *and* lunch, or my name isn't All-Wise!"

It wasn't, as she later learned. But even if she'd known then, it wouldn't have made her feel any better.

The gnome who called himself All-Wise took them to his cave on the back of a big beast, like a bear with no head and leathery paws that were red as a sunset. Morlock appeared to be unconscious, but still alive; his clothing was torn and there were wounds on his face. Rhabia herself could not move, except to breathe and blink. Whatever he had zapped her with had a lot of staying power. The journey seemed endless; certainly hours passed as the headless bear lumbered after the gnome through the dense, high snow.

When they reached the gnome's cave, the headless bear shrugged them off onto the ground. The gnome took a flute or whistle from his gray smock; it looked like it was carved from brown bone. The gnome played a little tune, and the headless bear shrank until the gnome stopped playing, scooped up the tiny beast, and tucked it and the flute away in the same pocket.

He tossed Morlock's pack into the cave. Then he took Rhabia and Morlock, each by the collar, and dragged them (apparently without effort; he seemed to be strong as an ox, if nothing like as large) into the cave entrance. There was a large chamber filled with many peculiar things, like some sort of magical workshop, but the gnome didn't linger there. He hauled them to the back of the chamber, down a long tunnel covered with mirrors and odd writing, into a larger gloomier chamber deep underground where several iron cages dangled from the roof. There were mirrors and scribbling all over the walls here, too.

The gnome tossed them each into a cage and searched their persons with impersonal efficiency, taking all of their weapons and removing several inexplicable items from pockets of Morlock's clothes; finally he locked them in. Then he turned to Rhabia and, making an odd gesture through the iron gate, said, "You can speak and move. Is he"—a jerk of the bristly flat-topped head—"really Morlock Ambrosius?"

"Morlock, Ingrabe's son," she replied instantly. "He's a tinker, passing through this area. We—"

"You are a very poor liar," the gnome crowed, "as well as being remarkably ugly. You should strive for excellence in all things. This is the watchword I have made the . . . er . . . watchword of my life."

Something in the cave smelled rather strongly of rancid fat and as he moved around, Rhabia realized it was the gnome. She also realized that his "fur" was not really fur. It appeared to be a carpet of long yellowish gray warts completely covering his skin. They glistened in the light of the flameless lamp; she guessed that he rubbed fat on himself to protect against the cold.

"This isn't good, is it?" she said, more to herself than him.

"It's better than good!" the gnome responded. "Everything here, everything I am, is the best. I am All-Wise, All-Strong, All-Beautiful!"

"Your smell is pretty strong, anyway," she said scornfully. He could kill her if he wanted, but she wasn't going to flatter him.

But the gnome took it as a compliment, with a smirk twisting his warty face. "Oh, true: very true! A powerful and pleasing scent, refined and carefully aged animal fat mixing with my natural fragrance. I envy you for being able to smell it so clearly, and for the delight of seeing me for the first time. I would wish I were you, if you weren't so horribly ugly."

"Watch that!" she snapped. Maybe she wasn't some rose-petal goddess, but she had her share of admirers.

"Can't bear to," All-Wise (etc.) admitted cheerfully, averting his eyes from her to a smudgy mirror hanging nearby. There was one of these almost anywhere one looked, all over the walls of the dingy place. Dim flameless globes set over some of the mirrors provided a bare minimum of light. Wall space not hidden by mirrors was thickly larded with graffiti—Rhabia couldn't read a lot of it, but the name (?) NURGNATZ was repeated over and over. "But don't worry!" All-Wise said generously. "*You* can look at *me* as much as you like. The effluvium of my beauty is inexhaustible, no matter how many hungry eyes feed on it."

At this point Morlock began to move sluggishly on the floor of his cage and All-Wise began to scream, "Wake up! Wake up! You're missing everything!"

Morlock's head jerked and his eyes opened. "What am I missing?" he croaked.

All-Wise made an impatient gesture, as if it pained him to have to explain the obvious. "Me."

"Eh," said Morlock.

"Something wittier please, Morlock—much wittier!" All-Wise sneered. "Try to match my high standard of conversation! You'll never make it, of course, but the effort should inspire you to undreamed-of heights! Why, just the other day I was saying to myself—"

"What is it you want?" Morlock cut in.

The gnome looked confused. On the one hand, Rhabia reflected, Morlock had interrupted him. On the other hand, it was a fresh opportunity to talk on his favorite subject: himself.

"Want?" he said querulously at last. "I want to give you your finest hour! I want to give you a chance at greatness! I want to give you a golden opportunity that—"

"Can be described only in clichés, it seems," Morlock observed dryly to Rhabia.

"I'm going to cut you open and eat you," All-Wise snapped. "That way, you will be mingled with my greatness, although I don't expect you to be grateful for it."

"We're not," Rhabia confirmed.

"But I'm tired of your insolence!" the gnome screamed at Morlock. "Tired of your lies! Tired of your slander!"

"Whom have I been slandering?" Morlock asked, glancing around the dim mirror-encrusted room.

"Me! You claim to be the master of all makers—"

"No."

"—when you know full well that *I* am the greatest of all makers!"

"I never heard of you until today, Nurgnatz."

"That's an obvious lie, since—" the gnome began, and then interrupted himself to scream, "Hey! My name is All-Wise!"

"These walls are covered with love poetry to someone named Nurgnatz," Morlock replied. "The one I can see most clearly begins, 'Oh Nurgnatz, your thighs like thunder bestride the yearning world—'"

"Those were written by my many admirers!"

"They're all in the same handwriting and none of them is written higher than what is eye-level for you. But I take it you admit your name is Nurgnatz."

The gnome ground an ugly yellow tooth or two and then snapped, "It *was* Nurgnatz. I changed my name to reflect my true nature! All-Wise, All-Strong, All-Beautiful!"

"Why did you ever call yourself Nurgnatz, then?" Rhabia wondered.

The gnome glanced darkly at her and said, "It was my sister's idea. We agreed to name each other."

"And what did you name her?" Rhabia asked.

"Glundoschlunk," Nurgnatz admitted. "But she was ugly. You can't imagine how ugly she was!"

"About four and a half feet tall, flat head, covered with yellow-gray warts," Morlock guessed.

"It's a good start," Nurgnatz admitted modestly. "But she never anointed her warts with tallow! Often they exhibited a dry encrustation! Is this not repellent?"

"In context, no."

"After eating dragon-dung cakes she never rinsed her mouth with dreck-ooze! Does this not disgust you?"

"Not as much as you do."

Nurgnatz laughed indifferently. His ego was unassailable; he simply didn't believe Morlock. Rhabia was leaning forward against the door of her cage, staring with unguarded interest at the gnome. He turned toward her and, without warning, leapt forward, his fangs bare. Rhabia jumped back, but not before she felt a shock like a hammer-blow on her left hand. Looking down, she saw blood pouring from two stumps. Looking up, she saw her two middle fingers dangling like burst sausages from Nurgnatz's yellowish gray lips, blood streaking the warts below his mouth like a beard. He sucked them into his maw and began to chew.

Rhabia swore more or less continuously as she wrapped up her wounded hand in a bandage torn from her clothing.

"Well, I was hungry," Nurgnatz replied, as if that explained everything. He turned back to Morlock. "I'm wasting too much time here. I wanted to ask you how to get into your backpack. I'm sure there are some interesting items in there that could enhance my reputation, making up in some slight way—"

"I had some problems with thieves," Morlock interrupted, "so I set a seal on it. You won't be able to open it."

"That's *my* point, Morlock; do try to keep up. I can't get it open, and I want to. How do I go about it? I'm going to eat you anyway; there's no point in your stuff going to waste. Do be reasonable."

Morlock said, "Death and Sleep are brothers. I am not afraid of dying, as long as—" He broke off abruptly.

"As long as what?" Nurgnatz prompted him. "What is it that frightens you more than Death or Sleep?"

Rhabia heard all this dimly through a red haze of pain and anger and shame. She was sick at the thought of being mutilated, and the torn flesh of her finger-stumps felt as if there were little fires, growing more intense all the time, and she was furious at Nurgnatz for biting her and at herself for letting it happen. She was even angry at Morlock, who just stood there in his cage and gaped uselessly at her. The burning pain in her wounded hand reminded her somehow of the message set on fire by the wound in Morlock's hand, and she suddenly thought of a way to get revenge on the gnome who had mutilated her.

She laughed harshly. "I know what he's afraid of," she said to the gnome. "I'll tell you."

Morlock looked at her as if he'd been slapped, and the gnome turned with relief to his more cooperative witness. "Well?" Nurgnatz said.

"I'll tell you if you promise me something," Rhabia said slowly.

"Don't!" shouted Morlock.

"What is it?" Nurgnatz asked.

"I want you to kill me before you eat the rest of me," Rhabia said dully. "I don't want to be eaten piece by piece."

"Hm," Nurgnatz said slowly. "It's rather a great concession, as I like my meat fresh and fresh. Still. Very well."

"Don't do it!" Morlock urged. "He's lying to you!"

"It's fire," Rhabia said swiftly, before she could change her mind. "Morlock's terrified of it. I had to make the campfire and cook the food all through the trip—"

"Eh," Morlock said weakly, "it's woman's work."

"We'll see about that," Nurgnatz said thoughtfully. "I've a grill upstairs I haven't used for ages. Shall we try it out, Morlock?"

"You wouldn't dare," replied Morlock glumly.

"You forget I am All-Wise, All-Strong, All-Brave—the compendium of all the virtues! We'll test yours in a little while," he leered, and scampered back the way he had brought them.

Morlock said nothing but reached into his boot and drew out a little piece of metal. He reached through the bars of his cage and tossed it to Rhabia. She caught it with her unwounded hand and looked at it. It was an odd little thing, like a long blunt needle with many flexible joints. She'd never seen anything like it, but she was very much mistaken if it wasn't a lockpick.

Rhabia looked at Morlock. There must be some reason he wasn't saying anything—maybe Nurgnatz was (or could be) listening just outside the door. She gestured toward the door of her cage, as if to say, *Shall we go now?*

Morlock held up his hand (*Wait!*) and then gestured with his hand toward himself and then waved in the direction Nurgnatz had gone. She guessed he was telling her to stay where she was until Nurgnatz came back and took him away.

She gestured at him and herself and then more urgently toward the cage door. *Let's go now!*

He gestured at his shoulders. She didn't get it at first, then she realized he was saying, *What about my backpack?*

She gestured at him, then herself, then at her own shoulders, meaning, *Is a backpack worth your life or mine?*

Rather unimaginatively, he gestured at his shoulders again, which Rhabia interpreted as, *I'm getting my damn backpack.*

She shrugged and stood pat. After all, it was barely possible he knew what he was doing. If Nurgnatz wanted what was in Morlock's backpack so bad, maybe he shouldn't get it.

Morlock was pointing solemnly at his head, then at Rhabia. *You're pretty smart*, she read this.

"And cute, too," she replied aloud, in a Nurgnatzian burst of self-esteem, and turned away to staunch her wounds.

Time passed. Crouching in a corner of her cage, Rhabia actually fell asleep for a while, in spite of her pain, and the cold, and her fear. But when Nurgnatz returned with his headless bear in attendance, her head snapped up and she leaped to her feet. The bear was walking upright, Rhabia saw dimly through sleep-bleared eyes, and its red forepaws were actually hands of a sort—with seven or eight fingers each, and at least three thumbs per hand.

Nurgnatz opened Morlock's cage and stood back. The headless bear rushed in before Morlock could dodge out, and it grabbed him with four arms—an extra pair extruded from the headless bear's belly to help it keep the crooked man captive. Then it lumbered out of the cage and went to stand by Nurgnatz.

"See you soon, my dear!" carolled the gnome, his warty chin still stained with her blood, and he dodged out of the many-mirrored chamber again. The headless bear, carrying Morlock, lumbered swiftly after.

She waited until their sounds had vanished, following them up the tunnel, and then she got to work with the lockpick. Her wounded hand hurt more than ever, and every time she had to use it the stumps started bleeding again . . . but fortunately she was right-handed. And, anyway, this was life or death; she couldn't worry about minor discomforts, or even major ones.

She had picked a few locks before, for lockbox owners who had lost their keys. (She wasn't a thief.) This lock was trickier than any she had tackled; Nurgnatz was evidently almost as gifted as he thought himself. But the lock-pick was handier than any she'd used before; several times it seemed to move on its own to turn the tumblers back. Eventually she was free and gratefully pocketed the little device.

Now the program was a little hazier. But there was one obvious way out: the way she had come in. Unfortunately, that was also the way Nurgnatz and his headless bear had dragged Morlock. Still . . .

She crept carefully up the long tunnel leading away from the many-mirrored room. There were mirrors on the wall of the tunnel, too, and more love poetry from Nurgnatz to himself. Unfortunately there were no branches to the tunnel, only little lightless alcoves along the way, full of bones and bad smells.

When she was investigating one of these to see if it was the entrance to another tunnel a dry dead voice said, "Make stop."

Rhabia leapt back. She wished she had a weapon—but, on balance, the voice hadn't sounded dangerous.

"Make who stop what?" she asked the unseen speaker.

"Make me stop. Make him stop. Make him make me stop. Stop. Please stop." The dead voice droned on in the dark.

There was another sound along with the voice—an often repeated, soft squishing sort of noise. She couldn't place it. She stepped over to one of the dim flameless globes buried in the wall and pulled it loose and returned to the alcove where the dry hopeless voice was begging for something to stop.

After she saw what was happening she wished she had passed on without looking. A pudgy white-skinned man was sitting there on the floor of the alcove. Over half his body the skin and fat had been torn away so that the raw red muscle glared at her in the dim light of the globe. As she watched in horror his fingers reached out and tore away a strip of his own skin. Then he tossed it in a metal dish that sat nearby him on the floor. This was the constant squishy sound she had been unable to identify.

"Don't do that!" she yelped.

"Don't! Don't! Don't!" he begged. "But he makes me. He makes me make myself. Make me stop. Make him make me stop."

Nurgnatz had placed a compulsion on the man; that was clear. It was also, unfortunately, clear why. The imprints of Nurgnatz's clever little hands were painted in blood around the rim of the metal dish. Nurgnatz liked skin and fat, and he was making the man strip his own flesh off. Occasionally Nurgnatz would stop by and have a snack. . . .

Rhabia turned away, causing the man to panic. The tone of his voice didn't change, perhaps could not change, but he said faster than before, "Stop. Stop. Make it stop. Make me stop. Stop." All the while his hand continued stripping away little bits of his own flesh.

Maybe Morlock could do something for him, Rhabia thought desperately. But Morlock was likely to have enough to do in helping himself. She couldn't help this man, but she couldn't leave him behind, begging the empty dark to make it stop. That maternal instinct again; what a nuisance it was!

"Listen," she said, turning back to the man. "There's only one way I can make you stop. Do you understand?" She put the light-globe down on the ground.

"Make it stop," he said, the eyes in his mutilated face meeting hers eagerly as she took hold of his half-raw throat. "Make me stop. Make me stop. Make—" Then he couldn't talk anymore. His hand stopped tearing at his flesh, but she held on until she was sure he was dead.

"A little of this, little of that," she whispered, staring at her hands. She had never strangled anyone before. The exertion had been agony to her wounded hand, but that's not why she was weeping silently as she turned away.

She came at last to the end of the tunnel, which was its beginning in the upper chamber of Nurgnatz's cave.

There was a big pit in the center of the cave now. The pit was full of blazing coals. Over the pit stood a large metal grill, and on the grill lay Morlock Ambrosius, trussed hand and foot with chains. The chains were bound with leather strips to stakes thrust into the ground at the head and foot of the grill. It was apparently pretty hot; she could see the air wiggling over the grill, and Morlock's clothes were smoldering.

Nearby stood Nurgnatz, poking at Morlock uncertainly with a long fork. "Ready to talk now?" the gnome rasped. He patted Morlock's backpack, on the floor of the cave next to him. "If I have to, I'll burn this stupid thing. What good will anything that's in it do anyone then, eh? You made the stuff; don't you want it used?"

"Not by you," said the smoldering maker through clenched teeth.

Nurgnatz continued to proffer reasonable arguments why Morlock should do everything that Nurgnatz wanted, and Morlock continued to reply with terse refusals.

Rhabia stopped listening. Her attention was transfixed by the backpack—specifically by the sword grip emerging from the sheath hidden in the framework. If she could get hold of that somehow, maybe something could be done. But the trick would be to get past Nurgnatz, who was stronger than he looked. Fortunately, she thought as she edged forward, the headless bear or whatever it was didn't seem to be present.

Unfortunately, it *was* present; Rhabia just didn't see it because it was behind her. She discovered this when it grabbed her by her upper arms and lifted her off the ground.

"Oh—" she began, then shut up. Mere profanity could not begin to express her frustration and despair.

Nurgnatz turned to look at her with his gorgeous dark eyes. It was hard to read expression on his wart-infested face, but he seemed pleased to see her. "Ah, my dear. Mustn't be anxious. All in due time; we will become as close as you desire. But may I say that I found your fingers quite delicious. In fact, perhaps," he said, moving closer, "perhaps just a snack—"

Rhabia waited until he was close to her, and then kicked him as hard as she could in his face. She had the satisfaction of feeling his snout crunch against her toe-caps.

He reeled back, squealing a raspy scream. "Why is it always this way?" he wailed, wiping blood away from his nose and licking it off his fingers. "Nobody loves me." Lick. "I live here all alone in splendid isolation—" Lick. "—with no one to enjoy my beauty—" Lick. "—and whenever—"

"Look, Nurgnatz," she cut in. "Eat me if you can, but don't ask me to feel sorry for you. Tell it to your sister."

"She hated me. Everyone hates me, and all I want is to be loved!"

She suggested he perform an act which was sometimes a gesture of love, but not in this case. "With that toasting fork of yours," she added.

He whistled oddly. The extra pair of arms extruded from the headless bear's stomach and gripped her legs firmly. "I will love you," the gnome said quietly, "in my own way. And you will be one with me, and, for a while, I won't be lonely anymore." He sidled toward her.

"Nurgnatz," Morlock said, no longer through clenched teeth. "Turn me over. I'm done on this side."

The gnome, annoyed at the interruption, wheeled around and stabbed Morlock viciously with the fork. The tines entered his shoulder and sank deep. Nurgnatz drew the fork out and was going to stab him again, but never got the chance. Blood from Morlock's wound fell on the hot coals and burst into a cloud of orange flame.

Nurgnatz screamed and jumped back from the fire. Meanwhile the fire was eating away at the leather thong binding Morlock's wrist-chains to the stake. He pulled the chains loose and sat up to quickly untie the thong binding his feet-chains. In seconds he had rolled off the grill, although his hands and feet were still chained.

"Hey!" Nurgnatz shouted, in apparent disapproval.

Morlock, holding out his hands, called, *"Tyrfing!"*

Morlock's sword leapt out of its sheath, flew across the fire pit, and landed in his outstretched right hand. He gripped it with both hands and held the blade at guard.

"Not bad," Nurgnatz said, with professional courtesy. "A talic impulse woven into the crystalline lattice of the blade, I suppose?"

For a wonder, Rhabia actually understood this. In her years of doing a little of this, a little of that, she had learned a very little about magic. And she knew what tal was: the quasi-material force by which living souls impelled mere matter into motion. Every living consciousness was haloed with tal. Morlock must have implanted some tal into the sword, so that it would come to his hand when he spoke its name.

"Impressive, in its rather primitive way," the gnome said superciliously. "Still, have a look at this!"

Nurgnatz muttered a few words that Rhabia didn't quite catch. A golden sword dropped out of the ceiling and stood at guard opposite Morlock.

To Rhabia's dismay, Morlock was obviously dismayed. He stared at the blade hanging in midair and essayed a tentative cut at its grip. The golden blade executed exactly the same move, and the two magic blades clashed in midair. Morlock withdrew his sword to guard, and the golden blade mimicked the act.

"A talic construct?" Morlock speculated.

"Precisely. You really are almost my equal—at least professionally," Nurgnatz added with a vain smirk. "It perceives the talic impulses of your intended action before you have time to execute it, and matches its action to yours."

"You used the tal of your dead victims, I suppose?" Morlock asked.

"Some of them. I find that the extraction process spoils the flavor of the meat."

Morlock nodded. "Interesting. Still, tal is produced only by a living consciousness. Every action your construct takes depletes its reserves of tal. Eventually it will run out and have to be recharged."

Nurgnatz snickered. "Oh, it can outlast you, Morlock; don't worry about that."

Morlock had hooked his foot around one of the legs of the grill, and he flipped it into the air at the golden sword. It executed the same move as before, severing the grill in midair. The two unequal chunks of iron fell to the floor of the cave with dull thumps, as heavy as Rhabia's heart.

"Oh, I forgot to mention," Nurgnatz added smugly. "It learns. Any attack or defensive move you make, it can remember and use at any time."

"Is this as bad as it looks?" Rhabia called out to Morlock.

"Nothing," said Morlock, "is as bad as Nurgnatz looks."

The gnome, evidently considering this a joke, threw back his head and laughed. Morlock quickly crouched down (the golden sword opposite him mimicking the position of Tyrfing). He shifted Tyrfing to his right hand alone and scooped up coals from the fire pit with his now-free left hand. He tossed the coals at Nurgnatz.

The gnome's laugh turned into a rippling screech. The fiery coals set alight the grease thickly layering his warts. "My warts!" he cried desperately. "My warts! My beautiful warts!" He ran around the cave frantically, patting at the flames, which only spread to his greasy bloodstained hands. At last he dodged out the dark cave entrance and rolled in the snow outside.

Morlock tried to follow him, but he was hampered by the chains on his feet and a sudden attack of the golden sword. He was forced to stop and defend himself and, apparently by reflex, slashed in counterattack, teaching his opponent a new move. It used the attack instantly, forcing Morlock to retreat past Nurgnatz. He gave the grovelling gnome a good stomp as he passed, but it wasn't enough to disable his enemy.

Nurgnatz rolled to his feet and started sputtering. "You burned a great hole in my warts! It'll take a century to regrow them the way they were! And then the others will be that much longer! I'll never be the same again!"

Morlock shrugged (somehow expressing total indifference to Nurgnatz's wart-care regimen) and backed away slowly. The golden sword followed, making occasional cuts at him, which he met without counterattacks. It was obviously difficult for him to restrain his swordsman's impulses to attack, but he seemed to be playing a waiting game as he disappeared into the darkness beyond the cave, followed by the golden sword.

Nurgnatz growled impatiently, and then began to whistle. Rhabia found that the headless bear holding her was starting to move toward the cave entrance.

"Morlock, look out!" she called. "We're coming for you!" That didn't sound quite right. "I mean—"

"Understood," Morlock's laconic reply came from the darkness outside.

The headless bear carried her out of the cave and past the whistling gnome.

The snowstorm had ceased, but some of the drifts would be hip-deep on a tall man. Morlock was not especially tall, and he was hobbled by chains on his legs.

The sky above was clear. Somber Chariot glared over the eastern horizon, but there was another light in the sky, a dim gray light. By it, Rhabia caught sight of Morlock, floundering away from an attack by the golden sword. He caught each slash of the golden sword on the edge of his, but all the time he retreated, step by hobbled step backward.

The whistling commands of the gnome drove the headless bear to run a great circle and dash at Morlock from the side. The crooked man hopped out of the way, but the chains tangling his legs caused him to fall.

Rhabia thought the fight was over. But the golden sword didn't know how to attack something lying on the ground.

Nurgnatz realized this belatedly and issued a whistling command that sent the headless bear back toward Morlock, no doubt to stomp him as he lay struggling in the snow. But by then Morlock had rolled to his feet and was hobbling backward again, deflecting slashes from the golden sword.

Rhabia was getting dizzy trying to follow the fight from her moving vantage point in the grip of the headless bear. But at least it was a little lighter now, and easier to see things.

The gnome was beginning to whistle a command to the headless bear again when Morlock called out, "I underestimated you, Nurgnatz."

The gnome broke off his whistle to respond, "Of course! Ugly people like you always assume that we beautiful people succeed by beauty alone. We could, of course. At least I could. But my other virtues drive me to omniform excellence. Yes, omniform excellence," he repeated, pleased with the phrase. He rounded his yellowish gray lips to whistle again.

"'Omniform excellence!' Morlock said, dodging back from a cut by the golden blade. "What is that, exactly?"

"Excellence in every form, you stupid, ugly crooked man!" squeaked the gnome angrily.

"Tell me, since you must know," Morlock said, backing away again so that Nurgnatz had to shamble forward to hear him, "are the forms of excellence infinite in number?"

Nurgnatz held forth for some time on the different types of excellence. He summed up his disquisition some considerable time later with the modest suggestion that there was in essence one true type of excellence, the state of being Nurgnatz, but that this one excellence had a potentially infinite number of Nurgnatzian attributes.

"Ah," said Morlock. "Light begins to dawn."

"Yes, of course," Nurgnatz said querulously. "I should think by now you would understand—"

"I meant literally," Morlock observed.

Nurgnatz gaped at him for a moment, then swung around to see the brightness imminent at the top of a nearby hill. The silver light of Chariot had given way to the reddish gray of dawn. Nurgnatz wasted no time screaming but bounded instantly toward his cave.

But the snow was very deep, the ambient light already in the air was stiffening his gnomish limbs, and Morlock had retreated very far from the cave entrance. Nurgnatz was only halfway between Morlock and Rhabia, yet in the grip of the long-unmoving headless bear, when the tide of golden light swept up and left him a still gray statue of a terrified, fire-scarred gnome.

The golden sword fell and was buried in the snow, its activating spell cancelled by the death of its caster.

Rhabia also fell to the ground, dropped by the headless bear. It went down on all fours and wandered away, past the stone image of its former master, into the snowthick woods beyond.

Rhabia climbed to her feet and went to meet Morlock, already hobbling toward her through the drifts of snow. His face was gray with weariness in the gold light of morning. Maybe he was immune from fire and had flammable blood, like all those crazy legends said. But for the first time, as she looked at him, he looked as if he might really be centuries old—and feeling every second of it.

"Better get those chains off you," she said gruffly. This damn maternal instinct of hers kicked in at the weirdest times.

"There are some tools in my pack," he said.

She sniffed. "That's what we risked death for? A hammer and chisel?"

He turned to spear her with his searching gray eyes. "*You* risked death to help me, when you could have walked away. I won't forget it."

"Ah." She waved her wounded hand in dismissal. "It evens out. I lost my bonus from Thyrb, but I bet I can sell that gnome statue for ten times what Thyrb was going to pay me. So the debt runs the other way, really. I at least owe you a decent breakfast when we get to town."

"I don't think—"

Her maternal instinct didn't have to put up with anyone thinking at her. "Listen, pal," she cut in. "I've had a long day and night of men who think the damn world revolves around them. So you will eat your damn breakfast and thank me nicely for it afterward."

There was some more negotiation on this point, but in the end she had her way. And it was after that memorable breakfast that Morlock offered her a job that bid fair to free her from Thyrb and his ilk forever.

XV

Interlude: How the Story Ends

The merit of an action is in finishing it to the end.

—Genghis Khan

I t was the last day of the season of Motherdeath, and new Valona's egg-sac had fully grown in. That day they had a rare daylight implanting. The Sisters watched as the males of the tribe wove their dance about young Valona, fertilizing her eggs, reverencing her and the life she represented. Then she implanted her first eggs in old Valona. The first eggs of a Khroi mother were supposed to be very lucky, and those implanted in an old mother doubly lucky. So good days were obviously in store for the horde. Gathenavalona tried to be happy, and she was a little.

After the ceremonies and the afternoon feast, Gathenavalona went to the Mother's Nest. She found Marh Valone waiting outside.

"Why are you here, Gathenavalona?" he asked. His harmonies implied it was not a rhetorical question.

"You knew I would be, it seems," she replied.

He gestured expectancy.

She gestured compliance and said, "I promised to tell her the whole tale of Motherdeath, back when she was only Dhyrvalona. I wish to keep my promise." Her harmonies vibrated with determination. She would fight, if need be, to keep her word.

"That is a good story," Marh Valone said earnestly. "It is the story of the change that began and has not yet ended. The realization that the gods may not hate us, that our own actions can harm us or save us. The Khroi slept for centuries in dreams of the gods' hatred. Now we have begun to wake up. You can be a part of that new day, Gathenavalona."

"Not as Gathenavalona," she begged. "Give me a new name, and a new destiny."

Marh Valone's three mouths issued a quiet harmony of resignation, grief, and gladness. He reached out with one palp-cluster and traced the line of one of her jaws, an almost shocking gesture of intimacy between a grown male and a grown female.

"You will have a new name and a new destiny," he said. "Do you know what I feared? Many a Gathena will kill herself, or her charge, in the time of anointing or afterward. As always, you make me proud."

She gestured gratitude and an inability to speak.

He waved her past. "Go then. Keep your promise to her. When you emerge from the nest, I will have a new name for you, a new task."

Gathenavalona passed by him and climbed into the nest.

New Valona's bulk nearly filled the vast Mother's Nest. She had grown so much after that night of the first anointing.

Her limbs had thickened and grown; her body was more massive, especially her neck with the enormous burden of her egg-sac. Her internal organs had swelled to support her greater size—most of them, anyway. She crawled along lengthwise, of course: she was too enormous to stand on her hind legs and ped-clusters. All her palp-clusters had become heavy, padlike ped-clusters. She had regrown the quadrilimbs that all Khroi are second-born with; they were as massive as her other legs.

Valona's eyes fell on her old nurse, standing at the entrance to the nest. Gathenavalona looked in vain for any glint of recognition in those eyes. The transformation wrought by the royal jelly magnified the body many times, but the enormous ovaries in a Mother's abdomen seemed to crowd out most of the room for the brain. Mature Khroi mothers never spoke, and it was hard to say what they understood.

Valona caught sight of a trough of food at the base of her nest. She moved toward it, grunting with excitement.

Gathenavalona thought of her promise to Dhyrvalona. She thought of Marh Valone's promise: a new name and a new destiny.

She kept her promise. As young Valona ate to sustain her vast bulk, her old nurse told her how the story ended.

XVI

Spears of Winter Rain

Words also, and thought as rapid as air,
He fashions to his good use; statecraft
     is his,
And his the skill that deflects the
     arrows of snow,
the spears of winter rain: from every
     wind
He has made himself secure—
     from all but one:
In the late wind of death he cannot stand.

—Sophocles, *Antigone*

As the ice storm raged about him, the crooked man stood in a cleft of the mountains watching another crooked man walk a twisting path through the shattered icy stones of the rockslide to the west. He saw the man fall among the ice-glazed stones, saw him struggle to his feet again, saw him continue his slow meandering way eastward.

"A plodder," muttered Merlin, and shook his head. It was the only way Morlock would ever reach anything, the older Ambrosius decided: by finding out where it was and walking straight toward it, literally or metaphorically. Well, it was a way to get somewhere. Unfortunately, it left you open to observation and attack by your enemies, a fact Morlock had never learned, apparently.

Merlin shook his head and sighed. This had been a long hard struggle, and it was nearly over. In a way, he would miss it, he decided. That was why he was withholding his final weapon. But that was not the only reason.

Merlin grimly noted that Morlock was not carrying his backpack. He had hidden it somewhere before coming to the confrontation he anticipated between himself and his father. Merlin's map of the future had predicted this, and that was why he planned to avoid any such confrontation.

They were high in the mountains, well above the treeline on the north face of the Blackthorns. Morlock, of course, was approaching from the west.

He knew where Merlin was, because Merlin was necessarily near the core-self of Nimue, and Nimue's shell and impulse-cloud together were able to tell where her final segment lay. They had told Morlock, and he proceeded to walk directly toward his goal, along the path Merlin had foreseen.

Several days earlier, Merlin had deliberately started several avalanches on the slopes above Morlock's future route, and halted them with a network of force-wefts. He had only been waiting until Morlock was directly in their path to loose the wefts. And now Morlock was, and if he did not loose them soon there was some chance that Morlock would be able to make his way out of the danger zone before the avalanche caught him.

Merlin took one last look at his only living son, then sighed. He took a rune-slate from a pocket in his left sleeve, and he broke it with his fingers. It was bound-in-state to the force wefts; once it was broken, they were no more.

The avalanche started. First there was a low rumble, and the man far below, antlike in his distance and his vulnerability, began to run. Of course, Morlock had been raised among mountains and he knew that sound well. The torrent of snow and ice and stone rolled down toward him like a tidal wave, took him, buried him, rolled onward until it exhausted itself on the slopes below. Soon enough the slide was quiet and the icy rain was glazing the fresh surface of snow. If Morlock hadn't had his neck broken or his body crushed in the avalanche, it was only a matter of time until he smothered. The long struggle between father and son was over.

Merlin sighed again. Unlike Morlock, he was an introspective man, and he understood how complex his own motives were. If Morlock had succeeded in reuniting Nimue's segments and negating the antideath spell, it would have been terrible; he would have been furious at his defeat and the loss of his beloved wife. But it would have been a relief, too: a relief to be free from the endless struggle against death. Death was an enemy even more plodding and relentless than Morlock, even harder to defeat. Now he would have to carry on that fight.

"And so I will," he decided. "I'll win, too," he added, because there was no penalty for bravado, at least when no one was listening.

"Anyway," he said to himself, "now I am the master of all makers again. By default." He scowled. Well, he reflected, in any fight the last man standing is the winner.

Merlin pulled his cowl over his head and stepped out of the cleft's shelter into the bright bitter rain. His cloak and his shoes did not get wet (a man does not reach the second half of his second millennium without being able to avoid these inconveniences), but still from time to time the wind turned and a dash of freezing rain stung his face. It was irritating, but he bore it. He had just won a victory, a great victory. No doubt he would feel the full impact of it presently.

Now it was his turn to meander across the treacherous ground he had used to kill his son. There was no reason to hurry, so he did not. He was careful to avoid using the sight—for one thing, he needed all his material senses to keep himself from Morlock's icy fate; for another he could not risk a confrontation with Nimue. It was possible that he might defeat her, in her divided state, but it would be difficult to defeat her and Morlock in tandem, and something told him that Morlock, though doomed, was not dead yet. In fact, as he passed by the western edge of the avalanche-field, his insight told him there was someone in visionary withdrawal. Morlock, no doubt: it was shrewd to go into withdrawal, reducing the body's needs almost to nothing, waiting for help to come. But there was no one to come rescue him; Morlock would die there of cold, if nothing else.

Merlin scowled again and turned away. It occurred to him that for most people, for the short-lived people of a day (like that Naeli woman, or Nimue herself, really), children were the chief weapon in the struggle against death. He had been forced to sacrifice one of his children to win a brief respite in his struggle against death—not even a real victory, just a respite. Perhaps death might not be merely a plodder, might be an extremely subtle antagonist who could sneak through your windows even as you were locking your door. Never mind. Merlin would not stop fighting because he did not know how to stop. If Morlock had chosen to fight beside him instead of against him, it would have been different; they might even have forced death to retreat a step or two. That would have been a famous victory.

A shared one, of course. Merlin had never been one for sharing out the glory. He cursed a little, shook some ice from his cloak, put his head down and trudged onward into the sharp stinging rain.

Eventually Merlin came to the place where he had first observed Morlock approaching. Then he had to go more slowly, consulting his map of the future every so often. Morlock might be dead, or merely doomed, but his intention still shaped the present and the future. It crossed with Merlin's . . . there. Down below in the crooked line of pine trees, abristle with heavy spikes of shining ice.

Merlin passed onward cautiously, not just because of the terrain. Morlock was clever enough to have laid traps for Merlin, anticipating this moment. (Not cunning enough to avoid the moment itself: that was reserved for a genius on the level of Merlin himself.)

There were no traps. He came at last to a clearing in the glittering ice-hung pine trees. The map told him that Morlock's pack was hidden here, but he saw nothing of it. Either it was not here or Morlock had placed a wilderment on it so that it was invisible.

Merlin smiled within the shadows of his cowl. He could go into rapture and use his trans-material senses to see if the pack and (more importantly) Nimue's two lost segments were present. But there were so many risks to this. Morlock and Nimue might be already in rapport, awaiting the chance to capture Merlin's fetch. Morlock might have fashioned some nonmaterial trap out of talic impulses. No, he could not engage in vision until he was surer of his ground.

But no wilderment is perfect. They create visual flaws where they merge with their environment. Merlin walked around the clearing, eyes open for clues: an icicle sparkling on the wrong side in the gloomy day's light, a twig that disappeared midway of its length, a misplaced shadow. Soon he had quite a list, and he charted them on a mental map of the clearing. The center of the wilderment was that locus . . . *there.*

Merlin walked toward a pine tree, no more remarkable than any others on the edge of the clearing. He was wary of traps on all sides, but there seemed to be none. He reached down into the space he had calculated as the wilderment's center. His hand disappeared, and simultaneously met the rough surface of Morlock's concealed backpack. He drew in a deep breath and hefted the pack out of the wilderment.

It took a couple of tries. "God Avenger, this thing is heavy," Merlin grunted as he finally dragged the thing into visibility in the unspelled center of the clearing.

His long hands leaped, as if of their own accord, to the lacings of the pack, then halted.

"Caution, caution," Merlin reminded himself. There was no hurry. He would go slow.

It was well he did. The pack was sealed with a spell to prevent theft, and there was a particularly nasty trap inside, for anyone clever enough to pierce the spell. Merlin counter-inscribed the spell and defanged the trap. There seemed to be no other barriers. At last he unlaced the pack and, with trembling fingers, lifted out a blue jar.

The rest he would leave for whoever found it. He scorned to loot the pack of the master of all makers: he was Merlin Ambrosius, and his name did not echo and re-echo down the centuries because he was a successful thief of other men's magic. He had what he wanted.

He was sure of it.

He was almost sure of it.

He kept remembering that empty jar Morlock had taunted him with in Aflraun. This jar was not empty—it had a certain heft to it. He spun it in his hands, and certain irregularities of weight suggested to him that the jar was bigger on the inside than the outside, as it should be if it was the right jar. Yes, this was what he was looking for.

He was sure of it.

He was almost sure of it.

Merlin badly wanted to ascend into visionary rapture and check: if Nimue's shell and impulse-cloud were in the jar, he would know immediately; likewise if they were not.

But he couldn't risk it. He was all too aware that this might be the ultimate trap, baited with exactly what he really wanted. If Morlock and Nimue were in rapport, waiting for him, everything he had done might be for nothing.

He raised the jar up over his head and threw it against a nearby tree root glazed with thick ice.

The ice shattered. The blue glaze on the jar shattered. But the jar itself didn't: it lay there on the ground without a crack.

Merlin nodded. If Morlock had foreseen this moment, he would have made the jar breakable, but with some sort of menace or trap inside. Morlock hadn't. Ergo, Merlin had found the right jar.

He was sure of it.

He was *almost* sure of it.

Merlin walked over and recovered the jar. He weighed the risks against each other, shook his head, and twisted the cap off.

From the jar's wide mouth flew the indistinct form of a bird, its feathers gleaming with every shade of dim green in the day's dull light. It passed three times around Merlin's head and returned to the mouth of the jar. By then, Merlin had already slumped unconscious to the glittering glazed earth. The jar fell there beside him.

The jar unfolded three long spindly legs from its base. It shook out three long spindly arms from its striated body. The jar-shaped golem rose from where it had fallen and stood uncertainly on the icy ground.

Spindly the arms were, perhaps, but strong. The jar-golem reached down and picked up Merlin's prone body. The jar-mouth, already wide, gaped wider and wider. The jar-golem dropped the sleeping sorcerer into its mouth. Then it clapped the lid back down across its mouth and wrapped its spindly arms tightly around the lid, sealing the container. Its spindly legs crouched down and it waited.

Time passed. Eventually, two women came through the glittering ice-fanged pinewood.

The jar-golem didn't move. They weren't what it was waiting for.

One woman said to the other, "Should we see if we can help Morlock?"

"Who, dear?" the other replied.

"Morlock."

"That's funny. My son's named Morlock. I've never seen him, not since he was born."

"He was here with us, just a while ago."

"Looking for his horse. Yes, now I remember. I told him to watch out for that troll under the bridge, but he's not one of the world's great listeners, is he, Voin dear?"

"Rhabia. My name is Rhabia."

"Oh, yes. I remember her well. She looked a little like you. Give my regards to her, if you see her. But I have to be getting on, my dear."

"I'd better go with. That's what he's paying me for, anyway."

"Really? How unimaginative of him. Young men in my days had livelier ideas, believe you me. Who is 'he,' by the way?"

"Doesn't matter. Are you sure you know where you're going?"

"Oh yes; not a doubt of it. My impulse-cloud and my shell are not very effective at coherent thinking—"

"You don't say."

"I thought I had said it. Oh, Christ, I'm so tired and confused. Never mind: thinking isn't required. I can feel my core-self is near, so near, and I'm tired, so tired. Frightened, too. Can you—can you—?"

The younger woman silently took the arm of the older woman and they passed onward.

The jar-golem waited in the bright clearing under the wet gray sky. Time passed.

Morlock was not expecting the mountain to fall on him and he was utterly unprepared for it.

A glance or two about told him that there was no way to escape the slide entirely. He could make it as far as he could and hope the slide didn't kill him, or . . .

He curled himself into a ball and summoned visionary withdrawal. He had just ascended to rapture when the avalanche caught him: the sensation was vaguely similar to being kicked by a giant wearing a cotton boot. Then he was above the level of sensation, adrift in the tal-realm.

Reasoning and intention are oddly distorted in vision. If you enter with a strong intention, in talic stranj with a focus of power, intentional action may be relatively easy. But Morlock had simply sought escape, and having found it, he drifted like a cloud in an otherwise empty sky: not acting, not really thinking.

Merlin passed nearby. Morlock noticed this without really concerning himself about it. Sometime afterward, he sensed Rhabia and two segments of Nimue pass by in the other direction.

Merlin, Rhabia. Nimue, but not all of her. That triad prompted a coherent thought. He descended a little in vision as a consequence.

The sun was going down beyond the rim of the world. The world was colder now, even the tal-world, and that made Morlock think, too. Evidently the avalanche had not killed his body outright. But the cold would kill his body soon.

Well, what could he do about it? Little, very little.

What did he have to work with? Little, very little.

How little? he wondered. In the tal-state he was freed from material limits of perception. He had nothing else to do. He tried to find out how small a thing he could perceive.

Time passed, but he was not aware of it.

Eventually he found himself contemplating the void of matter on a very deep level. Most of it was empty to his sight. But in the void moved tiny particles, more swiftly than others, infected with something like life, although they were not all alive.

Some parts of the slide had more of these than the others. There were some on the surface, where the last red light of the day was falling, through the ragged edges of the ice storm's clouds. There was a cloud of them enveloping his freezing body, moving away from it in the emptiness of the dead snow and ice.

Morlock reached out with his mind and started turning these specks of light and warmth back toward his body. The snow and ice around him grew colder, but against his skin there was a layer of warmth. Eventually his body, balled up like a fist, was floating in warm water within an icy womb deep within the body of the avalanche field.

The maker in Morlock, never absent even when unconscious or asleep, was pleased. It was a temporary solution to survival underneath the avalanche.

Of course, it was only temporary. Morlock pondered alternatives.

Eventually, he began to bend the pathways of the particles of heat, denting the side of the icy womb and then breaching it. He used the heat to whittle away an icy tunnel with a core of warm water, angling the tunnel downslope. His unconscious body rolled along with the water downhill into the tunnel, along its length.

The water broke through the side of the avalanche field and ran out. Morlock's body slid afterward and bounced downhill over the glazed slope, like a badly made ball, eventually coming to rest against a rocky obstruction.

Morlock was pleased again. This looked like a permanent solution.

Of course, it created a new problem: his soaked body, exposed to the wintry night air, was losing heat even more rapidly than it had under the avalanche. He wasn't sure if he could weave the paths of the heat particles in the air as he had in ice and water; everything seemed to move more rapidly. It was an interesting problem, and he thought a little bit about solutions.

But whatever he came up with, it would not be a permanent solution. Eventually the source of heat within his living body would fail and he would die.

Morlock was not afraid of death; he had seen too much of it. It didn't trouble him that he had things to do, obligations unmet, because he knew that everyone leaves a trail of broken promises when they die. He would leave less than some.

On the other hand, there were things he wanted to do, problems he wanted to solve, things he wanted to make. He wondered if he could make an object solely out of the heat particles he saw dancing through the midst of the material void: a heat sculpture, a heat tool, a heat weapon. If he died now, he would never do that.

Morlock was not afraid of death, but given the alternative, he found he preferred life. He dismissed his vision.

The weight of the dark cold world fell on him. The cold was an agony, but under it burned darker, deeper pain from his bruised and battered body.

He forced his stiff aching limbs to unbend.

He was shuddering in the bitter dark rain so much that he could hardly make his limbs obey him. But he somehow made his way across the avalanche field, like a frozen sea that lurched occasionally under his feet, to the clearing where his pack and the jar-golem were.

The jar-golem rose to stand: this was what it had waited for.

As for Morlock: there were flames in the nexus, dry clothes in the pack, and the man who was trying to kill him was trapped in a jar. It looked as if he would live long enough to do some more making.

Night was much deeper and the storm had changed from sleet to snow by the time Morlock made it at last to Merlin's cave in the cleft of the mountains.

He expected to see signs of destruction, and he did find some. There had been a doorway securing the cave, but water had filled its frame and frozen till it burst outward. He saw two pair of footprints in the rubble: Nimue's and Rhabia's, no doubt.

Beyond the broken door was a stone stairway with a two-headed watch-beast—one side orange, the other purple. Both sides were dead, their gaping mouths stopped with frozen water.

Morlock passed down the stairway into Merlin's lair and came at last to an oval room in which lay the bodies of two women, one dead and one dying.

On the far side of the room Morlock saw his mother's body, lying motionless amid a shattered block of warm ice.

On the near side of the room lay Rhabia. She had been caught by a trap: a steel hoop had passed through one leg and bound her to the floor. She was struggling to stop the bleeding—an obviously long struggle which had so far failed, given the pool of blood surrounding her on the floor. She looked up and saw Morlock.

"Took awhile, didn't you?" she said with false bravado. He could see the relief growing, the fear fading in her eyes.

"I suppose," he said. He looked the situation over, then drew Tyrfing and broke the steel hoop on either side of Rhabia's wounded thigh.

"I'm going to slide it out," he told her. "It's going to hurt."

"Can't you put me to sleep with your green bird?" Rhabia said anxiously. "Like when you fixed my fingers?"

She flexed her hand where Nurgnatz had bitten off her fingers. Morlock hadn't really fixed them, simply replaced them with mechanical analogues that worked fairly well.

"No." He nodded toward the jar-golem, who had followed him into the oval room and was standing by the door. "Busy."

"Oh." She looked away. "All right, then."

She passed out before the metal was out of her leg. Morlock worked swiftly to sew up her wound before she woke. He wrapped her in a sleeping cloak and left her on the floor, since he was unsure where else he could put her safely.

The rest of the floor was dense with traps. Morlock made his way past them to where his mother's dead body lay.

The chunks of ice were warm as blood: Morlock didn't fully understand what they were. He suspected they were a product of water-magic, something perhaps he should know more about. But clearly they had been used to pre-serve (and imprison) Nimue's core-self. Her impulse-cloud and shell must have been able to break through the warm ice somehow and reunify.

Death would have followed almost instantly. As Morlock looked down on Nimue's face, he thought it looked different than he had come to know it from her shell. Was it because now she had joined with her core-self? Because she was dead indeed? He wasn't sure. He had never really known her, and now she was dead. Again.

He shrugged. He cut a hole in the side of the cave and buried her there, carving on the wall beside her the same epitaph he had used the first time he buried her.

By then, Rhabia had regained consciousness. He made a fire on the floor, as if they were in the middle of a wood, and brewed some redleaf tea to help her heal and replace her blood. She drank it with many complaints, clearly relishing the warmth, and when it was done she obviously felt stronger. Tossing aside the cup she said, "Do you want to know how it was?"

Morlock thought about what he had seen. "No. Unless you think there is something I should know."

"That's more thinking than we bargained for. You'll agree I carried out my part?"

Morlock went into his pack to get the agreed-upon sum of gold and handed it to her. The gold meant nothing to him; he could have easily have doubled the amount, or given her as much as she could carry. But he knew that the gold was important to her, not only for itself, but as a symbol of independence. The bag of coins he handed her had the exact amount they had agreed on back in Seven Stones.

She shook it with some enthusiasm. "No more working for Thyrb," she exulted. "Maybe I can even set up my own retreat."

Morlock nodded.

"Well," she said after a few moments, "I think I'll be getting out of here. Especially if the guy who dropped that mountainside on you is just asleep in there."

Morlock nodded. "Go back the way you came," he suggested. "It seems to be clear of traps."

"Right." She turned to go, paused, turned back. "Think you'll ever be back up Seven Stones way?"

Morlock thought about how angry Merlin would probably be when he freed himself. He thought about Roble and Naeli and her children, and how much they had suffered from knowing him. He thought of Stador, dead under a head of rocks in the Kirach Kund. "No," he said.

"Oh. Good-bye, then."

"Good fortune to you."

She left, and he turned away to explore the rest of Merlin's cave.

Eventually, he found what he was looking for. In a room that looked more like a butchering shed than a wizard's workshop, he found a metal dish with a pair of silver eyes in it.

They looked at him—quizzically, perhaps with a little fear, certainly with recognition. He recognized them, too: they belonged to his horse, Velox.

"Hello, my friend," Morlock said, not sure if Velox could hear him, not sure if he would understand if he did. He was never sure about Velox.

Merlin, of course, had been lying when he had told Morlock that Velox was dead. Morlock had suspected as much. For one thing, he wasn't sure that Velox could die. An unusual beast in many ways.

Velox's separate pieces all seemed to be present in the dreadful blood-soaked room. Morlock settled down to reassemble them. He was tired, his body battered and aching, but the task itself gave him strength. This was a deed he had set himself to do, and it was near to completion now.

Slowly, the immortal steed took shape in the stony womb beneath the mountain.

Trapped in the jar, the old man struggled against his bonds of clay and sleep.

Already far off, the wounded woman walked away through the long cold night.

APPENDIX A

CALENDAR AND ASTRONOMY

1. ASTRONOMICAL REMARKS

The sky of Laent has three moons: Chariot, Horseman, and Trumpeter (in descending order of size).

The year has 375 days. The months are marked by the rising or setting of the second moon, Horseman. So that (in the year before *This Crooked Way* begins) Horseman sets on the first day of Bayring, the penultimate month. It rises again on the first of Borderer, the last month. It sets very early in the morning on the first day of Cymbals, the first month of the new year. All three moons set simultaneously on this occasion. (The number of months are uneven—fifteen—so that Horseman rises or sets on the first morning of the year in alternating years.)

The period of Chariot (the largest moon, whose rising and setting marks the seasons) is 187.5 days. (So a season is 93.75 days.)

The period of Horseman is 50 days.

The period of Trumpeter is 15 days. A half-cycle of Trumpeter is a "call." Calls are either "bright" or "dark" depending on whether Trumpeter is aloft or not. (Usage: "He doesn't expect to be back until next bright call.")

The seasons are not irregular, as on Earth. But the moons' motion is not uniform through the sky: motion is faster near the horizons, slowest at the zenith. Astronomical objects are brighter in the west, dimmer in the east.

The three moons and the sun rise in the west and set in the east. The stars have a different motion entirely, rotating NWSE around a celestial pole. The pole points at a different constellation among a group of seven (the polar constellations) each year. (Hence, a different group of nonpolar constellations is visible near the horizons each year.) This seven-year cycle (the Ring) is the basis for dating, with individual years within it named for their particular polar constellations.

The Polar constellations are: the Reaper, the Ship, the Hunter, the Door, the Kneeling Man, the River, the Wolf.

There is an intrapolar constellation, the Hands, within the space inscribed by the motion of the pole.

This calendar was first developed in the Wardlands, and then spread to the unguarded lands by exiles. In the Wardlands, years are dated from the founding of New Moorhope, the center of learning. The action of *This Crooked Way* begins in the 464th Ring, Moorhope year 3245, the Year of the River. But in the Ontilian Empire, the years are dated from the death of Uthar the Great, a system that came into widespread use north and south of the Kirach Kund.

2. THE YEAR OF *THIS CROOKED WAY*

The novel begins early in the month of Brenting, 333 A.U.
48th Ring, A.U. 333: Year of the River

1. Cymbals.

New Year. Winter begins.
1st: Chariot, Horseman, and Trumpeter all set.
8th & 23rd: Trumpeter rises.

2. Jaric.

1st: Horseman rises. 13th: Trumpeter rises.

3. Brenting.

1st: Horseman sets. 3rd and 18th: Trumpeter rises.

4. Drums.

1st: Horseman rises. 8th and 23rd: Trumpeter rises.
Midnight of 94th day of the year (19 Drums):
Chariot rises. Spring begins.

5. Rain.

1st: Horseman sets. 13th: Trumpeter rises.

6. Marrying.

1st: Horseman rises. 3rd and 18th: Trumpeter rises.

7. Ambrose.

1st: Horseman sets. 8th and 23rd: Trumpeter rises.

8. Harps.

1st: Horseman rises. 13th: Trumpeter rises.
Evening of the 188th day of year (19 Harps):
Chariot sets; Midyear—Summer begins.

9. Tohrt.

1st: Horseman sets. 3rd and 18th: Trumpeter rises.

10. Remembering.

1st: Horseman rises. 8th and 23rd: Trumpeter rises.

11. Victory.

1st: Horseman sets. 13th: Trumpeter rises.

12. Harvesting.

1st: Horseman rises. 3rd and 18th: Trumpeter rises.
6th: Chariot rises, noon of 281st day of year. Fall begins.

13. Mother and Maiden.

1st: Horseman sets. 8th and 23rd: Trumpeter rises.

14. Bayring.

1st: Horseman rises. 13th: Trumpeter rises.

15. Borderer.

1st: Horseman sets. 3rd and 18th: Trumpeter rises.

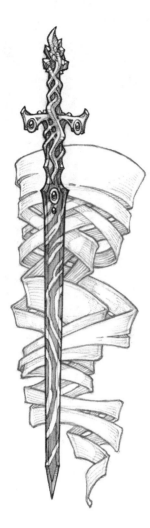

Sources and Backgrounds for Ambrosian Legend

hen the Allied forces firebombed Dresden in 1945, their real target was, of course, the Dresden Museum of Occult Antiquities, the infamous Übersinnlichaltertumswissenschaft-museum, which was believed to be the site of the Axis magical weapons research program. Destruction of the central complex was so complete that we will never know whether the fear was justified.

Because it was considered bizarre and questionable even by that institution's unusual standards, the Von Brauch collection had long been exiled to a basement storage facility off the main site. For that and other fortuitous reasons, a significant amount of the collection survived, including an almost undamaged holograph copy of Von Brauch's so-called *Gray Book* (*Liber Glaucus*), which until recently was our best source of information about the sorcerous Ambrosii.

I actually had the chance to see this codex when the museum reopened to the public a few years ago. Note taking, or any kind of image making, is forbidden by the curator. (Supposedly this is for the safety of the visitors: "a little knowledge is a dangerous thing" etc.; more likely it's so that the museum can sell copyrighted images in its splendid gift shop.) But, while a docent was distracted, I managed to scratch out an awkward version of Von Brauch's manuscript map of the continent of Laent—a map which has never,

as far as I know, been published. This sketch was used by the talented Chuck
Lukacs to create the map that adorns this book.

But I can't, and don't wish to, deny that most of my knowledge of Von
Brauch comes from the magisterial edition with commentary by H. N.
Emrys (Amsterdam, 1967), the capstone of a career devoted to the Ambrosian
legends. Emrys took some criticism for her agnostic approach to the so-called
authenticity question—whether these legends represent an actual tradition of
storytelling about Merlin's family or whether they were the mere inventions
of a pseudonymous fantasist. (No principality of "Brauch" has been discovered on the map of Germany, and it looks as if Von Brauch, like many of
those-who-know, operated under a *nom de guerre*.) Folklorists will long
remember Corvino's searing review of Emrys' lifework, comparing her stance
on the "authenticity question" to Jung's tacit endorsement of UFOlogy.

Emrys's vindication was a long time coming, but nowadays her agnosti-
cism seems almost too conservative. With Gabriel McNally's publication of
a rich selection of Khroic *ekshal* (Minneapolis, 2000), with translations and a
theoretical framework of tonal notations, we can now be certain there are not
only one but several independent traditions of storytelling about the
Ambrosii. The "authenticity question" has now been replaced by the "historicity question"—that is, "Do the Ambrosian stories contain some core of
historical fact (like the Trojan War legends) or are they purely imaginary?"
It's an interesting issue, one I don't propose to address (since my interests are
more mythographic than historical), except to point out how rare purity is.

The legendary material we have falls into three groupings, which naturally have some overlap:

1. Stories about Merlin Ambrosius, particularly before he becomes
   entangled in the history of Britain.
2. Stories about Ambrosia Viviana, and her rise to power over a significant portion of Laent. (Stories about Merlin and Nimue's other
   daughter, Hope Nimuelle, are less common, for obvious reasons.)
3. Stories about Morlock Ambrosius, the so-called master of all makers.
   It's this third group that is the most various and the most problem-
   atic. In some, he is a helpless drunk. In some, he is merely a cardboard

villain—Richard III without the charm. In some, he is improbably (almost tediously) noble. The Khroi incorporated him into their malefic angelology. Old Danish stories tell about his confrontation with Wayland Smith. The Canterbury recension of Mandeville's *Travels* includes a description of his workshop which is as ingenious as it is implausible.

These stories may each work (or not work) on their own, but they don't work together. It's not a question of historicity—I again waive any discussion of whether the stories are "true." It's that they don't cohere. In a small way, the traditions about Morlock resemble those about Hercules: they can't be stitched together to create a mythic biography (as can be done for Perseus, for instance, or Hrolf Kraki, or Atalanta, or many another legendary hero). So, in representing some of these legends in fictional form, I am not attempting to create a prose epic about Morlock, a multivolume Morlockiad. (Folklorists will recall the sad case of C. Linwood, who hysterically insisted that no reviews be made of his "eikosapentalogy" based on the legends of Uthar the Great until the twenty-fifth and final volume of the work was complete. He died before the project was more than a quarter finished, and today the work is almost unknown.) I'm just trying to tell some of the Morlock tales that are interesting, in ways that suit the particular story (or set of stories).

In retelling the legends about Lord Urdhven's attempted usurpation (in *Blood of Ambrose*), it seemed best to use the form of a Bildungsroman or "education of a hero," especially since the scant stories we have about Lathmar VII the Rebuilder tend to illuminate apparently contradictory traditions about Morlock and Ambrosia. It's a familiar form, too—perhaps overfamiliar. As Gabriel McNally recently wrote to me, "You can't swing a dead cat in the fantasy section of any bookstore without knocking three or four of these pig-tender-becomes-king books off the shelf." (I was intrigued by this image of the respectable philologist swinging dead carnivores in bookshops, but in later communications he insisted that it was just a thought experiment and that, anyway, the charges had been dropped.)

With *This Crooked Way* I turned to another venerable form in popular American fantasy, the episodic novel or "fix-up." Episodic novels have a bad reputation these days, and I don't think that's entirely undeserved. But this is a very traditional form in sf/f generally and sword-and-sorcery in particular. For some, that would be no recommendation at all. The past is dead. The future is now. The reason to jump off the cliff is that no one has done it yet. But when it comes to cliff jumping, I am not especially innovative. I like to look down and see a deep, soft carpet of my predeceased predecessors before I leap. In any case, the episodic novel meshes well with the segmented nature of the sources (which I have cobbled together from Von Brauch and McNally's translations of the Khroic song-cycles).

One of the reasons why I decline to involve myself with the historicity question is that it hinges on the material reality of Morlock's world and its relationship to our own. Opinions about this differ. Both the Khroic *ekshal* and Von Brauch's *Gray Book* refer to an area described (or named) as "the Sea of Worlds" (*Mare Mundorum* in Von Brauch's Latin; in Khroic, *Ver*[tone 1A]-*Thel*[tone 3B]-*Tre*[tone 7C]-*Lor*[tone 2ABC]). The Sea of Worlds is supposed to be an area between worldlines which can be navigated by those-who-know. As far as McNally is concerned, Von Brauch and the Khroi are independent witnesses whose testimony establishes beyond question the reality of the Sea of Worlds (and the worldline in which most of the Ambrosian legends are set). Doubting them is like "doubting the existence of the Ohio Turnpike, just because one has never driven on it." It's safe to say that most of his colleagues feel differently; the issue unquestionably played a role in his denial-of-tenure, a matter which is still under litigation (*McNally v. the University of Mackinac et al.*).

Nonfolklorists have proposed a "many worlds" hypothesis that might leave some possibility for Dr. McNally's controversial views. Thakurjeet Kaur, the eminent Indian-American physicist, spent her last years crafting a theory to accommodate the different models of quantum decoherence she considered valid, or at least potentially valid. Insofar as I understand it (which isn't much), she argued there was a probabilistic density that causes similar worldlines to collapse and merge, leaving a "world gap" that isolates and defines fundamentally dissimilar worldlines. This "world gap" might be functionally equivalent to the legendary Sea of Worlds. Whether it is navigable or not, or whether it even exists, is a question I leave to quantonauts more adventurous than myself.

ABOUT THE AUTHOR

James Enge's fiction has appeared in *Black Gate*, *Flashing Swords*, and everydayfiction.com. He is an instructor of classical languages at a midwestern university.

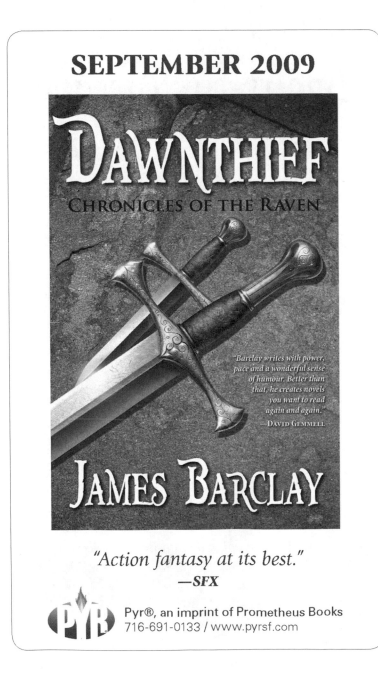

OCTOBER 2009

"Noonshade *is an epic tale and Barclay tells it with a mastery that is astonishing for only a second novel.*"

—SF Site

Pyr®, an imprint of Prometheus Books
716-691-0133 / www.pyrsf.com

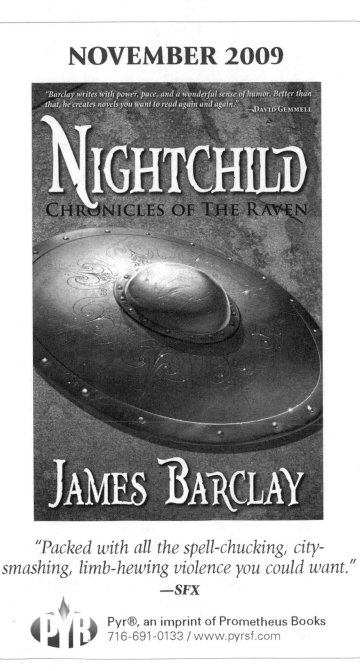